BURNING BRIGHT

Book One of The Extraordinaries

MELISSA MCSHANE

Night Harbor Publishing

For Hallie,
who knows why

CONTENTS

PROLOGUE

Elinor dreamed of fire, the unseen ground beneath her burning and the air white with heat, and woke to find her dream a reality. The walls of her bedroom were ablaze, the varnished floorboards slightly less so, and fire rolled across the ceiling in golden waves. Heat struck at her with an intensity that dried her nostrils and mouth and made her eyes feel roasted. She felt no fear, merely sat with her arms around her knees, her white, flannel nightgown tucked over her feet, and marveled at the fire's power and beauty. She had never seen such color. It made every memory she had of this dismal room seem even more faded and dispirited. Then the heat battered at her again, and she realized she would die if she did nothing.

So she reached out from within herself, and extinguished it.

It vanished between one heartbeat and the next, leaving behind the cold ash and charred beams of a long-dead fire. Patches of wallpaper here and there lent a leprous look to the walls. She heard screaming from somewhere nearby; that, and the void left by the fire's howl, filled her ears with a dull ringing sound. *I believe this is the strangest dream I have ever had,* she thought. She blinked to moisten her eyes, inhaled the dusty, acrid smell of wood smoke, and knew she was not dreaming.

"Elinor!" Her mother, her long braid of greying hair bobbing behind her, ran as far as the doorway and stopped short. Her full-lipped mouth dropped open into a perfect oval. "What foolish thing have you done now?" She held a candle at arm's length and peered into the bedroom, throwing shaky, grey shadows over the grey and black char as her hand trembled. Behind her, Elinor's younger sister Amelia hovered, her eyes sleepy.

Elinor looked around the room. The thick yellow curtains were burned at the edges and in irregular spots, but otherwise intact; the rumpled sheets of the bed where she sat were speckled with ash, and black stripes of char streaked the bedposts and the carved walnut foot-board. "It was a fire," she said, boldly, unable to give her mother a truer answer either of them would understand.

"A fire? However did you manage that?" her mother exclaimed.

"Come, mama, is it not obvious? Elinor has finally developed talent," said Amelia, taller and slenderer than Elinor and impossibly beautiful even in her sleep-disheveled state. She put a delicate hand over her mouth and coughed rather dramatically. "I suppose it is to be expected she should manifest as something so dreadfully vulgar as a Scorcher."

"And your Shaping yourself to fit the current fashion in beauty is not itself vulgar?" Elinor snapped.

"For shame, Elinor. And it's nonsense. You are far too old to manifest."

"I agree," said a deeper voice, and the two women made way for Josiah Pembroke. He was magnificent even in nightcap and gown with his feet shod in slippers embroidered with purple and gold flowers. "And yet this is unmistakable. Have you been concealing things from me, daughter?" He crossed the room to stand a few feet from her, his feet kicking up puffs of ash where he trod, his hands clasped over the expanse of his belly.

Elinor met his eyes with a calm directness that concealed the discomfort and fear she always felt when her father brought his attention to bear on her. She brushed ash from her nightgown and resisted the urge to take her braid in her hand, like a child clinging to a parent for comfort. "I have not," she said. "I dreamed of fire and woke to find it real. I would not conceal such a thing even were it possible." She did not for a moment consider pretending the fire had some natural origin; she knew in her bones that it was *her* fire, that she had created it, and it both loved her and would have killed her had she not subdued it.

Her father examined her with those dark grey eyes that looked black in the flickering lamp light. "Then tell me, if you would be so kind," he said, "did the fire extinguish itself?"

Elinor shook her head. "It was I who did it," she said.

Her father walked toward the window, drumming his fingers on his arm, then reached out to rub a blackened fold of the curtain between his thumb and forefinger. When he turned back to regard her, he was smiling, and Elinor's calm, expressionless demeanor cracked at the edges, because it was the smile of a predator. "Not only a talent," he said, "but an Extraordinary one. Do you see the possibilities, daughter?"

Elinor shook her head, though now that he had suggested there were possibilities, she could not help but try to imagine what they might be.

Mr. Pembroke's smile broadened. "In time, I think you will," he said.

CHAPTER 1

IN WHICH ELINOR ARRIVES IN LONDON, TO HER DISMAY

It was only Elinor's imagination that the black-clad butler, upon opening the door to their rented London house, drew back farther than was strictly necessary to let her pass. Her father's enthusiasm for telling the world he had an Extraordinary Scorcher for a daughter would not have extended to sharing the news with the employment agency.

She followed her mother into the narrow front hall. It was not a welcoming house, here on the unfashionable side of Mayfair, its plain, striped wallpaper cold blue and white, its walls devoid of paintings or portraits that would have made it seem more homelike. The air smelled of a harsh, astringent cleanser and, beneath that, the dust the cleanser was intended to eradicate. Elinor made immediately for the stairs. It had been a long journey, and she wanted nothing more than to rest in some room far, far away from her parents' scrutiny.

"Why is this house so cold?" Amelia said, removing her velvet-lined bonnet with reluctance and dangling it by its ribbons. "Do you suppose they use that horrid-smelling substance so we'll be impressed at how thoroughly they've cleaned? Really, you would think, with as much as papa is spending on this place, the servants might at least make it comfortable."

"Mr. Pembroke, only listen! We have had callers already," her mother cried. She waved two calling cards in the air as if they were tickets to a grand opera.

"Have we?" Mr. Pembroke took the cards from his wife's hand, glanced at them, and dropped them back on the salver. "No one of any consequence. Elinor, where are you going?"

"I... wish to rest before dinner," Elinor said, her hand grasping the newel.

Mr. Pembroke cast his iron-grey gaze silently on her for the space of several breaths, during which time the back of Elinor's neck prickled with apprehension. Surely he could find nothing to criticize in such an ordinary request? "Very well," he said finally. "Choose what room you will. I suppose you won't want my permission to light a fire in your grate, daughter?" He laughed at his poor joke, and Elinor smiled weakly and made her escape.

Behind her, Amelia's drawling voice battled with her mother's higher-pitched twitter. Small mercy: if she were forced to attend social gatherings where she would be on display like a cake in a shop window, she at least would not have to endure her younger sister's presence there.

She chose a bedroom as far from her parents' suite as possible, a little room her sister would not try to whine or wheedle away from her. It looked like an afterthought, tucked into an odd corner, with only one window that looked out on the rear of the house and massive furniture that might have graced a medieval manor. Elinor had to step sideways around the wardrobe to squeeze into her bed, which was tall enough to require the use of a stepstool to climb into it. The furnishings were so out of place they might have been placed there in storage. However, it had its own fireplace and was only steps from the water closet, an amenity their own home in Hertfordshire did not have. Elinor used it, then returned to her room, removed her gown, and hung it carefully on a peg in the wardrobe, shivering; despite the sunshine, it was unseasonably cold for April.

She stood in the center of the room in her shift and stays and traveling boots and hugged herself, rubbing the goose-pimply flesh of her arms. She was certain her father had no idea how he cowed her, that he saw only the smooth, indifferent visage she presented the world when she was in his presence, and she intended that he never discover the truth. If he but once realized how afraid of him she was, his casual cruelties would become intentional torment, for Josiah Pembroke despised weakness and showed no mercy to anyone who displayed it. One person in all the world who terrified her, and he was her own father.

She rubbed her arms harder. Why was this room still so cold? The fire—no, the grate was cold, fuel laid on the hearth but not lit. The unlit fire was an empty space inside Elinor's mind, the potential for flame clamoring at her to become real, so she obliged it with a thought.

Instantly the coals glowed as hot as if they'd been lit half an hour before, and small orange-yellow flames stretched out toward her, their heat caressing her bare limbs. She crouched down on her heels to feel the warmth on her face, and resisted the urge to take the fire into her hands, where it would surely burn her. Instead she molded it with her desires, made it stretch far up into the chimney, then spread out, puddled like water over the hearth.

She removed her kid boots and slid between the cold, slightly clammy sheets, moderately uncomfortable in her stays but unwilling to wait for her mother's maid Mostyn to help her remove them. *Suppose I could summon and extinguish a fire so swiftly it could warm these sheets without scorching them?* That *would be a useful skill.*

She lay on her back, staring at the ceiling, and went over the short list of uses for an Extraordinary Scorcher talent appropriate for a lady. *Putting out house fires. Lighting fires in the hearths. Lighting the stove when it goes out.* It was an extremely short list. *I suppose I could offer to light a gentleman guest's pipe, but I can't imagine why I would volunteer to make a pleasant room stink of tobacco.*

She'd hoped to become a Speaker like her father and her sister Selina, years ago when everyone assumed she would manifest at eleven or twelve like anyone else of her social class. Elinor wished more than anything to have the talent to communicate by thought with her beloved older sister and dearest friend. But talent never came for the asking; her own situation was evidence enough of that.

Her father's delight in her Extraordinary talent was understandable. Had she been a son, she would not have been nearly so valuable. It was illegal for a gentleman to purchase a bride for the sake of her talent, of course, but there was no law against a man presenting his new wife's parents with a generous gift, and Elinor was certain any man her father considered suitable for her would feel very generous indeed.

But her father's primary interest was in seeing her married well, which to him meant a nobleman with the right talent. Mr. Pembroke had spent a lifetime studying everything there was to know about talent—where it came from, how it manifested, but most importantly what children might result from the pairing of two particular talents. Elinor was certain when he contemplated her marriage, all his concern was for her potential offspring and where they might fit in the pages of the heavy folio Elinor thought of as his "breeding book." Oh, yes. She was a valuable commodity.

A knock on the door was followed immediately by Mostyn, short and angular with her cap askew on her blonde hair, awkwardly carrying Elinor's trunk and banging its corner against the door frame. "Excuse me, Miss Pembroke," she said in her colorless voice. Elinor turned her face to the wall and pretended to sleep. She listened to Mostyn opening drawers and thumping the trunk lid, and eventually drifted into a genuine slumber.

⚜

"I don't see," said Amelia, her perfect rosy lips drawn up in a pout, "why I cannot go out in society as Elinor does. Why, you can bring two daughters out with very little more expense than one, and you will not have the burden of a second trip to London." She leaned around the servant who was setting out dishes for the second course to plead with her mother with large, cerulean eyes.

"You are too young, my darling," Mrs. Pembroke said. "You shall have your season in good time."

"I shall be eighteen in two months. That is not such a vast gap. Papa, please do reconsider!"

"Your mother is right," Mr. Pembroke said. "Besides, I am sure you don't wish to share your sister's attention."

"She may have half the attention paid to me, and welcome to it," Elinor said. She stirred green peas around the plate with her fork. Her stomach had not quite recovered from the lurching, jolting pace of the coach; her lack of appetite had nothing to do with her place at her father's left hand, a new "honor" accorded her as an Extraordinary to which she was not yet accustomed. She would far have preferred her traditional seat by her mother, but her father was nothing if not committed to reminding her at every opportunity of her new status.

"Oh, Elinor, this will be *so* much more satisfying than your last visit to London!" Mrs. Pembroke said. "I assure you, social engagements are far more pleasant when you have plenty of admirers. And you will have so many admirers!"

"Yes, having a talent makes all the difference," Amelia said with a sneer. Elinor smiled pleasantly at her and twitched her right hand. Amelia started back in her seat, clutching her knife as if to wield it against her sister. Elinor picked up her own knife and cut her meat. It was petty, tormenting Amelia with the threat of using her Scorcher talent against her, but Elinor had been the victim of her younger sister's scorn for too many years to feel guilty about it.

"You need not fear, daughter," Mr. Pembroke said. "True, you will be much courted, but you may count on me to keep the less desirable men away. I assure you, no one titled lower than an earl will approach you. My daughters deserve the best. Although I would not scoff at fifty thousand pounds a year!" Mr. Pembroke laughed, and Mrs. Pembroke and Amelia added their titters to his.

Elinor smiled politely and allowed her father to serve her another slice of ham. She thought of the pig who had died so they could enjoy it, and felt sympathy for it. If her father could hang a sign around her neck with her asking price and talent specifications on it, he would do it without a second thought.

"Have you Spoken with Selina, papa?" she asked, trying to turn the conversation elsewhere.

"She intends to call on us tomorrow morning."

"Oh, Mr. Pembroke, but I intend to take Elinor shopping tomorrow! She requires almost an entirely new wardrobe."

"We can go later in the day, mama." Elinor said. "I do so want to see Selina. It seems forever since she last visited."

"Four months is hardly forever," Mr. Pembroke said, "but your affection for your sister is laudable."

Mrs. Pembroke sighed dramatically. "Very well, Elinor, we shall postpone our trip, but I expect you to be cooperative. Our last visit to the warehouses was terribly disappointing."

"Elinor is far too sober-minded to care about such things as gowns," Amelia drawled. "I know I should make far better use of my time were I in her position."

"Patience, my darling," Mrs. Pembroke said, patting Amelia's hand. "It will be your turn soon, and what fun we shall have!"

"I wish to see you in the study after dinner, Elinor," Mr. Pembroke said. Elinor maintained a serene expression, but under the table her hands gripped her napkin and twisted, hard. "We should discuss how you will present yourself at Lord Ormerod's ball in six days' time."

"I know how to behave in society, papa," Elinor said. *Calm, placid, like a still pool.*

"I have not forgotten how insipid you were when we first brought you to London, how little effort you made to encourage suitors," Mr. Pembroke said. "I was willing to overlook your behavior then because you had so little to recommend you and were unlikely to receive an offer however you behaved. Things are different now. You have a desirable talent, and I will not see you squander this grand opportunity. Do you understand me?"

So little to recommend you. Elinor's stomach churned again. She clung to her outward serenity like a drowning man clutches a rope. "I understand you perfectly, papa," she said. "I will submit to your instruction." *And then I will ignore it. I may have an Extraordinary talent, but the law says I cannot be forced to marry against my will, and you, dear papa, have no idea what my will is like after living under your disdain for twenty-one years.* The brave thoughts faded away immediately. She tried to imagine herself saying such a thing to her father, but succeeded only in making herself feel more ill.

"Very well." Mr. Pembroke smiled at Elinor and covered her hand with his; it took all the willpower she had not to jerk away from him and instead smile pleasantly back. "And don't fear, Elinor. A Scorcher talent in a lady is undesirable, true, but it is well known that Scorchers produce powerful Bounders and Movers, and any nobleman wishing to better his fortunes would be a fool not to see your value. And an Extraordinary Scorcher talent—my dear, you are the only one of your kind in England, the only one in a century—do you not see how desirable that makes you? It is not beyond possibility that this time next year, we will be visiting London as the guests of our daughter, the Duchess!"

"And only think what you may do for your sister!" Mrs. Pembroke gasped. "Oh, Amelia, would you not like to be brought out by your sister?"

"She must marry first, mama," Amelia said, glaring at Elinor. "It is a pity she is so plain. But then, I've heard good talent makes a lady beautiful beyond her birth."

"It is a pity you have nothing more to recommend you than the face you have so carefully Shaped," Elinor snapped. Amelia gasped, then broke into theatrical tears.

"For *shame*, Elinor," Mrs. Pembroke said, and patted Amelia's hand.

"And she is not to be reprimanded for commenting on my appearance?"

"Amelia is younger than you, and is still learning to curb her tongue. She lacks your self-control," Mr. Pembroke said. "I expect you to behave with greater self-restraint."

"Yes, papa," Elinor said, casting her eyes down so he would not see her anger, but not without first flicking a quick glare at her sister, who went white.

"I'm sure I beg your pardon, Elinor," Amelia said. "We none of us can help the way we're made."

Whether that was an apology, or another, subtler dig, Elinor could not decide, but she chose to let it pass. "I apologize for my quick words," she replied. "I think I am more tired from the journey than I realized. May I retire early, papa?"

"You are clearly overwrought, so I will excuse you this once, daughter. We will speak tomorrow."

"Do not forget, Elinor, we *will* be attending to your wardrobe after Selina's visit is completed," Mrs. Pembroke said as Elinor was about to leave the room. "I think it is not too much to ask that you take an interest in your appearance."

"Yes, mama," Elinor said, and escaped to her room.

The fire rose up in response to her entrance, and she soothed it as she would an anxious puppy. She knew it was not truly alive, but it amused her to pretend it was; she refused to entertain the notion that she did so only because she was so desperately lonely now that Selina was married. If only she had had a Speaker's talent! She certainly did not envy Amelia her talent, since Shaping, unless one had the Extraordinary gift of Healing others, was useful only for making oneself pretty, and Elinor was accustomed to being the plain one. But to speak to Selina every day...

Elinor stretched out her hand to the fire, and the flame mirrored her gesture. Where had this strange talent come from? Her father had not discovered a single Scorcher in his lineage for a dozen generations. Her mother, talentless but pretty, was out of the question as a source for Elinor's talent; Mr. Pembroke thought too well of himself to believe his wife had ever played him false. At any rate, Elinor resembled her father too closely for that to be possible, with her chestnut hair and heavy, dark brows, her iron-grey eyes, her too-strong chin that on her father looked manly and on Elinor looked stubborn. Her heritage was a mystery, and one Elinor had no interest in solving.

She drew back from the flame and undressed, awkwardly fumbling with the lacing of her stays until she could wriggle free of them. She was to be launched on society in the manner of one of the Navy's ships of the line, rigged and outfitted for the duty of marrying well and producing dozens of talented babies for her noble husband, all thanks to this unexpected talent—and yet she could not say, if she were given the opportunity, that she would ask for it to be taken away. The fire was like a part of her that had been waiting all these years to awaken, and the idea of losing it, even after only four months' time, made her feel ill.

The sheets were still clammy because she had come to bed before the maid had brought the warming pan, but she rubbed her bare feet together to warm them, then bade the fire bank itself. She felt as if she were in two places, her solid body here in the slightly damp bed, her ghostly self snuggled securely into the fireplace. It was a strange but comforting feeling, and she lay awake enjoying her dual state for close to an hour before falling asleep.

ELINOR ROSE EARLY THE NEXT MORNING AND WENT QUIETLY DOWN the stairs to collect the newspapers. Her father never failed to arrange for their delivery, no matter where he was. She settled into an over-stuffed chair in the unfriendly drawing room decorated in mauve and eggshell blue and opened *The Times*. Such ghastly news out of Notting-hamshire these days, those men striking in darkness, burning and smashing looms in the name of their "General Ludd." And now Parliament was talking of making those actions a capital offense. Napoleon's men overrunning Spain, his ships armed with Scorchers wreaking havoc on the Royal Navy's proud fleet. Reading the newspaper certainly put her own problems into perspective.

She heard the faint sound of the door opening, the murmur of the butler's voice—she had no idea what his name was—and then, more clearly, "I know perfectly well Miss Pembroke is at home, and you need not trouble yourself inquiring."

"*Selina!*" Elinor threw the paper to the floor and leapt from her seat, meeting her sister halfway down the stairs and nearly bowling her over in her enthusiasm. Selina, Lady Wrathingham, laughed and embraced her tightly. "I'm so glad you've come," Elinor said into her ear. "I have missed you so much."

"I've missed you too. Now, shall we sit and talk? I knew you would not mind if I came early, but I wanted you all to myself for an hour." Selina pinched Elinor's cheek gently. "And I intend to breakfast with you, which I realize is a shocking imposition, but if one is a viscount-ess, one is allowed to break with tradition, especially in the bosom of one's own loving family."

"I can think of no greater pleasure," Elinor said, taking her sister by the arm and leading her upstairs to the drawing room. "I will tidy these papers away—sit, sit, and feel free to remove that horrid bonnet."

"You think it horrid? It's new."

"Puce has never been your color, Selina."

"You may be right. Oh well, I suppose I'll have to order another." Selina handed Elinor a loose sheet of newsprint and removed the offending bonnet, revealing dark-blonde hair that shone in the diffuse light from the windows. "I don't know how you can bear to read about all the misery in the world. I know it makes me positively ill with anxiety."

"I like knowing things. And it's not all miserable. The Royal Navy has just announced the commission of half a dozen new ships, smaller and faster to fight these awful pirates coming out of the West Indies."

"You see? Horrible pirates preying on our shipping lanes."

Elinor laughed and shook her head. "I see there is no convincing you. But there are far more interesting things to talk about. How are my dearest nephews?"

"Very dear indeed, though poor Jack has had a terrible cough all week. Colin is beside himself at being deprived of his favorite playmate." Selina cast her eyes down demurely and smoothed her fur-lined grey pelisse over her stomach. "And I expect to give them another companion before the year is out."

Elinor threw her arms around her sister again, laughing in delight. "Such wonderful news! John must be bursting with pride."

"He does dote on his sons fiercely," Selina agreed. "Though I believe he would be just as happy with a daughter."

"Of course he would! You are so lucky in your family, sister. If I believed I could be half as happy—" She stopped, biting her lip.

Selina took her hands and squeezed, gently. "I know why mama and papa have brought you to town," she said. "They treat you differently now that you have an Extraordinary talent."

Elinor nodded. "All these years of being the non-talented one, and then one night... I don't understand it, Selina, but there it is. And now nothing will do but that I marry some duke or earl I neither know nor care for—" The tears she hadn't shed for four months choked her. She swallowed hard, and went on, "This is not the life I wanted."

"What life did you want? Certainly not to be Miss Pembroke, spinster daughter of Josiah and Albina Pembroke, living in their house and eating their food with no home nor portion of your own."

It felt like a rebuke. "You sound as if you agree with them."

Selina shook her head. "I apologize, dearest, that's not what I meant at all. I'm simply asking what you *do* want, if it's not living with papa for the rest of your life or marrying some chinless duke."

"I want..." Nothing sprang to mind. "I want to be free to do as I choose. If I marry, I want to marry someone I can at least respect or even love, not because he has the right talent—and I certainly want to marry someone who cares for me and not this...this *gift*, I suppose you could call it, though that raises the question of who gave it me. God, possibly. But mostly I want not to feel I owe my every breath to someone else. I don't want to be *grateful* all the time, Selina, and papa never fails to make me feel as though everything I am and have and will be is due to him."

"I wish I knew how to give that to you."

"So do I."

Selina patted her hand compassionately. "Do you not think it even remotely possible one of these titled lords might be someone you could love?"

"I suppose." Elinor shrugged. "But with papa spreading the news of my valuable talent as if he were advertising a horse for sale, I doubt any of them will look at me as more than a breeding animal."

"Oh, don't, pray don't talk like that! You are breaking my heart." Selina's enormous fur muff fell off her lap and rolled a little way across the floor. "Elly, you deserve so much more than that!"

"Tell it to papa. He might listen to Lady Wrathingham. He is certainly not interested in Miss Pembroke's opinion."

"If I thought it would do any good...you know he has only your best interest in mind."

"Or what he believes is my best interest, which coincidentally aligns in perfect harmony with what Josiah Pembroke wants."

"You cannot think so cynically of him."

"Can I not?" Elinor sighed. Selina was right; he might terrify her, but he did believe he was securing her happiness in helping her attach the right man—even if his definition of right failed to match hers. "I beg your pardon, Selina. I am simply so discouraged. You know how miserable my first season was. Mama assures me this will be different, but I fear it will simply be miserable in a different way."

"Well, you needn't fear, because I intend to introduce you to many men who will see you for yourself and not for your talent," Selina said. "And papa cannot force you to marry according to his wishes, you know."

"I know. But he's threatened to protect me from 'undesirables,' which makes me want to find one of them and propose marriage immediately."

Selina laughed and bent over to retrieve her muff. "I should like to be there when you do!"

"For shame, Selina, intruding on a private moment like that. Hand me that muff, and do remove your coat. I think it is late enough that I can demand breakfast from the staff. Will you join us afterward in our tour of the warehouses? I shall be so much happier if I am not left alone with mama and Amelia, who I am certain will find a way to be included in the party."

"Has our darling sister changed much since I last saw her?"

"Her cheekbones are higher and I believe her waist is narrower, not that anyone will notice. If she is not careful, someone will snap her in half like a piece of straw."

"I've often wondered what it must feel like, to a Shaper, shifting bones and muscles around like that." Selina linked her arm through Elinor's as they descended the stairs. "Like snakes slithering around beneath the skin, I imagine."

"The snake is certainly a creature I associate with Amelia."

"I should probably reprimand you for being so cruel, but it's hard to do so when I agree."

CHAPTER 2

IN WHICH A BALL TURNS OUT TO
BE A DISAPPOINTMENT

The chaise rattled and jounced over the cobblestones, forcing Elinor to cling to the edge of her seat or be tossed into her mother's ample lap. She wished her father had not hired this shiny, expensive carriage that exposed her to the gaze of everyone they passed. Anxiety was making her stomach churn as if she had eaten something poisonous.

She smoothed wrinkles out of the skirt of her apple-green gown and wished she had not given in to her mother's cries of joy over the fabric. Elinor was certain her mother's pleasure in her daughter's Extraordinary talent began and ended with the fact that Elinor was no longer limited to wearing white muslin in public despite her youth and unmarried status. Her new wardrobe was filled with silks and satins Elinor believed were far more suited to a matron than to her.

They had argued over colors, insofar as Elinor was inclined to argue over something so superficial. Mrs. Pembroke had refused to consider any of the colors Elinor preferred on the grounds that they were too dark, too intense, too rich for a girl just out; when Elinor had pointed out she was, in fact, several years removed from the schoolroom, Mrs. Pembroke had said, "And *that* is precisely what we do not wish anyone to realize." No doubt her mother's greatest hope was that the three years since Elinor's come-out had erased fashionable society's memory of that awkward, unremarkable girl.

"Remember, Elinor, what we discussed," Mr. Pembroke said. "You will be the object of much talk this evening; you must appear to be insensible of it. Demure, polite, respectful—many tonight will watch to see whether your Scorcher talent has made you wild and unbiddable. Stand up with anyone who requests the pleasure of a dance, but show no preference. It will not do for you to seem anxious to make an attachment on your first social appearance, especially so early in the season. There will be time enough for that when I have examined the aspirants to your hand in depth. This evening is for making you known to the fashionable world."

"What of supper?" Elinor said. She had no idea of where she stood in precedence—did an Extraordinary Scorcher outrank a baroness?—and the thought of stumbling through the crowd and being pitied or scorned by everyone else made her cringe inside yet again.

"You have no need to fear. I will ensure you have a suitable partner when the time comes."

Elinor nodded and lowered her eyes, certain she was the picture of serene young womanhood. Her stomach tried once again to turn itself inside out. She looked at her shoes, silvery-green to match her gown. It must be her imagination they felt so tight; they had fit very well when she'd tried them on two days ago.

They waited in line to be deposited at Lord Ormerod's front door for twenty minutes, during which time Mrs. Pembroke chattered about Elinor's prospects, and her gown, and her hair, and her jewels, and then about her prospects again until Elinor was certain she would be violently ill all over the carriage. She might even have welcomed illness if she hadn't been equally certain her father would sponge her down and send her inside anyway. She swallowed hard and pretended to pay attention. This would not be so awful. Selina would be there, not all the men could be as horrible as she feared, and she did enjoy dancing. And her father would likely be far away from her for most of the evening. Not so awful, at all.

Lord Ormerod's mansion stood several stories tall, all its windows golden with light. The house was full, though not so full as to require them to push their way through the crowd. Somehow Lord and Lady Ormerod were not present to greet them, though her parents seemed to think nothing of this social gaffe, and although Elinor heard her name announced, she did not think anyone farther than five feet away from the door did. She could cherish her anonymity for a few minutes more.

It was a beautiful house, or would have been had it not been so full of people. Elinor tried not to gape at the ornately carved tables and chairs, the paintings by famous masters, or the delicate marble statuary placed at random throughout the house as if Lord Ormerod or his wife simply had so many beautiful, expensive things they could leave them wherever they wanted. How her father had secured an invitation to this place baffled her.

She passed through hot, cramped rooms that smelled of sweat and perfume that attempted to cover the sweat, and emerged into the ball-room, its high ceiling rimmed with gilt and painted to resemble a midday sky. The clouds made an interesting *trompe l'oeil* effect, poised to drift across the ceiling and block the rays of an invisible sun, though the actual light was provided by three chandeliers shedding their sparkling brightness over the floor far below. Men in tightly-fitted coats and knee breeches vied with women in muslin and silk draped with gauze for the prize of having the most colorful garb. Elinor felt out of place, though her own gown was as fashionable as any. She always feared, at such gatherings, that she was seconds away from saying or doing something awkward that would make everyone stare in astonishment at her gaucherie. Her father's presence at her elbow did nothing to ease her discomfort. Her gaze passed once more over the crowd, seeking out Selina. The ballroom was large enough to feel cool by comparison to the rest of the house, though it was lit with candles enough to—

—to set the roof ablaze, make the wax run like clear-white liquid to rain on the parquet floor—

—and Mr. Pembroke put his hand on the small of her back and urged her forward. "Do not be overwhelmed by this, daughter," he whispered in her ear. "Your destiny is even grander."

Elinor nodded. She dared not look up at the chandeliers again—

three of them, who truly needed three chandeliers filled to bursting with the finest wax tapers?—but there was fire *everywhere*, lamps on the walls, candles above her head, and it pleaded with her to give it freedom. She clenched her fists and walled away her awareness of the fire. It could keep her anxieties company.

A tall woman gowned in maroon velvet and an equally tall man with an enormous pot belly approached them. "Mr. Pembroke, Mrs. Pembroke, welcome," the woman said. "And this must be Miss Pembroke. I am Lady Ormerod. I am happy to meet you." She did not seem happy. Her lips were white, as if she were holding in some strong emotion, and she did not offer Elinor her hand in greeting.

"Mr. Pembroke, such a pleasure!" The man, by contrast, held out his hand and pumped her father's with enthusiasm. "And this must be your charming daughter—no, I mistake myself, Mrs. Pembroke, you look younger every time I see you!"

"Oh, my lord, you are *such* a charmer!" Mrs. Pembroke said, giggling and allowing the man to raise her hand to his lips.

"Miss Pembroke, may I introduce my husband, Lord Ormerod," Lady Ormerod said.

Elinor bobbed a polite curtsey. Lord Ormerod raised a quizzing glass to his eye and surveyed her. "What an attractive young lady," he said. "And not a trace of... that is to say, talent never shows itself on the skin, does it?"

"I believe not, my lord," Elinor said, trying to sound demure, although what demure might sound like she had no idea.

"Very attractive indeed. Welcome to my home, Miss Pembroke, I am honored indeed to welcome you." His welcome seemed genuine, but Elinor was conscious only of Lady Ormerod's almost palpable tension and... yes, it was fear. The stomach-churning knot in her stomach clenched again.

"I am so happy you could join us this evening, Miss Pembroke," Lady Ormerod said. "And such an...interesting...talent you have. I am sure I have never heard of its like."

"My daughter is rare indeed, my lady," Mr. Pembroke said, laying his hand on Elinor's shoulder. "I hope you will make her feel welcome. She has little experience in society."

Elinor went red with embarrassment. Fortunately, it seemed Lady Ormerod interpreted her scarlet cheeks differently. "Of course, I am certain she will be extremely popular, Mr. Pembroke," she said, and her voice seemed fractionally warmer. "Miss Pembroke, allow me to make introductions for you."

She guided Elinor around the ballroom so rapidly Elinor was unable to remember more than a few names, and barely able to apply those names to the correct faces. "Lord Landon... Mr. Fitzhenry... his Grace, the Duke of Wannisford... oh, Lord Adelburn, here is someone you *must* meet." A short, heavyset young man turned to greet Lady Ormerod, then regarded Elinor with mild interest. "Miss Pembroke, this is the Earl of Adelburn."

"Charmed," the young man said. Elinor curtsied, then wondered if she had done it correctly, because he looked at her as if he expected something more. In the face of his inquiring stare, her carefully planned conversational gambits abandoned her. Lady Ormerod cleared her throat, and the Earl transferred his stare to her. "Oh," he said. "Miss Pembroke, may I solicit your hand for the first two dances?"

"Ah... of course, Lord Adelburn," Elinor stammered.

"If you'll excuse me?" Lady Ormerod said with a smile, and retreated more rapidly than Elinor thought was good manners.

She turned her attention back to the Earl, whose inquiring stare had deepened. "I, ah, that is, my lord, I am afraid I know little of London society. Are you a frequent guest of Lord and Lady Ormerod's?"

"On occasion," Lord Adelburn replied. "I beg your pardon, but you're the Scorcher girl, aren't you?"

Elinor's cheeks flamed again. "I would not refer to myself in quite that way, but yes."

"Didn't mean anything by it. I meant, you're the one everyone's talking about."

"Are they?"

The musicians struck up the first dance, and Lord Adelburn offered Elinor his hand and led her to where the couples were gathering. "Talking of nothing else, it seems. What is an Extraordinary Scorcher talent, anyway?"

Elinor made her curtsey and reached to take his hand with her gloved one. "I am able to shape and extinguish flame as well as ignite it."

"Is that all? That sounds uncomplicated."

"I suppose it is."

They made the next few passes in silence, and Lord Adelburn said, "I'm not good at making conversation."

"Neither am I, my lord. Perhaps that makes us well suited as dancing partners?"

He laughed, an uncomfortable gulping sound. "Perhaps it does." He had a pleasant smile, and Elinor responded in kind. This was not as terrible as she'd feared.

When their two dances were over, Lord Adelburn bowed to her, said, "You're not what I expected," and was gone before she could reply. Did he believe, as her father had suggested, she would be hoydenish, unmannered, and ungovernable, simply because she could shape fire? She did not know what was more unsettling, the young Earl's ignorance or Lady Ormerod's fear. She moved off into the crowd. Surely Selina would be here somewhere. Her sister had a lively sense of humor and had buoyed her spirits so many times during that first, disastrous season. And she had promised to find Elinor unsuitable partners.

Then Lady Ormerod was at her elbow again, saying, "My dear, here is someone you simply must meet," and once again Elinor was being led to join the line with barely enough time to learn her partner's name. She danced, and was offered punch, and danced again, and while she was not exactly enjoying herself, she was forced to admit Mrs. Pembroke was correct; this was very different from her first, unsuccessful season. *Though I cannot imagine how Selina managed it, falling in love in a succession of crowded ballrooms. Oh, Selina, where are you?*

"Miss Pembroke, I do hope you are enjoying yourself," Lady Ormerod said. "May I make known to you Lord Huxley?"

"My lord," Elinor said, curtsying, then looked up and had to look further up to meet the tall gentleman's bright, merry blue eyes. He had a crooked smile that made him seem to be laughing at some private joke; if he was, it was not a cruel one. He bowed to her, his smile widening, and offered her his hand.

"Miss Pembroke," he said, and his voice was deep and pleasant. "Dare I hope you will be my partner for the next two dances?"

"It would be my pleasure," Elinor said, and found she was telling the truth. She was no romantic; she did not think Lord Huxley looked at her the way a lover might, but the admiration in his eyes told her that he saw her, and not her Extraordinary talent. She accepted his hand with more than usual pleasure.

"I hope you are enjoying London, Miss Pembroke," Lord Huxley said as the music began. "The city has so much to offer."

"I have not seen much of it as yet, my lord. We have been in town only seven days."

"Do you enjoy the theater?"

"I have been only once or twice, my lord. I am afraid you will think me sadly provincial."

He smiled that crooked smile at her. "I would only think that," he said, "if I believed you did not intend to remedy that lack."

"And you can make that judgment based on five minutes' acquaintance?" She smiled back at him.

"I pride myself on my ability to read a man's—or a woman's—character in her eyes. Yours clearly indicate you have a daring soul."

Elinor blushed. "Have I?"

"Indeed. Do not deny it; you have the appearance of a young woman who, when she is told 'no,' wants to know 'why not?' "

"I think you are mistaken, my lord. But I imagine you intend a compliment, so I thank you."

"Do you believe it wrong for a woman to be inquisitive?"

"I believe inquisitiveness, in either sex, has merit in its place."

Lord Huxley laughed. "Such a demure answer. You are not what I expected, Miss Pembroke."

"You are not the first to tell me that this evening, my lord."

"I think you must not know many other Scorchers, Miss Pembroke. They tend to be rather erratic in their conversation and actions. An Extraordinary Scorcher... the assumption is you must be even more like a Scorcher than a Scorcher, if you take my meaning. Yet you are quiet and polite, and you blush so prettily—yes, there it is again." Elinor found herself unable to meet his gaze. "And yet I imagine who you truly are is somewhere in the middle of those extremes."

"Forgive me, my lord, I am not accustomed to such frankness in conversation with someone to whom I have only just been introduced." He was remarkably perceptive, was Lord Huxley, and she could not decide if that discomfited her or not.

"I meant no offense. I find you interesting, Miss Pembroke, and I fear I sometimes presume too much on a new acquaintanceship."

"I am not offended, simply...you are the first tonight who has been willing to be so honest. I find I enjoy it."

The music came to an end, but when Lord Huxley had made his bow, he offered Elinor his arm. "It is my good fortune to be your partner when supper is announced," he said. "May I escort you? I should enjoy continuing our conversation."

"Thank you, my lord," Elinor said, blushing again. She felt as foolish as a girl just out of the schoolroom, blushing at any provocation, but despite his age—he was probably in his late thirties—he had a charming smile and seemed genuinely interested in conversing with her.

She still did not see Selina when they sat down to table, and this distracted her sufficiently that her dining partner drew her attention to it. "Has my company palled so quickly?" he asked with that lopsided smile.

"I had hoped to see my sister here," she admitted. "It is not like her to be so late."

"Your sister is Lady Wrathingham, is she not? I am afraid I haven't made her acquaintance, but she is well spoken of in all the best circles."

"She is a dear, and I hope it is nothing serious that has delayed her."

"Surely not. Will you make me known to her, when she arrives?"

"I will, if you wish it."

"I do. I find I am interested in meeting the relations of someone as remarkable as you, Miss Pembroke."

"Now you are flirting with me, my lord. That cannot be proper."

"Since you are the only one of your kind in all of England, I think referring to you as remarkable can hardly constitute flirting."

This time, Elinor controlled her blush before it spread. "My father said the same, about me being the only one of my kind. Is that true?"

"He is the one from whom I heard it, and everyone knows Josiah Pembroke is the authority on the history of talent in England."

"I see." She applied herself to her food to cover her confusion. Lord Huxley had spoken to her father—but that did not necessarily mean he—on the other hand, he was exactly the sort of man her father intended for her—and he *had* escorted her in to supper—

"You are unexpectedly silent. May I ask what thoughts occupy your mind?" Lord Huxley said.

"I was thinking about dancing again," she lied. "I do enjoy it, and it is pleasant to stand up with people one has *not* known all one's life."

"I regret only that your great popularity militates against my dancing again with you, Miss Pembroke," Lord Huxley said with a smile.

Elinor returned his smile, but automatically. He was *too* smooth, *too* well-mannered. Elinor did not think herself repulsive, but neither did she believe a man like Lord Huxley would be interested in someone like her unless she came with a sizable dowry. Or, in her case, an Extraordinary one. The warm feeling his attention had generated inside her chest died to nothing. She wished desperately that Selina would appear and they might find a quiet place where Elinor could pour out her misery.

She managed to endure the rest of the supper, and Lord Huxley's now obviously insincere compliments, without bursting into tears or setting the table aflame. When the assembled company rose from the table, he offered her his hand once again, but instead of leading her back to the ballroom, he took her through another room and opened a door at its far end. "I am persuaded you are over warm, and some cool air will do you good," he said.

Elinor, confused, passed through the door and found herself in a small garden behind the house, and was struck once more by the unfamiliar smell of London, the acrid scent of the fog mixed with the more distant sour-sweet odor of the Thames. The night air was chilly, and although it did clear her head, it was not entirely pleasant; her thin gown was little protection, and goose pimples rose up on her arms and prickled her cheeks. She shivered.

"My lord, I am grateful for your concern, but—" she began.

"No need," he said, and put his arms around her and pressed his lips to hers.

She was so startled that at first all she could do was stand motionless and allow herself to be kissed. The sleeves of his coat rubbed her bare arms with a roughness that against her chilled skin felt harsh; his mouth tasted of beef and wine gone vinegary in combination with it. Then she came to her senses, and tried to push him away to no effect. His grip around her shoulders tightened, and his lips grew hard and insistent against hers. Furious, she beat at his chest until he finally released her, smiling that crooked smile. She took several steps backward and wiped her mouth with the back of one hand.

"My lord, I do not know what I have done to make you believe I would welcome such attentions," she said, her voice trembling with fury, "but I assure you I am not the sort of woman who appreciates them."

"It is to your credit that you shy away from me," Lord Huxley said. "It is obvious from your reaction you are unfamiliar with the ways of men, and I find that most attractive." He reached out and stroked her cheek; she jerked away. "You need not fear me, Miss Pembroke. I shall teach you to enjoy my embrace."

"My lord, I sincerely believe that to be impossible. Pray allow me to return to the ball."

He chuckled. "Truly remarkable." He opened the door for her and took her hand when she tried to pass through it. "I look forward to our next meeting."

"I anticipate you will wait long before that happens," she retorted, pulling her hand free and making her escape. No one seemed to have noticed her absence. She scanned the crowd for Lady Ormerod's blonde head and, having found it, moved rapidly in the other direction. She left the ballroom and began opening doors at random, knowing only that she needed to find a place where she could be completely alone, not caring that it was both improper and rude for her to be wandering through her host's home uninvited and unsupervised.

Is this what I am to be subjected to? she thought. *Will everyone believe I am so desperate to be wed that I will accept any impertinence?* She rubbed her lips again, harshly, trying to forget the feel of Lord Huxley's mouth on hers.

She opened yet another door and stepped into a dimly lit room that smelled of dust and disuse, moonlight filtering through tall windows whose heavy blue or black drapes were tied back with finger-thick ropes, their tassels brushing the floor. A pianoforte shrouded in white sheets stood in one corner; the angular shape of a harp similarly covered stood in another. A long, darkly upholstered sofa with a high back faced the pianoforte at an angle, while pale chairs with narrow legs and cushions matching the curtains stood here and there throughout the room.

Elinor closed the door behind her and went to sit on one of the chairs, covering her face with her gloved hands. She might be entitled to cry, to feel sorrow for herself, but that would do nothing except ruin her complexion and make her a figure of pity when she eventually returned to the ball. *And I suppose I do have to return sometime. It's a pity there's no way for me to summon our carriage and make my escape out the back door.*

A discreet cough sent her leaping from her chair, clasping her hands in front of her as if she were a child caught stealing lumps of sugar from the bowl. "You probably shouldn't be here," said the man now sitting up from where he had been reclining on the sofa.

"Well, neither should you," she retorted, embarrassment giving an edge to her tongue.

"I live here. You don't."

"If you live here, you ought to be with your guests, not... not *skulking* in dark rooms."

"Where I can startle innocent young ladies, you mean?" The man was tall, with light-colored hair that seemed grey in the dim light of the music room, and he wore a dark suit of an unusual cut. He came around to the back of the sofa and leaned against it, as relaxed as if startling innocent young ladies was something that came naturally to him. "And they're not my guests, they're my cousin Harry's."

"Is Lord Ormerod your cousin, then?"

"Distant. Third cousin, or some such. And I was at the ball until fifteen minutes ago. I *thought* this was a room where a man might have some quiet, away from all that din."

"I didn't realize I was a *din*, all by myself," Elinor said.

"You're quiet enough, but I thought if you were here for an assignation, I should make myself known before the situation became awkward."

"*Assignation?*"

"It's not uncommon, at these doings. You didn't come here to meet your beau?"

"How *dare* you insult me like that? I am a *gentlewoman!*" Was it something in her appearance, that made men assume she was open to any amorous advances?

"It's the gentlewomen who are most often the ones sneaking off to quiet rooms like this—"

"Do not say another word, you...*Captain*," Elinor sputtered, realizing his strange dark suit with the white facings and the braid along the cuffs was actually a naval uniform. "I came here because I—actually, I think it is none of your concern why I came here, but I assure you it was not for some clandestine meeting. Or are you so quick to accuse me because *you* are waiting here for some...*doxy?*"

"I assure you, I don't need to make assignations in dark, uncomfortable rooms," the captain said, his light eyes as colorless as his hair in the dim light. He sounded amused, which infuriated Elinor. She cast about for something cutting to say, but he continued, "And I do apologize, miss, if I offended you. It was an honest mistake."

"I wonder you do not have to apologize constantly, if your assumptions are all 'honest mistakes' like that one," she said.

"I won't apologize for saying what I think, and that's true." He crossed his arms over his chest; she thought he might be examining her, and she blushed with more anger.

"If you are quite finished staring at me, I'll leave you to your quiet," she said.

She had her hand on the doorknob when he said, "Wait."

"Have you thought of some other insult to share with me, Captain?" she said.

There was a long silence. "No," he said finally. "It was nothing. A pleasure meeting you, miss."

"I wish I could say the same," she said, and regretted her hasty words the moment they left her lips. She wrenched at the door knob and let the door shut loudly behind her. Why had she said that? He hadn't intended to insult her, and she'd been so rude...but she couldn't go back and apologize, she would sound so foolish, and he probably hadn't been insulted anyway. Her face flamed with embarrassment. With luck, she would never see him again, and eventually she would forget how awful she'd been to a perfect stranger.

It took her some time to retrace her route, since she had not been paying it much attention when she passed through the house the first time, but again no one seemed to have noticed her absence. Selina still wasn't there. Lady Ormerod's blonde head bobbed at the far end of the ballroom. Elinor resolutely didn't catch the eye of anyone who might feel obligated to ask her to dance and went in search of her mother.

She found her in one of the salons off the ballroom, playing whist and laughing like mad at something her partner had just said. "What is it, Elinor dear?" she asked.

"I have the head-ache, mama," Elinor said, pressing the back of one gloved hand to her forehead in what she hoped was not too theatrical a way. "Do you suppose we might leave soon?"

"My dear, it is only now gone one o'clock! But if you are ill... Theodosia, do take my cards, and Elinor, you sit here and sip this punch, and I will find your papa."

It felt like an age before Mrs. Pembroke reappeared, saying, "Mr. Pembroke has gone to summon the carriage, and I'm sure I don't need to warn you not to tease him, because he was not happy at having to leave so soon. He becomes so *intense* when he discusses politics, you know!"

But Mr. Pembroke did not seem angry. In fact, he looked almost smug when she sat down in the chaise across from him. "I think we may call tonight a success, Elinor," he said.

"May we, papa? I am so glad."

"Indeed. You comported yourself very well. I cannot tell you how many compliments I received on your behalf. I hope you found the evening enjoyable?"

Right up until I was assaulted, and then was horribly rude to someone who didn't deserve it. "Yes, papa. It was gratifying to receive so much attention."

"Particularly from certain quarters, eh, daughter?" Mr. Pembroke chuckled.

"I... don't understand, papa."

"You made at least two conquests tonight—surely you cannot be unaware of this? Of course we cannot consider Mr. St. George's offer, he is far too old and has no title, but Lord Huxley—"

Elinor gasped. "Papa, you cannot mean to say Lord Huxley has made me an offer?"

"And why should he not? You are precisely what he is looking for in a wife. Granted, he is as yet merely his father's heir, but eventually he will be Earl of Lymington, and the Huxleys have some of the strongest Bounder talent in the country."

"But...but he hardly knows me!"

"Which is why I told him I was unwilling to entertain the notion of your becoming engaged so soon after arriving in London. You will meet him again in company, several times, and I assure you he is committed to fixing your interest with him. He has good manners, he is not too old—"

"Nearly twice my age, or I miss my guess!"

"Oh, Elinor, you are being foolish!" Mrs. Pembroke exclaimed. "Handsome, talented, wealthy, titled—you cannot expect to do better. I am so *happy* for you I could cry!"

A knot of acid began forming in her stomach again. "Papa, you said it would not do for me to make an attachment on my first appearance."

"And you will not. I expect Lord Huxley will not formally make you an offer until you have met some four or five times more."

"But what of...did you not say you wished me to have many offers, that you could consider them?" Her head began aching in earnest, as if the jaws of an invisible trap were closing over it.

"I did not anticipate you drawing the notice of someone as eligible as Lord Huxley. We will be joining him at the theater in three nights' time; he said you expressed an interest. Do you not see how he cares what will please you?"

The knot of acid threatened to overpower her. "Papa, I do not—he made improper advances to me, and I am persuaded I cannot like him."

Mr. Pembroke waved this away. "It is not uncommon for men to be carried away in the presence of a woman to whom they already feel an attraction," he said. "You are young and unfamiliar with the ways of the world. Don't be missish."

"Papa," Elinor exclaimed in desperation, "I will not accept an offer from Lord Huxley."

Mr. Pembroke's pleasant demeanor faded. "What I hear you saying," he said, "is that you refuse to be obedient to my wishes."

"No, papa, I—"

He leaned forward and gripped her knee painfully hard. "I will not hear 'no' from you, daughter," he said. "You may have no thought for your future, but I assure you, I have. I have indulged your freaks far longer than I should have, given you latitude to do as you pleased, and now I expect that indulgence to be repaid. Do not think I will support you forever. You will marry, you will marry well, and you will be grateful for my interference on your behalf. Do you think a man like Lord Huxley would ever have paid you the slightest heed had I not brought your talent to his attention? Your mother is correct—you cannot expect to do better, and, I might add, you could very likely do worse."

Elinor's eyes watered from pain. "You cannot force me to marry," she whispered.

"I can make your life a misery if you do not. Imagine yourself cut off from every pleasure, your allowance vanished, your movements restricted. No more parties, no more balls, no social visits. I will forbid you the library and the newspaper. Choose that, or choose to marry. There is no third way." He squeezed harder, and she gasped.

"Mr. Pembroke, do not—"

"Be silent. Elinor, you are not a fool. You must see what I am doing for you is best. It will make you happy. *Think.* You cannot believe I enjoy causing you pain."

Elinor opened her mouth to speak and gasped again as his grip on her knee grated against the bone. "I understand," she whispered. A few teardrops spattered the green silk, leaving marks that would probably not come out. Mr. Pembroke loosened his grip and patted her knee before withdrawing his hand.

"Then everything is settled," he said in a perfectly normal voice. "You need not rise early tomorrow, daughter. We keep London hours now."

Elinor nodded. Mrs. Pembroke, uncharacteristically silent, reached out as if to pat her daughter's knee, but withdrew before she touched her.

Elinor submitted to Mostyn's care—her mother, as if in apology, sent the woman to Elinor first—and then sat in her nightdress on the edge of her bed, staring at the fire. Its flames burned low and Elinor did not have the energy to rouse them. Lord Huxley's crooked smile came to memory. It would not be so bad, would it? At least he was interested in her, though how much of that interest was due to her talent she had no idea. He was friendly, amusing, attractive, wealthy— or so her father said—and someday he would make her a countess. She felt his mouth pressed against hers once more and went to her knees and scrabbled under the bed for the chamber pot, which she found just in time to be sick into it.

Afterward, she scrubbed her mouth with her sleeve and laid her forehead against the counterpane. Her father might dress it up any way he liked, but she was being sold on the market as surely as if she were a two-year-old filly. Whatever Lord Huxley wanted from her, she was certain it was not entirely her talent.

She carried her chamber pot to the water closet and poured it out, wrinkling her nose at the stench, then climbed into bed and pulled the blankets close under her chin. Live as a slave in her family home; live as a slave in Lord Huxley's mansion, or estate, or wherever it was he lived. There was no third way. *And I never did apologize to the captain. Not that it matters now.*

She fell into a restless sleep and dreamed of Luddites smashing her father's house, dreamed she was one of their number and set the place ablaze, then woke terrified the dream might have been real, though she had not unconsciously burned anything since that first night four months ago. She slept again, and dreamed of her father as the captain of a Caribbean pirate ship, and set his ship on fire over and over again until she woke in the cold April dawn, a third path clearly outlined in her mind.

She dressed in a dark-green merino walking gown and matching spencer, good quality clothing with no frills, clothing that declared her a serious, responsible person. She put her hair up, something she had been doing for herself since her first, failed season, tied her good grey bonnet with the silk lining over it, and threw a cape over the entire ensemble. She examined herself in the mirror; her heavy brows made her look fierce, which in this case might be a virtue. She straightened her hem, went downstairs, and had the butler summon a hackney.

She waited in the entry, pretending to be calm, terrified that some Pembroke or other might break with tradition and wake early, come into the hall, and want to know where she was going. Finally, the carriage arrived at the front door. She climbed into it unassisted, rapped on the roof, and said, "Take me to the Admiralty."

CHAPTER 3
IN WHICH ELINOR BRAVES THE ADMIRALTY

Elinor had never been to Whitehall, and was disappointed to see that its blocky architecture looked exactly the same as the parts of London she was familiar with. She had thought such an important seat of government would be more distinguished. The Admiralty was housed in a series of unassuming red-brick buildings situated around a central courtyard, surrounded by an imposing colonnade in which stood a small, square entrance barely tall enough to allow her carriage through.

Even at this hour of the morning, the courtyard was already busy with men, in uniform and out, passing through the entrance and in and out of various doors opening on the courtyard. She paid the hackney driver and stepped down into the yard. She saw no other women, but she held her head high and strode across the expanse to a pseudo-Grecian entry with four columns that looked entirely out of place against the modern brick façade. No one stopped her.

Inside, she stood, uncertain as to her next move. The marble floor beneath her feet reflected her as a grey smudge marring the smooth whiteness. A fire blazed in the long fireplace, doing its best to warm the bleak room but failing in the effort; the chairs flanking the fireplace were likely the only beneficiaries of its heat. More doors led off this chamber, ahead and to her left, neither of which gave her any clue as to where she should go.

Her uncertainty mounted, growing within her like an approaching fog she was powerless to stop. It was not too late to go home, to turn and walk out the door as if she'd merely been curious about the interior of the Admiralty and had now satisfied her interest. She half-turned, took a step toward the front door—*no, if I am to leave it will be because the First Lord rejects my plan, not because I am a coward.*

She looked desperately from one door to the other, wishing she dared choose one, afraid to choose incorrectly. Her continuing hesitation brought her the dubious assistance of a man in livery, who said, "Is there something I can help you with, miss?" as if certain there was not.

"I wish to speak with the First Lord of the Admiralty," she declared, squaring her shoulders and burying her hands in her skirt so their trembling would not betray her.

The functionary, surprised, said, "Do you have an appointment, miss?" His voice clearly conveyed he could not imagine anyone like her having an appointment with such an august personage as the First Lord.

"I think Lord Melville will want to speak with me when he knows what information I bring," she said, keeping her gaze steady and calm in contrast to the man's growing consternation. She hoped the First Lord was a reasonable man. Her plan hinged on it.

"Miss, I think you have been misinformed...the First Lord is a very busy man, and no one can simply walk into this building and demand an audience."

"I repeat, sir, Lord Melville will wish to speak with me."

The functionary blew out his breath in exasperation. "Miss, I'm afraid I will have to ask you to leave." He reached out as if to grasp her shoulder, hesitated, then stepped forward and made a little shooing motion with his hands that would have amused Elinor if she were not so agitated. He looked like a hen trying to get a recalcitrant chick to obey.

She clenched her fists, which were now shaking so hard she was certain he could not help but notice. She looked over the man's shoulder at the large fireplace where the cheerful fire crackled a welcome at her. "Sir, I believe something is wrong with your fire," she said.

The functionary reflexively looked over his shoulder. "I see nothing wrong. What do you mean?"

She raised her hand, knowing drama could sometimes win the day when reason and logic could not. "That," she said, and made an unnecessary gesture of dismissal as she commanded it to go out.

Five people passing through the room stopped in their tracks, and Elinor heard someone gasp. The liveried man took two steps backward in astonishment, then turned to look at her, his jaw hanging slack and his eyes wide. "You—" he began, then seemed to lose track of his words.

"I," Elinor said, and gestured again. The fire reappeared, as high and bright as if it had never been extinguished. "Shall I show you again? Or will you take me to see Lord Melville?"

The functionary nodded, his mouth hanging open slightly. "Follow me, miss," he said.

Elinor followed him down some broad, marble-paved corridors, too nervous to pay much attention to her surroundings. She kept her gaze directed at the functionary's back as they passed men in uniform or livery so she would not have to see their reactions to her presence, though she imagined their attention pressing on her back like a blunted knife, too dull to pierce skin but painful nonetheless. Her unwilling guide led her to a heavy oak door that looked exactly the same as all the others they had passed. The man opened it, hurrying inside without waiting for her to precede him. "My lord," he said, his voice cracking, "this young lady wishes to speak to you."

This room was high-ceilinged, paneled in oak with windows along one wall that let in the grey morning light. A long, green-topped table occupied most of the middle of the room, and a fireplace, its fire laid but unlit, interrupted the paneling on her right. Long cylinders that might contain maps hung above the fireplace. Across the room, a clock several feet in diameter set into the wall swept out the time above a pair of globes larger than she could encircle with her arms, bracketed by a pair of narrow glass-fronted bookshelves. It was big and masculine and overpowering and because of that, Elinor relaxed a little; the room was trying too hard to intimidate, like a large man blustering at the world who does not know his trouser seat is torn.

At the far end of the table stood a high-backed chair, in which was seated a man with a handsome face and slightly disordered hair who looked up at her entrance. Two Admirals standing near him, leaning over the table to examine a large sheet of paper, glanced at her and then gave her longer, more astonished stares, while a fourth man wearing a post-captain's epaulettes stood looking out one of the windows and did not acknowledge her entrance.

The seated man said, "Grafton, have you taken leave of your senses?"

"My lord, please...give her five minutes," Grafton said, glancing at Elinor with no small measure of fear.

"No, not five seconds. Young lady, I do not know how you enticed this man to bring you here, but I am astonished at your want of conduct. Please leave before I am forced to have you escorted out."

In addition to the fire laid in the fireplace, there were unlit lamps in sconces along the walls and a decorative lamp she guessed was some kind of ship's lantern on a table below the windows. Another lamp of translucent, cloudy glass some three feet in diameter hung high above the table, shedding only a dim light on the proceedings below. Elinor wondered that the dimness did not bother the First Lord, who surely must be squinting at whatever his paper said.

She shivered and drew her cape more closely about herself. "Your room is too cold," she said, and lit every fire in the room at once. The fire on the grate roared in its joy at being set free, filling the fireplace and stretching two feet up the chimney. The lamps on the walls flared seven inches in the air and set liquid wax pouring over the sconces to drip on the floor. The ship's lantern made a popping sound; Elinor quickly soothed that fire and hoped it had not damaged the lamp too badly.

Melville leapt to his feet, knocking his chair over; the man nearest the fireplace stepped away from it, shielding his face from the raging heat of the fire; and the man by the window glanced down at the burning lantern next to him, then turned around to look at Elinor and crossed his arms over his chest, reclining against the wall. In that stance, despite his face being backlit by the morning light streaming through the window, Elinor recognized immediately the captain she had met the night before. She took an involuntary step backward, then turned her attention on Melville. He had gone from startled to furious.

"You dare come into my offices and play Scorchers' tricks on me!" he shouted. "Grafton, remove this woman at once!"

"I apologize. I seem to have made your room too warm," Elinor said. It astonished her that she sounded so calm. "Let me correct my mistake." She extinguished all the fires with a thought, leaving the room with only their residual heat. Without the scant light of the overhead lamp, the room seemed even colder than before, the wan, blue-grey light from the windows making the four men look as if they were made of wax. Elinor hastily relit the overhead lamp, which lessened the effect but did not eliminate it. Her anxiety melted like the candle wax. She had taken an irrevocable step, and there was no going back now.

"Grafton—" Melville began, then realized what she'd done. His face fell into the same mask of astonishment the functionary's had borne only minutes before. "You—" he said to Elinor, then seemed to run out of words.

"My lord, this is Miss Pembroke," the captain said, advancing toward the table with his hand on the hilt of his sword to keep it from swinging. "She is, as you may have realized, an Extraordinary Scorcher." He made a slight bow in her direction. "We were...introduced yesterday evening."

"Captain," Elinor said, bobbing a slight curtsey. He didn't seem to hold her rudeness against her, but he didn't exactly seem friendly either. Where had he learned her name? "My lord, I apologize for the display, but I wanted you to take me seriously. I wish to offer my services to the Royal Navy."

The room went perfectly silent. Elinor refused to allow herself to blush. This was her third path, and she would not let them deny it to her. "It is well known that the Navy is fighting a losing battle," she said. "Pirates are harassing British merchant ships, disrupting our trade, while Napoleon's ships are interfering with the convoys supplying Lord Wellington in the Peninsula. Our Navy is the jewel of our military forces, but most of our ships are too heavy to successfully defend against the smaller, faster privateers and pirates, and as I understand from reports in the newspapers, we cannot afford to split our forces now that Napoleon has closed off European ports to our trade. To make matters worse, most of the enemy ships bear Scorchers in greater numbers than we currently have, and they have destroyed or captured many of the ships we depend on to defend our fleet, forcing our shipyards to scramble to replace them."

She took a breath. "My lord, I believe you can use someone with my talent. I am capable of rendering those attacks useless; my power at igniting fires is unmatched; and if enough of our enemies realize that tangling with our ships will bring only death and disaster, they will look for easier targets elsewhere."

She was not actually certain of her second point, as she had never yet had reason to test the limits of her power, but she could feel the fire call to her, and believed if she asked it, it would rage hot and bright enough to immolate this building and everyone inside. The image sickened her.

The silence persisted for a few seconds more, then both Admirals spoke at once, their words tangling in the air so they never reached Melville's ear. The First Lord bent to right his chair, then sat in it, fixing his eyes on Elinor's. Years of turning a calm visage to her father's scorn and anger kept her from flinching at the intensity of his gaze. "Hold a moment," he said, and the admirals went silent. "You are a woman," he continued.

"I realize that. I have been a woman my entire life. Do you think a woman might not feel some desire to defend her country?"

"Women do not serve in the Navy. For a well-born woman, even an Extraordinary, to do so is unthinkable."

"Yet you would accept my offer were I a man. You need me, my lord, and I think under such circumstances, neither of us can afford to entertain such niceties as pertain to my sex."

One of the admirals said, "My lord, she's not wrong."

Melville looked at him in astonishment. "Stanhope? You, of all people, entertaining this radical notion?"

The admiral stabbed at the map with his forefinger. "Six merchant vessels lost in the last month, my lord. And that upstart Wellington has been foaming at the mouth, complaining that we are not making any effort to keep that rabble of an Army of his from starving to death. If she were a man, you wouldn't think twice. You would probably have gone out of your way to recruit such a talent. And you know the government expects all Extraordinary Seers, Shapers, and Bounders, male *and* female, to serve four years in the Army's War Office. We've been rejecting female Extraordinaries based on long-standing naval policy, but it might be time for us to rethink that policy. If this young lady is willing to take the risk, I say we allow her to."

"That's preposterous!" the other admiral said. "Miss...Pembroke, was it? Miss Pembroke, you have no idea what conditions on shipboard are like. You know nothing of the privations of war. We cannot guarantee your safety, let alone that you will be treated with the respect a gentlewoman deserves. There is little privacy, the men behave in a coarse fashion that will surely offend your delicate sensibilities, and what they will think of any unmarried woman who—they may offer you insult—"

"I believe any Scorcher is more than capable of defending against such assaults," the captain drawled.

"But no lady should be subject—"

"I appreciate your concern, Admiral," Elinor said. "You are correct that I have never experienced such conditions as obtain aboard a ship. I am, however, willing to endure if that is what I must do."

Melville shook his head. "I don't like it."

"We haven't become the preeminent naval force in the world by failing to innovate," the admiral Melville had addressed as Stanhope said. "Consider it, my lord. Those da— those accursed pirates fleeing before *us* for a change."

"But your reputation—" the other admiral began.

"Need not suffer if you do not publicize my involvement," Elinor said, smoothly heading off his objection. "Although that does bring me to the second part of my offer."

"And what is that?" Melville said. Elinor thought his opposition might be weakening. What she was about to say might cause him to throw her out of the office entirely.

"My services do not come free," she said, "much as my offer is made in a spirit of patriotism. I want fifteen thousand pounds, invested in the funds, available to me in full when my term of service is complete."

All the men except the captain burst out in torrents of speech. Elinor waited patiently, clenching her shaking hands in the folds of her skirts, until she judged their outrage had died down somewhat. "Gentlemen," she said, raising her voice to carry over the din, "you have already addressed an important point: I may well be throwing my reputation away by my actions. I must have the assurance that I will be able to support myself if I do, in fact, end up ostracized by society."

"Fifteen thousand pounds is out of the question," the First Lord said, his face red. "Out of the question. We are stretched to the limit as it is. Do you have any idea of the cost to His Majesty's government of our sailors' pay alone, young lady? I cannot approve it."

"I am well aware England has invested a great deal of money in this war," Elinor said. "It is one of the primary points of contention between Whig and Tory and the subject of much debate for those who care about the future of our kingdom. I am also aware that the cost of a new frigate is much greater than the sum I am requesting, and we continue to require more of those since, as I mentioned before, our enemies persist in destroying or capturing them. You might think of me in terms of...of adding another ship to your fleet, in which case fifteen thousand pounds is a rare bargain. And I will forgo my share of the prize money I would otherwise be entitled to as a, well, a sailor aboard one of His Majesty's warships. Whatever my rank within the Navy would be."

"It is impossible. I cannot justify such an expense."

"My lord," Stanhope began, "her logic—"

"Admiral Stanhope, you should be the first to argue against such an extravagance!"

"Because I am in favor of reining in our expenses? If we accept Miss Pembroke's conditions, we save the cost of another ship as well as the time it would take to build one. I have seen an enemy Extraordinary Scorcher in action off the coast of Panama, my lord.

Used wisely, Miss Pembroke's abilities could tip the scales in our favor."

"My lord," Elinor said. "I realize I am asking you to take a risk. If it turns out I am wrong, and I can offer the Navy nothing, then our agreement is void." She put her hands on the table and leaned forward to look the First Lord in the eye. "My lord, no one knows I came here today. I can walk out of this office and return to my old life if you refuse me. But I don't want to do that. And I don't think you want me to either."

"My lord—"

Melville cut off the second admiral with a gesture. He ran the fingers of his left hand through his hair, revealing the secret of why it looked so disordered. "Your family cannot possibly approve this course of action."

"I am of age, sir, and an Extraordinary. My family may disapprove, but I am free to make my own decisions." *And I will endure when my father most certainly casts me off.*

The First Lord intertwined his fingers on the desk before him, possibly to prevent himself from rumpling his hair still further. For a moment, he seemed to be looking past her, contemplating some unknown future. Then he brought his gaze to bear on her, and for a moment it contained a degree of calculation so similar to the expression she had often seen in her father's eyes that her hands shook again. "Miss Pembroke," he said, then went silent again. "Miss Pembroke, are you certain you understand the implications of what you offer? This is not the life you were raised to. Admiral Pentstemmon is correct; we cannot guarantee your safety, let alone your comfort. There are superstitions about women aboard ship that may cause many seamen to treat you with a lack of the respect you are no doubt accustomed to. And you may find yourself without a life to return to. I repeat—are you certain?"

Elinor took another deep breath. "My lord," she said, "the life I was raised to has not turned out to be as satisfactory as you imagine. I had far rather take this chance than stay at home and continue as I have always done."

Melville looked at her for another long moment. He extended his hand. "Then I welcome you to the Royal Navy, Miss Pembroke."

Admiral Pentstemmon threw up his hands and turned away. Stanhope also extended his hand to shake Elinor's. "Admiral Stanhope," he said. "Your talent is remarkable. Can you do it at any time?"

"I can," Elinor said, "though I have had it only four months and have yet to discover its limits."

"Remarkable," Stanhope said. "I would like to see the looks on those villains' faces when they come up against you."

Elinor smiled, though now that she'd achieved her goal, her certainty wavered. Not her certainty that she had made the right choice, nor that she could endure shipboard life; she feared she had made these men promises she would not be able to keep. She lit the ship's lamp once more and gave that flame space in her mind. Yes, if she chose, she could feed it until it broke free and encompassed the room. Whatever her limits might be, burning a ship was not beyond them.

"I think concealing your presence will give us an advantage in this fight. We shall proceed as quickly as possible, so word of this has no time to spread," Melville said, removing paper and ink from a drawer next to his seat. "Your word as an Extraordinary is binding in itself, but I think a short document outlining our agreement will be a valuable surety for both our sakes—if you've no objection to these gentlemen witnessing?"

Elinor nodded. It was probably a good idea to define exactly what actions on her part would qualify as benefiting the Navy, in case the penny-pinching First Lord thought to cheat her later by saying she had not performed to satisfaction. Even so, she did not think the talentless Melville would dream of cheating an Extraordinary, however much political power he wielded. She read the document twice, signed, and handed the pen to the First Lord to do the same.

He swept the nib across the paper with a flourish and waved the paper in the air to dry it. "Excellent. Miss Pembroke, how soon can you be ready to leave?"

"Tomorrow," Elinor said, feeling certainty return. She had only to pack her clothing and bid farewell to Selina—why *had* her sister never appeared at the ball?—and, she supposed, tell her father she was leaving. The temptation to simply leave him a note was profound, but she refused to be a coward any longer.

"Excellent. Fortunate all around you came today, Miss Pembroke. The need for secrecy prohibits my putting you under the command of the Navy Board, as we do our Speaker corps, so instead I will assign you to Captain Ramsay. It is better, I think, that we keep you outside the chain of command. You will answer directly to him, though I expect you to treat the other officers with respect."

The captain had come to full attention as Melville spoke, and almost before he was finished, said, "You want her to serve on *my* ship, my lord?"

"Do you have a problem with that, Ramsay?"

Captain Ramsay fixed his eyes on a point some five inches above Melville's head. "Wouldn't Miss Pembroke's talent be better applied closer to home, sir?"

"I want those pirates dealt with. We need those American trade goods, and we need the merchant fleet to regain its confidence in us, after all those losses we've sustained. Let the ships of the line protect the Peninsular convoys. Unless you are telling me *Athena* is not up to the challenge?"

Ramsay shook his head. "No, sir."

"You are already acquainted with the young lady, and you are the man on the spot. If I assign her to another ship, I will have to inform yet another man of the secret. I will already have to tell Admiral Durrant, and he will...at any rate, I think I need not tell you not to spread this around."

"No, sir."

"Very well. Your orders are what they were an hour ago—proceed west to join the fleet. Cover the shipping lanes, engage any enemies you meet, take prizes where you can and burn the rest." He handed Ramsay a sealed packet of paper.

"Yes, sir."

"And stop giving me monosyllables. The *Athena* is our newest ship and the fastest, and you have distinguished yourself by taking more prizes than any other man of your rank. You are the obvious choice.

Dismissed, Captain, and...don't warn your crew. We both know they will not be able to stay silent."

Ramsay brought his gaze down to meet Melville's eyes. "They won't like that, sir. They'll feel betrayed."

"You may tell them you will have a special passenger, but that is all you will say until you are safely out of harbor. It's regrettable, Captain, but I know you see the reason in it."

Ramsay glanced at Elinor. "I do," he said, but his neutral air had turned into something less friendly. Elinor's heart sank. She'd prepared herself for the possibility the crew might not like her, but she'd hoped at least to have a captain who wanted her there. And he'd seemed so accepting of her plan, right up until it turned out he was a part of it.

"Thank you, Captain," she said, and offered him her hand.

After a moment, he took it, but released her as quickly as good manners allowed and left the room.

"If you will give me your address, I will send a carriage for you tomorrow morning," Melville said. "Pack lightly and sensibly; you will be responsible for your own dunnage. Ramsay knows his business and his officers will treat you with respect, but you should not expect them to neglect their duties to wait on you."

"No, Lord Melville, and I am accustomed to doing for myself," Elinor said.

"I hope you won't regret this, Lord Melville," Pentstemmon said.

Melville looked at Elinor. "So do I," he said, and shook Elinor's hand again. "Good luck, Miss Pembroke."

Elinor curtsied to each of the admirals in turn, then found her own way out of the Admiralty Building and back through the courtyard to the street, where she waved down a carriage. Safely inside the hackney, she sat rigidly upright in the center of her seat, clenching her hands once more to keep them from shaking. "Wrathingham House," she commanded, and the carriage lurched into motion. She would tell Selina first, swear her to secrecy, then return home and pack her belongings. She would not face her father until tomorrow morning, when it would be too late for him to stop her. It had nothing to do with fear.

CHAPTER 4

IN WHICH ELINOR EMBARKS,
LITERALLY, ON HER THIRD PATH

D ear Father,
    Dear Sir,
    Papa,
Father,
When you read this, I shall be beyond your reach.

She'd purchased a cheap trunk on her way back from Selina's house, daring the shopkeeper to make an issue of it, and smuggled it up to her room in terror that someone might see her. Her success at keeping it all a secret seemed miraculous. Half an hour before dawn, she had stood outside the front door, waiting for the First Lord's hackney and feeling grateful that the butler had no previously undiscovered talent that would let him see through the wood of the door. Now she clasped her hands in her lap as the hackney, black and anonymous and smelling a little of mildew, rattled along the cobblestones toward the docks. She sat well back and did not look out the windows, fearing notice even at this early hour despite the emptiness of the streets.

Halfway to Wrathingham House yesterday, she had realized that telling anyone, even Selina, what she intended made it likely she would be locked in her room until she agreed to give up her mad scheme.

46

She'd pushed her relief to the back of her mind, told herself she was not being a coward, and kept herself perfectly composed during her visit with her sister, who had no more sinister reason for her absence from the ball than a sudden head cold.

Selina had listened indignantly to Elinor's story of her encounter with Lord Huxley and their father's demands. "He cannot believe you will submit to this plan," she said. "Come to stay with me, dearest. You must know you will always have a home here."

"I will remember that, but I do not think things have come to such a pass yet," Elinor said, feeling horribly guilty at lying to her beloved sister. "I have not given up on finding another solution."

I am not insensible of the fact that for my entire life, I was beneath your notice—until I developed a talent that brought not only myself but you into prominence. How concerned were you for my happiness half a year ago, when I was still, in your eyes, nothing?

They were crossing the Thames now, its sickly stench flooding her nostrils, and Elinor covered her nose with her handkerchief and looked out across the wide river to watch the ships traveling downstream, around the curving banks to who knew what destination. None of them were Navy vessels, but that was the extent of her knowledge about ships. She was going to be in the way on board...*Athena*, Lord Melville had called the ship. She would do stupid things, and they would all resent her; this was the worst idea she had ever had and it wasn't too late to turn around, was it? She could live with Selina, be her companion...her poor, dependent companion, doomed to face the same fate as if she'd remained at home. She tried breathing through her mouth, which made the smell only marginally better. She was not going back; nothing this future held could possibly be worse than what she was leaving behind.

But you are correct in one thing: I have only two paths ahead of me, even if I disobey you and refuse Lord Huxley's offer. I must either marry, or remain dependent on you for the rest of my life. The first fills me with dread, the second with abhorrence. I have discovered a third path, and I intend to follow it.

They left the Thames, and its stench, behind, and entered a part of the city Elinor had never imagined she might visit. Spring had not come to these streets, which stank as badly as the river had. The buildings crowded together as if for company, but were in such a state of disrepair it seemed impossible anyone could bear to live in them, their roofs sagging and gapped where shingles were missing or broken, their windows cracked and patched with brown paper or stuffed with rags.

The streets here seemed to be in the same condition as the houses, for the carriage bounced more than usual as they passed through the district, though Elinor thought the driver was also driving faster than he had leaving her father's house, as if afraid of what might happen were he stopped. It seemed impossible that this was the same London as the one she'd left behind, all those enormous buildings weighted down by history. She pushed the heavy hood of her cloak back; she'd worn it not for warmth but for anonymity, and aside from the dirty children who raced alongside, no one was paying any attention to her or her carriage right now. Plenty of time to be stifled when she reached the docks.

Don't search for me; as I said, I am beyond your reach. If my departure causes you any pain, I apologize for it, though I think your pain will be more for your lost alliance than for your lost daughter. Believe me when I say this course of action is better for all of us; I gain a life of my choosing, and you lose an undutiful, rebellious daughter who would never be able to satisfy you. If you wish, you may give my love to mama and Amelia, for I do love my family, however my actions might imply otherwise. Farewell, and I hope someday you will be able to forgive me.

She'd posted a second letter to Selina, its contents more loving but equally uninformative. She was far more concerned about what Selina might think of her disappearance, and had struggled for several hours the previous day trying to decide how much to tell her so her imagination would not be tortured with possibilities. In the end, she had said simply she was going to travel, that she would be gone for some time, and Selina was not to worry about her—though she knew her sister would ignore that instruction.

The thought of Selina's suffering made Elinor press her handkerchief to her eyes. She refused to cry. She would not enact Captain Ramsay any tragedies; he already didn't like the idea of her presence aboard his ship, and she intended to give him no reasons to further regret the First Lord's plan.

Ten minutes more brought the carriage back within sight and smell of the Thames, and Elinor leaned forward once more to see her destination. A forest of slim masts had sprung up ahead, their sails furled, and beyond them more ships moved past, these with sails puffed out to catch what little breeze there was. In the distance, the skeleton of an enormous ship sat in a cradle, swarming with tiny figures. Her anxiety faded, replaced by curiosity and the beginnings of excitement. These were the Deptford docks, and somewhere among these ships was the one she would call home for the foreseeable future.

She sat back and pulled her hood up, peering past its sides as the carriage turned to pass parallel to the small boats that served as transport between the ships nearer the center of the river and the shore. Men went past hauling burdens, singly or in pairs, carrying crates or rolling barrels or coiling lengths of rope or hauling any of dozens of objects whose purpose she couldn't begin to guess. They shouted to one another in unintelligible accents, their voices blending with the cries of birds and the rumble of cargo being loaded by men who looked as if they could lift a ship out of water and bring it to the cargo instead. A good number of them wore little more than short, loose breeches, which both fascinated and embarrassed her. It now occurred to her that the seamen aboard *Athena* likely didn't wear as many clothes as she was accustomed to, and they probably would not change their behavior to suit her sensibilities. She hadn't even boarded the ship and already she was out of her depth. *Hah. A nautical metaphor.*

The carriage came to a halt, and the driver climbed down and opened the door for her. "Let me help you into the boat, miss," he said.

Before Elinor could protest, she was handed down into a rowboat shining with fresh black paint, manned by two seamen who looked younger than she was. "*You're* going t' *Athena?*" the nearer one said. His front teeth had a gap between them, and when he said *Athena* it came out as *Asena.* He glanced back at his partner, who shrugged.

"Just take the lady to the ship, and keep your opinions to yourself," the driver said, handing down Elinor's trunk. "Good luck, miss."

Elinor twisted around in her seat to watch him drive away, and when she turned to face front again, the young seamen had begun pulling at the oars in straight, smooth strokes. They were facing the wrong way, or at least Elinor thought they ought to watch where they were going instead of where they'd been, but they didn't seem concerned they might run into some other boat. Both seemed fascinated with her, and Elinor wished she could pull her hood over her face again, regain that anonymity.

"Goin' t' the *Asena*," the sailor said. "Wotcher goin' there for?"

"Are you one of *Athena*'s crew?" Elinor asked. The young man nodded. "Then I suppose you will learn that once we're there, won't you?" Captain Ramsay likely resented her for his not being allowed to forewarn his crew about her presence. Elinor ruthlessly shoved her anxieties away again—plenty of time to entertain them in private, once she...*oh, no, will I even have a private place to sleep? Don't people on ships sleep in hammocks? I will never be able to sleep in a hammock. It's fortunate I can't swim, or I would risk the Thames and go home.* But she knew she wasn't going back, even if it did mean sleeping in a hammock, surrounded by a hundred sailors.

They came out from among the great ships being loaded at the docks, into smooth, murky water the color of grey, smoked glass, and the young men, again without looking, steered the boat so it was pointed at a large ship anchored a short distance away. From here, she could clearly read the word ATHENA painted across the rear of the ship. It was beautiful, all sleek curving lines contrasting with the straight masts and cross-beams, its black paint and yellow trim fresh and bright, its sails bundled along the masts white in the morning sun. They were approaching the side of the ship from the rear, which gave it a foreshortened look and prevented Elinor from seeing whatever figurehead might be mounted at the front; would they have put an image of the Greek goddess there?

A bay of six glass-paned windows across the rear of the ship looked out of place, as if someone's sitting room were trying to emerge from the ship's curved posterior. She counted the red-lined gun ports—thirteen, so *Athena* carried twenty-six guns, and more—she couldn't tell how many—on the deck above. The ship looked enormous to Elinor, though based on the number of guns it was actually small compared to the 74-gun ships of the line that were the pride of the Royal Navy. Lord Melville had called *Athena* one of their fastest ships, but Elinor had trouble believing anything that size could possibly be fast. *That,* however, was an opinion she planned to keep to herself. She had heard sailors were proud of their ships and didn't like outsiders criticizing them. At least she knew better than to call it a boat.

It loomed larger as they neared it, the oarsmen not slowing down at all. Elinor gripped the rough edge of her seat and bit her lip to keep from screaming at them to stop before they crashed into the ship. Just as she was certain she would be finding out whether or not she could swim, the seamen dipped the oars, and the boat turned, slowed, and came to a neat stop next to *Athena's* side, barely kissing the wood without leaving a mark.

Wooden cleats affixed to the ship's side ran from the waterline to the deck, high above, like a primitive ladder. Climbing it would be impossible, even if she weren't wearing a gown. "I can't climb that," she told the men, reddening with embarrassment. She was not even aboard ship and already she needed special treatment.

"Identify yourself!" A head, darkly backlit against the lightening sky, peered down at them.

The first seaman stood up, rocking the boat so Elinor had to grip the edge of her seat again. "Lady comin' aboard! Send down the bo'sun's chair!"

Moments later a bundle came into view, high above, and was slowly lowered toward them. It turned out to be some kind of seat that did not look stable, a tangle of canvas and rope that, once untangled, hung limp like a child's swing. The seaman helped Elinor arrange herself in it, holding the ropes while she tried to balance in its exact center and simultaneously keep her gown from hiking up; the other young man stared at her slack-jawed and did not offer to help. The gap-toothed sailor strapped a harness around her and shouted again.

Elinor gasped as the "chair" jerked into motion. She kept a firm grip, for despite how securely she was fastened into it, she felt terribly unsafe. She carefully kept her eyes fixed straight ahead, insisting to herself she was safe, truly she was; they had handled the whole transaction so matter-of-factly they must do this all the time, and there was nothing to worry about.

The seat rotated slightly, and she gripped the rope so tightly the fibers cut into her palm as her view went from being one of the ships moored at the dock to the smooth black side of *Athena*, so close she could have touched it if she'd dared let go of what she was clinging to. The young seaman shouted something up at her, but she couldn't make it out. A gull swept past, croaking its shrill cry; she squeaked involuntarily and cringed, then felt like a fool. *It's only a bird. And you're not dangling what feels like twenty feet in the air with nothing beneath you but a tiny wooden boat and who knows how many feet of filthy water.*

Soon her eyes were level with the deck, then she rose above it and realized the seat was attached to a spar and its ropes were being pulled on by several men who acted as if her slight weight was almost impossible for them to manage. A couple of crewmen came forward to help her out of the chair; they both looked puzzled at her appearance, as if they hadn't been expecting her. Which, of course, they weren't. "I would like to speak to Captain Ramsay, please," she said.

They looked at one another, then at her, their expressions of puzzlement deepening. "The Capt'n?" one said. "Wotcher want w' the Capt'n?"

"That's my business," Elinor said in her most patrician manner, softening it slightly with a serenely smiling visage. She was barely able to understand his thick accent. Yet another problem she had not considered when embarking on the madness that was this journey. Behind her, the ropes and pulleys creaked again. She hoped it was her... dunnage, yes. It was like learning a foreign language.

"Whom have you brought on board?" A dark-haired man wearing a lieutenant's epaulette approached her. He sounded irritated. "We are not expecting—I beg your pardon, who are you?"

"I have business with Captain Ramsay," Elinor said in that same firm tone.

"And what business is that?" The lieutenant had bad skin and a nose that turned up at the tip, which gave him the appearance of a somewhat seedy elf.

"Private business. Can you conduct me to him, Lieutenant?"

The lieutenant looked her up and down, almost leering, as if he had a suspicion of what the captain's private business might be. *Again I wonder if there is something about me that makes men believe I am open to the most immoral practices.* "Certainly," he said. "Follow me."

There was rope *everywhere*, tawny, thick strands strung like a giant child's cat's cradle from the masts to the sails and from there to the deck, where it was wound round pegs and an enormous spool with spokes emerging from it. Men swarmed over the deck, hauling more rope and wooden buckets and other things she did not recognize; they stepped around Elinor, glancing at her, but did not pause in their activities. They were surprisingly quiet, speaking just above a normal volume, rarely shouting out to their fellows but appearing to understand one another quite well nevertheless.

Elinor looked up at the sails and observed more men clinging to the masts and the cross-pieces—she ought to at least learn the names of the ship's parts, if she were to be even nominally a part of Captain Ramsay's crew. They were beginning to unfurl the white sails, and Elinor wondered if the wind would be sufficient to take them out of harbor or if they might be stranded here at Deptford for days. Days during which her father could search for her.

She closed her fists until her nails cut into her palms. Her father might think to ask the butler, who knew Elinor had hired a hackney the previous day and might have heard her instruct the driver to take her to the Admiralty. Then he might manage to find someone there who had seen her...she unclenched her fists. Lord Melville and the two admirals would say nothing. Her father would not be able to find her. And even if he did, Captain Ramsay would not allow him to drag her, screaming, off *Athena*. Probably.

The lieutenant led her past a grating over a large, square hole in the deck to a set of steep stairs—Elinor was tempted to turn around and go down them as if they were a ladder, but the lieutenant seemed quite casual about descending them, and she already disliked him enough not to want to show weakness in front of him—and into a noisy, crowded place filled with sweaty bodies and cannons larger around than she was.

Men shouted past each other and laughed at jokes she couldn't make out, told in accents she couldn't understand. The walls curved just the slightest bit, and the ceiling was low enough the lieutenant had to duck a little to avoid cracking his head on the beams. It was lit only by the sunlight coming through the gun ports and by brass lanterns giving off an orangeish light; she heard the noise decrease, and as her eyes adjusted to the dimness, she saw the men nearest her were staring, their silence spreading outward until Elinor felt deafened by it.

She turned and hurried to catch up to the lieutenant, who had moved without hesitation beyond the stairs to a door whose carved moldings belonged in a country house rather than on board a ship, an unexpected contrast to the flimsy wall into which it was set. Beyond that was a tiny, windowless room with another door, on which the lieutenant knocked and said, "Captain? You have a...visitor." He looked at Elinor over his shoulder and smiled; it was, again, nearly a leer.

Elinor responded with a smile of her own, innocent friendliness concealing her irritation. *I wonder what that smile of yours will look like when you learn we are shipmates?*

Half a minute later, the door opened, revealing Ramsay in the process of buttoning his jacket. "Miss Pembroke," he said, "please come in. Thank you, Mr. Livingston, that will be all." Elinor glanced back before the door closed and saw, for a moment, a hint of disdain touch the lieutenant's eyes.

This room was brightly lit by the morning sun pouring through the clear glass of the windows, two of which were open to catch the brisk air and the sound of seabirds *kraaawing* across the river. With pictures adorning the walls, it had a comfortable, home-like look. Less domestic was the pair of swords mounted one above the other on the wall to her right, the longer one decorated with gilt and a tassel, the shorter one plainer with signs of use. There was another door to the left, smaller and flimsy by comparison to the others, and a couple of covered objects Elinor realized after a moment were small cannons. They were a reminder that this room, as homelike as it seemed, was still built primarily for war.

Two couches upholstered in brown leather, with a short oak cabinet resting between them, fit nicely into the space beneath the windows, though why they were attached to the walls, she could only guess—to keep them secure in bad weather, perhaps? A long table stood near the furthest left-hand window where the light would fall most brightly on its surface, with a log book open on it, and a chair was drawn up to it at an angle as if someone had just got up, for example, to answer the door.

"You're earlier than I expected," Ramsay said.

"This is apparently what the First Lord meant when he said he would send a carriage in the morning," Elinor said. This was the first time she had seen the captain in full light. His face was long and interestingly bony, his nose a little crooked as if he'd broken it once and had it imperfectly set. He wore his light-brown hair cut short and swept back from his face, which again had that neutral expression she'd seen in the Admiralty, and his eyes were a startling blue against his tanned skin. Elinor had heard seamen grew weathered and prematurely aged because of their exposure to wind and wave, but despite the faint lines at the corners of his eyes, Ramsay didn't look old, merely as if he were contemplating a puzzle he was not certain he could solve.

"Where is your companion?" he asked.

"My—?" Elinor flushed. "I have no companion."

Ramsay's eyebrows went up. "No companion? Miss Pembroke, do you have no care for your reputation at all?"

"I cannot expect another woman to endure what are apparently the privations of shipboard life," Elinor retorted. *And I cannot afford to hire a duenna or abigail.*

"You know what society will think if word of your...adventure...gets around."

"I am depending on you to see it does not, Captain."

Ramsay's lips tightened. "That's quite an expectation. Mr. Selkirk has the boys in charge; none of our officers have wives aboard. And duenna is not among my duties."

"I apologize, Captain. Please believe I do not hold you responsible for the keeping of my reputation. I meant only that I know you will do your best to conceal my presence here. And I think my being an Extraordinary is some protection."

"Protection from overt censure, possibly. I still think you should have a companion."

"Where do you suggest I find one at this juncture?"

Ramsay shook his head and turned away from her so she couldn't see his expression. She clenched her fists. This was so *stupid*, this assumption that because she was a woman, her virtue was irreparably stained the moment she was alone with a man not related to her anywhere but the drawing room of her own home. She felt like burning something, anything to give relief to her pent-up frustration and anxiety and fear, but she did not want to appear ungoverned and dangerous in front of this man.

Finally, Ramsay looked back at her, his expression as calm as if she weren't an impediment to him, which she was certain she was. "If that's your decision, Miss Pembroke...well, I suppose it doesn't matter so long as we can conceal your presence. We will set sail around noon, and I'll ask you to keep to these quarters until we are underway."

Elinor nodded. Ramsay looked as if he wanted to say more, shook his head, and went to take the short sword off the wall. He strapped it to his waist, picked up his hat, and said, "*Athena* is the newest design for frigates—the captain's quarters have a little more space, so we'll be able to accommodate you nicely. This is the great cabin. Please feel free to make use of it whenever you want. I keep a few books in that cabinet you're welcome to."

He slid open a panel Elinor had thought was a wall, revealing a tiny space containing a bench with a hole in it. "The quarter gallery. The, ah, sanitary facilities," he clarified when she looked at him in confusion. "We call it the head. And over here is where you will sleep." He opened the second door to reveal another tiny chamber mostly filled with a strange, boxy-looking bed. Ramsay Moved the narrow, long chest sitting on the bed, making it rock, and lifted the chest to shoulder height.

"But...this is your bedroom," Elinor said, looking at the chest.

"Not anymore. Now it's yours."

"I cannot take your room, Captain."

Ramsay removed his hat and turned his full gaze upon her. "Miss Pembroke," he said, "I could hardly call myself a gentleman if I didn't see to your comfort. I'll be bunking out here. Don't trouble yourself on my account."

"But—"

"The First Lord put you under my command, yes? Then I'm

making this a command. I'll return shortly." He put his hat back on and was out the door before Elinor could protest further.

She gave the bed a little shove—it was mounted in a way that made it sway at her touch—and went back to the great cabin to look out the windows. They provided her with a view of the river traffic headed into London or toward the sea. Not all the ships had sails; some were propelled by oars, a few near the shore by long poles, but mostly it was sails as far as she could see in both directions. She imagined what it would be like to look out these windows and see nothing but water, and she shuddered, excited and terrified by the thought.

The room Ramsay had indicated she was to sleep in was little more than a windowless cubby illuminated only by one of those orange-tinged lamps. She wondered what other frigates were like, if this were representative of "more space." At least the bed wasn't a hammock, even if it did move alarmingly like one.

Two of the sailors brought her trunk into the room, and she unnecessarily tidied its contents when they were gone, reflecting on how strange it felt to wear only a boned chemise and shift rather than stays, which she had left behind knowing she would be unable to don them without assistance. She smoothed the wrinkles from her favorite evening gown, white rose-figured gauze over pink silk, then hung it on a peg in the narrow cupboard; she had no idea when she would wear it, but she hadn't been able to bear the thought of Amelia snatching it up as she was certain to do with the rest of Elinor's wardrobe, once it became clear she was not returning. Never mind that she wouldn't be able to wear any of it; Amelia could never bear anyone having the advantage of her.

She returned to the great cabin and took a turn around the room. The wall into which the door was set appeared impermanent, as if it were designed to be removed, though why that should be necessary she had no idea. She looked out the windows, then sat on one of the couches. There was another sliding door on the opposite side of the room to the head, and before she could contain herself, curiosity drove her to open it.

The space beyond, matching the size and shape of the head, would have been small even if it hadn't held Ramsay's chest and a neat bundle of fabric hanging from the ceiling. She pushed on it and watched it sway; so this was what a hammock looked like when it was not in use. Windows looked out across the Thames toward the ship under construction, filling the little room with light. She slid the door shut and then took a few startled steps backward as the cabin door opened and Ramsay entered. Elinor quickly turned away, her cheeks red. "Will you show me how to work the windows, Captain?" she asked to cover her confusion.

Ramsay showed her how to turn the latch and prop the windows out of the way. "Keep them closed during heavy weather, obviously," he said, then gestured for her to take a seat on the sofa. "We have a few things to discuss, you and I."

Elinor took a seat and crossed her hands neatly on her knees, and waited for him to speak. He looked at her as if he expected her to say something, then shrugged.

"Sailors can be superstitious about women on board, though it's not that uncommon an occurrence," he began, "and they are terrified of fire. Getting the ships to accept Scorchers on board has been a battle, especially since none of them have your ability to contain fire. On the other hand, sailors are also superstitious about Extraordinary talents, in a good way—they see them as a sort of divine providence. So between the two of us and Peregrine Hays, the surgeon, that should offset their fears. Somewhat."

"You're an Extraordinary?"

He nodded. "Mover."

"You can *fly*?"

His lips twitched in a fleeting smile. "That's the definition of an Extraordinary Mover, Miss Pembroke."

"I've never known an Extraordinary Mover before."

"Well, I'd never met an Extraordinary Scorcher before, though I gather no one in England has in a century."

Elinor flushed. "According to my father," she said in a low voice. She knew she sounded resentful, but if he noticed, Ramsay didn't react.

"At any rate, you should be prepared for some of the crew, and possibly some of the officers, to steer wide of you and make warding signs in your direction. As long as they don't grow abusive, you should ignore that behavior. I think a few victories in which they can see your talent directed against the enemy should make them less antagonistic."

"I will do my best not to give them cause for resentment."

"Let's hope that makes a difference. You're not to wander beyond the captain's quarters and the quarterdeck. I'll show you exactly what that means when we're underway. The men don't need you intruding on their space. They're good men, at least most of them are, and they know I expect them to behave honorably, but you have an ambiguous status here, and I can't guarantee some of them won't be stupid enough to offer you insult. You're free to defend yourself, but I don't want you offering provocation."

Elinor was annoyed at his implication that *she* might be the one causing trouble, but decided not to challenge him.

Ramsay went on, "I will have one of the midshipmen instruct you on ship's rules and regulations, mainly so you won't get in anyone's way, though you will be expected to obey the rules that apply to someone in your position. If I give you an order, you follow it. If one of the officers tells you to move, you move. But I will be the one directing your attacks, when the time comes. You will eat with me and my officers, and dinner is as formal an occasion as we can make it, though judging by what you're wearing now you'll look more formal than the rest of us. Any questions?"

"Yes," Elinor said, her irritation getting the better of her at last. "Will your antagonism interfere with the performance of my duties here on your ship?"

He looked surprised. "I don't feel any antagonism toward you."

"You are certainly giving an excellent impression of a man faced with an insurmountable annoyance."

Ramsay closed his eyes and drew in a deep breath, then released it slowly. "Miss Pembroke," he said, his eyes still closed, "your presence here causes me some difficulties, it's true. This ship is embarking on its maiden voyage, half the crew and a third of my officers have never sailed with me before, and the Atlantic journey isn't the easiest to make."

He opened his eyes, and again she was startled at how blue they were. "I'm not happy about having to explain your presence and then deal with the consequences while I am, at the same time, trying to integrate over one hundred men who don't know me into my crew. And you are a civilian, and civilians make trouble simply because they don't understand what life on a Royal Navy vessel is like—and before you come over haughty at me again, I believe you will do your best not to be a problem, but you'll make honest mistakes that will still cause trouble. But I also think your talent will be invaluable in this fight, so I'm willing to face all those potential problems for its sake. I just don't think it's reasonable for you to expect me to be happy about doing so."

"I...think I understand, Captain. I wish there were a way to do this without so many problems."

"If that were possible, this wouldn't be the Royal Navy." His lips twitched in that faint smile again, making Elinor wonder if he were even capable of stretching his lips wide enough for a real one. "We will meet with my officers in the great cabin in about an hour, when they're all aboard. You'll hear two bells—two bells of the forenoon watch; you should probably start becoming accustomed to our timekeeping aboard ship. I think it's fair to tell the officers what's happening before the rest of the crew knows. And, Miss Pembroke... for what it's worth, all things considered, I'm glad to have you on board."

He nodded to her and left the room before she could think of a suitable reply. *That* was at odds with his demeanor and his lecture to her about proper behavior. For a moment, he had been much more like the man she had met in the Ormerods' music room. Remembering that meeting still made her blush, though she didn't know why; he certainly hadn't behaved as if her rudeness had affected him at all.

She went to lean against the windowsill and watched the ships pass by in the distance. A few hours, and *Athena* would join them, and it would be too late to abandon this course. That would not matter; she already knew she would not turn back.

CHAPTER 5

IN WHICH ELINOR HAS A SMALL PROBLEM, WHICH LEADS TO A LARGER PROBLEM

linor slid the door to the head closed and leaned against it. Well. This was certainly something she should have come prepared for, and having been caught unprepared, she felt embarrassed and foolish and angry all at once. What was she to do? Her wardrobe was not large enough that she could afford to use one of her shifts for rags. She would have to ask someone for help, but the thought only deepened her mortification.

After three days at sea, she barely knew enough to put names to faces. First Lieutenant Beaumont was polite but impossibly distant; Lieutenant Livingston, who'd "welcomed" her aboard, continued barely civil; Lieutenant Fitzgerald was awkward and bumbling in her presence. The midshipmen pretended not to notice her. The assortment of men who held positions somewhat lower than the commissioned officers but a good deal higher than the crew baffled her, the officers' servants avoided her, and as to the crew... after hearing someone, in a none-too-low voice, refer to her as "the captain's bit of muslin" a second time, she had not needed Ramsay's warning to stay away from their territory, much as she longed to visit the place where the livestock were kept below.

Ramsay. He'd introduced her to his officers, and then to the crew, and such was the force of his personality that there had been silence from the former and a subdued murmuring from the latter. But Elinor was certain none of them believed she could do what she claimed. She pounded her fist against the sliding door. If she could only prove herself—but there was no practical way to do that, not without damaging the very thing that kept them all alive. She could ask Ramsay for a solution to her problem, but she would...she would be *damned* if she kept crawling to him for help. Ramsay didn't permit profanity on his ship, but that didn't stop the men from swearing when they thought an officer couldn't hear, and Elinor was surprised at how many vulgarities she'd picked up in her walks around the deck. Just thinking the word made her feel sinful. It was a good, strong, hot feeling that countered the griping ache below her stomach.

No, there *was* someone she could speak to, wasn't there? She'd met the Extraordinary Shaper Peregrine Hays once, that first day, when she shook hands with each of the officers and he had given her an absent smile. He had a room on the deck below, a place Ramsay had forbidden her to go, but surely he could not expect her to abide by that rule under these conditions? She had a medical problem and needed assistance. Ramsay would simply have to accept that.

Passing through the main deck, even for the short distance from the great cabin to the stairs of the companionway, never failed to make her feel like an outsider. A breeze from outside, carrying the odor of salt and damp canvas, only made the fug of the deck stronger, and she tried to pinch her nostrils closed without actually putting a hand to her face.

The source of that fug, the muscular, barely clad men smelling of sweat and tart-bitter blacking from the guns, paused in what they were doing as she passed. Most stepped well out of her way, refusing to meet her eyes, but a few moved only enough that she had to brush against them as she passed. Their grins told her they knew exactly what they were doing, and she had a brief but vivid daydream of setting their grimy trousers or shirts on fire, seeing those leering grins turn to terror. It made her sick to think herself capable of even imagining such a thing. So she ignored them. *They aren't hurting you,* she told herself, *and you have endured worse than this.* At least none of them had ever offered her violence.

She went down the companionway to the deck below—if only people would talk to her, she could learn the names of things!—with her spine stiffened and her eyes fixed straight ahead, followed by the sounds of unintelligible commands and the soft chime of the bell on the quarterdeck, marking out time according to some system she still didn't understand.

In contrast to the warm, crowded, noisy main deck, where cannons were everywhere underfoot, this deck was practically bare. A few hammocks were strung and occupied, but at nearly noon most of the sailors were elsewhere, their hammocks rolled and stowed in nets in the rigging on the weather deck. Ramsay had told her this provided more protection for the crew during the battle, with the rolls of heavy canvas deflecting the sharp spears of wood flung up by cannonballs plowing the length of the deck. The image had made Elinor queasy, but she had controlled her reaction rather than let Ramsay believe her a coward.

Above her head were the cleverly devised tables that lowered from the beams at mealtimes, and Elinor moved more quickly, because it was only a few minutes until the sailors' noon meal and not even Ramsay interfered with that. Ahead of her, and to her right, were three doors set into the same kind of movable partitions that formed the forward wall of the great cabin. She hesitated for a moment, then knocked at the nearest. No one answered.

She was about to knock at the next door when the first opened and a man leaned out. He was entirely bald, his reddened scalp speckled with brown, and he wore a dingy white shirt half tucked into his trousers, which he was holding up with one hand. The other was pressed to his stomach. "You," he said, sounding surprised. "Wot deck we on then?"

"I—" His question made no sense. "I am looking for Mr. Hays," she said, trying to regain her equilibrium.

The bald man blinked slowly, then clapped a hand over his mouth and ducked back into the room. Sounds of retching and the stink of vomit drifted through the door. Elinor put her hand over her own mouth to hold in a completely inappropriate laugh. Shortly, the man reappeared, somewhat paler than before, and said, "You want the surgeon?"

"Yes, please, if you'll just—no, I can find him myself if you'll only tell—"

The man was fastening up his belt and tucking in his stained shirt properly. "Time I was seein' him meself, missie. Don't think I got no more o' they thunderations pent up in me belly, like to see me own innards next time." He opened the door to her right and indicated she should enter.

More doors lined the walls of a sizeable room illuminated dimly by a bulbous glass lamp hanging above a polished wooden table, around which were arranged several spindle-backed chairs—this must be the gunroom, where those officers who hadn't been invited to dine with the captain ate. It smelled musty, like a room infrequently aired out, which made sense since it was probably often below the water line. Ramsay's table was elegant, set with a linen cloth and silver and crystal that to Elinor seemed completely out of place, and the food was excellent, so Elinor had felt some pity for the officers who didn't receive an invitation.

Now, taking in the excellent craftsmanship of the furniture and the beautiful lamp of pale amber glass, she realized they did not need her sympathy. Possibly their dinners were more lively affairs than the captain's, though it was likely, even probable, that her presence had had a chilling effect on the conversation at the captain's table these last three evenings. Or perhaps Lieutenant Beaumont and Mr. Worsley, the purser, who'd joined them on those three occasions, were both naturally taciturn. They had been the three most uncomfortable dinners Elinor had ever endured, and considering her relationship with her father, that made them very uncomfortable indeed.

The bald man went around the table and opened a door without knocking. "Mr. Hays, yon missie's got business w' you, and I needs summat to still this pit o' mine," he said.

"Mr. Bolton, I told you I cannot dose you further—oh, Miss Pembroke," Hays said, stepping through the door and peering at her as if he had forgotten his spectacles, which surely a Shaper had no need of. "If you are suffering from *mal de mer*, I am afraid I have no Healing for it. Mr. Bolton, return to your room and do try to sleep this time."

"Man can't sleep w' this fire gnawing at 'is innards," Bolton said, putting a hand over his stomach for emphasis.

"Then perhaps you should not eat meat that has gone off, even on a dare. I have given you plenty of water, and do not make that face; it's clean and will help your system recover from the Healing. Go now, and remember—sleep."

Bolton made a face, but left, nodding at Elinor as he went. His unexpected... it was almost friendliness, and it had startled her so much she had nearly forgotten why she had come seeking out Hays in the first place. "Mr. Hays, I have a somewhat delicate problem," she began.

"Ah. I expect your menstrual cycle has begun. If you are suffering from the attendant physical complaints, I believe I can help you, though, alas, even Extraordinary Shapers cannot change the laws of biology in this respect." He smiled and tapped the side of his nose knowingly.

"How did you—"

"It was evident in my initial assessment of your physical condition. Have a seat, please." Hays guided Elinor to a chair; she pulled away from his hand, anger growing in her.

"You intruded—how *dare* you invade my privacy in that manner!"

Hays was at least six and a half feet tall, a crane of a man who had to bend far over to keep from hitting his head against the low ceiling, and now his eyes, which had previously seemed unfocused, came to rest on her with an unnerving firmness.

"Miss Pembroke," he said, "you must know little of the Royal Navy, and I beg pardon that you were not informed of this, but it is Navy regulation that officers and crew submit to a physical examination by a qualified Extraordinary Shaper before embarking on any voyage that will take them out of British waters. It is a practice that has eliminated some of the worst medical disasters that in the past were distressingly regular. Your arrival was so irregular I unfortunately had to perform that examination in an ad hoc manner, but now—"

"I see," Elinor said, her cheeks still flushed. "I... you're correct, I did not know. I apologize."

He waved it away and drew up another chair. "No need to apologize. Give me your hand." His own hand was unexpectedly soft for someone who treated battlefield injuries, and whatever he did when he closed his eyes, Elinor felt nothing, except, eventually, a lessening of the ache in her belly.

"You are in perfect health, Miss Pembroke," Hays finally said, releasing her hand. "And your talent is remarkable."

"Thank you, Mr. Hays, but I do not understand how you can say that when you have never seen me use it."

He smiled and patted her hand as if he were much older than the fifty-odd years she estimated his actual age to be. "Your talent is written throughout your body," he said. "They all are, you know, bred in the blood and bone, but Scorchers are all ash and char, and you are living fire. Perhaps that is a bit too poetical, but Shaping is a kind of poetry, did you realize?"

She grasped the part of that speech she did understand. "Living fire?"

"Did I say that? Sometimes I am carried away by beauty," Hays said. "It's true I know nothing of your talent, but I imagine you must feel great joy when you are surrounded by your element."

Elinor nodded. "I do."

"There you are, then," Hays said, patting her hand again. "If there's ever anything else I can do for you, Miss Pembroke, please don't hesitate to ask."

"Actually, Mr. Hays, I was wondering if you had something I might use for rags," Elinor said, flushing again. Why she should be embarrassed to ask this of someone who had seen her most private inward parts, she didn't know, but embarrassed she was.

Hays felt no such embarrassment. "Of course," he said, and Elinor followed him out of the gunroom, down the steps to an even lower deck—she felt wickedly pleased at her disobedience—and to a storeroom, where he gave her an armful of rolled bandages. "I keep many on hand, so please ask if you need more," he said.

"Thank you, but I think this will suffice." Elinor bobbed a curtsey and made her way back up the stairs.

The noise of the main deck made an unpleasant contrast to the quiet below. Elinor clutched her bundles to her chest and tried not to look furtive, feeling certain every man there knew what she was about. She turned to go to the great cabin and bumped into one of the seamen, dropping one of the rolls in her surprise. Over the man's shoulder, she saw Lieutenant Livingston standing near the companionway to the quarterdeck, watching the interaction, his face expressionless. "I beg your pardon," she said to the man, and bent to retrieve the cloth.

She felt a sharp twinge in her rear end, and stood upright with an outraged squeak, rubbing the place where the man had pinched her. More rolls fell. "How dare you!" she exclaimed.

The man grinned at her and winked. "Rub up 'gainst me any time, bob-tail."

Elinor looked over at Livingston, who hadn't moved. More men stopped to watch, men coming from behind, men's heavy footsteps on the companionway. "Step out of my way," she said, and cursed the quaver in her voice. The sailor's grin became wicked.

"Stand aside *now*," said Ramsay, descending the last few steps at speed and taking in the situation with a glance. He grabbed the sailor's shoulder and shoved him in Livingston's direction. "Confine this man pending his punishment," he said. "The rest of you, back to work unless you want to join him. Miss Pembroke, my cabin. Now." He took her elbow and dragged her toward the great cabin, past the Marine sentry; she was too shocked to protest his rough handling. She clutched at her remaining bandages, unable to remember why she held them.

Ramsay slammed the door behind them and turned on her. "I told you that space was off limits," he said in a low, furious voice. "What the devil were you doing? You are *under orders*, Miss Pembroke, though you don't wear a uniform, and I do not make suggestions."

His anger snapped her out of her confusion and roused some anger of her own. "I needed the surgeon, Captain, on a feminine matter I'm certain you'd prefer I didn't elaborate on. I did nothing wrong. It was that man who offered me insult."

"Had you not been there, he would have gone about his work and would not now be facing punishment."

"You blame *me* for his coarse behavior?"

"These are not the sort of men you're accustomed to. They know I expect them to behave honorably, and most of them live up to that expectation, but there are always some who lack the will to discipline their baser instincts, and changing that is beyond my power. Blame is irrelevant, Miss Pembroke. What matters is that you disobeyed my instruction, and now I will have to have a man flogged for it."

Elinor's mouth fell open. "*Flogged?*"

"Discipline must be maintained, Miss Pembroke. I've gone three years without having to resort to the cat, but I cannot allow these men to believe you are vulnerable to that sort of familiarity."

"But surely—it was unpleasant, yes, but such a harsh—"

"If that man had showed that sort of disrespect to an officer, the punishment would be the same. This is a ship, Miss Pembroke, a floating community of three hundred men crammed together in a space half the size of my cousin Harry's mansion, and we officers main-tain our position by virtue of our skills and our leadership, which includes enforcing obedience to the laws and regulations that govern us. Those men will not follow weakness, and every one of them will witness that flogging and know it's a just punishment."

"Or they will resent me further for being the cause of it!"

"He knew your position and abused it. A little resentment is far better than another, more serious assault on your person." Ramsay narrowed his eyes. "This isn't the first incident, is it?"

Elinor looked away. "I would hardly call sidelong looks and muffled laughter an incident, Captain."

Ramsay's lips shut in a thin line and he walked to the window, leaned against the sill and stared out over the sea. "And I will have to do something about Livingston," he said in a quieter voice. "I can't have an officer flogged, even if I think it might do him some good."

"Mr. Livingston did nothing wrong."

"He did *nothing*, and for that there must be a consequence."

"Then—what will it be?"

"I don't know. As satisfying as it would be to humiliate him in public, that would only make him more difficult to work with. So it will have to be something else."

"You do not like him."

Ramsay turned his head quickly. "I spoke out of turn. Ignore my remarks."

"And I know he doesn't respect you, though he is good at concealing that," Elinor added. "He is new to your command, so he can hardly have had time to develop a dislike of you personally."

"Miss Pembroke, do you intend to disregard everything I tell you to do?"

"I hardly think you are allowed to command me in what I think, Captain, and I *think* you would prefer Mr. Livingston elsewhere."

Ramsay shook his head in exasperation and went back to staring out the window. "Livingston has no talent," he said, "and he is resentful of those who do, and doubly resentful of someone like me possessing an Extraordinary talent."

"Someone like you?"

"Someone not of superior birth. He's the second son of a viscount and would like that to matter more here aboard ship than it does."

"Then he no doubt resents me as well."

"Yes, and thinks the men's disrespectful treatment of you reflects badly on me as your...sponsor, in a sense. Which satisfies his need to see me at a disadvantage."

Elinor sat on one of the couches, some distance from Ramsay. "If I could only show them..."

"I can't arrange for an enemy ship to sail into our arms, I'm afraid."

She glanced up to see him watching her. "You think this entire venture is meaningless."

"I hardly think *you* are allowed to put thoughts into my head, Miss Pembroke."

She laughed, but said, "*Do* you, then?"

"No." His lips twitched in a smile. "I think we've not been at sea long enough to declare it a failure. We've not even reached Gibraltar."

"Are we stopping there?"

"I think not. No need for supplies, no deliveries to make. We'll stop at Tenerife instead." His good humor fell away, as if he'd remembered why he was there. "I will have to ask you to remain here for the rest of the day. I hope you can see why."

"I intend to stay well out of the way until the whole display is over, never fear, Captain."

Now Ramsay's smile was grim. "Oh no, Miss Pembroke, you will be present to see that man flogged. Everyone witnesses. It may convince you not to ignore my instructions again."

"It's barbaric!"

"This is a hard world. I said before you'd make mistakes because you don't understand it. You ought to see the consequence of your mistake."

Elinor bowed her head and looked at her hands, still clutching the rolls of cloth. "You are right," she said, "and I regret the incident."

"Not as much as I do, that I failed to head this thing off before it came to this," Ramsay said. "Maybe it was inevitable, but if you're to blame, I'm to blame as well. It speaks to a failure in my leadership if I can't discipline my men without resorting to that level of punishment. I never enjoy seeing a man flogged, even if his crime warrants it." He sighed, and turned to go. "It will be tomorrow morning after breakfast. You might...want to eat lightly."

Elinor, still staring downward, heard the door close quietly behind him. It was so grossly unfair, blaming her for the choice the man had made; even more unfair that the sailor should suffer so over something so insignificant. Then she remembered the leer on the man's face and how frightened she'd felt, surrounded by all those sailors who...

She hurried to the head and took care of her needs, refusing to face the memory. She didn't know if she could bring herself to burn a man, and besides, what good would that do if he took hold of her so closely she could not burn him without burning herself? Ramsay was right, they would continue to harass her unless an example was made. But such an example...she sank down onto the sofa and fumbled in the cabinet for a book, then tried to focus on the words. It was the seaman's fault that he believed she could be attacked with impunity—

what *was* a bob-tail, anyway?—but she felt guilty nevertheless, and witnessing the man's punishment might assuage some of that guilt.

⟡

"LASH HIM TO THE GRATING," RAMSAY SAID, HIS VOICE COLD, AND two sailors dragged Elinor's assailant forward and bound his hands to a grating propped upright amidships. The chill wind raised gooseflesh on the half-naked man's arms and back, making him look even more vulnerable. Elinor stood behind Ramsay, clasping her hands together and wishing she dared wrap her arms around her chest to warm herself.

Above, the sails of the mainmast snapped in the brisk wind, their whiteness standing out starkly against the lowering grey sky, the heavy clouds promising rain that would probably not interrupt the imminent flogging. The deck was crowded with men, sailors in their striped shirts and hats of all shapes, officers trim in their most formal blue coats with the white facings, hats in the fore-and-aft position, the red-coated Marines standing at rigid attention nearby in case of an uprising.

But the crowd was, to Elinor's eye, surprisingly subdued. They had listened to the reading of the Article of War the man had violated without protest and without casting vicious glances in Elinor's direction. If anything, they had seemed uncomfortable in her presence, which made her feel irrationally guilty again. She kept her eyes fixed on that naked back, which failed to arouse any feelings of prurience. Soon it would be striped with blood. She ought to feel hysterical, but instead felt only numb with cold.

"Bo'sun's mate, do your duty," the captain said.

A burly man stepped forward, the nine lashes of the cat swaying in the wind, and took a position about two feet from the unfortunate man. He brought his arm up, swung, and the man's strangled groan rose over the sharp crack as the many strands ending in tiny, wicked knots struck that naked back. The bo'sun's mate lashed him again, and again, and Elinor clenched her jaw to keep from groaning in sympathy. Tears sprang to her eyes that she willed to evaporate before they could escape to roll down her cheeks. She felt warm, now, as if a fire was burning inside her, though she was still as numb as ever.

She rubbed her hands together to warm them as the fifth strike landed. It could not be a fire within her; that was impossible. Yet she could still feel flames nearby, even though that was also impossible. How could anything burn on the ocean waves? She looked up and to her left, toward the heavens, and saw fire arcing toward them, a ball of pale fire, flickering white and yellow, falling out of the sky. She extinguished it without thinking and said, "Captain, there—"

"Miss Pembroke, this is not the time for you to display feminine frailty," Ramsay said in a low voice.

She grabbed his arm. "Fire," she said, and pointed to where another ball of pale yellow flame fell toward them. Ramsay's mouth fell open, just a little, then he shouted, "*Beat to quarters!*"

Instantly the deck erupted with motion, followed seconds later by the rhythmic pattern of drums somewhere farther along the deck. Elinor dismissed this second fireball with a wave, reasoning once again that dramatic gestures would be to her benefit, not that anyone was watching her at the moment. She looked lower, toward the horizon, and her heart pounded in her chest as she registered the presence, far too close to them, of a warship headed directly for *Athena*.

CHAPTER 6

IN WHICH ELINOR PROVES
HERSELF

Athena veered unexpectedly, staggering Elinor, who had nothing to hold on to. Two more fireballs at once now, both easily extinguished—what was their Scorcher thinking? Fire, yes, but so diffuse it seemed unlikely to ignite anything important. Ramsay had disappeared. Men pushed past her, and she stumbled, then retreated to the stern, out of everyone's way, and gripped the rail running the width of the stern, the taffrail, with both hands to keep from falling. No one heeded her in the confusion; no one stopped to tell her what was happening or what she ought to do.

She looked out at the distant ship, and anger rose up within her. *This* was why she was here, to use her talent in defense of her country, and she was being pushed aside and ignored exactly as if she were nothing but a talentless passenger, a burden to be endured but not respected.

She could feel the fire calling to her as her anger grew, heard it clamoring to be set free, and looked out at the enemy ship—how far away was it? Half a mile? She had never had reason to test the range of her talent, had no idea if her reach extended that far, but she closed her eyes and imagined the feel of the damp canvas under her fingertips, then set the fire free on the highest center sail.

For a moment, she thought she had failed. Then she felt the fire take hold. It was as if she were in two places at once, her body standing at the taffrail, trying to keep the ship in sight as *Athena* began curving around to approach the enemy ship and her sails impeded Elinor's vision, her—could you call it her soul? At any rate, the part of her that knew the fire as it knew itself—encompassing the distant fire and sending it flowing like boiling jelly down the sails, leaping from the mainmast to the other sails in glorious drops of molten copper. The ship continued its course toward them, burning like a tiny sun that lit the dull grey waves beneath it like a sunset. It was so beautiful it made her heart ache.

The noise of busy men scattering in all directions had grown louder, with overtones of surprise and fear and exhilaration. Cheering. "*God's blood,*" someone said from nearby, and Ramsay said, "Bridle it, sailor."

Elinor heard it all as if from a distance, her distant self consuming everything it touched and filling her small human body with a power that made her bones hum. The first sail to burn, the topgallant—and where had *that* piece of knowledge come from?—began to disintegrate, shedding large swaths of burning fabric onto the deck below. She felt herself falling with it, and staggered, gripping the rail more tightly. Hands took her by the elbows and steadied her. "Be careful," Ramsay said in her ear. "Don't overextend yourself. Talent has limits."

She shook her head. She didn't feel overextended; she felt alive, invigorated, as if she could go on burning the sails and the masts and the ship until they were nothing but ash. *Athena* was close enough now that Elinor could see the enemy sailors scurrying about, some even climbing the burning ropes with buckets in a futile attempt to save their ship. Some of the rigging collapsed, and two men fell to the deck, their screams like the distant whine of gnats. The sound woke Elinor from her fantasy, and she pulled away from Ramsay's grip and breathed deeply, smelling faintly the grimy smoke from the burning canvas. "What should I do?" she said, not certain if she meant to ask Ramsay for direction or to question her own motives.

Ramsay responded to her surface meaning. "Can you melt the cannons?"

Elinor shook her head. "I think that is beyond my capacity, Captain."

"Well, then, if you could avoid burning the masts, that will make it easier for us when we take her."

Elinor found where the flames were battering at the mainmast and extinguished them, shaped the fire to flow around the other two masts to the sails. "Will not the loss of the sails make her difficult to maneuver?"

"We can make up for that loss. I would prefer not to replace their mast."

Beaumont came to join them. "Looks like *Joyeux*, Captain. Amirault's probably pissing his trousers right now. I mean—I beg your pardon, Captain."

"I agree with the sentiment, if not the language," Ramsay said.

Athena continued to approach the other ship, which had stopped moving entirely. Elinor could see men clustering around the guns at the enemy's bow. Ramsay strode down *Athena*'s deck, calling out commands, and sailors gathered around *Athena*'s cannons as well, the ones near the bow of the ship, whatever that part of the deck was called, smaller and lighter than the twenty-six enormous beasts below.

More men scrambled through the rigging, hanging on despite the wind that had picked up and made her fire stream away from the damaged ship like a deadly golden pennant. *Athena* was going to pass perpendicular to the other ship, which Elinor didn't understand; surely it would make more sense to pass parallel, exposing more of the enemy to their guns. But she was just the Scorcher, not the captain, who at that moment returned to her side. "Can you extinguish the fire now?"

The way he phrased his request angered her. She turned her back on the enemy and folded her arms across her chest. "*Can* I, Captain?" she said, and extinguished the fire without a gesture, without a word.

Ramsay stared at her for a moment, then laughed. "I apologize, Miss Pembroke," he said, "for implying I doubted your ability. I meant, 'will you.' You might—"

A thump shattered the air, and Ramsay put his arm across her shoulders and shoved her down to the deck. A ripping sound followed, and then a splash somewhere to *Athena*'s starboard side, the one not facing the enemy. Another distant thump, this one missing *Athena* entirely, and then a rippling roar from *Athena*'s own guns as cannon after cannon let fly at the enemy. Elinor tried to stand, to see the effects *Athena*'s attack had on the French ship, but Ramsay continued to restrain her.

"We're not close enough," he shouted, and ran toward the bow, leaving Elinor to pull herself up from the deck. She was not certain how they could not be close enough, given that the enemy's cannonball had gone through one of *Athena*'s sails—at least, that was what she guessed the tearing sound to be—but *she* was certainly close enough, and with only a brief thought for what Ramsay might think of her acting on her own again, she remembered the first fireball arcing toward her, made one of her own, and sent it hurtling toward the enemy's deck.

It struck the ship's starboard bow and kept going, crossing the deck diagonally to exit on the larboard side near the stern. Men scattered, which made her laugh; none of them were injured, though what rigging was left had caught fire. She threw two more in rapid succession, paralleling the cannonballs fired from *Athena*'s stern guns, delighting in the phantom sense of flying with the fire. Was this how Ramsay felt, when he Flew? Or was it the power of the fire, its joy in being set free, that made her feel so exhilarated?

"That's enough," Ramsay said, once again at her elbow, and she startled. Across the waves, the French flag had disappeared. Had it come down with the rigging? "What does it mean?" she asked.

"It means they surrender." Ramsay was smiling broadly. One of his front teeth was crooked. *I wonder if that's why he smiles so tightly all the time.* "Pass the word below, Mr. Livingston. Do you feel well?"

It took Elinor a moment to realize he was addressing her. "I feel very well, Captain," she said. Her back ached a little for no reason she could imagine, but she felt invigorated, as if liquid fire ran in her veins.

"You should be careful. Overusing talent has a price. Though I think we haven't seen the limits of yours yet."

"They fired only twice."

"Yes," Ramsay said, smiling again, "that they did. I think you won't have any more problems with the crew, Miss Pembroke."

She looked around. There weren't many men on the deck by comparison to during the punishment, and most of them were still preoccupied with the guns, but those men handling the rigging cast covert glances at her, and she thought they were looks of either admiration or fear. "I suppose not," she said. Then she remembered, and asked, "What of the... the punishment?"

Ramsay's smile disappeared. "He'll take the rest of his lashes tomorrow, but I'll let Mr. Hays have a look at him in the meantime. More to the point, I'm afraid there will be a number of other men following him to the grating. That ship should not have been able to surprise us, and the men on watch who let it happen will also have to be flogged, and the lieutenant of that watch punished."

"I understand."

"Do you?"

"It was my talent alone that alerted you to the attack, Captain. How much damage would that ship have done to us if they had come close enough to use all their guns? Those negligent watchmen would have been responsible for the injury and deaths of so many men. I understand little of your methods of discipline in the Navy, but surely such a dereliction of duty must warrant a severe punishment."

Ramsay nodded. "And they will understand that as well. Bring us about for a boarding party, Mr. Wynn, and Hardison, signal to them to send their captain across. Mr. Beaumont, will you join me? You'll be taking the *Joyeux* in to Gibraltar."

Elinor turned in time to see Livingston's reaction to this; he looked first surprised, then angry, and opened his mouth as if to say something. Ramsay met his anger with a cool gaze, one eyebrow raised as if inviting Livingston to say whatever damning thing might come out of his mouth. Livingston closed his mouth into a tight line.

"Miss Pembroke, you should go below now, before you are fully visible to our friends," Ramsay continued. "And...thank you."

"Certainly, Captain." Reflexively she bobbed a curtsey as if he'd asked her to dance, then blushed, and Ramsay gave her one of those little smiles. Livingston, by contrast, turned his tight-lipped glare on her as she passed. So he blamed her for whatever it was the captain had done in giving Beaumont, not him, command of the *Joyeux*. It seemed Captain Ramsay had found a punishment for him, after all.

IN HINDSIGHT, SHE MIGHT HAVE GUESSED CAPTAIN AMIRAULT would have to be confined aboard *Athena*; he might be an honorable man, but even the most honorable man might be tempted to break his parole and attempt to retake his ship if he were allowed to remain on it. Reasonable it might be, but Elinor resented being trapped in her bedchamber nearly every hour of the two days it took *Athena* and her prize to reach Gibraltar. The young midshipman who brought her meals, St. Maur, could barely meet her eyes, let alone converse with her. She was forced to sit or lie on her bed, reading and re-reading the few books she'd thought to bring with her into her bedchamber exile, or staring at the ceiling while Amirault paced the great cabin outside her door.

In the evenings, she eavesdropped on the conversation at the captain's table and discovered that yes, her presence had been a damper, because at least eight people sat down to dinner each night and drank and ate with gusto, calling out toasts and roaring with laughter over jokes Elinor rarely understood. She fumed, and picked at her food, and determined she would have words with Ramsay about inventing some reason for her to be aboard that would allow her to roam free without raising Amirault's suspicions. Even a French captain would know a well-bred Englishwoman would not be without a female companion, and if in his captivity he were to spread the word of her presence there... It was astonishing that she could ever have considered her restriction to the quarterdeck and the captain's rooms an imposition.

On the morning of the third day, she woke to realize the ship's movement had changed from a pervasive swaying to a gentle rocking, barely perceptible after so many days on the open sea. She dressed quickly and sat on the edge of her bed, tapping her feet rhythmically and wondering if she dared venture out. Twice she stood and put her hand on the doorknob, twice she withdrew it and returned to the bed.

Finally, the door opened, and St. Maur looked in on her. "There's food laid on the table, miss," he said, still not looking at her. "Captain's gone ashore with Captain Amirault."

Elinor pushed past him and went to look out the window, careful not to stand where she might be seen. The blue expanse of the harbor was dotted here and there with ships, including *Joyeux*, which lay at anchor nearby. Golden sunlight struck the waves, which reflected the light in flashes that made Elinor blink and her eyes water. She had to look away, and instead watched the other ships. One of them must have just come into harbor, because its white sails were being furled; they looked like albatross wings, but, she presumed, conveying good luck rather than bad.

Beyond the water, far in the distance, a grey and green stone promontory rose high in the air, one side a sheer cliff descending to the shore, the other a gentler but still intimidating rise to the summit. It looked as if God Himself had dropped creation's largest boulder on the shore and let it lie there gathering moss for a thousand lifetimes. Heedless of who might see her, Elinor stepped forward and pressed her palm against the glass. At this distance, her hand exactly covered the Rock of Gibraltar and made the blue sky seem bluer against her fair skin. Impossible that it was the same sky that covered her father's house in Hertfordshire.

"Captain said to tell you, don't go up on deck, and...he said, exactly, 'don't argue with St. Maur, it's not his fault you're trapped,' " St. Maur said, his face crimson.

Elinor sighed, exasperated with Ramsay and impatient with the timid midshipman. "Mr. St. Maur, I do not intend to argue with you, but I do not need an audience at my breakfast," she said, and St. Maur was out the door almost before she'd finished saying it. She sat down and tucked into hot eggs, kidneys, toast, and coffee, along with fresh peaches Midshipman Hervey, the ship's Bounder, must have brought that morning. Elinor recognized an apology when she saw it. Hervey had also brought *The Times* along with the mail, and Elinor felt almost civilized as she read and ate. Ramsay set an excellent table.

The door opened again, and Dolph, the captain's steward, entered. Elinor wasn't certain what that was, exactly; he cooked the captain's food and tidied the captain's chambers and washed the captain's laundry, but he wasn't a dogsbody, and he wasn't a valet either. Dolph laid down a plate of sausages with his usual clatter and grunted at her. Elinor smiled at him, which made him frown harder and leave without saying anything.

She speared a sausage and bit into it with more force than necessary. She'd stopped trying to befriend Dolph after only two days' voyaging, but she wished he weren't so actively antagonistic toward her. She had the impression he resented her, though she was not sure if this was because she was a woman, because she was taking up even a small amount of the captain's attention, or if he just didn't like cooking for two.

"Good morning," Ramsay said, entering the room and seating himself across from her. "Captain Amirault is safely in custody ashore, and I regret it didn't occur to me to come up with an explanation that would give you the freedom of the ship while he was here."

"It was extremely unpleasant, Captain."

"I did apologize, Miss Pembroke. Do you have any ideas? You could be a missionary en route to Jamaica to convert the heathen."

Elinor looked over the top of her newspaper to see him looking back at her, perfectly straight-faced, but with a humorous gleam in his eye. She lowered the paper. "I think I should be a respectable but impoverished woman going to stay with my brother and his wife."

"Who are, naturally, overjoyed to add another member to their household, what with their brood of seven children and a maiden aunt."

"But I dote on my nieces and nephews and will be a fine, useful addition to the family, unlike the maiden aunt, who sits in the parlor and criticizes everything Hester does."

"Who is Hester?"

"My sister-in-law, of course. I cannot believe you are so sadly ignorant of my relations."

"Again, I beg your pardon. But what about Ernest? You see I didn't forget about him."

"Ernest?"

His eyes went wide with shock. "The young man from the next

plantation over who's intended to be your husband, of course! Miss Pembroke, think how upset he'll be to learn of your indifference!"

Elinor laughed. "Captain Ramsay, things are by no means settled between Ernest and myself!"

"I'm glad to hear it. You should at least meet the young man—" He began laughing as well. "Miss Pembroke, I had no idea you had such a sense of humor."

"Neither had I, to be honest, Captain." She folded the newspaper and offered it to him, but he declined with a wave. "I feel it has been years since I last laughed so much."

Dolph brought another plate for the captain, who began eating with the neat efficiency that seemed to characterize everything he did. "I hope you realize we're all grateful for the capture of *Joyeux*," he said, and laughed again. "Amirault couldn't stop talking about you—not you specifically, but our *feueur*, and he kept asking to meet you. I don't know if he wanted to shake your hand or strike you, but I think he felt vindicated by your prowess. Something about how no one could have been expected to stand up to that kind of assault. Well, if it makes him feel less humiliated... Amirault's a decent sort, and it'll sit hard with him to have to be ransomed."

He took a few more bites, but with an air that said he wasn't finished speaking, and Elinor sat in some impatience waiting for him to continue. "So please don't take what I'm about to say as a denigration of your efforts."

"You have me positively on edge now, Captain."

He shook his head. "It's only that we were extremely lucky," he said. "Their Scorcher fired off those shots far too early, which gave us plenty of warning even though our watchmen didn't see them coming. And based on what I've seen in ship-to-ship combat, he also wasn't very powerful. If Amirault hadn't made so many mistakes, if you hadn't made up for the failings of our watchmen, *Joyeux* would have fired at least one full broadside before we were prepared to respond. *Joyeux* isn't made to repel Scorcher attacks, either. Where we're going, many of the ships treat their sails with flame retardants, have fire-fighting gear handy, use tactics even you may have trouble overcoming. I think it's important you know not all our combats are going to go that well."

"I appreciate that, Captain. I did feel as if it were all too easy."

"It was, and it wasn't." He chuckled again. "You didn't see the men when those sails went up in flames. Throwing fireballs is one thing, but that ship was three times as far away as any of us had seen a Scorcher ignite a fire before."

Elinor gaped. "I...had no idea, Captain," she said. It surprised her how unsettled this knowledge made her, when she had been so matter of fact about her talent during the battle. "I know I have power," she said, "but it seems almost absurdly great. And I feel—I felt as if I had not reached my limit. It is rather like asking one's father for a pony and getting a stable of thoroughbreds instead."

"It is," Ramsay said. "I am rated at ten thousand pounds—Moving capacity, you understand—and I think I could push that limit if I had to. That's three thousand pounds higher than the previous record. I loaded the cannons on *Athena*, two at a time, in about three hours, because we were in a hurry to get her finished and loaded. I felt almost ridiculous tossing them around like that, and the way they all looked at me—" He broke off. "At any rate, I do understand what you mean."

"When did you manifest, Captain?"

"Late." He smiled wryly. "Not as late as you. I was fourteen when I manifested Moving and fifteen when the Extraordinary talent appeared. Do you think your having an Extraordinary talent was the reason you manifested so late?"

Elinor shrugged, thinking, *He changed the subject very quickly just now.* "Most of the records we have about talents are lists of manifestations, not details. It has been barely fifty years since that sort of thing has been noted. Of course there are multitudinous genealogies, breeding records, titles of nobility granted over the centuries." She could hear, again, the bitterness that filled her when she thought of her father's passion. "One thing we do know is there are so few Scorchers not only because English talent does not tend in that direction, but because so many of them die when they manifest."

"Burn themselves to death?"

"And their families, sometimes. The trade in attempting to predict what talents will result from a particular pairing thrives in part because parents want to prevent that sort of thing."

"I thought it was all fakery and lies."

"At worst. Most of the diviners genuinely believe in their divinatory methods—astrology and chiromancy are extremely popular. But they're no more accurate in their predictions than if they'd chosen them at random. Those who apply logic and reason to the problem are somewhat more successful." She thought of her father's breeding book and suppressed a shudder. "I understand some Greek natural philosophers have embarked on a more thorough study of the mechanisms that cause talent to arise, applying modern scientific principles, but that is the extent of my knowledge."

Dolph entered the room and began clearing the table, ignoring them both. Ramsay scooted back a little, out of his way, and said, "It will be a while before we leave, and I would prefer you not show yourself above, since we failed to tell everyone about your family on Jamaica. Is there anything I can bring you?"

"More books? Since I understand we have a long voyage ahead of us."

He made a slight bow of acquiescence. "You may have the freedom of the ship once we've left harbor. I believe you've gained the respect of the crew and you'll have no further problems."

"But you'd prefer I not intrude on their space any more than necessary."

He smiled, displaying that crooked tooth. "You are a mind reader, Miss Pembroke."

"I think not. They're mythical."

He laughed. "Good day, Miss Pembroke."

"Good day, Captain Ramsay."

When both he and Dolph were gone, she went to look out the window at the steep face of the rock, then opened it to let the cool sea air flow through the cabin and dissipate the smell of sausage, which had become rather pervasive. Climbing the rock would be far too difficult, even on its sloping side, but how would it feel to stand at the summit and look back down at *Athena*, riding gently on the waves that entered the harbor? Had Ramsay ever done that, Flying across the grey-green expanse to light on the tip of the Rock?

Peace, tentative like a new shoot of grass, began working its way through the anxiety she had been carrying with her for a week. She who had never been more than one hundred miles from home in her life was now nearly ten times that distance away and preparing to go even farther. *Thank you, papa, for driving me out of my tiny life into something so much vaster than I imagined. Thank you for thinking so little of me that I was forced to find a place where I was valued. Thank you.*

She leaned on the casing of the open window and drew in a deep breath of salt air. Ramsay was only partly right; the crew probably feared her as much as they respected her. But she had a place on *Athena* now; she had fought for it, and she was beginning to feel as if she belonged there.

CHAPTER 7
IN WHICH ELINOR'S SHIPMATES
ARE INTRODUCED

It seemed to Elinor, kneeling on one of the couches to lean against the open window frame, that she had never known what blue truly was until she saw the waters of the harbor at Santa Cruz de Tenerife, deep and rich and so clear she could see to the bottom of *Athena*'s hull where it curved away below the stern. If Plato was right, and there truly was an ideal form of all objects, this was surely blue in its most perfect state.

The town of Santa Cruz came all the way up to the shore, surrounded by stony walls interrupted by the fortress of San Cristobal, the blocky towers at its four corners overlooking the bay where *Athena* was anchored near a dozen other ships. They had sailed in at dawn, so Elinor had seen little of the storied shores of the island, with its golden sand and lush greenery, but its mountains lay like sleeping giants that might choose to roll over and crush the town at any moment. That had been Hays' colorful metaphor when he had described the island to Elinor two days before.

"The mountains are volcanic, you understand," he had said, "and actively volcanic at that. There was an eruption only fourteen years ago—well inland from Santa Cruz, and I am told it affected the town very little. Still, I think it's quite exciting, don't you?"

"More unsettling than exciting, Dr. Hays," Elinor had replied. "I hope we will not be subjected to another such event."

"It's unlikely. And the mountains generally give plenty of warning before they wake. I am hoping to travel into the interior some distance; *Serinus canaria* and *Fringilla coelebs* are fairly common throughout the Atlantic islands, but *Regulus regulus teneriffae* breeds nowhere else. Would you care to join me?"

Elinor had laughed and shook her head. "I am afraid I did not come prepared for a journey into the wild. I intend to walk along the shore and enjoy the feeling of a surface that does not roll beneath my feet."

Now she surveyed the city and wondered if she would get her wish. The red-tiled Spanish roofs and white stucco walls of Santa Cruz were easily visible from the harbor, a gleaming Mediterranean town in a tropical paradise. The buildings crowded together, however, rather the way they did in London, if London were drenched in sunlight that warmed the roofs and turned the drab walls bright. She could make out a few people walking the streets like ants struggling across a cobblestone path, but even this early in the morning the port teemed with activity, and longboats and dinghies crossed the harbor from ship to shore and back again. With almost three hundred men all wanting leave to visit the town, Elinor thought it unlikely any of them would want to escort her elsewhere, and she doubted Ramsay would allow her to wander around unsupervised.

The smell of eggs and sausage preceded Dolph into the great cabin. He banged down plates and a coffeepot and left before Elinor could seat herself. Coffee splashed from the spout of the pot, making an irregular brown stain on the tablecloth that Elinor chose not to mop up. It was Dolph's fault, after all, and she found a perverse pleasure in the thought of him doing extra work because of his dislike of her.

She poured herself a cup, stirred in a lump of sugar, sipped, and closed her eyes. With the burnt-chocolate smell of the coffee, the spicy scent of the sausage and the faint hot-water smell of the hard-boiled eggs in their shells (Dolph either couldn't do soft-boiled or was being spiteful again) she could almost imagine herself at home. Though at home she could not have heard the rush of the tide against the stone walls of the harbor, nor the cawing cry of seabirds diving past the open window.

"Good morning," Ramsay said, and Elinor quickly opened her eyes. "Ready to go ashore today?"

"May I?"

He took an egg and began peeling it. "Of course." The shell fell away in small shards, pitting the smooth surface with its reluctance to let go.

Elinor peeled an egg of her own. Hers was more cooperative. "I thought it might be unfair to ask someone to give up his time in town, since I understand there is little there to interest me."

"Not unless you like getting drunk and—that is, the pleasures of Santa Cruz are tailored to seamen, it's true," Ramsay said with one of his wry smiles. "And I'll take you myself. I can't say I'm interested in the pleasures of Santa Cruz either."

"Would that not interfere with your duties?"

Ramsay shrugged and flicked eggshell off his fingers. "I've already called upon the port admiral, and I can afford to take an hour or so. Arthur—Lieutenant Beaumont—isn't interested in going ashore at all. Something about not wanting to run into anyone he might owe money to. He's perfectly capable of handling any emergencies that might arise."

The door banged open, but instead of Dolph, Midshipman Hervey entered, breathless, carrying a knobby sack and a couple of parcels. "Mail for you, sir, and some things for Miss Pembroke," he said, giving the sack to Ramsay.

"The mail's late today," Ramsay said.

"I apologize, sir, I had to wait at the Admiralty, and then there was the bookseller's." Hervey handed two packages tied with string, one soft, one rectangular and hard, to Elinor, who immediately began tearing the wrapper from the latter. "Mr. Hervey, do not say you have found it?" she exclaimed.

"It's not as if it's that old, Miss Pembroke," Hervey said. "I can't believe you've never read *The Romance of the Forest*. It's really quite good."

"My mother disapproves of my reading novels. She prefers a good moral tale. I believe we own everything Hannah More ever wrote." Three volumes fell from the wrapper into her lap. "Thank you so much, Mr. Hervey."

"I believe I owe you, since you were so kind as to give me that other book. Didn't think I'd like it at first—it's not as exciting as anything Mrs. Radcliffe writes, but I came to like it immensely."

"I admit to being occasionally disconcerted to read my own name on those pages, but I promise you that did not influence my enjoyment of it! I wonder that the author signs herself only 'A Lady.' *Sense and Sensibility* is something any author could be proud of, and it's not as if it is improper for a woman to write novels."

"She might be shy of publicity. I hope she writes more of 'em. I was near on the edge of my chair when Elinor found out Edward was engaged to that bottle-head Lucy."

"Please use language more fitting to a member of His Majesty's Navy, Mr. Hervey," Ramsay said, but the amusement in his voice tempered the rebuke.

"I beg your pardon, sir. Miss Pembroke, you'll have to tell me how you like *The Romance of the Forest*. It's one of my favorites."

"I'm certain I will enjoy it, Mr. Hervey," Elinor said. Hervey smiled at her again and bumped into Dolph as he left, nearly causing the steward to drop the silver serving dish he carried. Dolph muttered at his retreating back and set the dish in front of Ramsay, ignoring Elinor completely. Ramsay raised an eyebrow at Dolph and gave the dish a push. "I believe I've told you to serve Miss Pembroke first," he said.

Dolph looked at Elinor, who smiled at him, thinking, *You are the most unpleasant person I have ever met,* wishing she were an Extraordinary Speaker to send that thought into his unwilling brain. He picked up the dish and brought it to Elinor's side of the table, setting it down with a little more force than before, and dropped a smallish beefsteak on her plate. "Thank you, Dolph," Elinor said sweetly, and was rewarded by seeing his face, now turned away from Ramsay, twist into a scowl. He served Ramsay a considerably larger piece of meat and stomped out of the room.

Ramsay turned in his seat to watch him go, shrugged, and applied himself to his food. "I had no idea Mr. Hervey was so interested in literature," he said. "You've certainly brought out a side of him we've never seen."

Elinor brought a forkful of tender meat to her lips. It was amazing how well Ramsay ate. "I enjoy discussing books. I rarely have—had—the opportunity at home. But you seem not to have time to read, though you have a surprising collection," she added, indicating the cupboard under the window. Aside from suppers with his officers, Ramsay never sat still for longer than the half-hour he spared himself for meals, and sometimes he did not even grant himself that much leisure.

"Surprising how?"

"Ah—that is—" She had made the comment without thinking, and now blurted out, "I did not think a man like you would be so interested in poetry."

Ramsay's eyebrows lifted almost to his hairline. "A man like me? And what kind of man am I, Miss Pembroke?"

Elinor wished the floor would open and drop her into the gunroom below, onto the table to disrupt the officers' breakfast. It would be far less embarrassing than this. "I meant only...oh...you are a...a man of action, I think, and not...contemplative...and..."

He laughed. "Don't tie yourself into knots, Miss Pembroke, I take your meaning. I think there's a regrettable attitude about poetry, that it's the province solely of wan and wispy young men or women of extreme sensibility. I blame Wordsworth, with all his talk of buttercups and daffodils."

"I hardly think that is fair to Mr. Wordsworth. Some of his writing is quite serious and non-floral."

Ramsay laughed and waved his hand dismissively. "I should have known better than to make sweeping exaggerations to someone as well-read as you. I admit to having strong preferences in my literature. 'The Tyger,' for example, which surely *you* must be familiar with."

"I am afraid I do not know that one. It is not by Wordsworth, I know."

"No, a fellow named William Blake. Listen." He leaned back in his seat and laced his fingers together on the table top before him, then began speaking, his voice now lower and more intense.

"Tyger! Tyger! burning bright
In the forests of the night,
What immortal hand or eye
Could frame thy fearful symmetry?
In what distant deeps or skies
Burnt the fire of thine eyes?
On what wings dare he aspire?
What the hand dare seize the fire?"

The poet's words sent a thrill through Elinor, eerie and marvelous. "I think Mr. Blake must have known more than a few Scorchers," she said. "I feel my talent is much like his tiger, fierce and terrible and beautiful all at once."

"Nothing wan or wispy about that poem, is there, Miss Pembroke?"

"Not at all, Captain. Am I making unwarranted assumptions again when I suggest you must also like *The Rime of the Ancient Mariner?*"

"Hah! Coleridge must have gone to sea once. '*Water, water every where, Nor any drop to drink.*' We were becalmed three years ago off the coast of Panama and came close to dying of thirst, and I had to stop a couple of men from drinking the seawater. No, it is his 'Kubla Khan' that appeals to me, the contrasts, the ambiguity."

"I do not know that poem."

"It hasn't been published yet. I was lucky enough to attend a reading several years ago. I wonder that you know his poetry at all, if your mother was so scandalized by novels—she would definitely not approve of Coleridge."

"No, but she believes your friend Mr. Wordsworth to be representative of all poets, and I doubt it has ever occurred to her that a poet might write about the leprous Nightmare Life-in-Death who makes men's blood run cold." The words left her lips before it occurred to *her* that perhaps "leprous Nightmare Life-in-Death" was not a phrase a young woman ought to know, and she blushed, but Ramsay merely looked amused.

"Never fear, Miss Pembroke, I'm not scandalized," he said. "You don't seem to be afraid of what people think of you."

He had to be thinking of that night in the music room. "I simply act, sometimes, before I have thought out the consequences."

"It didn't seem that way in the Admiralty. You seemed to have considered all the possibilities when you approached Lord Melville."

"Not all. I—" She stopped, unable to tell him the truth. She hadn't considered how her leaving would hurt Selina. She hadn't realized she did care, at least a little, about what people would think of her when she returned to society if they knew she had been alone and unaccompanied on a ship full of sailors. "I didn't realize the living conditions would be so confined," she continued. "Not that I have any complaints, Captain, I merely intend to illustrate what I did not know to anticipate."

Ramsay had his elbow on the table, his chin propped on his hand, and was regarding her in a way that told her he knew she hadn't been completely honest with him. He teased apart a bit of egg with his fork, idly, stabbing with the tines at each piece. "Do you have regrets?"

"No." It was abrupt, too abrupt, but she had a sudden fear that if she admitted any of her worries, he might tell Hervey to take her back on his next trip, and she was *not* going back. "No," she said more casually, and gestured at the window. "Not when I have such an extraordinary view. I have never seen anything so beautiful."

"Where we're going, such sights are commonplace. If the West Indies were not so hazardous to the health, it would be impossible to prevent a mass emigration there. Though it's very hot in the summer. I wish these pirates followed the practices of their forebears and went north during the hottest months. We could cruise off Newfoundland and enjoy the breeze."

"I think you cannot mean you wish the pirates success in any way."

He laughed, a short, abrupt sound. "No, but as we're to chase after them whatever they do, I'd rather not swelter under the Caribbean sun. The Navy hasn't authorized cooler uniforms for tropical conditions."

"I sympathize completely, Captain."

He regarded her, his eyes narrowed in thought. "I imagine you do. We should see about getting you some kind of parasol. That bonnet seems insufficient protection."

"Please don't put yourself to any extra trouble on my account, sir."

"Miss Pembroke, you need to learn to accept gallant gestures in the spirit they're offered," he said, straight-faced but with that merry twinkle in his eye that said he was teasing her.

"I'm afraid I'm not accustomed to them, so you must make allowances for my ingratitude," she replied with a smile.

"You're not? You surprise me, Miss Pembroke." He pushed his chair back, leaving Elinor groping for a response to a statement she didn't understand. "We'll go in an hour or so, before the heat becomes too much, if that's agreeable to you."

"Of course, Captain," Elinor said. "Will you send someone to tell me when the boat is ready?"

He smiled, that crooked tooth peeking out once more. "Oh, we won't be using the boat. Not when we can take a more... direct approach."

Elinor sucked in a breath. "But, Captain—"

"Come now, Miss Pembroke, I can't believe the lady who bearded the First Lord in his chilly, dark den is afraid to try something new!" He smiled more widely. "I promise I won't drop you," he added, and shut the door behind himself.

Elinor's face warmed. Flying. Or being Moved, which amounted to the same thing. *I must put on a clean shift*, she thought, then stuffed her fist in her mouth to keep from laughing at herself. Of course Ramsay wouldn't expose her to embarrassment. But...*flying*...

She left the table before Dolph could enter to clear it and went up to the forecastle, adjusting her bonnet against the bright sun that was such a contrast to the dimly lit main deck. The sailors made way for Elinor as she made her way forward, touching their foreheads as if they were the brims of their nonexistent hats and avoiding her eyes. She was still uncertain, more than a week after the capture of the *Joyeux*, whether this was from fear or from awe, but she stayed well away from their territory nonetheless, remembering stripes of blood on a naked back. She stayed away from the gunroom, too, after her one visit, which had been an awkward, silent thing in which she could feel the discomfort of the officers like an ashy film over her skin.

Now she smiled and nodded, walking nimbly around coils of rope and dodging a group of men who, in response to a shouted command, swarmed up the rigging of the mizzen sails like so many squirrels. She was never going to understand their language, all that "Stretch out those tops'l halliards!" and "Clear that hawse!" Nor would she learn the difference between "hull up" and "hull down," but she could tell the topgallant from the mainsail and knew the difference between starboard and larboard. She was a beautiful ship, *Athena* was, and now that she no longer stank of fresh paint Elinor found it quite pleasant to stand at the bow as close as she could come to the figurehead, which was indeed the goddess Athena, and let the wind wash over her and through her as if it were trying to carry her away.

"Mr. Bolton," she said when she had reached her usual spot, "good morning."

Bolton paused in running his fingers over the place where two paler boards fitted between the planks of the darker, sun-weathered deck. "Mornin' to you, missie," he said. Bolton himself was as sun-weathered as the ship, his bald head permanently sunburned and marked with a constellation of brown freckles, but he looked much healthier than he had when she'd met him, vomiting into a bucket and complaining of stomach pains. He stood and stretched with a great popping of joints. "You'll be goin' ashore, belike?"

"I will."

" 'Tes best you not go to Santa Cruz, missie, it ain't a place for a young lady." Bolton squinted and looked up into the cloudless sky. "Don't much like cities, cold and crowded as they be. Open air and sun, 'tes what every man needs."

Elinor followed his gaze but saw nothing. "I intend to visit the shore," she said. "It looks so much different to the sea at Brighton. We went only once, and it was so cold and rocky... I did not realize the seashore could look so inviting."

Bolton nodded. " 'Tes a grand thing the sea is, wi' moods like a weather-cock, deadly as you like when she isn't smilin' at ye." He picked absently at a rough patch on the bow rail with the air of a man dissatisfied with the job he'd done and continued to watch the sky. "Yon," he said, straightening and pointing aft.

Elinor leaned out over the bow rail with her hand on the rigging and looked where he pointed. A distant speck no bigger than a pinprick seemed to hover in the sky on the larboard side of the ship, but as they watched, it grew and resolved first into an oblong shape, then into the figure of a man, dropping out of the sky to skim across the waves faster than a hawk stooping to its prey. Ramsay, minus his coat and hat, swept past them, curved around the bow and up again in a graceful arc, hovered briefly at the apex of the curve, then darted past the masts and rigging toward the stern and out of their sight.

"Fair makes my gut quiver, watching 'imself flittin' about," Bolton said. " 'Tesn't natural."

"Of course it isn't," Elinor said, laughing. "If it were, then everyone could do it."

" 'Tesn't natural," Bolton repeated. "But 'tes a beautiful thing else."

"Not like fire, then?" Elinor teased.

"Fire's got its own beauty. And any man c'n spark a flame, missie. Scorchers need no match nor flint, 'tes so. But no man c'n fly however he sets his mind to 't, 'cept he's got the talent."

"I think you're simply accustomed to Scorchers."

" 'Tes true my daughter's like to have given me a fondness for 'em. Nigh to leavin' the academy, she is, and her mum 'n me be reet proud o' her."

"You should be. I would have liked to join a fire brigade, if I'd been allowed."

"So you joined the Navy instead?" Bolton sounded amused. " 'Tes true you ain't stopped by not bein' allowed things."

"I had not thought of myself in quite that way, but I suppose I agree with you." Elinor straightened her sleeves and wished she dared put on her gown with the shorter sleeves. There was no one here to care what she looked like, and it would not be so bad to let the sun turn her brown, but she pictured herself returning to London... it seemed she did care more for the opinions of her social class than she imagined. Besides, if Ramsay and his officers could endure the sun in their heavy, blue undress coats, she could bear her muslin gown with the long sleeves.

"Miss Pembroke! I say, Miss Pembroke!"

Elinor closed her lips on a word she'd heard the bo'sun's mate say, put on a polite smile, and turned to watch the awkward, black-clad figure of Stephen Selkirk cross the deck toward her. How he managed to move in such a way as to interfere with the path of every sailor on the forecastle was a mystery to her, especially since he hopped and pivoted in an effort *not* to do so.

Bolton spat over the side, then said, "Excuse me, missie, got things t' do," and went well out of Selkirk's path past the bowsprit to clamber up the foremast rigging. He made no attempt to disguise the fact that he was fleeing.

"Miss Pembroke," the chaplain said, breathing a little heavily, "I'm told we will be permitted shore leave this afternoon. I'm quite looking forward to it, aren't you?" His thick, dirty-blond hair was tied back at the nape of his neck with a black ribbon, but some of it was slipping free to hang limp around his face.

"Indeed, Mr. Selkirk, I—"

"Such a glorious day for it too. Not too hot, not too cold."

"Yes, I can—"

"I wonder, Miss Pembroke, if you would allow me to accompany you ashore? It would be improper for you to wander the city unescorted."

More improper than being confined with three hundred men, unescorted? "I thank you, Mr. Selkirk, but I already—"

"Then that's settled. I look forward to it—"

"*Mr. Selkirk*," Elinor said, feeling desperate, "I already have an escort but thank you so much for your concern it truly is unnecessary." She drew in a deep breath.

Selkirk looked surprised. "You should have said so, Miss Pembroke. I'm not one to impose on others."

"I apologize, sir, for the miscommunication."

He waved his hand. "No matter. Would you care to walk with me? I find a stroll along the deck most bracing in the mornings. And we might continue the conversation we were having yesterday, I hope? About the nature of divinity as expressed in the natural world?"

"I should be pleased to do so," Elinor said, finding it difficult to maintain her smile. She took Selkirk's offered arm and tried to keep up as he dragged her along, wandering drunkenly among the tarry ropes and seeming unconcerned that he was making sailors step out of his way. The first time she had accepted his arm, she had felt awkward, terribly conscious that the contact would allow him to perceive her emotions. It would have felt intrusive even if she hadn't feared hurting *his* feelings with her mild dislike of him. But Selkirk had simply patted her arm and said, "Of course a lady of such great sensibility as you are would feel distaste for the setting in which you find yourself," and had never once since then realized how irritated he made her.

Had she encountered him at home, Selkirk would have been a mild annoyance, someone to be endured for an hour or two at a supper or a dance. Here, in the confines of *Athena*, he was both unavoidable and insufferable. His sermons displayed genuine piety, but his air of inviting confidences, of being permanently on the verge of solving problems one either did not have or did not want solved, made him someone Elinor wished she could avoid. But upon learning she was from Hertfordshire, and that they shared some mutual acquaintances, he had decided to make her the recipient of his friendly overtures, and she was too polite to reject him.

Besides, she told herself, barely regaining her balance after tripping over a bucket her companion had accidentally kicked into her path, *imagine how awkward it would be, meeting one another over the supper table almost every night, having snubbed him openly.* She clutched his arm a little tighter and he smiled down at her; she managed to smile in return. *But oh, how pleasant not to be the subject of his attention.*

CHAPTER 8

IN WHICH THERE IS FLYING, A
NEW FRIEND, AND AN
UNEXPECTED ATTACK

"**Y**ou have only to relax," Ramsay said, "to not resist."

"You cannot Move someone who fights you?"

"It's more difficult, sometimes impossible, if they're strong-willed enough. But you aren't going to fight, are you?"

Elinor cast a skeptical eye on the captain, impeccably turned out as if they were going to a dance rather than the seashore some half a mile away. "Could not Mr. Hervey transport me?"

"Mr. Hervey is already on leave ashore. Come, Miss Pembroke, you have demonstrated your talent for all of us. Let me do the same for you."

"But I saw you Fly this—aah!"

She felt the faintest pressure on her entire lower body, an invisible cushion that flexed when she moved, and then her feet left the deck and she hovered a few inches in the air. She flailed a little before realizing that, counter to her expectations, she did not feel awkward or unbalanced. She kicked her feet, but remained perfectly stationary. "Oh," she said.

"Back, the rest of you, it's not like you've never seen this before," Ramsay commanded, and the men who had been openly gaping pretended to return to work. "Are you afraid of heights?"

"Not to my knowledge." She was floating higher now, drifting toward the rail, and despite her words her heart was hammering. Suppose he dropped her? Suppose he lost control of both of them and they plummeted into the ocean? Suppose—

"Slowly at first, I think," Ramsay said, and then he was beside her, both legs drawn up as if he were sitting on a chair. Then she was over the rail and floating some twenty feet above the waves, and she gave another involuntary cry, remembering the bo'sun's chair—but she felt as secure, this time, as if she were seated on the sofa in the great cabin. More secure, even, since that sofa moved with the waves all the time, and had once flung her off during some rough weather.

The breeze, with its salt spray, threaded through her hair and caressed her cheeks and hands. She looked down at the waves beneath her, said "No!" and snatched at her shoe, then watched it fall away from her reaching fingers toward the white-capped crests. It came to an abrupt halt about three feet above the waves, then reversed its course until Ramsay plucked it out of the air and returned it to her with a bow made comical by his position in midair.

"Thank you," Elinor said, and squatted to put it on, only realizing when she was straightening again that she had not given one thought to the empty space beneath her. "This is...rather invigorating, actually," she said.

Ramsay smiled, the barest twist of his lips. "I think so. It's like swimming, except far, far better, of course."

"You can swim?"

"More or less. I think I actually Fly through the water more than swim, but as long as it keeps me from drowning, I don't care what it is. Care to go a little faster?"

"I think so."

The breeze became a wind, and then she was flying, skimming above the waves. This close to shore, they resolved themselves into long lines topped with white that curled and crashed against the dark gold of the beach ahead. She threw back her head and laughed with delight. No wonder Ramsay went Flying every day. If she had his talent, she might never come down to earth. It was almost as wonderful as letting the fire loose.

As she thought that, she registered the nearness of the shore, how the dark gold of the wet sand became the paler gold of the upper beach, and beyond that were numberless trees of varieties she had never seen before. The wind brought their green, wet fragrance to her nose, and she breathed it in and thought, *They would blaze high enough to wake the volcano*, and a chill passed over her. That she could even consider such an indulgence—

"Start walking," Ramsay said, coming back to Fly close beside her. "It will keep you from falling over when you land."

She obediently began moving her legs as they descended toward the beach, gradually losing speed, and then she was trotting along the wet sand, her feet making shallow dimples in the ground, and she came to a stop and tried not to breathe heavily as the earth reasserted its grasp on her. The land rocked beneath her as if it were *Athena*'s deck; she balanced carefully on the balls of her feet and prayed she would not fall over. "Captain Ramsay, I believe you were showing off," she said when she had composed herself.

Ramsay was still hovering two inches above the sand. "Possibly. But you have to admit it's a wondrous thing."

"It is." Elinor kicked the wet sand and a clump flew an inch or so before settling back to earth. "And this is a marvelous place."

"Some of the beaches are rockier than this, and they have more interesting wildlife, but I think your footwear would not survive it."

"I agree. Captain—" She hesitated.

"Miss Pembroke?"

"You did not need to put yourself out so for me."

Ramsay turned and began walking away down the beach, close to where the water rose and fell on the shore. Spent waves lapped at the soles of his boots. Elinor followed, somewhat higher on the sand; her footwear would not withstand a solid wetting any more than it would a hard, rocky shore. "There are many Extraordinaries serving in the Navy, did you know?" Ramsay said without turning his head. "The Admiralty spreads us out as widely as possible, to get the best use of our talents, and it's rare to have more than one on a ship. *Athena* may be the only one in the service with three." He kicked at a wave and made a splash that spattered his breeches. "And Peregrine, bless his heart, is rather focused on his scientific pursuits—I hope he doesn't become so caught up in his search for that elusive sparrow he keeps claiming is here that he forgets to return on time. Though it wouldn't be the first time I've had to hunt him down."

"And I am an Extraordinary."

"I realize it's a narrow thread to hang a friendship on, but…it's more than just talent, being Extraordinary; there's as big a gap between us and an ordinary talent as there is between a talent and a non-talented person. Arthur is a Speaker and my closest friend, and even he can't entirely bridge that gap." He turned and faced Elinor, but continued walking backward, completely unconcerned at the possibility of tripping and falling. "And you are interesting, Miss Pembroke. I've thought that since we met."

Elinor blushed and averted her eyes. "I…Captain, I have regretted not apologizing to you for my hasty words that night—"

"No need. I put you at a disadvantage, and you reacted as anyone would have. I didn't know who you were at the time—had to ask Penelope, Lady Ormerod that is, and I guessed you might have been under some strain that evening, what with all those people watching to see if you were going to burst into flame."

Elinor laughed, and said, "That would indeed be a show. Fire burns me as it does anyone."

"I didn't realize, but I suppose that makes sense." He looked past her shoulder, then to her surprise retreated to the dry sand, sat down and removed his boots. "We're out of sight of *Athena*," he said to her baffled face, "and I can afford to shed some of my dignity. And I've liked wading since I was a boy." He took off his stockings, tossed his coat over them, and trotted back down to the water, wading in until the waves were past his ankles. "You might try it, Miss Pembroke," he called. "You can hardly be worried about your respectability at this point."

Elinor gasped, then laughed. "I think I am extremely respectable"—she removed her shoes—"and demure"—she tugged off one stocking, then the other—"and I think the proof of that is in my enduring Mr. Selkirk's company without snubbing him in self-defense."

She walked down the shore to join Ramsay, lifting her skirts a little to keep them out of the water.

"If he's disturbing you, I can stop inviting him to dine at my table," Ramsay said. "I can barely stand the man myself, man of God or no." He dug his toes into the soft sand as a wavelet washed over his bare feet.

"He is too self-absorbed to respond to any but the strongest deterrent, I think, and I cannot bring myself to give him that. It is not his fault he is a...a..."

"A shallow, prating fool covered with a veneer of faux holiness?"

"That seems unfair to him. At least his faith seems genuine."

"Possibly. But he thinks his Discernment gives him more of a window into the human soul than the simple ability to feel others' emotions."

"And he seems to misinterpret what he *does* perceive. I thought Discerners were, well, more discerning than that."

"Some are simply more skilled than others, I suppose. Fortunately, he's not an Extraordinary Discerner and has to touch people to feel what they feel, because he wouldn't be able to avoid knowing how disdainful I am of him. He probably means well, but I don't like him trying to be everyone's best friend and confidant. It's intrusive and inappropriate. I'd like to have him reassigned, but I'm afraid no one else wants him either. And the truth is he's not a bad man, and I'd feel guilty giving him such a decisive shove when he's always been respectful of me. Though I'm afraid he sees me as a heathen in need of converting."

"He sees *me* as a kindred spirit. I am quite cast down wondering what it is about me that he sees as his kin."

Ramsay laughed at that. "You did make the colossal mistake of admitting you were from Hertfordshire. I have never seen anyone try so hard to discover common acquaintances." He kicked up some water, splashing Elinor's hem and making her dance quickly backward. "My apologies."

"Pray do not ruin my gown, I have only the four."

"You travel light, for a gentlewoman."

"I did bring my best evening gown, Captain."

"I'm afraid I can't give you that kind of entertainment, but I think I could arrange a concert, if you enjoy the fiddle and flute. Mr. Worsley can play most of Beethoven's Fifth on the nose-harp—"

"Stop, pray, or I shall be unable to breathe from laughing!"

"But it's all true! We have several Welshmen, you know how they are for singing, and Hawkes and Geneally on the starboard number five gun carry their fifes at all times. Of course they won't play for the officers, but you can sit in the companionway and listen to their dulcet music."

Elinor covered her mouth to hold in her laughter. "I depend upon you to arrange it, Captain."

"My pleasure. And now I think we should dry off and return to the ship. Even in springtime the afternoon sun in these latitudes can be brutal."

They Flew back at much greater speed than before, Elinor spreading her arms wide to pretend it was the wind buoying her up. She felt her spirits buoyed as well, but not by the wind; it was good to have a friend, and Ramsay was right: there was a divide between her and the other talents on the ship that simply didn't exist between her and Ramsay, or even between her and Hays. It had been a long time since she had felt so comfortable with anyone but Selina. She looked up to where Ramsay Flew overhead, looping about while keeping her perfectly level, and felt that kinship Selkirk didn't have; she knew joy in an Extraordinary talent when she saw it.

❦

The sun had fully set, and the lamp swaying gently over the captain's table turned the windows into a row of mirrors that reflected Elinor's face poorly. Her eyebrows looked particularly fierce tonight, though that could be the shadows. She traced their line on the glass, then snatched her finger away when the door behind her opened and men's voices preceded Ramsay and his officers into the great cabin.

"Good evening, Miss Pembroke," the captain said. "Won't you join us?"

He held the chair to his left politely while she sat, then there was a

general scraping of chairs and shifting of bodies as the men joined her.
Dolph and two other seamen, all of them dressed as nicely as they
could manage, began bringing dishes out. The table was not large
enough for proper removes, but Dolph always managed at least two
courses: plain food, but delicious.

"Thank you," Ramsay said as Dolph set out a tureen of clear soup,
and dipped the ladle into the broth to serve Elinor only to be interrupted by a discreet cough.

"If you would allow me to say grace, Captain?" said Selkirk, one
hand half-raised as if he were answering a prim schoolmarm's question.
He turned his saintly expression on Ramsay, and Ramsay let the ladle
fall with a small splash, sitting back in his chair and gesturing his
permission. Selkirk nodded, clasped his hands in front of him and
bowed his head; around the table, the other officers adopted varying
poses of reverence. Elinor bowed her head, but looked sidelong at
Ramsay, who had rested his elbows on the table and propped his head
on his clasped hands. Elinor had seen this drama play out with little
variation every evening Selkirk had joined them at the table, but she
judged Ramsay's seeming indifference to religion had more to do with
his disdain for Selkirk than for any innate impiety.

"Our Father," Selkirk began in a loud voice, and Elinor turned her
attention elsewhere. When Selkirk began his grace with Our Father, he
always followed it with a homily Elinor was certain was inappropriate
in a blessing over food. The soup would probably be lukewarm when it
finally reached her bowl.

"In Thy name, amen," Selkirk said. Elinor muttered her reply with
the others. Ramsay proceeded to serve Elinor as if he hadn't been
interrupted.

"I hope you enjoyed Tenerife, Miss Pembroke," he said, sounding
far more formal than he had on the beach that day. "We should remain
in harbor here a few more days, let everyone stretch their legs."

"And then stretch them again when we round up the men,"
Livingston said, irritated. "All of them drunk, probably."

"Let them work it out ashore," Ramsay said. "Give them a chance
to enjoy themselves before the real work begins. They'll work better if
they know they're being treated fairly."

"Generous of you, Captain," Livingston said, and raised his glass to Ramsay before draining it and pouring himself another. Ramsay returned the salute with a tight smile and took a sip from his own glass.

"I'll be going ashore again tomorrow," Hays said. "Still on the hunt for *Regulus regulus teneriffae*. Absurd how well the little creature has hidden itself from me; the place is supposed to be thronged with it. Though Tenerife is unique in more ways than its fauna, since it has those active volcanoes."

"You mean it might go off again?" Gibbons said, his thin face going pale enough to make his spots stand out red against the background. Elinor privately thought him too young to be a lieutenant of anything, let alone of a detachment of Marines.

"Oh, no," Hays laughed, "it's unlikely. And even if it does, we'll have plenty of warning. There's nothing to fear."

"I don't know—"

"Come, man, show some backbone," Livingston drawled. "Don't be letting the side down in front of the ladies." He directed a lazy smile at Selkirk, who reddened. Livingston's cheeks looked red too. Elinor had not been watching him, but she was certain he had had more than a few glasses of wine already.

"Mr. Livingston, would you mind passing that dish by your elbow?" said Sampson Brown, who had been silently making his way through his meal until then. The sailing master was round and had a fringe of black hair circling his head that made him look like a medieval monk. Elinor could not remember hearing him speak before. He communicated with Ramsay through a system of grunts and nods that was as good as a language for both of them, and she thought they must be good friends, because Ramsay frequently invited him to join him for meals.

Livingston straightened in his seat and handed the platter across. As he handed it over, Hays said, "I believe I may have to go some distance farther inland to find what I seek."

"That won't be possible on this trip, Mr. Hays, but I'll keep it in mind," Ramsay said. "Sampson, I'd like some of that, if you would pass it this way."

Brown grunted and handed it over. Livingston poured himself another glass of wine and drank deeply. "Don't suppose the rest of us'll see much more than the harbor," he said.

"Plenty of time for that when we reach Bermuda," Beaumont said. "Unless you know more about our orders than what's on the paper."

"Admiral Durrant will give us more detailed instructions," Ramsay said, "though I can't imagine they won't have something to do with the Brethren of the Coast."

"Excuse me, Captain, but who are the Brethren of the Coast?" Elinor said, lowering her fork.

Livingston laughed. "Thought you were well-read, Miss Pembroke. You've never heard of them?"

"They're a group of men who've been directing the activities of the pirates along the American coasts and in the Caribbean," Ramsay said, overriding the beginnings of Elinor's angry retort. "Admiral Durrant has yet to capture or kill any of them and...saying they're a thorn in his side is an understatement."

"I apologize for my ignorance, Captain"—Elinor shot a glare at Livingston, who smirked at her while topping up his wine glass again —"but I thought pirates were independent operators. From what little I have heard, they sound more like... like Italian outlaws holding wealthy captives for ransom."

"A hundred years ago, they *were* more independent. The closest they came to organization was Henry Morgan's loose band of pirates and privateers. But now Rhys Evans, their leader, controls almost all the ships, tells them where to go and which ships to take and how to treat the captives. His strategy is to encourage the merchant ships to convince their governments to pay an ongoing ransom in exchange for the pirates not molesting their ships."

"It's working, too," said Beaumont. "Spain gave in about three years ago and the pirates haven't attacked them since. Well, the Brethren pirates haven't. There are still independents working the seas, but if Evans catches 'em, he makes an example of 'em."

"I imagine it is not a pleasant example. Please do not describe it to me."

Ramsay nodded, his face grim. "Evans would like to be the second coming of Henry Morgan, them both being Welshmen and all. It's why he took the name Brethren of the Coast, though they're nothing near as honorable as Morgan's band, which considering the kind of men who sailed with Morgan is saying something. The Admiral is furious at his fleet's inability to find their headquarters, let alone capture any of the Brethren leaders, which is why I imagine we will be directed to do so."

"So you might want to practice that fire-slinging you do," Livingston said. He poured himself yet another glass—was that five now, or six? Elinor had thought there was a rule, perhaps even an Article of War, prohibiting drunkenness, but Livingston seemed not to care about his condition.

"Mr. Livingston, I think you should pass me that bottle," Ramsay said. "May I offer you wine, Miss Pembroke? Watered, of course."

"Bet she took more than that from you today," Livingston muttered, casting a sly glance at Elinor.

She gasped. Ramsay stood with a force that knocked his chair over, slamming his fist on the table, making his plate and Elinor's rattle and the bottle fall on its side. "Apologize to the lady *this instant,*" he snarled.

Elinor, her eyes wide, clutched her napkin in her fists, feeling her cheeks burn. Wine trickled from the narrow mouth of the bottle. Livingston sat up, his face as white as Elinor's was red.

"Miss Pembroke, I apologize," he said, though he looked more afraid than penitent. "I have had too much to drink and allowed that to override my good judgment. I sincerely beg your pardon."

"I...I accept," Elinor said. Beside her, she could almost feel Ramsay quivering with fury. She didn't want to look at Livingston, but she was afraid to look anywhere else, afraid of what she might see on their faces.

"It's your good fortune I'm not allowed to call you out, Livingston," Ramsay said, his voice like sharpened steel. "Make such allegations about my character again, and I don't care who your father is, you'll be back in London as fast as Mr. Hervey can carry you. Get out of this cabin, and I don't want to see you again until you're sober enough to appreciate the tongue-lashing I'm going to give you later."

Livingston pushed back his chair and stood, wobbling. "Sir," he said, then turned and left the room, letting the door swing shut behind him.

"I truly beg your pardon, Miss Pembroke," Ramsay said, righting his chair and taking his seat.

"It's not your fault, Captain," she said, proud that her voice remained calm. The idea that anyone might think she and Ramsay... such an innocent thing, spending an hour alone together...*who knew my reputation could be on such shaky ground, even here?* "Mr. Livingston was clearly in his cups, and I'm certain he would never have said such a thing if he were sober."

"That's not an excuse, but you're more generous of spirit than I am." Ramsay set the now-empty bottle upright and tried mopping the stain with his napkin. "Dolph's going to be angry, me ruining his table-cloth like that."

"I assure you, Miss Pembroke, no one could possibly believe such a thing of either you or Captain Ramsay," Selkirk said, reaching across the table to pat her hand. Elinor successfully resisted the urge to snatch it away.

"Livingston's an ass," Brown said, still placidly eating. "Always thought so."

"He's an ass with connections," Beaumont said, then glanced nervously at Elinor. "Excuse my language, miss. Captain."

Elinor waved a weary hand. "I think there is no better word in the English language for him," she said, "and I am not sure why you put up with him. Could he not be transferred elsewhere?"

"West Indies or no, this is a prime posting," Ramsay said, "and we're likely to take many prizes before we're done, which means possible promotions for my lieutenants. Lord Copley wants great things for his son and pulled several strings to get him posted to *Athena*."

"You should have given him *Joyeux*, Miles," Beaumont said. "Would've spared you some of that bile."

"I had good reason not to," Ramsay said, flicking his gaze briefly toward Elinor. "And I think Livingston's dislike of me is deeply seated enough that nothing's going to change his feelings."

"Should I be worried about mutiny?" Gibbons said.

Ramsay shook his head. "Livingston's animosity won't extend beyond me. He wants his career to thrive, and if he has any sense, he's working on a nice speech that will convince me not to destroy him."

"Can you do that?" Elinor asked.

"He probably believes I can. There's certainly much I can do to impede his progress."

"Boy's still an ass," Brown said.

"Watch your language, Mr. Brown. But I agree with you."

Elinor picked up her fork again, saw how her hand trembled, and laid it down before it could betray her. "Would you have challenged him to a duel, Captain?"

"Dueling is illegal, and that goes double for Extraordinaries," Ramsay said, sounding as though he'd bitten off something sharp. "But —" He gripped the bottle's neck like a club. "I'll put the fear of God into him, or at any rate the fear of me, and he won't trouble you again, Miss Pembroke."

He stood, glass in hand. "Gentlemen, let us toast the King." Elinor never knew what to do during that little ritual, but it seemed sitting quietly was acceptable, because Ramsay had never corrected her. So much of what they did was impenetrable to her.

"Well, Captain, I must say that's the most entertaining meal I've had in a long time," Hays said, pushing back his chair. "I don't think I'll stay for drinks, if you don't mind."

"And I think I shall retire," Elinor said, "so, good evening, gentlemen." They all pushed back their chairs as she rose and made her curtsey, then she went to her room, where she sat on the bed and stared blindly at the wall. Livingston's white face rose up before her mind's eye. She did not think his comment had come solely out of the bottle; it must have been something he'd thought about before. The memory of her pleasant walk along the beach went sour. She *was* in Ramsay's company often; their bedrooms *did* adjoin to some extent—would others have drawn the same conclusion?

I've been too careless, she thought, *and I cannot allow myself to forget I am the sole guardian of my reputation, here aboard ship.* Yet her relationship with Ramsay was perfectly innocent; what did she care if low minds assumed otherwise? *Let enough people believe your virtue is...flexible...and*

you will endure far more than idle gossip. Bad enough you can't avoid Mr.
Selkirk; imagine trying to stay out of the way of someone whose intentions are
far darker. Captain Ramsay can't have everyone on this ship flogged.

A knock at the door, then, "Miss Pembroke. Would you mind
coming out here?" After a pause, Ramsay added, "All things considered,
I probably shouldn't enter your bedchamber even if there's no one
around to see it."

Elinor pushed open the door. Ramsay had already turned away and
was standing with his hands gripping the back of his chair. "I apologize," he said without looking at her. "It never occurred to me anyone
here might question my honor, let alone yours."

"You have done nothing to apologize for, Captain. Mr. Livingston
has reason to wish us both ill," Elinor said. "He spoke out of spite."

"And hit a plausible target. How many others are thinking the same
way?"

"Does it matter?" Ramsay's tense, distant stance made Elinor forget
she had the same concerns. "Captain Ramsay, I have so few friends
aboard ship that I cannot afford to lose one. Can it not be enough that
we know ourselves to be honorable?"

He turned his head to look at her, his blue eyes shadowed. "Miss
Pembroke, do you honestly believe your presence on this ship can be
hidden forever? You have to protect yourself against that day. Arthur
or Peregrine will dine with us from now on, and I'll sling my hammock
in the lobby outside the great cabin—"

"You will never get any sleep if you do that!"

"I'll never get any sleep if I'm worrying about what people think
I'm doing behind closed doors. Forgive me, Miss Pembroke, but I
believe I told you that you need to learn to accept gallant gestures
when they're offered you." He smiled, but there wasn't any humor
behind it.

"I think this is the wrong decision, Captain."

"It's the only decision left to me. Good night, Miss Pembroke." He
pushed the chair in, bowed to her, and went into what would no longer
be his bedchamber.

Elinor stood there a few seconds longer, her mouth agape, then
retreated to her cabin and once again sat on the bed staring at the wall.

All her innocent pleasure, poisoned by a few vicious words. It infuriated her that her honor was such a fragile thing in the eyes of the world that it could be tainted by the merest accusation of improper behavior. Ramsay would still be friendly, but under such constraints they could never become true friends.

Loneliness struck her as it had not since her first night aboard *Athena*, when she had cried a few self-indulgent, homesick tears and reproached herself for choosing her third path. And they would be setting off across the Atlantic soon, a journey of almost three weeks that at the moment seemed like three years. She felt like kicking Livingston, or setting him—no, not setting him on fire, *never think like that, not even idly*—but she could happily see him flogged if it meant being allowed to be Ramsay's friend.

She put on her nightdress and lay on her bed, atop her blankets. *At least Mr. Selkirk will be company for you.* She groaned. It was going to be a very long three weeks.

CHAPTER 9
IN WHICH ELINOR MEETS THE ADMIRAL

T he sound of a distant drum woke Elinor from her reverie, a pleasant daydream in which she was walking in the fields near her family's home in Hertfordshire, and she sat up and rubbed her forehead where it had pressed against the window frame. Could they have encountered another ship, here where there was nothing to see but waves and sunlight and—no, that wasn't a bird, it couldn't be.

She left the great cabin, and as she neared the companionway, the drumming resolved itself into the sound of men's boots beating a tattoo across the deck and up the ladder. The smell of hot wood and tarred rope drifted past them, along with shouts made incomprehensible by the brisk sea wind that carried those too-familiar odors. She halted outside the captain's quarters and watched them pass, and when the flood had abated, she followed them up the ladder and, blinking, into the fierce midday sunlight.

To her dark-adjusted eyes, the men climbing the rigging with more than usual alacrity were black insects with too few legs, skittering against the sails that blinded her. More men crowded the larboard rails, jostling for position, a few climbing onto the ship's boat to have a better view of whatever it was they were all looking at, then leaping down when a shrill whistle and a shout from Lieutenant Fitzgerald brought them to order. Elinor blinked away the last of the light-blindness and touched the shoulder of the nearest man, saying, "I beg your pardon."

The man turned, jerked away from her in surprise, then nodded and began shoving. "Out o' the way for Milady! You there, shift a leg, din'cha hear me? I said *move!*"

A passage wide enough for two people to walk with arms linked opened up to the rail, and Elinor moved forward. They had fought two more battles, guided to their targets by the Admiralty's Seers and Speakers, after leaving Tenerife, sinking one and capturing the other. In both cases she had brought her talent to bear on the enemy with some success, though nothing as spectacular as *Joyeux,* and her displays had won her supporters even as they had terrified others. They called her Milady, bowed when she passed, and went out of their way to make her comfortable. Ramsay, on observing this, had smiled one of his little smiles, but said nothing, and Elinor, torn between embarrassment and relief, had settled on the latter and responded to her admirers with friendly gratitude.

She smiled at the man, who bobbed his head. "What are we looking at?" she asked. The horizon was as empty as it had been for the past eighteen days.

" 'Tis land, Milady," the man said, " 'tis Bermuda. We're here!"

Elinor shaded her eyes and saw the faintest fuzz like mold growing on the surface of the sea. "Land," she breathed. "Land!"

"You've seen it, now back to work," Beaumont said, and the men scattered, casting glances at the horizon over their shoulders as they went. "We're still a good ways out, but with this wind it shouldn't be long," he told Elinor. "And Mr. Hervey will Bound in shortly."

"Is that important?"

"You're to go directly to Admiralty House from *Athena* rather than taking a carriage from Ireland Island, where the docks are. It minimizes the number of people who will want to know who you are. Mr. Hervey will take you and the captain."

"Why cannot Mr. Hervey go now? Surely he is not limited by distance."

"Mr. Hervey's never been to the Caribbean before and doesn't know the House's signature. He'll have to Skip there, learn the signature, and come back."

"I don't understand what that means."

Beaumont scowled. "I—Mr. Hervey, would *you* answer Miss Pembroke's questions? I beg your pardon, but I must return to my duties." He left her with a nod, and Elinor ground her teeth. Beaumont was always perfectly polite, but it was also perfectly clear that he wished she were serving elsewhere. He might be Ramsay's best friend, but they were as different as fire and ice.

She looked to where Hervey stood on the far side of the quarterdeck with the other midshipmen working their navigation calculations, saw him turn in her direction, and then he was in front of her with a faint popping sound as if a cork had been drawn. She stepped backward in surprise, and he laughed. "Beg pardon, Miss Pembroke, I didn't mean to startle you. You wanted to know about my talent?"

She laughed with him, but faintly, for he had startled the air from her lungs. "I cannot believe we have never discussed it," she said. "I suppose we have been too preoccupied with literature."

"That's more interesting than talent, *I* think," he said. "Besides, there's not much to tell. I can Bound to a place I don't know so long as it's within my range, and I can Bound anywhere in the world if I know its signature."

"And a signature is—?"

Hervey leaned on the rail and let his hands dangle. One foot kicked at the mass of hammocks strung in the netting. "Bounders have to recognize where they're Bounding to," he said. "So lots of public places, and some homes, have Bounding chambers. You'll see when we go to Admiralty House. They're these white rooms with symbols painted on the walls, easy to remember. *Athena's* is near the bowsprit, by the heads. Just a little space, but that's enough."

"But you must know *Athena* well enough that you would not need a Bounding chamber, surely?"

Hervey laughed. "Don't I wish! With Bounding, you have to keep all the details of a place in your head, so complicated places, like my Great-Aunt Fanny's sitting room with all her fol-de-rols, nobody but an

Extraordinary can Bound to. And no Bounder, Extraordinary or otherwise, can Bound to an outdoor place, with everything moving and changing all the time. I need the simplicity of a Bounding symbol. Best I can do is Skip from one end of *Athena* to the other."

"So," Elinor said slowly, "if I wanted to keep you out of a Bounding chamber you knew, I would have only to alter it in some way you cannot expect."

Hervey eyed her admiringly. "You're devious," he said. "That's exactly what they do in the Army to keep enemy Bounders out."

"But I do not see how an enemy Bounder could enter a concealed location to learn its signature in the first place."

"You have to have a Seer with a gift for drawing. And it's risky even for an Extraordinary Bounder if the drawing's not perfect. That's why we don't keep a book of symbols for Bounders to learn. Better to get the first-hand experience."

"So what is your range?"

"About five hundred feet."

Elinor looked out at the green fuzz in the distance. "But we will surely be in port before you are close enough to Bound there."

Hervey laughed. "That's what Skipping is. I take a sight and Bound as far as my range lets me, then I take another sight and do it again, over and over until I'm where I want to be."

"But will you not fall into the sea? That seems dangerous."

"Have to be fast. Like skipping a stone over water. You go fast enough, you don't sink." Hervey chuckled. "Don't worry, Miss Pembroke, I've been doing this a good, long time now. You should watch me go!"

"I think I may have to, if only to reassure myself you will not simply sink like a skipping stone that has reached its limit!"

Ten minutes later, Hervey stepped up to the bow and tucked his hat under his arm. Ramsay handed him a flat packet. "Don't stay for a response," he told the midshipman. "Admiral Durrant will want to... discuss those orders, and he might not care whom he discusses them with."

"Understood, sir," Hervey said, then tipped his hat at Elinor, tucked it under his arm, and vanished. She leaned well out from the bow and saw a tiny figure appear high in the sky several hundred feet ahead of them. She had only just fixed her eyes on him when he began to fall, and she cried out—then he vanished again, and was the merest speck of a gnat in the distance, and then he was gone.

Elinor turned to face Ramsay, who was smiling. "My stomach is always in knots when I see him do that," he said. "Though I've never seen him dampen so much as a toe."

"May I see the Bounding chamber while we wait for his return, Captain? I find I am curious about what Mr. Hervey does."

Ramsay smiled, that little twist of a smile, and bowed her down the companionway. "As you have already captivated half the crew," he said, "I believe you may go anywhere you like."

Some time later, Elinor was reading in the great cabin when a knock at the door preceded Ramsay's entrance. Elinor's fist always clenched when he knocked; it should not have been necessary. They should not have allowed low minds to ruin their friendship, and she had not resigned herself to the necessity.

"Mr. Hervey's back," he said, "and we will leave as soon as you are ready."

"Will you think less of me if I admit to some nervousness about such a mode of transportation?" she asked with a smile.

"Since we know less about the mechanisms of Bounding than of any other talent, you're right to be nervous. I can only assure you that I've been Mr. Hervey's passenger more than a dozen times, and nothing has ever happened to me."

"And if I admit to nervousness about meeting Admiral Durrant?"

Ramsay's good cheer dropped away. "I'd like to tell you that's unfounded. You should keep in mind that the First Lord wants you here, and Admiral Durrant is too honorable to disobey a direct order. And, honestly, if he's going to argue the point he will probably argue it with me, not you. So you could be nervous on my behalf if you like."

"I should prefer not to be nervous at all. I think I will change my gown and comb my hair, if you don't mind, Captain."

Ramsay inclined his head. "We'll be waiting for you when you're ready."

Elinor dressed with great care in her second-best gown, her best being her evening gown, which would be entirely inappropriate. She brushed out her hair, pinned it up, and hoped she did not look as haphazardly gowned as she felt. If only she had more than a hand mirror...She sighed, smoothed the fabric over her hips, and went to open the door of the great cabin.

Ramsay and Hervey were both wearing their dress uniforms, though Ramsay looked relaxed and Hervey stood like one of the masts, unmoving and stiff. "We're doing this in here because it's awkward and can look undignified," Ramsay said. "Hervey has to carry anything he takes with him when he Bounds, which means he will need to carry each of us for the second it takes him to slip between places. I apologize for the indignity—"

"But surely he cannot lift *you*?" Elinor exclaimed. Ramsay had at least four inches on Hervey and certainly outweighed him.

Ramsay's lips twitched. Hervey said, "He's not *that* heavy," and went red. "I'm stronger than I look."

"I beg your pardon, Mr. Hervey, that was rude of me. I was simply surprised. Will you go first, Captain?"

"I will, if only to reassure you." Ramsay stepped closer to Hervey and hooked his arm around the midshipman's waist; Hervey, with a sidelong glance at Elinor and even redder cheeks than before, put his arm around Ramsay's waist in return. Ramsay looked as if the whole thing was as ordinary as peeling an egg.

"On three," Hervey said, and the two of them counted together aloud. When they both said "three," Hervey heaved, Ramsay's feet left the floor, and the two of them were gone. Elinor found she was holding her breath, and let it out in a drawn-out hiss. *Oh, he'll have to hold me, too, and that will be so awkward for him. And for me. Oh, I cannot see how Captain Ramsay could do this so many times and not feel embarrassed.*

After a few minutes, Elinor heard footsteps, then Hervey opened the door, his face flushed as if he'd been running. He held out his arms. "I don't mean any disrespect, Miss Pembroke," he said, "and you know I think of you as a sister, so don't... don't..."

"I am determined this will not be awkward for either of us," Elinor said, and allowed him to put his arms around her and circled his shoulders with her arms. "Have you not Bounded with a woman before?"

"No."

He was right; it was like embracing her brother, if she'd had a brother. "Count to three." She counted off with him, and on three—

—she was transparent, empty, her body a gauze shell that might float apart if she forgot who she was. She couldn't even feel Hervey's arms around her; there was no air, not that she needed air, no light even though she could see her body—

—and she was herself again. Hervey released her and stepped away quickly. "That wasn't so bad," he said.

"It was very strange." The room they were in was little bigger than a closet and was lit by frosted glass lamps behind which burned tiny, happy flames. Its walls were white plaster, and on the wall opposite the French doors, also white, was painted a complex symbol of irregular angles, red and blue. "If that is what you think of as simple," she said, pointing at it, "I am amazed at your ability to remember even one of these."

"I know about forty," Hervey said. "That's average. Some Bounders know as many as two hundred." He pushed open the French doors and Ramsay looked up from where he'd been contemplating his boots.

"You'll wait for us in the front hall," he told Hervey, and offered his arm to Elinor. "Though it isn't as if you need my assistance walking," he said.

"I am not certain of that, Captain," Elinor said, taking his arm. The ground beneath her heaved like *Athena's* deck. "It feels as though Bermuda would like to throw me into the sea."

"You'll be fine," he said, and proceeded down the corridor, forcing Elinor to wobble along beside him and Hervey to trail behind. By the narrowness of the hall and its plain, somewhat cracked dingy white plaster, she guessed they were in the servants' annex. Chicken and carrots were cooking somewhere nearby, and she heard voices mumbling as if through water. The smell of soup made Elinor's stomach quiver with hunger.

A woman came out of a door ahead of them, and Elinor gaped in astonishment. She had never seen anyone with such dark skin, like melted chocolate without cream, nor black hair that crinkled tightly around her face. The woman didn't look up, though Elinor could tell by the way she looked so fixedly at the floorboards that she was aware of them. A slave? Elinor half-turned to watch the woman go, then had to quicken her pace to avoid slowing Ramsay down. Perhaps he was so accustomed to seeing slaves that this one was a commonplace. Elinor glanced once more over her shoulder; the woman was gone.

"When we meet Admiral Durrant, say nothing, no matter how angry he makes you," Ramsay said in a low voice. "I'll do the talking for both of us."

"I beg your pardon, Captain, but why?"

They emerged into a wider hallway, high-ceilinged with smoothly finished walls painted cream and trimmed with rust-red moldings. Candles behind glass chimneys clung to the walls every two feet, casting flickering shadows over the floor and ceiling and imperfectly lighting the way. The floorboards were narrower and paler than Elinor was accustomed to, a warm brown that appeared to be its natural color, and her wobbly feet ticked across them like clicking beetles. Aside from the gilt-framed portraits of men in naval uniform lining the walls, they were the only ones in the hall, and her footsteps and Ramsay and Hervey's heavier treads echoed off the paintings.

"Admiral Durrant is a good strategist and a courageous man, but he is also a misogynist who's not as intelligent as he thinks he is," Ramsay said, "and he doesn't think Scorcher talents are any more use than parlor tricks in this war. If he heeds you at all, he will be hoping to make you look irrational and ungoverned so he can justify sending you home. So don't rise to his insults."

"But surely an Admiral must be a gentleman also?"

"Gentleman, yes. Well-mannered, no. Don't be surprised at his rudeness. As I said, he will be looking for ways to be rid of you."

Elinor shook her head. "I thought the admiral had to follow the First Lord's instructions."

"There's following, and then there's following. He'll stick to the letter of his orders but he won't put one finger outside their literal meaning."

"But then how shall we ever be effective?"

Ramsay reached up with his free hand and squeezed hers where it lay on the blue wool of his jacket. "By being cleverer than he is."

They passed through a pillared hall with double doors large enough to wheel a cannon through, also unpeopled, where Hervey left their procession and went to sit on one of the benches carved of the same rosy brown wood as the floor. Potted miniature trees with dark-green, sharp-edged leaves scented the air with a dry, sunny smell. "Where is everyone?" Elinor asked. "I cannot believe this house is so large that all its officers can simply disappear into it."

"All gone home, or to supper," Ramsay said. "Admiral Durrant didn't want anyone to see us arrive. And if you were wondering, it's because he doesn't want to have to explain why you're here, not because he cares about your reputation. He doesn't like that the Admiralty can tell him what to do, here in his own fief."

"You seem to know a great deal about him."

"This isn't my first time in the Caribbean."

They proceeded down more windowless, empty, portrait-hung white corridors until Ramsay stopped in front of a pair of doors with oval, iron knobs and looked at Elinor with an unreadable expression. Then he pushed the door open and entered. Elinor followed him, her pulse pounding in her ears like the drum beating to quarters.

The sun had dipped below the horizon during the time it had taken Elinor to dress and for Hervey to bring them both here. Picture windows lining one wall revealed a yew shrubbery brushing against the glass, beyond which lay a strip of lawn, grey in the shadows, and for a moment she imagined herself looking out over her mother's garden back home, and shivered. Farther in the distance was a dense grove of trees, indistinct in the dim light, but their outlines told her they were utterly alien, despite the effort to make the garden a piece of England.

The house had to be part of that effort, and she was surprised to see how closely this room resembled that of the First Lord in the Admiralty building in London. There was the same table, this one's surface shining mirror-like, reflecting the chandelier poised high above it; there was the fireplace, unlit, though in this climate that was more reasonable than it had been in the First Lord's frigid chamber; there map cylinders hung over the fireplace, cords dangling that would allow them to be pulled open for display without removing them from the wall. The brick-red carpet with its intricate black and gold pattern might have come from the same stall in some eastern bazaar.

Even the tableau was the same: three men gathered at the far end of the table, heads bent over a sheet of paper covering half the mirrored surface. Two of the men looked up as they entered; the third continued to trace a line along the paper with a slender baton about a foot long. "This puts them *here* and *here*," he said.

Ramsay removed his hat and tucked it under his arm, rested his other hand on the hilt of his sword, and came to a sort of relaxed attention that was outwardly correct but hinted that he thought himself the equal of any man in the room, rank notwithstanding. Elinor clasped her hands in front of her and fixed her gaze on the third man, whose continued inattention to their entrance was rapidly becoming an insult. The man on his left fidgeted, casting quick glances at him as if hoping to catch his eye, then flicking his gaze at Ramsay with what looked like an apology.

The man on his right, by contrast, bowed to Elinor, then gave her his full attention; he was handsome for a man probably her father's age, his silvering brown hair tied back with a black ribbon, with warm brown eyes and a full-lipped mouth that curved into an unpleasant smile. His gaze dropped from her face to her breasts. She suddenly wanted to cover herself with her hands, to turn away, anything to keep him from staring at her body as if he wished he could use his hands rather than his eyes to examine her contours. Lord Huxley's undesired attention had been far, far more welcome than this.

Finally, the man in the center raised his head. "Good evening, Captain Ramsay," he said. His voice was as dry as his skin and as brittle; this was a man whom the sea and sun had weathered into tree bark. "You bring interesting orders."

"Admiral Durrant, sir," Ramsay replied, but said nothing more.

"And this is the Scorcher," Durrant continued, not looking at Elinor. "A slender reed to hang a strategy on."

"You have my report on the success of that strategy."

"Yes." Durrant sat, followed by the other two, the man on the left hesitating again as if expecting Durrant to offer his visitors chairs as well. "Only three successes."

"The point of sending *Athena* here is to increase that number."

"The *Athena* is still only one ship. How do you expect to prevent the pirates who roam freely through these waters from striking in several places at once?"

"That's up to you, sir. I expect your understanding of the tactical situation to guide our efforts."

"Hmph." Durrant rested his chin in his hand, creasing his onion-paper skin. "I don't like it."

"Sir."

"Admiral, they're here now, and we need to put them to use," said the fidgety man. His vowels were strangely accented and he continued to divide his attention between Durrant and Ramsay. "The Colonial fleet has had a great deal of success with Scorchers—"

"And even more success with a full complement of ships, Wood. We don't need talents, we need *ships*. We don't need a girl barely out of the schoolroom who may faint at the first sign of violence."

Elinor opened her mouth and then closed it abruptly as Ramsay stepped firmly on her foot. "Miss Pembroke has already seen combat," he said, "and she's very level-headed."

Durrant dismissed this with a wave. "We'll see if that's true, I suppose." He beckoned to Ramsay to come forward, and once his foot was removed, Elinor followed him. Only the leering man paid any attention to her, and Elinor wanted to scrub her skin with sandpaper to rid herself of the oily feeling his gaze left on her body.

She tried to keep Ramsay between them, but he stepped up to the table to look at what turned out to be a map of the Caribbean, and the leering man came up close enough behind her that she could feel his breath on her ear, hot and smelling of fish. She tried to focus on the map, though the contours of the islands were obscured by tiny printed words radiating out from the coastlines and curved lines filled the seas following those same contours. She identified Bermuda, a dot well north and east of the rest of the islands, just as the admiral said, "You probably don't know much about the situation here."

Ramsay said, "Not much. Only that over the last thirty years a group of pirates styling themselves the Brethren of the Coast, in homage to Henry Morgan probably, have organized the individual ships into a single unit which they use to terrorize cities into paying protection money. And that Spain, fighting Napoleon on the Continent and facing rebellion in their Latin American colonies, capitulated to their demands three years ago, which means that any Spanish ports are potential pirate havens. It's probably important that they prosecute their war against us by treating their captured merchant crews with gentility, so those merchants will put pressure on their governments to give in and pay what the pirates demand. Of course they haven't realized that, as the saying goes, once you start paying Danegeld you never get rid of the Dane, but it means we are fighting a war of public opinion as well as a literal war. But other than that, sir, I don't know much."

Elinor bit her lip. Durrant looked as though he wasn't sure if Ramsay was making fun of him. He cleared his throat and said, "We've received intelligence that puts a number of pirate ships under the command of Hugh Bexley, one of Evans' chiefs, sailing from Havana tomorrow or the next day to make a run up the American coast, passing between Florida and the Grand Bank of the Bahamas."

He traced a snaking line with his baton, which flexed as it touched the map. "We don't have enough ships near Cuba"—he glared at Ramsay, then at Elinor—"so part of our fleet is leaving Bermuda and assembling *here*"—tap, tap at a spot north of the long chain of islands that paralleled the ragged coast of Florida—"to intercept them. You'll be cruising north of Saint-Domingue to catch any ships trying to take advantage of our ships drawing northward."

"Admiral, with all due respect, that seems like a waste of a valuable resource," said Wood. "You've never seen an Extraordinary Scorcher in battle before. I have. Believe me, you want the girl as close to the action as you can manage."

Elinor ground her teeth to keep from objecting to "girl." Ramsay said, "I believe the First Lord wanted *Athena* to take a more active role in this war."

"The First Lord isn't the man on the spot, is he?" Durrant thwacked the map with his baton. "You'll sail where I tell you, and my judgment is that you'll best serve us off Saint-Domingue, guarding our flank. Unless you think your five minutes' assessment of the situation is superior to my seven years of successfully fighting off these vermin?"

"No, sir," Ramsay said. "We're happy to go where we are needed.

Sir, might I ask about the enemy's tactics? So we will be prepared when we encounter them."

Durrant had been leaning forward, palms flat on the map, and now he sat back, smiling as if he'd beaten Ramsay at some game neither of them admitted to playing. "Sullyard, the historical map," he said, and the man standing far too close to Elinor brushed against her as he went to the fireplace and unrolled another map of the Caribbean, this one showing only the islands within the Caribbean Sea. Black X's made patterns between the islands as if marking the ocean currents.

"This is a record of all the victories we've won," Durrant said. "You can see the patterns show they follow our trade routes and look to pick off weak or unguarded targets. We used to focus on convoy duty, but since Spain's turned up its fluffy white tail, we've tried to take the battle to the pirates. They have smaller, lighter boats and can slip through channels our heavier vessels can't navigate. We've commissioned a number of Bermuda sloops, and I had *hoped* for a few more frigates, but God forbid I tell the Admiralty what to do."

He walked around the table and smacked the hanging map with his baton. "So watch the shores, Ramsay, watch the currents, and see if you can't manage to bring some of these bas—" He seemed to notice Elinor for the first time and cleared his throat again with a great hocking noise. "Take prizes if you want, but don't let any of them escape."

"Yes, sir. What about these rumors of the pirates' intelligence gathering network?"

"What rumors? Are you listening to rumors?"

"No, Admiral, but word gets around. Is it true they've Seers tracking our ships' movements?"

"*That is a damned lie*," Durrant shouted. "If I could find the blackguard who's been spreading that lie, I'd have him strung up at the point in Port Royal by his tes—that is," he corrected himself, the angry flush fading from his cheeks, "I'd make an example of him. It's sedition, that's what it is, trying to demoralize good men. Don't listen to rumors, Ramsay, it's a weak and cowardly thing to do."

"Yes, sir. If you'll give me my official orders?"

"Sullyard?" The man went to a row of drawers behind Durrant and removed a flat packet tied with red ribbon and handed it to the admiral, who tossed it at Ramsay. Ramsay caught it neatly out of the air and bowed to both the admirals in turn.

Elinor quickly bobbed her curtsey and exited the room ahead of Ramsay, who waited only long enough to hold the door for her before striding off down the corridor so quickly she nearly had to skip to keep up with him.

"Captain—"

"Wait until we return, Miss Pembroke. Too many listening ears." The halls were completely empty, so Elinor could not imagine who might be listening to them, but she kept her mouth shut as Ramsay strode through the halls and into the entrance.

Hervey shot to his feet and said, "Captain—"

"Take Miss Pembroke back, then return for me. I'll meet you at the Bounding chamber," Ramsay said, and walked away without waiting for Hervey's assent. Elinor was certain the dumbfounded look on Hervey's face matched her own. Hervey shrugged and put his arms around her. "On three, Miss Pembroke," he said, and again there was the sensation of being completely incorporeal, and then they were in the cramped, whitewashed Bounding chamber, lit by a single lamp, with a few slashes of dark green or black paint on the forward bulkhead. Elinor had barely regained her balance before Hervey was gone again. She took a moment to breathe deeply, then realized she ought to exit the chamber so Hervey could return to it.

At this hour, just after nine o'clock in the evening, the lower deck was crowded with hammocks and men wheezing and snoring. The hammocks were strung so closely together that one man's feet brushed against another man's head, and it was so hot Elinor could not understand how they were able to sleep at all. The motion of the ship beneath her feet was the gentle bobbing of *Athena* at rest, soothing to her spirits after the meeting with the admiral. She folded her arms across her chest and waited. If Ramsay thought she would be willing to wait patiently in the great cabin for an explanation, he was sorely mistaken.

Only a few minutes passed before the flimsy wooden door banged open and Ramsay stepped out, followed closely by Hervey. Ramsay took her arm and steered her between the hammocks and their occupants reeking of stale sweat and spirits. He seemed unsurprised she had waited for him.

"Thank you for keeping quiet," he said. "I know it was difficult."

"I believe my foot will never be the same, Captain," she retorted.

Ramsay laughed. "It was all in a good cause, Miss Pembroke." He pushed open the door to the great cabin and turned to Hervey. "Get the lieutenants up here, and Mr. Brown. Whoever's on deck, you're taking over for the next hour."

"*Me*, sir? Yes, sir. But—what should I tell them?"

Ramsay smiled at Elinor, a wicked, delighted grin. "Tell them we're going to war."

CHAPTER 10

IN WHICH THEY ARE NOT ALLOWED TO GO TO WAR, BUT DO SO ANYWAY

"I beg your pardon, Captain," Elinor said, "but it sounded very much as if Admiral Durrant intended us *not* to go to war."

"What did I tell you, Miss Pembroke, about us being cleverer than he?" Ramsay held the great cabin door open for her, then brushed past her to open a long cabinet and take out two rolls of paper. "Help me lay this out, would you?" He unrolled the first cylinder and spread it on the table, where its edges extended past the tabletop. It threatened to roll back up again, and Elinor found a cruet and the silver salt cellar to pinion the edges.

Then she walked around the table until she could see it right way up. It was, as she expected, a map of the Caribbean, but far finer than the admiral's and with fewer labels along the coasts of the islands. It also showed most of the North and South American coastlines, also labeled, with country borders sketched in more palely than the black outlines of the islands.

"If you please, would you give us a little more light?" Ramsay said, and Elinor fetched candlesticks and set the candles burning so she could see that the map was colored in green and blue and yellow, with a few specks of purple near the edges and solid green over most of the North American continent. Yellow predominated along the shores of the mainland, with two large blotches of green, and one of the islands was particolored blue and yellow. "Do you understand what you're looking at?" Ramsay said.

Elinor traced the outline of the yellow peninsula protruding from the northern continent. "Admiral Durrant said this was Florida, which is Spanish territory, so I gather whatever is colored yellow belongs to Spain. And the rest of North America is our American colonies, so I presume green is British possessions and blue must be French."

"Very good—ah, gentlemen, please join us. Miss Pembroke, if you'll be seated?"

The lieutenants took seats around the table and Sampson Brown stood behind Ramsay. None of them looked surprised to be hauled away from duty or their beds. "Not good news, Miles?" Beaumont said.

"Oh no, Arthur, the best news," Ramsay replied with a smile, and quickly recounted the conversation of the board room.

When he was finished, Livingston said, "Begging your pardon, Captain, but I don't see how our being stuck in the ass-end of nowhere constitutes good news."

"Mr. Livingston, watch your language. Admiral Durrant thinks that's what he's doing, but he hasn't given any thought to how we're getting there," Ramsay said. "More important, though, is that he confirmed that the pirates have learned to use Seers to locate our ships and steer clear of them."

"I thought he denied it," Elinor said.

"With the vehemence of someone who would like an unpleasant fact to be untrue. For an Extraordinary Seer to compel Visions of particular places or objects, he—or she, my apologies—must have something on which to focus. The implication is that someone within the Admiralty is passing information to the pirates, and the admiral takes that accusation of treason personally. So he declares loudly that it is impossible.

"The First Lord, on the other hand, informed me that the War Office's Seers have discovered that the leader of the Brethren of the Coast is an Extraordinary Seer who has discovered how to direct his Vision without a focus. The Admiralty has been scrambling to learn the secret and deploy it against Napoleon, or at any rate to defend against Evans' use of it, but we are far from a solution."

Ramsay went to the writing desk and dug through the drawer, came up with a pencil, and returned to the table. He pulled out his belt knife and began sharpening the tip, flicks of wood and lead flying in the candlelight. "Admiral Durrant means well, but he's set in his ways—you know that, Miss Pembroke—and it takes a preponderance of evidence to change his mind. We're going to provide that evidence by eliminating that pirate squadron and proving that *Athena* and her resident Scorcher are of far more use than a handful of frigates."

The quiet Lieutenant Fitzgerald leaned forward. "Where did you say our fleet would be?"

"Here." Ramsay drew an X on the map.

"And we're going to assume the pirates know that."

"Yes."

"Then..." Fitzgerald put his finger on a spot on the largest yellow island and drew an invisible line along its coast and past Florida. "This is what the admiral thinks the pirates' route will be."

"It would make sense. They've the advantage of the prevailing winds," said Beaumont.

"Correct," said Ramsay. "So the question, gentlemen, is—what route would allow the pirates to most effectively attack our waiting fleet, and take it unawares?"

The three lieutenants bowed over the map. Brown crossed his arms and watched over Ramsay's shoulder. "If the fleet's attention is southward, then this route through the Bahamas would take them up and around so they could attack from the north," said Livingston, his animosity gone for the moment.

"And our fleet would be beating against the wind the whole time," said Beaumont. "The pirates would have the advantage of surprise."

"And if they took the channel between Providence and Eleuthera, and then came around east of Abaco and took advantage of that row of keys...good Lord, they'd be thumbing their noses at England the whole way!" Fitzgerald looked stunned. Ramsay looked smug.

"Now, gentlemen, and Miss Pembroke, we should remember our orders," he said. "We've been ordered to the coast of Saint-Domingue, and I intend to follow that order. So we will take *this* route, here between the Bahaman islands, and if we happen to run into any pirates along the way, we will do our duty as instructed by Admiral Durrant himself. Is everyone clear?"

Fitzgerald's stunned look gave way to amazement. Beaumont and Livingston looked almost as pleased as Ramsay. Brown snorted and pushed past the captain, putting his stubby finger on the yellow island. "Don't suppose you know when they were leaving?" he said.

"Tomorrow or day after."

Brown snorted again. "Fair enough. Lay out that other map and let's see if I can plot us an interception. But I can tell you right now it'll probably be off Nassau, which is close to poetic justice."

Ramsay nodded, then said to Elinor's puzzled expression, "Providence Island was a pirate haven about a hundred years ago. We drove them out by making it... unprofitable for them to stay there."

Elinor nodded. "I see. But, Captain, what I do not see is how *Athena* can defeat several ships, even if they are smaller than she is."

"Well, Miss Pembroke," Ramsay said, the smile giving way to the wry quirk of his lips, "that would be where you come in."

⚜

IT WAS EASY TO BELIEVE, HERE IN THE OPEN OCEAN BETWEEN Bermuda and the rest of the world, that *Athena* was the only ship that ever sailed the seas. How any two ships might cross paths across that grey-green expanse was a mystery to Elinor, but Brown and Ramsay, plotting their location twice a day, seemed completely unconcerned that they might sail all the way from Bermuda to Saint-Domingue without encountering any other ships, let alone the pirates they were searching for. But she was only the Scorcher, not the captain, so she paced the deck or pretended to read in the great cabin and tried not to think about the upcoming confrontation.

"We can't afford to take more than two prizes," Ramsay had told her the day after their impromptu council of war. They had been alone in the great cabin, heads bowed together over a sheet of paper, and Elinor felt as if Livingston's crass remark was no longer an impediment to their friendship. Still, she made no comment on the propriety of their situation, not wanting to draw attention to it and risk Ramsay deciding he might be damaging her reputation. "We simply don't have the manpower to sail more than three ships, even over such a short distance as from the Bahamas back to Bermuda."

"Is there nowhere closer you might bring prizes?"

"Port Royal in Jamaica is the only other major harbor we have out here, and it's a good deal farther. Besides"—Ramsay smiled, a wicked light in his eye—"I want Admiral Durrant to get a good look at our success."

Elinor returned his smile. "For my part, I share that sentiment, Captain."

"At any rate," Ramsay continued, "we can't make a plan of attack until we see how many ships we're facing, but we can strategize in general."

He sketched the outline of a ship with one mast and three sails, a large, roughly trapezoidal one and two smaller triangular ones. "This is a Bermuda sloop. We've commissioned several of these because they've a shallow enough draft to chase the pirates into coastal waters a ship like *Athena* can't navigate. Unfortunately, the pirates have several of them as well. They're fast, well-built, and maneuverable, and we waste a great deal of shot trying to sink them.

"Now, the pirates are making this run up the coast to strike at Colonial targets, which means they'll have larger ships for the transport of cargo and the sloops for protection—as small as they are, they can still do plenty of damage. So your primary role will be to burn through those masts and leave the sloops dead in the water. We'll pick them off after we've captured the primary vessels."

"I am not certain how quickly I can accomplish that."

"You're the one who knows your abilities, but if you start a fire on the sails as well, they'll be preoccupied with fighting several fires at once. Keep in mind, though, that those sails are likely to be fire-resistant."

"Do we carry any of the substance they spread on the sails to make them so?"

"Yes, and I should have thought of that. Ask Mr. Ayres for that and some canvas."

Elinor sighed. "Mr. Ayres does not like me much."

"He'll have to learn to behave himself. For what it's worth, I think he's more afraid of you than disapproving."

"That is not much comfort, Captain."

Ramsay leaned back in his seat and ran his hands through his hair, pushing it back from his forehead. "I served under a few captains who ran their ships on fear rather than respect, and I swore I'd never do that. I think I've succeeded. But there are still men, some of the newer men, on this ship who fear me."

"You have the power of life and death over them, as their captain. That seems fairly frightening to me."

He raised his eyebrows. "Surely you're not frightened of me, Miss Pembroke."

Elinor thought of her father, his cold-iron eyes, his rough grip bruising her knee. "Of course not," she said, as lightly as she could manage. "I simply understand what it is to be afraid. Though I think those men who fear you must never have served under a real tyrant."

"What is it you fear?" Ramsay's expression was curious, as if he'd unearthed an ancient object he could not identify.

"Nothing, now that I have the power to defend myself," Elinor lied. "And you?"

Ramsay's eyes went distant. "Things I have no power to prevent," he said. "Losing this command. Being stuck in England on half-pay waiting for another ship. I dislike being subject to the whim of the Admiralty, so I do whatever I can to prove I'm worth keeping. Much as you said."

"So your desire for taking prizes, that is not—"

"Not what?"

Elinor blushed. "I was about to say 'mercenary,' but I know you are not that."

"Do you? I admit I am as fond of money as the next man, but no. And I don't crave fame; it's only the outward appearance of what I do want, which is security."

"The First Lord said you held the record for most prizes taken."

"That was an exaggeration. It's not as if anyone keeps score."

"From what little I've seen of the Royal Navy, I think that is untrue."

Ramsay laughed. "Miss Pembroke, you're positively dogged in your pursuit of truth. Do you have no scruples about leaving a man his privacy?"

"You choose to answer my questions, so I cannot imagine you are terribly worried about your privacy either."

"Very well, I insist you answer some questions as well. One question."

"You fill me with dread, Captain."

"Why did you come to the Admiralty that day?"

It was not a question she was expecting, and a clever rejoinder caught in her throat and choked her. "I—"

"It can't be that complicated a question."

She looked down at her hands, then back at Ramsay, whose smile belied the serious look in his eyes. "My—I was faced with the necessity of choosing between two lives, neither of which appealed to me. And I had no outlet for my talent in my own world."

"They must have been far more than unappealing, for you to take such a desperate step. Didn't it worry you that you might never be able to go back?"

"What had I to go back to?" She wished she could take the words back even as they escaped her tongue. This was a far, far more intimate conversation than she had ever dreamed of having with anyone. "Forced marriage, or a lifetime of being someone's poor relation? If that is what my good reputation earns me, I cannot think much of it."

"You can't be forced to marry against your will. That's the law."

She laughed a short, bitter laugh. "It is remarkable in how many ways one can be forced to a decision without having a knife to one's throat."

Ramsay nodded. "And so you chose the Navy."

"Even so."

"Well, I'm glad you did." Surprised, Elinor looked up to see him smiling at her from where he leaned back in his chair. "Quite aside from the thrill of seeing an enemy ship go up in flames, I appreciate your company."

"Enough that you risk tainting my reputation by being alone with me?"

He laughed. "I wondered if you'd notice that. I realized I missed your conversation, and, as you pointed out, we *are* two honorable people, and I thought—to the devil with Livingston and his low mind. And I *did* leave the door open a bit."

Elinor laughed with him, feeling an unsuspected weight lift from her heart. "Such power an open door can have. I am humbled before it."

"If Livingston becomes a problem again," Ramsay said in a lower voice, "you could always burn most of the way through his hammock ropes and listen for the thump."

"Oh, Captain, how dare you fill my mind with such a nasty trick! I must try it immediately." She had smiled at the image of Livingston sprawled awkwardly on the deck, and Ramsay had laughed at her calculating expression.

Now she left the great cabin and came up to the quarterdeck to enjoy the fresh, salty air. Ramsay had been right, all those weeks ago: there was not a single unattractive vista in the Caribbean. Elinor stood at the taffrail, her parasol shielding her face—Ramsay was correct; the bonnet was not enough protection from the tropical rays—and watched another perfectly green coast slip past, the turquoise waters surrounding it turning to robin's-egg blue where they met the cloudless sky.

They were far enough from the island that its trees and bushes and grasses were a single emerald blur, but they looked so...lush was the best word to describe it, a word that sounded almost vulgar, but there was nothing proper or restrained about the verdant growth. It made her long to kilt up her gown and go wading along the line where the surf struck the golden shore.

She had finally decided not to care what people thought and donned a short-sleeved morning gown that seemed to draw the breezes even as it allowed her arms to be warmed by the sun. Bolton had warned her to keep to the shade as much as possible, that the sun's rays were powerful in these latitudes and sunburn was painful, but so far Elinor's arms remained pale and unmarked.

"Don't it make you wish someone would write about it so everyone back home could know what it's like?" Hervey said, coming to stand beside her. "Makes all those Gothic horrors seem like a dream."

"Or possibly a nightmare. Besides, I believe the point of reading something like *The Castle of Otranto* is to make one grateful one's own life is not nearly so dramatic. A novel set in the Bahamas would necessarily have the opposite effect, and I wonder at how popular it might be."

"*I'd* read it. O' course, we're living it now."

"True. I wish we could walk along that shore. The sand looks so fine and white."

"It'd only get in your shoes and your hair."

"Mr. Hervey, I thought you were a romantic."

"Not about sand."

"Mr. Hervey, if it's not too much trouble, would you mind returning to your duties?" Livingston drawled. Hervey touched his hat to the lieutenant and then walked away without another word. "I think you should not distract the men, Miss Pembroke, if indeed you can help yourself."

"You mean, as you are distracted right now, Mr. Livingston? Unless your duties include rebuking me for innocently standing here and observing the beauties of nature." She wasn't certain what insult his remark had been meant to convey, but it nettled her, and she remembered Ramsay's comment about hammocks and fire and began to think seriously about it.

"You ought not to be on the quarterdeck when we are not in combat, Miss Pembroke."

"I believe that's the captain's decision, not yours."

"Yes, and the captain's judgment couldn't possibly be compromised where you are concerned."

Elinor snapped her parasol shut and rounded on him. "Mr. Livingston, are you perhaps under the impression that I am a defenseless target of your spite? We both serve the Royal Navy in our separate ways, though I begin to wonder exactly what your purpose on this ship is, when you do not have me to vent your impatience on. I can hardly help having a talent, and I do not understand your jealousy of it."

Livingston drew in an outraged breath. "I, jealous? You mistake me."

"Then I apologize for my mistake. But I am not mistaken that you and I cannot have anything more to say to one another. Good day, Mr. Livingston."

Livingston stepped closer and snarled, in a low breath, "Say what you like, I know what you truly are, *bitch*."

Elinor brought her hand up and around and slapped him so hard it made her palm burn. Livingston screamed. She was about to shout something awful at him when she looked at her hand and joined her scream to his, because her hand was on fire, burning white-gold across the lines of her palm and over the backs of her fingers like a flickering glove. A faint charred handprint marked Livingston's left cheek, and his hands groped at it as he wept.

Elinor felt no pain, nothing except the surge of pleasure she always felt when wielding fire, a pleasure mixed with terror that she could not turn the fire off. She shook her hand as if trying to rid herself of something unpleasantly sticky, threw her parasol away and slapped at the fire with her free hand, but the fire only transferred itself so that both her hands were burning. Another scream formed in the back of her throat.

"Relax," Ramsay said from behind her, "and do whatever it is you do when you extinguish fire." He had his hands on her shoulders, steadying her, and she closed her eyes and tried to stop shaking. *It's like any other fire, you just tell it to go out*, she told herself, and when she opened her eyes the fire was gone, and Livingston was kneeling on the deck clutching his face.

"Forgive me," she began.

Livingston looked up at her and shouted, "You dare—"

"Be silent, Mr. Livingston," Ramsay said, stepping away from Elinor and cutting across Livingston's words with that voice that could carry from one end of *Athena* to the other. "I've no doubt whatever Miss Pembroke did to you, however unexpected, was thoroughly deserved. Mr. Hays can Heal that mark. See him immediately."

Livingston leaped to his feet and took two steps toward the

captain, who stood his ground in the face of Livingston's rage. "You and—"

"Mr. Livingston, I make allowances for how overwhelmed you must be right now," Ramsay said, more quietly but with no less force. "Say nothing I will be forced to take notice of. Now, get below."

Livingston clenched his fist. Ramsay shifted his weight as if preparing to take a blow. They stood like that, eye to eye, for several seconds until Livingston swore and turned away, storming down the ladder in a way that boded ill for anyone coming up it. Ramsay watched him go, not relaxing his stance until Livingston's head had completely disappeared down the companionway. Then he turned to face Elinor. "Can you explain what just happened?"

To her chagrin, Elinor found she was blinking away tears. She cleared her throat and said, "We were arguing—Mr. Livingston insulted me terribly—I should not have struck him, but then I was..." She held up her hand, which looked like a normal hand that had never considered setting itself on fire.

"You should have—"

"*Ships, Captain!*"

Ramsay's head whipped around to look up at the boy clinging to the masthead, and then he was in the air, his hand clapped to his hat, hovering next to the lookout. He brought his spyglass to his eye. "Five...six ships!" he shouted down. "South southeast." He Flew back to alight on the deck. "Raise the Spanish colors. Let's see if they're the ones we've been looking for," he shouted. "Topmen aloft, and wait for orders! Mr. Wynn, keep us on a steady course. We have the wind, and if they turn and run we still have the advantage. We're a lone Spanish ship, unsupported and easy prey. No one out here to see the pirates breaking their agreement."

"Captain, six is too many. We have to run," said Beaumont.

"I'm not going to make that decision until we can get a clearer look at them. If four of those ships are Bermuda sloops, we've nothing to worry about. *Athena* outguns any sloop they have, and we can outrun any larger ship that might give us problems. Stop worrying, Mr. Beaumont." Ramsay was smiling, but Elinor could see his eyes, and they did not look so assured as his words suggested.

"Captain," she said in a low voice only he and Beaumont could hear, "if this is too much for us to handle, surely no one would fault us for refusing to engage with them."

"Two things I have faith in, Miss Pembroke," Ramsay said, his eyes still fixed on the horizon. "One is this ship and her crew. The other is you. Don't give me reason to doubt that."

Elinor's cheeks heated up until her head felt as though it might burst into flame, an image that worried her now that it seemed possible it could happen. "Captain, that is a heavy burden to bear. I'm still barely tested—"

"Miss Pembroke, go and stand at the bow and wait for my command," Ramsay said. "Remember what we discussed. The sloops first. Then come back to the quarterdeck and wait for new orders."

"I—" Elinor looked at Beaumont, whose face was unreadable, then back at Ramsay. "Yes, sir," she said, and moved forward across the deck in a daze, forcing sailors to step out of her way until she reached the bow. She stood as close to the bowsprit as she could, looking out at the distant white daubs of sail on the horizon. He had faith in her. She hardly thought she deserved it, but he had made it impossible for her to refuse him.

She gripped the rail hard and watched the sails, unblinking, until her eyes were dry and painful. The usual noises of sails snapping, planks and rope creaking, men calling out to one another all seemed so much louder than usual. She reminded herself the pirates were far too distant to hear any such thing.

She glanced at Ramsay, who once again had his glass raised to his eye, and sniffed. Something was burning nearby. She looked down and shrieked because her hands were once again aflame and were burning black handprints into the rail. Bolton would be annoyed she'd damaged his ship. She snatched her hands away and willed the fire to go out. Why, *why* was this happening, and why now, when she could not afford to explore the mystery?

Minutes passed, half an hour, an hour. The sails had resolved into ships: still tiny, but even Elinor could see them distinctly. She shifted her weight. She desperately needed the head. She fidgeted a moment longer, then dashed for the companionway, hoping to avoid Ramsay's eye. Relieved, she quickly returned to her post. The ships weren't any closer. How far could she reach? Not that far, she decided after some inner contemplation. And Ramsay had said to wait for his command.

She turned and leaned against the comforting bulk of the rail and watched the men at the wheel. Beaumont stood with his head thrown back in a stance that indicated he was Speaking with someone. Ramsay paced along the quarterdeck, occasionally consulting with Brown, speaking to the helmsman, or looking through the glass. Waiting was causing her stomach to curdle, though it had nothing to curdle because noon had come and gone with no meal. She was too anxious to eat.

More time passed. The ships were close enough now that she was certain she could burn them if necessary. She glanced back at Ramsay, but he wasn't paying any attention to her. *Soon, soon, let it be soon.* What was he waiting for? The pirates flew no colors, had not attacked them —suppose this was merely a merchant convoy? Attacking them prematurely could be disastrous; waiting for them to attack first could be fatal. She gripped the rail again and waited to see if her hands would again catch fire, but nothing happened.

There were four of the Bermuda sloops spaced around two larger ships, both smaller than *Athena*, but still sizable. If they had gun ports, they were closed, because their sides were uninterrupted white planking trimmed red. Were those pirate colors? Didn't pirates fly black or red flags with horrific images on them? The smell of smoke, again, and Elinor swore, then clapped a burning hand to her mouth. The fire didn't hurt her face, either. This was a terrible time for her talent to manifest a new and disturbing aspect.

All at once there were flashes of light on the other ships' decks, then the crumpled thump of cannon fire. Cannonballs whistled through the air to land short of *Athena*'s stern, and the foremast caught fire. Black flags bearing white skulls and hourglasses shot up to fly above the two larger ships as the gun ports flew open, revealing the gaping mouths of rows of cannons.

"Raise colors!" Ramsay shouted, then, *"Miss Pembroke! Now!"*

Elinor took in the scene before her, fixed her eyes on her targets, and swept the sea with fire.

CHAPTER 11

IN WHICH ELINOR
DEMONSTRATES HER TALENT TO
AN UNWILLING AUDIENCE

A ll four of the sloops' masts caught fire at once, turning them into gold-red pillars of flame pointing at the cloudless sky. For nearly a minute, they burned untouched. Then Elinor felt the tugs at her attention that told her the crews were attempting to put out her fire. She extinguished *Athena*'s foremast and tried to increase her own fire's power, but quickly discovered she could not control all four fires and also extinguish the ones the enemy Scorcher, or Scorchers, tried to light. She was barely able to defend her fires against the buckets of water and the sprays of a strange liquid that snuffed out whatever it touched.

So she changed tactics. She left three of the fires to burn as they would, kept part of her attention on defending *Athena*, and turned the rest of her focus to the fourth ship, the one closest to *Athena*. The part of her that was fire observed that that ship had eight guns on its deck, which looked absurdly large for the slim, elegant craft. It was a pity they would have to sink her. She ran the fire down the mast like fingers stroking fur, and found a place above the heads of the desperate crew.

She had, as a child, spent time in the kitchen watching Mrs. Branton, the cook, prepare all sorts of foods, and had been fascinated to see her slice cheese with nothing more than a thin wire. "It's the tension, love," Mrs. Branton had told her. "Pull it tight enough and it'll slice through near anything."

She peeled away a long, long string of fire and looped it around the mast, crossing its ends and, picturing the cheese-wire, pulling tight. She could feel the fire understand her intent and pour into the groove she was burning into the mast, devouring the wood as if racing to see which flame could reach the center first.

The mast fell before that happened. Eaten away on all sides like an apple, supported only by its fragile core, the mast cracked and fell like an ancient pine, rocking the ship and tossing more than a few men over the side. Elinor had no time to feel pity for them; her attention returned to the other three ships, where she discovered one crew had managed to put out her fire completely. *That is unacceptable*, she thought, and set the mast afire again, this time extending the flames across the sails to keep them occupied.

She had practiced for hours, learning how to burn away the thin resin that soaked into the canvas and left it pliant but almost impossible to ignite. Now she *leaned* on the fire and rejoiced in the green-blue flame the resin made, a color resembling that of the shallows surrounding the nearby islands. Two fireballs in quick succession flew at *Athena*'s deck from both the larger ships, and Elinor made them vanish like mist. She laughed at the marvelous quickening of power that ran through her, pulsing in time with her heartbeat.

Someone grabbed her from behind. Another man tackled her legs. She was flat on the deck and furious before she registered that they were telling her to get down, stay down, and a cannonball struck the rail five feet from where she'd been standing, showering the three of them with a hail of prickling splinters. Suddenly the world was echoing with shouts and screams and the whistling of cannonballs, a deafening contrast to the silence that had surrounded her in her concentration.

She shouted, "I cannot leave yet!"

They ignored her and half-dragged, half-carried her to the quarter-deck, where they handed her over to Ramsay. He pushed her toward the stern and shouted, "Stay down! I told you to return when I called!"

"The sloops are not yet destroyed!"

"So do it from back here. And stay down!"

Elinor stood long enough to survey the battle. The ship whose mast she had cut down lay rocking on the waves, its crew clambering over fallen rigging and sails in a vain attempt to rejoin the battle. The enemy Scorchers, wherever they were, were still trying to burn *Athena's* masts and sails, but Elinor's skill at switching her concentration from putting out fires to starting them was growing, and *Athena* was barely singed.

One sloop was still burning green-blue. One of the others had nearly succeeded in putting out the fire; she flicked a command at it and it blazed hotter than before. Fire consumed the deck of the third, and men were screaming and leaping from it into the sea, where they disappeared from her sight. She felt neither guilt nor sorrow over that; she had no time for such indulgences.

Of the larger ships, one had clearly received the brunt of *Athena's* long guns; its sails were shredded and its deck splintered, but it was still valiantly trying to bring its guns to bear. As she watched, two of those guns flew off the deck and plummeted into the sea, one dragging a screaming pirate with it. Apparently they were close enough for Ramsay to use his talent against the enemy. The other ship was in far better condition and was working its way around to put *Athena* between itself and its consort.

Athena's deck was a tangle of fallen rigging and shattered wood, and a few men lay fallen and bloody where they had not, or could not, be retrieved by their fellows. *Athena* shuddered as its guns pounded at the damaged ship again. Elinor extinguished yet another fire on *Athena's* main topsail and began putting some effort into lighting the battered ship's sails.

"*Miss Pembroke!*" shouted the captain. Elinor caught herself and realized one of the sloops, the one whose crew had nearly extinguished its fire, was sailing toward the battle despite the small-arms fire from *Athena's* Marines. It had been well to starboard, out of the path of both pirate ships, and Elinor had not thought it worth expending her talent to do more than keep its deck ablaze. Now it was steadily making its way against the wind toward *Athena*. Either its captain was brave or foolhardy, but Elinor recognized in him a clever adversary who would require her to change tactics. She assured herself that the other two fires were burning steadily—the one with its deck ablaze was listing heavily to one side and would no longer be a threat—then turned her attention to the last sloop.

They had done something to the deck—oh, they had poured the resin over it, and her fire could not spread across it. Clever. She hoped no one else came up with that solution. They were coming closer, and she would not be able to burn the treated sails in time. The guns, could she melt the guns? She reached out to let fire caress the brass barrel of one, and knew she could make it run like liquid, but again, not in time. Surely they could do little damage to *Athena*, but Elinor could not bear the thought of losing even the few lives the sloop might manage to take.

It took her only a second to know what she had to do, another second to be repulsed by it, and a third to summon the fire and turn every man on the sloop's deck into a screaming, fiery pillar.

She didn't even have to maintain her control. They staggered, and waved their arms, and some of them found the rail and toppled over it, leaving it smoldering behind them. Others fell to the deck, convulsing and crying out. She watched, dispassionate, because nothing about the scene made sense to her; the screaming men might have been animals keening in the night.

Then one of the men bobbing in the ocean seemed to look at her, though he could hardly have identified her from this distance, and his face was blackened and unrecognizable as human. She jerked as if waking from a nightmare, stuffed her hand in her mouth to keep from screaming, and extinguished the remaining human fires. Then she hung over the taffrail and vomited clear liquid and cloudy yellow bile onto the stern windows.

She tried not to imagine what it must smell like on that deck, roasted meat and melted lacquer and burned paint and smoky, charred wood, and vomited again until she felt she had nothing left in her. Her back ached as if she had been beaten, her spine was a streak of sharp pain, and her abused stomach was still trying to turn itself inside out. She swallowed, gagged on the bitter taste of her saliva, and pushed her hair out of her eyes where it had fallen sometime during her exertions. She had—she could see that blackened face in memory, and wanted to curl into a ball and crush that memory out of existence.

It's not over. I have to save Athena. *This has to be worth it.*

She turned the green-blue sails to ash that sifted down over the unburned pirates, looped the mast with fire and brought it down on the sloop's deck, then spread that fire out to cover every inch of the planking, forcing herself not to listen to the screams as men leapt from the burning ship into the unwelcoming Caribbean waters. She burned a hole near the waterline of the listing sloop to encourage it to sink quietly, and watched for a moment as water bubbled up around it; there was no one left on its deck.

She looked around for something else to do. Ramsay was gone. All the lieutenants were gone. It seemed the cannons had swept the crew off the decks to carry them away into the sea, or possibly all the way to the Bahaman islands surrounding them. The helmsman Mr. Wynn was still there, stolid like a block of granite, and a few sailors manned the 12-pounders at the bow, and a handful of others scrambled about doing the same incomprehensible things they always did.

The much-battered pirate ship lay a few lengths off the larboard side, and Elinor could hear distant cries, the ringing clash of metal on metal, and the echoing blasts of small arms fire. *Athena* was tethered to the other ship, but Elinor heard no noise from it.

She rested her hand on the mizzenmast, found she needed its support because her back hurt as if she'd torn it open, and leaned more heavily on it as she said, "Mr. Wynn, what has happened?"

"Ha' took 'un," he said, nodding at the larboard side ship, " 'n 'sall o'er but 't scrappin'. Yon giv'un 't colors, like t' droppin' 'er drawrs." He pointed toward the silent ship to starboard.

Elinor understood barely two words of that. "Does it mean... we won?"

Wynn nodded. "Ayuh."

Elinor took a few paces toward the nearer ship, glanced over at the other one, and her legs gave out and she sank to the deck, shivering so hard she thought she might rattle the planks. "Tell Captain Ramsay I have gone below," she said to the air, and crawled down the companionway ladder until she could stand and walk, still shaking, to her bed.

She lay down, but had no intention of sleeping; when she closed her eyes, she could still see the sloop's deck spotted with short, fiery pillars that screamed and thrashed.

I didn't have a choice it was their fault I had to save the ship what have I done?

That blackened face floating in the grey-green water stared at her.

I killed him. I have killed a man. Dear Lord, I have killed dozens of men.

How many pillars was it? She couldn't keep from counting, then lost track and had to do it again before giving up. *At least sixty. How can they possibly fit so many men into those tiny ships?* And all of those who drowned because they couldn't swim, weren't they to her account, too? She had been a fool, a *damn* fool, to go so blithely to war without real- izing that the primary purpose of war was to kill the enemy so he would not kill you.

She hugged her knees to her chest. She had done the right thing. She had protected the ship. She wasn't the only one who'd killed; the gun crews killed the enemy too. If she understood Wynn at all, some of *Athena's* officers and crew were on that battered ship right now, fighting and killing pirates to take control of the ship and keep them from killing anyone else. Was she so much better than they, that killing in defense of ship and country was beneath her?

But it wasn't the killing—or not entirely the killing. It was that she'd done it with fire. Her precious, beautiful talent that filled her with such joy, used to turn men into so many piles of bone and ash and grease.

She held her hand well away from the bed and set it afire. It still didn't hurt. It was gold and lapis and ruby and a dozen other precious stones, limning her fingers with fire, and it was so beautiful it was impossible to think of it being used to destroy—and yet wasn't that the point of fire, ultimately, to destroy? Even fire that gave heat to a house had to destroy coal or wood to do it. She flexed her fingers and drops of fire fell away from her hand, dimming and going out before they struck the floor. Frenzied, she tore at her clothes and flung them away until she stood naked next to the bed and set her whole body alight.

Smoke rose from the floor, and she drew the fire up until she seemed to be wearing flaming trousers, but otherwise let it pour over her, her face, her hair, her chest and bottom and legs. The fire consumed her misery and her fear and filled her to bursting with joy. *This* was what the fire was for, this intense, beautiful feeling that hurt no one, and with that thought she again felt guilt and despair and began sobbing.

Her tears spat and hissed as they struck her fiery cheeks, so hot they did not even leave traces of steam. She cried, her sobs barely audible over the crackle of the fire as it burned and burned and did not consume her. When she had cried herself out, she extinguished the fire and staggered with weariness and pain all down her spine. So it was not completely harmless, after all. But she could endure any amount of weariness if only she could feel that way again.

She dressed and put on her shoes and sat on the edge of her bed, waiting. Someone had to have seen what she'd done, which meant Ramsay would know, and although Elinor did not think he would detest her for it—he was too rational and generous of spirit—he would never be able to treat her the way he had before. And that would be the end of any friendliness from the crew. How likely was it that those men would believe she might not turn her talent on them?

Someone knocked at her door, startling her. "Miss Pembroke?"

"Yes, Captain?"

"You disappeared rather thoroughly. I thought I'd check to see that you were still with us."

"I think I should be asking whether you still *want* me with you."

Silence. Then Ramsay said, "We captured both ships, though unfortunately Bexley killed himself rather than be taken prisoner. One of the ships surrendered without a fight. Apparently the sight of men burning like torches made them consider the benefits of not trying our patience."

"I am glad to hear it."

"You should be. You performed brilliantly today and saved many lives."

At the cost of others. "That is why I'm here, Captain."

She heard him make an impatient sound, and then he opened the door and entered. His sleeve was black with blood and he had a blood-stained handkerchief tied securely around his upper arm. "Stop that," he told her.

"Captain, your arm—"

"Hays will fix it later. You need to stop indulging in self-pity. You're alive. They aren't. That's all that matters." He closed the door and sat on the floor to lean against it.

"I beg your pardon, Captain, but you don't know a... a *damn* thing about it."

"Language, Miss Pembroke. You think I don't?"

Elinor shouted, "How could you possibly understand?"

Ramsay leaned his head back and closed his eyes. "I killed a man when I was fifteen," he said.

Elinor, ready to shout again, closed her mouth in astonishment. He sounded so weary, and yet so matter-of-fact, that she could not think of a reply.

"It was murder, actually, nothing less than murder. I'd had my first posting and there was this other midshipman who wouldn't stop harassing me—the details aren't important. I...wasn't good at controlling my temper—"

Elinor made an incredulous noise, and Ramsay smiled without opening his eyes. "Nothing like killing someone in a murderous rage to teach you to bridle your emotions. He went too far one day. I struck out with my talent, threw him as hard as I could at the bowsprit and cracked his skull. He fell into the water, and when I pulled him out, he was dead."

"If it was...murder...were you not punished?"

He smiled again. "That was the day my Extraordinary talent manifested. I Flew to pull him out of the water and then as fast as I could to the nearest Extraordinary Shaper. The service—let alone the government—can't afford to waste an Extraordinary by executing him, even if he deserves it. So it was quietly hushed up and ruled an accident. They said I was too powerful and didn't know the extent of my Moving capacity. Which was correct, but not true. If you see what I mean."

"I think so."

Ramsay opened his eyes and looked at her, clasping his hands loosely on his knees. "You're more disturbed by having used your talent to kill those men than you are about their deaths."

Elinor gaped at him. He added, "I have this magnificent, beautiful talent. Moving is—it's as if you can feel these currents, all around, and you Move things through them and it's unbelievable how good that feels. And Flying is a hundred times better. And I used it to take a life for no better reason than I was tired of being teased. So yes, I do know what it's like. And I honestly can't tell you what to do about that. Fire is meant to destroy, after all. But it doesn't taint you or your talent that you've used it to kill. I swear to you that's true."

So much of what he said mirrored Elinor's own thoughts that for a moment she could not find a response. Finally, she said, "Everyone will be afraid of me."

"Does that matter? That is, does it change who you know yourself to be?"

Elinor shook her head. "But it is an uncomfortable feeling."

"Well, don't worry about it. You forget half these men have sailed the Caribbean before and know what pirates do to Navy sailors when they capture them. It's a good deal less pretty than burning to death. The other half are being told stories about it. By now every man on this ship believes your actions have paid back in equal measure everything those pirates have ever done to us. They may be trying to put your face on the figurehead as we speak."

Elinor gasped and then laughed, covering her face with both hands. "That is far worse than being feared."

"That is a good attitude to have." Ramsay pushed himself up and, after a moment's thought, extended his hand to her. "You've made a tremendous sacrifice today, and I want you to know I appreciate it. Would you care to join me for supper? Only the two of us, unfortunately, as Livingston and Fitzgerald are in command of the prizes and the others are all engaged in putting *Athena* to rights."

His hand was warm and firm and his smile made all the rest of her disquiet fade. "I do not call that *unfortunate*, Captain," she said.

CHAPTER 12

IN WHICH THERE IS AN
UNPLEASANT DEVELOPMENT

Despite knowing that the prizes were under their control, even if one of those doing the controlling was Livingston, whose abilities she doubted, Elinor could not help worrying. Her imagination presented her with scenarios in which the pirates might break free of their prisons, wrest control of their ships and turn their guns on *Athena,* sailing helplessly between them.

She spent many hours on deck, pacing from side to side and making plans for how she would destroy the ships if that became necessary, until Ramsay guessed what she was doing and confined her to the great cabin. "You're making the men nervous," he told her, "and that's affecting the ship. So stay here. Read a book. Write in your diary. Anything that will keep you off the quarterdeck."

"Am I a prisoner now?"

"I think it would be difficult to keep *you* locked up on what is essentially a floating box of wood. So I'm making it a forceful suggestion."

Elinor made an exasperated noise, but did as she was asked. She needed to catch up on her diary, which she pretended was a series of letters to Selina, and finding a way to explain what had happened in the battle was difficult. More difficult was the realization that for the first time, she was concealing things from her sister, albeit a fictional version of her sister—though who could say she might not someday be able to give it to her? In the end, she simply glossed over the deaths and said only that she had burned the ships' masts so they were unable to maneuver, which was true as far as it went.

Captain Ramsay, she wrote, *has turned out to be a true friend, which surprises me as I did not expect ever to call a man "friend." I suppose it is because all the men I have known, apart from papa, have either been indifferent to me because we have nothing in common, or far too interested in me as a potential bride. It is in part because of the talent we share and in part, I think, because we do have much in common, though our backgrounds could not be more dissimilar; his mother is dead, his father a tenant farmer who was thrilled to see his son escape that life of drudgery. Whatever the reason, I am glad to have a friend, because this place is not at all what I am accustomed to.*

"Elinor?" Hervey stuck his head into the room while simultaneously knocking. "We'll be in Bermuda before nightfall. Captain wants you at Admiralty House with him in four hours."

"Thank you, Stratford." They were such good friends now that they made free of one another's Christian names, though only in private —*and how strange that the captain and I remain formal despite our friendship. I suppose it would be bad for discipline if I treated my commanding officer with such informality.* "I admit to being nervous. Admiral Durrant seems rather erratic. He may still decide my contribution is unnecessary."

"That was a pretty decisive victory, Elinor. I think even the admiral would have trouble saying you didn't pull your weight."

"I hope you're right." Elinor closed her diary. "I may need new clothing soon. I tore and burned my gown during the battle, and my long-sleeved one is simply unbearable in this heat, which leaves me with one morning dress and my poor, unnecessary evening gown."

Stratford pulled out a chair and sat at the table. "Well, there are plenty of ladies in Bermuda; they must get their clothes from someplace."

"Or they make their own. I am a poor seamstress. I have always been grateful that my family could afford to pay others for that service, though I feel it is a terrible extravagance."

"What's a terrible extravagance?" Ramsay entered the room, put his hat on the table and ran both his hands through his hair. "If I had my way, there would be a Caribbean uniform that was nothing but cotton breeches and linen shirts."

"We were also speaking of dress, Captain," Elinor said, "because I fear I will have to sew my own, and I am terrible at it."

"Oh, there are seamstresses in Bermuda. You think Admiral Durrant's wife makes her own clothes? Hardly."

"The Admiral is married?" Elinor covered her mouth as if she could hold back her astonishment.

"And well you may sound shocked. She's a lovely woman and quite the hostess. The Admiral clearly has charms that are not on display to lowly captains and Scorchers of ambiguous status."

"Must I go with you?"

Ramsay mock-glared at her. "Yes, you must, because I want Admiral Durrant to have to put a face to the destruction. He needs to be clear to whom he owes most of this victory. Otherwise *Athena* is nothing more than a particularly effective warship."

"You flatter me, Captain."

"It's hardly flattery if it's true."

Beaumont flung the door open with more than necessary force. "I've Spoken with Admiralty House," he said, "and they want you there now."

Ramsay scowled. "They said four hours."

"You can argue the point if you want. Just get another Speaker to relay it. They were unpleasantly testy."

"Fine. Miss Pembroke, are you ready?"

"Will five minutes be too much of a delay?"

"Since I'm changing into my dress uniform, no. Mr. Hervey, wait here."

Elinor was changed and ready before Ramsay, who finally emerged from his cubby looking elegant except for the scowl on his face. He picked up a packet of papers, tucked it inside his jacket, and said, "Let's go."

The Bounding chamber was, of course, unchanged from their first visit. The servants' hall outside the chamber, however, was considerably noisier. Dark-skinned men in short trousers and loosely-woven shirts and women in bright-patterned skirts passed their little party in both directions, carrying stacks of linens or basins or sometimes nothing at all. They avoided Elinor's eyes and stepped wide around Ramsay. The voices that had previously sounded like they were coming through water were clearer now, though Elinor still could not discover their source.

When they reached the entrance chamber, her question was somewhat answered: men in uniform wearing insignia of all ranks thronged the room in groups of two or three, seated on benches or standing and admiring the paintings decorating the walls. Their conversations sounded much like chattering geese gathered around a lake shore, each man honking away trying to be heard over everyone else.

One or two of the men glanced at Ramsay and Elinor, then turned away, unimpressed. Ramsay ignored them all and passed through the chamber into the series of windowless halls they'd seen before. Uniformed men, some carrying papers, passed them without acknowledging them, though a couple of them glanced at Elinor—to her surprise, they were admiring glances. It filled her with such confusion that she stopped paying attention to where they were going, and was startled to see the iron knobs and the door which Ramsay threw open without knocking.

This time, Admiral Durrant, Admiral Wood, and Sullyard were joined by two captains. One seemed to be Durrant's contemporary, though as he was as weathered as the admiral, it was impossible to guess his true age. The other was a younger man perhaps half a decade older than Ramsay, with blond hair that hung loose around his face and an expression so blank it had to be intentional.

Durrant, seated at the head of the table, made no game of pretending not to see Ramsay this time. "Good afternoon, Captain," he said, sounding as if the words were being wrung out of him. "Your report."

Sullyard came forward, his eyes constantly flicking toward Elinor, and accepted the packet Ramsay handed him. Durrant took it from Sullyard, snapped the wax seal and unfolded it. He read, lips moving slightly, while the men around him stood and shifted. Wood looked uncomfortable, but Elinor judged it was nervous rather than physical discomfort; the two strangers looked as if they were trying to read over Durrant's shoulder without appearing to do so. Elinor resolutely avoided looking at Sullyard. Ramsay was as collected and indifferent to the delay as ever. She shifted from one foot to the other and wished her shoes were more comfortable.

"Interesting," Durrant said, squaring the papers in front of him. "And quite the coincidence, happening upon the pirate squadron on your way to take up your post."

"Yes, sir. It was a harrowing experience."

"I can imagine. I'm not pleased you weren't able to bring that damned Bexley in alive."

"We didn't anticipate that he would take his own life rather than be captured, sir. I take responsibility for that."

"You should." Durrant shifted his gaze to Elinor, startling her. "Four ships, young lady."

"Yes, sir," Elinor said, wondering what line of questioning he intended to pursue.

"Luck, I suppose. You never having been in combat before."

"No, sir. That is, it was not luck, sir."

"Impossible," said the older man. "No Scorcher could possibly destroy four sloops in an hour."

"I beg your pardon," Elinor said, "but we have not been introduced, Captain...?"

"Vaughan," the man said, spitting the word at her.

"Captain Vaughan, I feel certain you do not intend to call either Captain Ramsay or myself a liar. I realize you are unfamiliar with the capacities of an Extraordinary Scorcher, but I assure you destroying four sloops in—did you say an hour? Time does fly when you are in battle—is certainly not beyond my abilities." She moved her foot away from Ramsay's boot, but he made no motion to step on it.

"No one's questioning your veracity," Admiral Wood said. "It seems as though you made good use of your resources and exploited the pirates' ignorance." It sounded like a prepared speech, but one Elinor hoped might be effective. Wood might be only a Colonial admiral, but she thought he was an important ally.

"I believe they were as surprised as we were," Ramsay said, "since I'm sure they thought that channel would be unoccupied."

Durrant scowled at him. Elinor bit her lip to hold back a smile. "You may have had a tactical advantage," he said, "but it was still luck that you happened upon them."

"That's true of many encounters with the pirates, sir."

"Possibly." Durrant folded the paper again and handed it to Sullyard without looking at him. "Congratulations," he ground out, "on your success."

"Thank you, sir."

"Thank you, Admiral Durrant," Elinor couldn't help adding. Durrant glared at both of them.

"I'll have new orders for you in a few days, Captain Ramsay, after we've reassessed the situation. In the meantime, keep your men under control; this isn't Portsmouth. Vaughan, Crawford, the same goes for you. Now, all of you, dismissed."

Elinor allowed Ramsay to hold the door for her, then took his arm again. "Is that—" she began.

"Not here, Miss Pembroke."

"Ramsay!" They turned to see the other captains following close behind. Vaughan pushed past them without a word, but the other man, Crawford, strolled up to join them. "Quite the victory, eh?"

"I was merely doing my duty, Crawford," Ramsay said, and now tension echoed in his voice, and his muscles were tight beneath her fingers.

"Oh, that we could all aspire to do our duty with such success as you've found," Crawford said. He looked briefly at Elinor and dismissed her. "I believe if we threw you into a shit-heap you'd come up covered in diamonds."

"Please watch your language in front of the lady," Ramsay said.

"My apologies, miss. I assumed you'd be accustomed to it, being surrounded by sailors all day. I wonder you're able to keep even a shred of... gentility."

Elinor squeezed Ramsay's arm, hard. "I feel honored to serve with such brave men as are aboard *Athena*," she said. "The First Lord did say it was the best frigate in the Navy."

Crawford's smile vanished. "Quite the compliment."

"Oh, no, I believe he was simply being accurate. He did not strike me as someone who gives compliments."

"Crawford, good to see you again, but I have things to do," Ramsay said, smoothly cutting off whatever Crawford was about to say. "Miss Pembroke?"

Elinor had to trot to keep up with him. "Captain, do slow down!"

"Not if there's any chance Crawford might try to follow us. Mr. Hervey, come."

"But I was enjoying—"

"*Later*, Miss Pembroke. There's no love lost between me and Crawford, and much as I was enjoying your little battle of wits, which by the way he was not equipped to fight, I'd rather not give him any more grounds to hate me than he already thinks he has." He handed her off to Stratford and pushed open the door to the Bounding chamber. "Back to the ship."

But Stratford, when the white walls of *Athena*'s Bounding chamber rose up around them, gripped Elinor's arm before she could exit. "It was over a woman," he said in a low voice. "They both courted her and the captain won her heart."

"But...is he married, then?"

"No. She cried off a month after they were engaged. She's married to some rich Cit now. Captain never talks about it, but then why would he? But it's why Captain Crawford hates him." He shooed her out of the chamber and shut the door. Elinor stood looking at it. How long ago had that been? He certainly didn't act like a man who had been crossed in love, not that she would know what that looked like.

The door banged open, startling her. "And now we wait to see whether Durrant has learned to use us more efficiently," Ramsay said, tucking his hat under his arm. "We have probably given Wood more leverage, which is excellent. He's a good man, if a trifle too aware of his subordinate status."

"Is he a subordinate, then? I believed him to be a high-ranking officer in the Colonial fleet, given his comments."

"Oh, yes, he's the admiral's American counterpart. He ought to be Admiral Durrant's equal, but the admiral being who he is, this pirate hunt has become more a British-led operation aided by our Colonial forces. Wood's a smart man, though, and you can be certain he's maneuvering the admiral to make better use of your talent."

He held the door of the great cabin open, and the smell of roast pork mingled with the sweeter, greener aroma of fresh peas greeted them. "Supper, and just in time. Meeting Crawford always makes me ravenous."

⚜

Midshipman St. Maur escorted Elinor into Hamilton the next morning, Stratford being occupied with ship's business. Four of *Athena's* crew rowed them across the Great Sound between Ireland Island and what Elinor couldn't help thinking of as the mainland. It was a long journey for the ship's boat, and Elinor felt some pity for the men, though they seemed to think nothing of it.

They hired an ancient carriage to take them the rest of the way, a poorly sprung contraption that smelled of damp, rotting wood, with tattered leather and seat cushions hard as rock. It was a silent ride, with both of them looking out the carriage windows, Elinor because she was fascinated with the sheer variety of plants and trees in all shades of vibrant green, St. Maur because he couldn't bring himself to look at her. After interacting with him some half a dozen times on the Atlantic voyage, Elinor had realized the midshipman was in the throes of an adolescent passion, which changed her feelings about him from annoyance to amused pity. She regretted it, a little, that Ramsay had thrown them together today, but perhaps an increased proximity would help the young man overcome his unrequited love.

Hamilton was a beautiful town nestled into the curve of one of the blue and sand-gold bays that Elinor was beginning, to her dismay, to take for granted. The buildings were tropical, blindingly white stone with large windows to receive the breeze blowing off the harbor, but the construction, the wide streets laid out in straight lines, the regularity of the roofs and doors, were all modern British design. It was a young, exuberant, thriving town, its streets thronged with men and women, mostly colored, and Elinor had to stop herself staring at them, wondering how many were free and how many slave.

She slid the carriage window open and fanned some of the sea breeze toward her neck. The sun was not terribly hot that morning, but the day was humid and the air clung to her like a damp second skin.

St. Maur muttered something. "I beg your pardon?" Elinor said, leaning forward.

"I said we're in Pembroke Parish," St. Maur said. "Thought that might be interesting to you."

"It is, Mr. St. Maur. I wonder if the founder could be related to me."

"Named after the third Earl of Pembroke."

"Really? Then probably not. My family is old but not titled. You seem to know a great deal about it."

"I was born here."

"Mr. St. Maur! I had no idea! I don't suppose you have leave to visit your parents?"

St. Maur had gone increasingly red during the course of this conversation. "Not today, miss."

"Born in Bermuda. How exciting!"

He shrugged and went back to looking out the window. "I suppose."

Elinor concealed a smile behind her hand. They were passing through a cool, shaded alley of cedar trees, lined in places with broken stone walls that were waist-high to the people strolling along, none of whom seemed inclined to hurry their journey. She felt a little indolent herself. No point in hurrying, was there, when the warm sun and the moist air relaxed her so. She closed her eyes and enjoyed the flickering of light falling through the leaves to brush her eyelids.

In town, she purchased a gown in a tiny shop run by a woman with charcoal-black skin and her hair wrapped up in a brightly patterned cloth, though it took nearly all her small store of money to convince the woman to sell it; it fit Elinor imperfectly, but she could not afford to commission anything *Athena* might not remain in port long enough for her to collect.

Then she coerced St. Maur into taking her on a tour of Hamilton. There was not much to see; St. Maur explained that the capital at St. George, his home town, had far nicer and more elaborate architecture, but Elinor was charmed by the simplicity of the houses and the friendliness of the citizens. Eventually they wound up at the harbor, where Elinor stayed on the road rather than tease St. Maur by asking to walk barefoot along the beach.

Ships of all sizes, from single-mast boats to vessels almost the size of *Athena,* stood at anchor in the harbor; others lay fully upon the shore, hulls tipped to the sky, while men scraped their bottoms free of barnacles and other growth. She watched one ship cross the harbor in a wandering path, tacking into the wind, and gazed after it until it cleared the harbor and its tawny sails disappeared around the point.

Legs aching from her unaccustomed exertion, sweat dampening her back and beneath her arms, she drifted off against St. Maur in the longboat and jerked awake when in her half-aware state she realized his posture was more rigid than usual, his hands and arm too still. Elinor swallowed a laugh and apologized to the young man, whose cheeks were maroon. She reached down and trailed her fingers in the warm water, and watched *Athena* grow as they approached her, thinking about what they might have for supper and how nice it would be to wear her new gown at the table.

But when she reached her bed cubby, she found a letter, creamy thick paper sealed with black wax, lying on the rough, slightly wrinkled blanket. She dropped her parcel on the bed and picked up the letter, whose rough rag texture caught at her fingers. Her name was written on the front.

She could not quite make out the seal in the dim lamp light, so she took the letter into the great cabin, where the smell of roasted chicken and rosemary promised a delicious supper, and held it up to the window to catch the fading sunlight as the sun began to dip like a bright orange below the horizon. It looked like an anchor, but was too blurred for her to make out entirely. She turned it over to look at her name again. No handwriting she recognized, so her family had not discovered her location, but who else would be writing to her?

She broke the seal and unfolded the letter. The smooth, curving copperplate did not match the handwriting on the outside of the envelope. Elinor was so struck by its beauty that she found herself halfway down the page with no idea of what she had read. She started over, reading more slowly. As the import of the words reached her, her fingers went numb, and she knew she was still gripping the paper only because she could see how her white hands clung to it. She stood, staring at the words without reading them, for a full minute before reading the whole thing through again, still barely comprehending the message.

Distantly, somewhere beyond the roaring in her ears, she heard the door open. "Ah, Miss Pembroke. Did you enjoy your outing?" Ramsay said, removing his hat and placing it on the little cupboard between the couches.

"Captain," Elinor said, and saw by his face that she had spoken so softly he could not hear her, so she repeated more loudly, "Captain, what ship is the *Glorious*?"

Ramsay began unbuttoning his jacket. "That's Captain Crawford's ship. Why do you ask?"

She held out the letter toward him. "Because I have been ordered to report there at once."

CHAPTER 13

IN WHICH ELINOR'S CIRCUMSTANCES CHANGE, AND NOT FOR THE BETTER

Ramsay stared at her for a moment, puzzled. He snatched the letter from her hand and read it silently. She could tell when he finished because his eyes came to rest somewhere in the center of the page for a few seconds, and Elinor had to make herself take a breath because the emotionless look on his face was far more terrifying than rage would have been. "Captain?" she said.

Ramsay thrust the letter back at her and was out the door, shouting, "*Mr. Hervey!*"

Elinor ran after him, crushing the paper in her hand so its thick creases cut into her palm. She went up the companionway at a run, felt her hair coming loose from its pins and shoved them back in so forcefully with her free hand their tips pricked her scalp. "Captain Ramsay, what am I to do?"

Ramsay swung around, his hand on the mizzenmast. "Stay here while I sort this out," he said. "Mr. Beaumont, take my place at table. Mr. Hervey, Admiralty House *now*."

Stratford, his eyes and mouth wide with astonishment, grasped Ramsay about the waist and disappeared. Beaumont, as astonished as Stratford if better at concealing it, said, "Miss Pembroke?"

Elinor tried to smooth the crumpled paper, then handed it to Beaumont, who read more slowly than Ramsay. He glanced once at Elinor before he came to the end. "I didn't realize you were subject to orders like this."

"Neither did I," said Elinor, "but I suppose—I mean, the First Lord did say I was to be under Captain Ramsay's command, and I thought that meant—Mr. Beaumont, will I have to leave *Athena?*"

Beaumont chewed on his lower lip and looked out across the Great Sound. "Don't worry. Miles won't let it happen." He didn't look as certain as he sounded. "Why don't we go in to supper?"

"Without the captain?"

"He insisted I do the honors. I wouldn't go against his instructions, however unsettled the situation is."

They were joined by Selkirk and Lieutenant Fitzgerald, but with Beaumont distracted and Fitzgerald nervous in Elinor's presence, she was left to converse with Selkirk, who seemed oblivious to the tension Elinor felt. His Discernment might or might not be strong—he had never been so impolite as to comment on her emotional state after the first time she'd taken his arm—but his powers of observation were remarkably poor for all he claimed great insight into the human heart. He persisted in chattering inconsequentialities without noticing that Elinor's responses were halfhearted or unenthusiastic.

She picked at her roast chicken while he prated away on something to do with cats, or possibly turtles. The smell of rosemary sickened her; it reminded her of unfolding the letter, reading that beautiful copperplate that wanted to tear her away from everything familiar.

It surprised her to realize how much she loved *Athena*, cramped and dark as it was; she even loved the terrible smell of rum that permeated the ship when they cracked open a new barrel to mix a fresh batch of grog for the men. Thinking of all the things she loved about the ship made her angry. She had fought and killed for *Athena,* and now Admiral Durrant wanted to take her from it? She was almost certain the First Lord's instructions had not given Durrant the power to assign her elsewhere. Ramsay would put him straight. This was all a horrible mistake.

"Miss Pembroke, if I might tempt you with another piece of chicken?" Selkirk dropped more meat on her plate without waiting for her assent. She smiled weakly at him and tried to take another bite, but it tasted bitter and too salty, like tears. "You seem out of sorts, my dear. Perhaps I might read to you later? We never finished that book of Catrynge's sermons you enjoyed so much."

"I thank you, Mr. Selkirk, but I think not this evening. I fear the sun has given me the head-ache," Elinor lied. In fact, she felt surprisingly vigorous considering her stomach was cramped with worry. A draft carried the smell of rosemary to her nose again; she snatched up an orange and began tearing at the peel, holding it close to her face and breathing the tangy citrus scent deeply.

"How terribly unfortunate, Miss Pembroke. Perhaps you ought to see Dr. Hays?"

"I believe rest is all I need, thank you."

"Then let me bring you lemon-water to bathe your forehead. It does wonders for the circulation and soothes even the tenderest—"

"*Mr. Selkirk*," Elinor said, unable to control herself, "I do not wish for lemon-water, or Dr. Hays, or anything but the comfort of my bed. I pray you, do not trouble yourself further."

"I see," Selkirk said, stiffly. "I apologize for my misplaced attention." He laid down his napkin and rose from the table. "I sometimes overstep when I am concerned about those for whom I feel—but I see I am renewing those attentions you find so intolerable."

"Mr. Selkirk—" She could feel the eyes of every man in the room on her, and wished she could melt like wax between the floorboards.

"No, you are correct, Miss Pembroke, I cannot offer you anything that will ease your distress." He made a perfunctory bow and went to the door only to cry out in surprise and pain when it was flung open in his face.

"I beg your pardon," Ramsay said, but he sounded not at all penitent. His voice was flat, emotionless, but Selkirk, his hand on Ramsay's arm where he had reached out to steady himself, gasped, snatched his hand away, and staggered out of the great cabin as if the flimsy door that had struck him had been made of iron.

Ramsay shut the door gently behind him and stood for a moment, looking down at his hand on the knob. "Captain," Elinor began.

"You're to pack your things and report to *Glorious* immediately," he said, "which I interpret to mean as soon as you've finished your supper. And that interpretation is the only thing I have power over." He went to the table and sat heavily in his chair at its head.

"But that is monstrously unfair! Captain—"

"Miss Pembroke," Ramsay said, still in that flat voice, "you are under orders like the rest of us. Admiral Durrant has determined you will best serve the Navy under Captain Crawford's command. The *Glorious* is to be made a special unit of Scorchers, you and three other men, for a mission the admiral didn't see fit to discuss with me. I have spent the last half-hour arguing with him, and all I accomplished was to be accused of disrespect and insubordination. So we are all to do our duty." He spat out the last word as if it tasted of sand.

Elinor looked at the men surrounding the table. "But I am certain this is not what the First Lord wanted," she said.

"So am I, but there's nothing I can do about it until Whitehall wakes up. Arthur, I want you Speaking to your contacts in seven hours —that should give them time to take their morning coffee. Mr. Fitzgerald, find Mr. Hervey and tell him to be ready to Bound when I have an appointment. Miss Pembroke..." Ramsay took her hand and squeezed it, almost painfully tight. "I will resolve this. Until then, well, Crawford may be an ass, but he's not a bad captain, and I'm certain he'll treat you well."

"Your face makes your mouth a liar," Elinor said.

He released her. "What am I supposed to tell you? I have no idea where Crawford's going or what instructions Admiral Durrant's given him. I don't even know if they understand your capabilities!"

"I am certain I will be able to endure whatever this new...adventure...brings," Elinor said with a wry smile, and he laughed once, bitterly. Elinor pushed her chair away from the table, prompting the men to stand, and Ramsay said, "You're finished already?"

"I find my appetite is not what it should be. Please excuse me, gentlemen." Ramsay looked as if he wanted to protest, and Elinor had to flee to her room because she had an unexpected urge to start crying.

She lifted her battered trunk to the bed and tossed her clothes into it, including her new gown, still in its paper wrapping. She looked at her evening gown, fingered the rose-figured white gauze over dark pink silk, and left it hanging in the cupboard like a promise she would return. Then she put out the lantern and returned to the great cabin, where Ramsay sat alone, eating chicken and boiled potatoes as if they were enemy ships he could dissect and consume. "Will I...is the boat ready?"

Ramsay nodded, not raising his head. "You'll take my gig. The coxswain has his orders. *Glorious* isn't anchored far away. I expect, from what the admiral said, you should be shipping out in the morning."

Elinor set her suitcase down with a thump. "Then why could they not allow me to stay the night?"

Ramsay laid his knife and fork down on his plate, neatly crossing one another, and finally looked at her. "This is every bit the power play you suspect it is," he said in a low voice, as if he feared eavesdroppers. "Your display convinced Admiral Durrant he needs your very valuable talent, and he doesn't want me taking all the glory of it when his nephew—yes, Crawford is his nephew—might benefit instead. This 'Scorcher ship' he's proposed sounds noble and tactically sound, but it's actually an excuse to promote Crawford's interests and, incidentally, give me a metaphorical poke in the eye. Miss Pembroke, I sincerely apologize for your being caught up in what is essentially a political battle."

"I did not realize I was a pawn," Elinor said, turning away toward the window. The sun had set fully and the air was a deep-blue haze that mingled with the darker blue of the water. "I had thought, having so much power, that I had some control. But I see how naïve I have been."

"What I fear is that the First Lord intended this all along. I swear to you, Miss Pembroke, I *will* return you to *Athena* if it's within my power to do so."

"I have faith in you, Captain."

He laughed that short, bitter laugh again. "Someone has to." He pushed back from the table and Moved her trunk into the air. "May I escort you to the gig, Miss Pembroke?"

She took his arm and, feeling as if she were walking to her own funeral, went up the companionway and across the deck for what might be the last time. Seamen came forward from the depths of the lower deck and crowded close to where the companionway opened up, their faces grave. Whispers grew to full-voiced murmurs, and then men were calling out farewells. Elinor couldn't stop herself shedding a few tears, struggling to keep them from turning into a flood.

By the davits that held the captain's gig, she turned and waved as it was lowered into the water. Now they were shouting "*Hip hip hurrah!*" and the coxswain and crew clambered over the side, then Ramsay himself helped her into the bo'sun's chair and she was lowered into the boat. She kept her eyes resolutely ahead, this time not out of fear, but because she dared not look up at the friend she was leaving. She took her seat, her trunk was settled, and the oarsmen began pulling with long, smooth strokes, taking her toward a new ship that could never be her home.

The ships in the new, partially finished harbor were visible only as gleaming lights high above the ocean's surface. "Hoy, the boat," someone called out from the first one.

"*Athena*," the coxswain replied, but the captain's gig didn't slow. Elinor watched them as the boat glided past each twinkling constellation, thinking, *This is the one*, and then, *No, this one*, when the first fell behind them.

After they had passed three ships, each hailing them and receiving the same response, the oarsmen turned toward a set of lights more numerous and higher up than the others, lights that resolved themselves into a ship quite a bit larger than *Athena* with the word GLORIOUS barely visible in the glow from the stern lanterns. "Hoy, the boat!" someone called out.

The oarsmen brought the boat up against the hull with a tap, and one of them shouted, "*Athena* for *Glorious!*"

After a moment, a shadowy head looked down at them. "Who's there?"

"Miss Pembroke from th' *Athena* wants to come aboard!"

"Wait a bit." The head disappeared. Elinor looked up in time to dodge a flying bundle that landed on the seat next to her: the bo'sun's chair. With the oarsmen's help, she disentangled the cords and settled herself. As she was jerked and tugged into the air, she closed her eyes and breathed in deep lungsful of briny, warm air tinged with the now-familiar smell of tar and lacquer and, more distantly, the musty smell of damp canvas. This was temporary. Ramsay would have her assigned back to *Athena* and Durrant would be put in his place. She could endure for a few days, or a week.

She opened her eyes in time to see the rail and the netting full of canvas bundles, then she was over the deck and alighting as easily as if she rode in bo'sun's chairs every day. "Good evening," she said to the sailors, unexpectedly crisp in their striped shirts and brown trousers.

Glorious smelled different from *Athena*, though Elinor could not identify the difference beyond noting that someone was cooking cabbage somewhere below. The upper deck was not flush the whole length of it; three steps on both the larboard and starboard sides led up to the quarterdeck, with the wheel centered in front of the mizzenmast. The deck was quiet, almost empty except for the handful of sailors who'd hauled her up. Everyone else would be at supper. Now these men stood in a rough semicircle around her, shifting their weight and staring as if they'd never seen a woman before.

"Could one of you please take me to see Captain Crawford?" Elinor said, and had a flash of déjà vu as she recalled having made the same request upon first boarding *Athena*, all those weeks ago.

The men exchanged furtive glances, and just as Elinor worked out they were each trying to pass an unpleasant task off on someone else, a lieutenant came quickly down from the quarterdeck, a little out of breath. "I beg your pardon," he said, "we didn't expect you quite so soon."

Elinor ground her teeth. He insisted on disrupting her life, but was unprepared for her arrival? It was one more way Crawford exerted his power over her. "Captain Crawford?" she said, not caring about politeness. The lieutenant's face flushed. He tipped his hat to her and indicated that she should precede him below.

The companionway looked much like *Athena*'s—*how long will it take me to stop comparing this ship to her? Will I be here that long?*—but the door to the captain's quarters was farther away from it and less finely crafted. Elinor felt obscurely gratified on *Athena*'s behalf. The lieutenant passed the Marine sentry on duty at the great cabin door, knocked, and received no response. With a furtive glance at Elinor, he knocked again.

This time the door was yanked open by Crawford, who shouted, "What the devil—" before recognizing her. "You," he said, less angrily. "I suppose you should come in." He turned and walked away without waiting for her; Elinor closed the door behind her. She hadn't liked Crawford before, and she liked him even less now he was the executor of Durrant's plan.

"Captain Crawford," she began, just as Crawford said, "Miss Pembroke—"

"Please go ahead, Captain," Elinor said. "I am certain you were going to answer whatever questions I might have."

Crawford sprawled on a three-sided settee in one corner beneath the windows. The great cabin was larger than *Athena's*, though its windows were the same, and the walls were bare except for the captain's swords, hanging on the starboard side near the quarter cabin's sliding door. The remnants of the captain's supper lay on the table; he had dined alone, but by the number of dishes remaining Elinor guessed he ate enough for two. How he kept that slim figure was a mystery.

He was an attractive man, with fine, strong cheekbones and a well-shaped mouth and straight nose, though his looks were spoiled by scowl lines etched into his face, and there were grease stains on his uniform. That Ramsay had won that young woman's heart over Crawford's blandishments made perfect sense to Elinor; Crawford might be objectively more handsome, but Ramsay's self-assuredness and quiet air of authority made him far more attractive on the whole.

"I don't know how Ramsay's put up with having a woman on board," Crawford muttered, then in a louder voice said, "I expect you to obey orders when you're given them. You won't get any special treatment here. Don't expect me to go offering you my arm all the time; I have no use for pretty manners on my ship. You'll be issued a uniform, and you and the other Scorchers will mess and bunk in the gunroom. In the morning I'll explain what the admiral's ordered us to do."

Elinor missed the last part of this speech because her mind had caught hold of a key phrase. "Issue me a uniform, Captain?"

"You're a member of my crew now, and you Scorchers will have your own uniform, something to set you apart from the rest. Durrant's orders. Besides, you're too conspicuous in that gown."

"I *beg* your pardon, Captain, but I will not sacrifice my modesty like that!"

"You'll do as you're told or suffer the consequences," Crawford said.

"And what, pray tell, would those consequences be? You cannot have me flogged, Captain!"

"No," he said, his voice going low and vicious, "but I can have you sent home, dismissed without pay. I think you don't want that."

The blood drained from her face. "You would not."

"I would. Now get down to the gunroom and talk to Lieutenant Fischer. I expect you to be properly clothed when I see you in the morning. Dismissed."

Furious, mute, Elinor hurried away, afraid she might not be able to control her tongue. Yes, Crawford would most certainly send her home if she refused to obey, and Elinor was beginning to understand how much power Admiral Durrant had over her. Home, with nothing to show for it—her reputation might not be ruined, but she would once again be trapped in a life of slow suffocation. She had no choice. *Oh, Captain Ramsay, find a solution quickly.*

She found the stairs leading down to the lower deck, where the noise of supper rose to meet her; the steps were battered, scarred from years of service the way *Athena's* were not, but they were also smoothed from the passage of hundreds of feet, and she stopped for a moment to breathe in the cabbage-scented air and calm herself. She would do herself no favors by being angry and recalcitrant.

She continued her descent more slowly, moving quietly so as not to draw the attention of the talking, shouting, laughing men pounding the tables. At least the deck was familiar in that respect; the men on *Athena* would be having their supper now as well, and afterward there was to have been music—she forced herself not to think of it, to focus her thoughts on the worn planks that creaked beneath her weight.

The gunroom had no door, only a great opening through which Elinor found a table, as well-used as the stairs, and a handful of men laughing over after-supper drinks. They all went silent and leaped to their feet when she appeared at the edge of the circle of lamplight over the table. "Miss," said one of the lieutenants, "uh, good evening, Miss." He was a little portly, with greying hair, and he didn't meet her eyes.

"I was told to report to Lieutenant Fischer," Elinor said.

"That's me, Miss. I, uh, there's a room for you, and I'll get you one of the new uniforms." He made no move to leave.

"She can share my hammock any time," one of the men said, none too softly, to his neighbor, who chuckled. Elinor's heart sank. How had she gone this long without threat of assault from her fellow officers?

"I thank you for the compliment, sir," she said, extending her hand as if offering to shake his, "but I fear you would find me an...overly warm companion." She lit her hand on fire and let the gem-colored flames spread across her palm and up her arm to the elbow.

The man swore and fell out of his chair backward in his attempt to get away from her. The others drew a breath in unison, making a sound like the wind sweeping through the sails. Elinor held onto the fire for a few seconds longer, then put it out. "Mr. Fischer, I believe you mentioned a room?"

"Uh," Fischer said, his eyes as wide as the plate at his left hand, and made a gesture with his hands that Elinor interpreted as meaning "follow me." He opened one of the doors, which was actually a rectangle of canvas hung crookedly within the frame, and showed her a cube of a space with nothing but her trunk in one corner and a bundled hammock and a small unlit lantern hanging from the ceiling. Elinor caught her breath. *I cannot sleep in a hammock.* She opened her mouth to protest, remembered Crawford's pleased, vicious smile, and shut it again. "Thank you," she said. "I am surprised you keep spare clothing aboard. I believed the men were required to provide for themselves."

"Uh, no, miss, Captain's very, uh, we were given Scorcher, uh, uniforms," Fischer said. "I'll be right back, miss." He closed the door, leaving Elinor in darkness.

Sighing, she once again kindled a fire and lit the lantern, whose clear glass gave off a brighter light than she was accustomed to. Hands on hips, she studied the hammock. There was a second hook in the ceiling some distance from the first, and by standing on the tips of her toes she was barely able to reach it.

She set about unhooking and disentangling the wad of rope and canvas until it dangled from its hook, limply, like sails when the air was still. Elinor lifted the canvas middle, which was stiff and heavy and did not look comfortable, then found the end of the ropes and began trying to loop them over the second hook. *Never mind being able to string it up, I do not believe I will ever get it back into that bundle. And Captain Crawford said no special treatment. I wonder if my dislike of him can possibly increase.*

Fischer pushed the door open with his foot. He held a pile of clothing that had not been folded and, atop that, a pair of clunky shoes and a floppy, wide-brimmed hat, all of which Elinor eyed with distaste. "Here you are, uh, Miss," he said, thrusting the pile at Elinor. Then he noticed the tangle of hammock and brightened. "Do you need help with that?"

"Would you please, Mr. Fischer? I have done my best, but I'm afraid this is my first time slinging a hammock."

Fischer showed her how to tie a secure knot and fix it to the hook. "I'll help you stow it in the morning. If there's nothing else?"

"No, thank you, Mr. Fischer." So he was at ease when it came to matters nautical. Maybe he could be convinced to think of her in that light, poor awkward man—she was merely a weapon now, as much a part of *Glorious'* arsenal as her cannons. "Good night."

Fischer nodded at her and closed the door behind himself. Elinor set her pile of new clothes on the hammock, which promptly swung and dumped them all on the splintery deck. Sighing, she picked them up one at a time and laid them gingerly across the canvas. It looked as though her uniform was a compromise between the commissioned officers' dress and that of the warrant officers, and she sensed Durrant's disdain for Scorchers in that decision to make them neither one nor the other.

There were trousers, not knee breeches like the lieutenants wore; a white shirt more finely woven than she expected; a waistcoat that would probably turn out to be too large; shoes that were *definitely* too large; and, of course, the floppy hat, its brim shapeless and the inside of its crown stained with what she hoped was salt water. She picked at it and turned up no lice nor nits nor other fauna that would love to transfer themselves to her head. Since she had forgotten her parasol back on *Athena*, and Crawford would no doubt have forbidden her to use it at any rate, this would have to suffice.

There was also a thin, red wool blanket, worn to the point of transparency in places, and a pillow that *did* have undesirable creatures crawling in it. She tossed it to one side, wondering if there were a way to burn the insects out without incinerating the pillow.

She folded her new wardrobe as neatly as she could, then slipped out of her gown and chemise and put on her nightdress before laying the new clothes atop her trunk. Then she turned her attention to the hammock. The canvas was stained, but (when she put her nose almost against it) did not stink of urine or anything else unpleasant.

She took a deep breath, turned her back on the hammock, took hold of the ropes on either side and tried to hoist herself into it. It rolled away from her and she slid, landing hard on her feet, her nightgown rucking up beneath her. She straightened it and tried again. And again. It took a dozen attempts before she held, jumped, and found herself seated in the canvas cradle—then promptly fell out again when she tried to turn herself sideways.

Ten more tries saw her lying gingerly lengthwise, her feet dangling. Slowly, afraid the hammock might realize what she was doing and dump her out again, she pulled her legs in and lay stiffly, motionless, only relaxing after several minutes passed and she had not fallen out.

Then she realized she had left her blanket in the corner.

She breathed deeply, willing her frustration and anger to seep away, then rolled out of the hammock, retrieved the blanket, and hopped back into her new bed without any trouble. The idea that she might have mastered what was surely second nature to even the rawest seaman eased the fury she could not quite rid herself of. She shifted an inch at a time until she rested completely within the hammock and had the blanket spread over herself. The ship's motion imparted a gentle rocking to the hammock, more noticeable than that of her bed, that was actually quite pleasant.

She lay, listening to the murmuring and occasional laughter of the officers outside her door, breathing in the familiar smell of warm, damp wood that characterized the mess deck on *Athena*, and the ridiculous tears she had been battling all evening slid down her cheeks until she wiped them ruthlessly away. This was temporary. Ramsay would resolve it. He might even have the problem solved before *Glorious* set sail in the morning. *But suppose he does not? Suppose the First Lord will not see him?* More tears. She hated her weakness. Crying would solve nothing. One ship was very like another, and she would be able to use her talent against the enemy no matter what ship she happened to be on. She and Crawford might even become friends.

She needed to stop lying to herself.

She extinguished the lantern and lay in the warm darkness, enjoying the movement of the hammock and the unintelligible murmur of voices that was as good as a lullaby, and eventually drifted off to sleep.

CHAPTER 14

IN WHICH ELINOR IS NO LONGER
THE ONLY SCORCHER

The sound of bells and the thunder of running feet jerked Elinor awake, and she had to grab hold of her hammock to keep from falling hard to the floor. Someone pounded against the wall near her canvas door. "Breakfast!" the man called.

Elinor squeezed her eyes shut to clear the confusion from her head. She was on *Glorious*. She was assigned to Crawford's special Scorcher unit. She was supposed to dress in trousers. She rolled out of the hammock, stumbling only a little, and set the lantern burning. No, it had not all been a horrible dream; she was still in her cube of a room on *Glorious*.

She stripped off her nightgown and dressed in her new clothes. Buttoning the flap of the trousers was more complicated than she had imagined, but other than that, men's clothing proved to be much easier to don than her gown and certainly easier than struggling into her boned chemise. She crammed her hat onto her head, slipped into her own shoes—the ones Fischer had provided felt like leather boxes on her feet—and stood for a moment, eyes closed, trying to relax. With her breasts flattened by the heavy fabric of her too-large waistcoat and her legs on display for the world to see, she felt humiliated—was this part of Crawford's plan, to keep her unbalanced so she would be more amenable to his commands? She felt as if she were about to step out of this room wearing nothing but her shift. She rubbed her hands over her legs, comforted by the rough, thick fabric that was certainly not that of her undergarments, took a few more deep breaths, and opened the door.

There were fewer officers at table that morning than the previous night, and only half of them looked up at her entrance. One of them stood and silently offered her a bowl and nudged a large spoon resting in a pot of burgoo. She had never had it before, though she had seen the men aboard *Athena* eat it, but she helped herself to a small serving and was then surprised when the same man scooped more of the gloopy mess into her bowl. "You'll be hungry later," he said in a gruff voice, and sat down and began shoveling burgoo into his mouth as if afraid someone might try to take it from him.

Elinor sat and began eating more daintily. It was gluey and bland, slightly salty, studded here and there with sultanas plump from their long immersion in the thick paste. She ate and tried not to think of the breakfast she would be having at ho—on *Athena*, and wondered that she had ever found Dolph's antagonism unpleasant. The silence in which these men ate was oppressive and made it hard for her to choke down her food.

When only a few spoonfuls remained in her bowl, Fischer appeared in the doorway and said, "Miss Pembroke, the captain would like to see you now."

Elinor gratefully abandoned her bowl and followed him up the stairs to the main deck, where they were met by an elderly man wearing glasses attached to a tape that went round his neck, coming down from above. He looked Elinor up and down, his brow furrowed, then shrugged and pushed ahead of Fischer to enter the great cabin before them.

It was a grey morning, the sun's light diffused by heavy clouds that made the great cabin dim enough that the lanterns had been lit. Crawford sat on the three-sided settee exactly as he had the previous evening, as if he had never left it. He had a low table in front of him and was reading documents, signing some of them and sorting them into neat piles on the seat to his right. He ignored their entrance, and

Fischer did not attempt to get his attention, so Elinor assumed he was aware of their presence and was simply demonstrating his authority over them.

Elinor covertly examined the old man, who'd walked to the window and was staring out, his hands clasped behind his back. Could this be another Scorcher? She had yet to meet one in person; encountering someone in combat did not count. The man's hair was grey and receded from his forehead, giving the impression of a whale rising from the deeps. He wore the same kind of clothing Elinor had been given, though his waistcoat was buttoned lopsidedly and was dark grey where hers was tan.

The door opened again, admitting two more men, also dressed as she was. One might have been younger than Elinor; his bright orange hair stood up in back, making Elinor itch to offer him a hairbrush. The other was middle-aged, with a paunch and thick jowls and chestnut-brown sideburns that threatened to engulf them. Both of them stared at Elinor, though the young man quickly turned away, and the older man pursed his lips as if in calculation. Elinor watched him warily. He looked and moved like someone with so much self-assurance it did not even occur to him that anyone might disagree with his opinions—no, that he did not consider himself to have opinions so much as make statements that were always, invariably true. She knew that look well. She had seen it on her father more times than she could count.

"Well," Crawford said, finally raising his head, "let's take a look at you."

The old man turned away from the window and fixed his spectacles on his nose, but made no move to join them. Crawford took no notice of it. "Admiral Durrant thinks you four are the best at what you do, and he's assigned you to this ship as an experiment with new tactics." He stood and walked past them to run his finger along the sheath of one of the swords on the wall, then turned around to face them. Elinor kept her gaze on him, but was aware the jowly man's attention was still on her, and it made her nervous. *He's not your father,* she told herself, *he has no power over you. He is only another Scorcher and not an Extraordinary at that.*

"Our fleet has established a system of confidential agents in cities throughout the islands that we believe harbor pirates," Crawford went on. "Each of these Speakers has a direct connection to Admiralty House to report the arrival of any pirate ship, along with any information he can gather about its crew, weaponry, and with luck, weaknesses. Those reports will be passed on to this ship so we can pursue whatever targets are most desirable. You four will be prepared to unleash destruction upon the foe under the direction of Fortescue, here." He waved a hand in the jowly man's direction, and Elinor's heart pounded more fiercely. "I expect you to follow his instructions and not waste my time looking to me or my officers for help. Any questions?"

He did not sound as if he actually welcomed questions, but the orange-haired man put up a timid hand and said, "Captain, are we to destroy all the ships?"

"Do you have a problem with that, Thatcher?"

Thatcher gulped and shook his head. "It's only that my previous captain, he wanted prizes, and..."

Crawford said, "I'll tell Fortescue when you're to take a ship, but Admiral Durrant has decided it's time to send a stronger message to these vermin, so more often than not we'll be burning the ships to the waterline. Any *other* questions?" No one spoke. "Very well. Fortescue, take your men to the gunroom and explain your tactics to them. We're sailing with the tide in two hours."

Two hours. It was still enough time for Ramsay to extricate her. Orange-haired Thatcher stood back to let Elinor pass, though the old man shouldered past her with a heavy tread as if she weren't there. She followed him and Fortescue back to the gunroom and took a seat at the table when the others did, crossing her hands neatly in her lap and sitting with her back straight and her chin high. She might be forced to dress like a man, but she could still behave with the manners of a lady.

"I hope you all realize I am sensible of the honor done me by being appointed our leader," Fortescue said, smiling with pretended humility. "I'm certain any one of us might do as well. But things are what they are, and I appreciate your deference to my instruction."

"Stop haverin' an' get to the point," the old man said, his Scottish accent thick enough that Elinor had trouble understanding him. "Ye're in charge, we ken, so get to tellin' us what to do already."

"If you want to put it that way, Ross, but I'd prefer to think of us as a coalition of equals."

Ross snorted and scowled at the surface of the table. Fortescue's smile didn't falter. "Since none of us have worked together before, I suggest we begin by sharing our various strengths. My ignition range is fifteen hundred feet, I can burn an area of three hundred square feet, and I can maintain my talent for half an hour before becoming exhausted. Ross?"

Ross scowled again and removed his glasses. He pulled out the tail of his shirt and began polishing them. "Twelve hundred feet, area five hundred square, twenty minutes."

Elinor and Thatcher exchanged glances. "I—" Thatcher ducked his head. "I can reach two thousand feet, and I think my area is about five hundred. I usually get exhausted before an hour is up."

Elinor took a deep breath. This was rather exciting, actually, discussing her talent with…colleagues, they must be. "I am afraid I cannot oblige you gentlemen," she said. "I am not certain of the extent of my talent. I know my range is at least two-thirds of a mile and I have never yet become exhausted from wielding fire. And the area I can set alight… what is the area of a main topgallant sail?"

Fortescue's expression had gone so blank his face might have been frozen. Thatcher said, "That's about eleven hundred square feet," in a faint voice.

"Then it is at least that much. Again, I apologize, gentlemen, but I have fought in only four battles to date. I hope I will not be too much of a burden." *I hope I will not fight beside you at all.*

"We will…make allowances for your inexperience, Pembroke," Fortescue said. He cleared his throat. Ross snorted, sounding amused. "I think we'll depend more on your extinguishing fires than starting them, at any rate. Our tactics are simple: direct fires at the deck and sailors to cause confusion, burn the sails if they haven't been treated—"

"I beg your pardon, Mr. Fortescue—"

"Fortescue, Pembroke. Let's have some comradeship here."

"Very well...Fortescue...I apologize if this is foolish, but can you not burn the treated sails?"

Fortescue gave her a patronizing smile that almost made her recoil, it looked so much like her father's. "The purpose of treating the sails is to prevent us from burning them, Pembroke. We do have our limits, you know. Even you."

Elinor waged a brief battle within herself, weighed the pro of making their tactics as strong as possible versus the con of looking offensively conceited, and said, "Actually, I have burned treated sails. It takes some effort, but the result is quite gratifying."

"Not possible," Fortescue said.

Elinor smiled sweetly at him. "I would hardly make such a claim were I not able to prove it, would I? If you can procure us a length of canvas and some of the retardant compound, I can demonstrate."

Fortescue looked as if he'd eaten something bitter with too many legs. "I would like to see you do this," he said. "I am not doubting you, of course, but it seems unlikely. And I have been in many more battles than you, my dear."

Hah. That "coalition of equals" is more a convenient fiction for you, is it not?
"Of course. And if I can teach you the secret, that will give us one more weapon they cannot defend against, correct?"

The bitter thing with too many legs was trying to climb back out of Fortescue's stomach. "Indeed. But I expect you, Pembroke, to focus on extinguishing fires and protecting the ship. Burning sails is secondary. Your...unique talent will be our secret weapon."

"I understand, Fortescue." So. Thatcher was nervous, Ross was surly, and Fortescue was arrogant. Elinor sent up a silent prayer that Ramsay would rescue her quickly.

꧁꧂

GLORIOUS LEFT THE DOCK ON SCHEDULE WITH NO WORD NOR appearance from anyone connected with *Athena*. Elinor stood at the stern, where she could barely see her beloved ship past all the other ones in the harbor, and prayed that a miracle would occur, that Stratford would appear on the horizon and snatch her up or Ramsay would step onto the deck and demand her return.

Nothing happened.

A week passed, and Elinor heard nothing from *Athena*. Of course, how could she? Stratford likely didn't know the signature for *Glorious'* Bounding chamber, and she didn't even know who Crawford's Speaker was or if Beaumont knew him well enough to Speak to him. Crawford was certainly not interested in including her in his plans; she was just the Scorcher whose talent would advance his career and make Ramsay look weak. She had forgotten to bring any books, and Crawford was no reader. The other officers showed no interest in making friends, and her fellow Scorchers, when they assembled, talked mainly of their talents and practiced setting fires Elinor extinguished.

She divided her time between her narrow, stifling cube and the deck, trying to find places where she would be out of the way of the sailors. Eventually she drifted into an empty spot on the forecastle near the bow, between the main stay rigging and the fore shrouds, and this became her accustomed place; the sailors never seemed to mind her presence, though they did walk wide of her, and she stood for hours looking out over the sea, thinking of nothing in particular. There were no mirrors on board, or at least none the officers were inclined to share with her, but she could see her hands growing brown and was certain her face, despite the shading brim of her hat, was doing the same.

She told herself she was not watching for *Athena* to come sailing over the horizon. After five days, it was true.

On the tenth day they had their first battle, a tepid affair in which she did nothing but swat fireballs out of the air. They burned and shattered the pirate ship and let it sink into the ocean, but it was not until Fortescue began recounting the events of the battle and making suggestions for improvement that Elinor felt her conscience wake up. She had no regrets for the deaths of those pirates—she had by now heard some of the stories Ramsay had alluded to, and they terrified and sickened her—but she thought she should at least feel *something*, some acknowledgement that she had taken lives, even indirectly. She wished desperately that she could talk to Ramsay about it. *You will probably never see him again,* she realized, and the thought left an aching, gnawing pain in the middle of her chest.

They fought two more battles during the third week, the first of which took over three hours and forced Elinor to take an active role when her colleagues reached the end of their endurance. When *Glorious* finally managed to smash the pirate's mainmast and board the ship to slaughter the crew—Durrant's orders were that they take no prisoners except any of the Brethren leaders they might find—Elinor was still fresh and invigorated, her blood pulsing with fire and the urge to turn the captured ship into a funeral pyre.

Then she met Fortescue's eye and felt as if he'd extinguished her. He was angry, he was jealous, and he was embarrassed all at once, and although he tried not to show it, Elinor had too much experience reading her father's expressions not to know what was going on inside her putative commander's head. She pretended not to see anything amiss and behaved matter-of-factly when they discussed the battle and how they might improve their strategy.

"I think, um, Pembroke ought to attack more often," Thatcher said as they gathered around the gunroom table, all of them with their allotted mugs of grog or rum, though Elinor never drank hers. "We might end our battles more quickly."

"Pembroke did excellent work today, but I think she's still better suited to defending the ship," Fortescue said, raising his cup to Elinor but not bothering to disguise the animosity in his eyes. "Unless you've discovered an Extraordinary talent, Thatcher?"

Thatcher ducked his head, rubbed his hands on his trousers, and said, "You're right."

Ross drank down his rum in a couple of quick gulps, blinked hard, and said, "I dinnae think we should all be attackin' at once. We cannae depend on Pembroke to press the attack if we're spent before the battle's won."

"I agree. We will spread out our attacks, take turns and perhaps extend our endurance that way. And possibly Pembroke can take a turn to give us all a breather, eh?"

Elinor nodded her agreement, but Fortescue's seeming concession did not fool her at all. He had no intention of allowing her to take the glory, as he saw it, of burning a ship to the waterline. She was ashamed of resenting their victories because they made Crawford look success- ful. It should not matter who defeated the pirates, because a victory for Crawford was a victory for the fleet. But she could not convince herself of that.

Four weeks, and they were running short on supplies, particularly fresh water. Crawford ordered them to set sail for Port Royal, which prodded Elinor out of the dull apathy she found herself in most days. She had heard so many stories about the former pirate haven and about the earthquake that had devastated the town in 1692 and turned it into a series of islands. The Royal Navy had built docks there, where they could observe any ship coming into Kingston, and it was at Port Royal that the Navy hanged pirates and left them in chains, dangling high where passing ships, many of them pirates, could see the fate of anyone who raised the black flag against Britain. It would be pleasant to go into Kingston, see the sights for an hour or two, anything to get her off *Glorious* and, possibly, back into a gown for even a little while.

"—until further notice," Crawford was saying as she came up the companionway and passed near the wheel, where he was having a low-voiced conversation with the helmsman. They both paused and looked at her, their faces blank and unwelcoming, but Elinor forged ahead anyway.

"Captain, if I may ask, will we be allowed to go ashore at Port Royal?"

Crawford smiled, a nasty expression. "There's not much to do at the docks, Pembroke."

"Then Kingston. I would enjoy taking an hour's walk on land."

"I think not."

His dismissal was so abrupt Elinor was goaded into forgetting he held her future in his hands. "Why not, Captain? I have no doubt you will allow the men some short time ashore. At least you know I will not become drunk or consort with loose women."

"I can't protect you ashore. And I'm not going to tell off one of my officers to do so."

"Then I will go with the other Scorchers."

"They won't want to be responsible for you either. You can stay on the ship and play lookout like you always do. What do you expect to see, on the horizon? Ramsay sailing in to snatch you away?"

Elinor gaped. "I beg your pardon, Captain?"

Crawford turned and stumped up to the quarterdeck, forcing Elinor to follow him. "He'd do it if he thought he could get away with it," he said. "He'd do almost anything if it would bring him glory. Selfish of him, really, trying to keep you on his poky little ship."

"That is not true. And *Athena* is not poky, whatever you mean by that."

"Come now, Pembroke, you were on the ship long enough to know *Glorious* outguns and outsails her. The Navy is much better served by having you here."

"Where I can play my part in covering *you* with glory?"

"I care only about serving king and country, Pembroke. *I* am not the one who foolhardily attacked a squadron of six pirate ships to make the admiral look bad."

"That is not what happened!"

Crawford shrugged. "I've known Miles Ramsay for years now, and I assure you his reputation within the Royal Navy is that of an ambitious, cocksure glory-hound who's won success more by luck than by skill. Consider yourself fortunate you're serving on *Glorious* now— Ramsay might have got you killed in one of his mad plans."

"And I assure *you*, Captain," Elinor said, forgetting all caution, "that I recognize jealousy when I see it. Captain Ramsay is no more a glory-hound than you are a...a gentleman. I have no doubt his successes taste like ash in your mouth because you know he will always be ten times the officer you are. At least he did not have to go running to Admiral Durrant as you did, looking for an advantage that would guarantee you success because your own abilities were insufficient!"

Crawford's mouth had fallen open, and now he was furious. "You *shrew*," he said, "I ought to have you flogged, and damn the consequences!"

"Beat an Extraordinary under your command? There would be consequences indeed!"

"*Get out of my sight,*" Crawford grated, raising his hand as if to slap her.

Elinor stood firm and met his gaze unflinchingly. Her own hand curled into a fist; arguing with her commanding officer she might get away with, but bringing her talent to bear on him might actually get her hanged, Extraordinary or not. Crawford abruptly turned away and strode to the taffrail, gripping it with both hands as if he intended to wrest it free and beat her to death with it.

Elinor, not hurrying, descended below and went to her cube, where she sat on her trunk and tried to calm herself. She was a fool. Ramsay did not need her to defend him to that sniveling, jealous *lump*. She would succeed only in bringing trouble down upon herself.

She leaned back against the thin partition that separated her cube from the next, closed her eyes, and concentrated on her breathing, in and out, in rhythm with her heartbeat. After several breaths she was relaxed enough to slip into a reverie, a familiar and comforting daydream in which she was having supper with the officers aboard *Athena*, and Beaumont made a joke that made Ramsay's lips quirk in that little smile of his, and she missed them all *so much*—

Someone pounded on her door. "Pembroke! Dinner!"

She wearily stood and tidied her hair. She would need to stay out of Crawford's way for a while. She could not bring herself to apologize to him, but perhaps time would let them both pretend nothing had been said. Perhaps.

After the noon meal, she risked going up on deck again and taking her place at the starboard rail. Ahead to starboard was one of the little islands, most of them unmapped, that sprang from the waters of the Caribbean like hillocks, verdant as every other scrap of land in this part of the world. Farther ahead there was another ship, the size of a fly skimming the water, sailing in their direction. She looked around; no one seemed worried about it.

"Shouldn't we be prepared for the possibility that it is a pirate?" she asked one of the sailors. He spat over the side, but grinned at her in a friendly way.

"Naught to worry about," he said. "Flyin' our colors. Matched our numbers. Cap'n's set a course for 'er."

"But... could it not be a ruse?"

"Nah, it's one 'o ourn," he said. "Fourth-rate like *Glorious*. Could be

Sandringham or *Breton*. We'll know when we can see 'er rigging. We'll stop along 'er and get the news."

"Oh," Elinor said, and went back to watching the oncoming ship, trying not to let hope take hold of her. Whatever ship this was, it would not miraculously bring orders that would free her from Crawford's command and put her back on *Athena* where she belonged. No, it would provide an hour's diversion, and then they would continue to Port Royal.

Not for the first time did she wish Durrant would give over his strategy of picking off the pirate ships one at a time and instead put his efforts toward finding and eradicating the Brethren's lair. If they could eliminate the leaders, it would break the back of the pirate consortium, and the Navy could easily defeat the rest. And then she could... what could she do? Go home? Receive her payment and set up a new life for herself?

For the first time, she realized she had never considered what her new life might be. If the First Lord kept his promise, she would have financial independence, even if on a small scale, but what else was there for her? Marriage, on her own terms? A business? She would likely fill her hours with the same tedious things she had left behind. No. She wanted more than that, but what kind of more it might be she could not say.

Minutes passed, and the ship slid closer. Elinor yawned and settled her hat more firmly on her head. She wanted to take a nap, but inertia kept her rooted to the rail, reluctant to leave until she'd seen what the ship brought with it. They were close enough now that she could see the British flag flying over it. She tilted her head back and squinted to look at *Glorious'* flag. They were flying signal flags as well as their kingdom's. It would be interesting to learn the signals, though Crawford would certainly refuse to teach her.

She leaned heavily against the rail and watched the approaching ship. Soon they would send up their own signal flags, responding to whatever message *Glorious* had sent. Soon... no, that was wrong. They should have sent up signals immediately. But the crewman had said the number signals were correct...

Elinor looked around; still no one seemed worried. It must be her mistake. Even so... She left her position and went to the companion-way. She could at least tell Fortescue they might need to be ready for an attack.

Thunder pounded from the clear sky, and Elinor was knocked to the deck as it heaved and cracked around her. Splinters filled the air, jabbing her legs and back and tangling in her hair. Thunder again, and something pierced her sleeve and sent a jolt of agony down her left arm. She reached up in a daze and tore a six-inch-long sharp, jagged sliver of wood from her arm and stared at it dully. She felt as if she were underwater, her limbs moving slowly, her ears numb and throbbing with her pulse. The sharp stink of gunpowder filled the air.

She raised her head, then staggered to her feet. Men lay bleeding all around her, their mouths open as if they were crying or screaming for help; she still heard nothing but the pounding of her blood. The enemy ship sailed past to starboard, cannons protruding from its sides like hungry mouths, smoke trailing from some of them. In the silence, it all seemed like a nightmare, something from which she would soon awake.

Then the starboard rail went up in flames, and Elinor felt as if she *were* waking, but from one nightmare into another. She extinguished the blaze and saw it break out elsewhere, again and again, always somewhere new as if their Scorcher were taunting her.

"Get Fortescue up here *now!*" she screamed at no one, anyone, and tried to regain her focus. They needed to press the attack, and that needed all four of them, because this enemy Scorcher was clever and cruel and Elinor wanted more than anything to find him and turn him to ash. She put out yet another fire, spared a grateful thought that he apparently did not know how to burn a treated sail, tried to manage a fireball but had to let it collapse when the capstan started burning.

"Stand back, Pembroke," said Fortescue, and raised his hands; he loved the drama of gesturing, and encouraged them all to do it, but Elinor never remembered. Across the gap, where the enemy ship had begun to maneuver around *Glorious* for another raking broadside, a section of the deck started to burn. Thatcher moved astern to cover the waist amidships, which meant Ross, whom she could not see, was most likely angling around to the bow.

Then the fire went out.

A second later, fire blazed on *Glorious's* deck as Fortescue turned into a screaming pillar of flame. Elinor, reacting without thinking, extinguished it, and Fortescue collapsed, still screaming. The capstan began burning again. Elinor ignored it and set the entire enemy deck on fire. *It has to be a mistake. Fortescue did it wrong.*

There was a moment in which fire wreathed the other ship's deck, and then the fire vanished. Elinor put out the capstan fire, her heart thudding painfully. "No gestures!" she screamed, and crouched and moved forward to help Fortescue, who seemed more shocked and terrified than injured. She felt dizzy with shock herself. Not just a Scorcher. An Extraordinary Scorcher. And one far more experienced than she was. They might already be doomed.

CHAPTER 15

IN WHICH ELINOR DISCOVERS
ANOTHER EXTRAORDINARY AND
HAS A VERY LONG SWIM

Fortescue's face was blackened and blistered, his clothing singed, and Elinor tried not to gag at the smell of burned flesh rising off his body. "It's an Extraordinary!" she screamed at him, guessing his near-immolation had prevented him realizing what they faced. Fortescue's eyes were wide and his breath came in quick, short pants, and he seemed not to understand what she said. Elinor shook him, failed to get a rational response, and let go of his shirt-front, allowing him to fall backward to the deck. This was her battle.

She could understand nothing of the screams and shouts that filled the air on *Glorious'* deck, whether orders or cries for help, and the mad scrambling over the rigging and the sails shifting to bring the ship about made no sense to Elinor as she extinguished one fire after another. All she could tell was that the enemy had the wind, and that was bad for *Glorious*.

Smaller fires erupted on the pirate ship's deck, each going out as quickly as they appeared. If that Scorcher could extinguish fires as he simultaneously ignited them... *Don't panic. You're as strong as he is. Maybe stronger. Think.* However capable he was of doing two things at once, his fires were much smaller than hers, so either he could not manage a large fire while dividing his attention, or he was not capable of

186

anything larger. *If he could set a larger fire, he would do so. Take the fight to him.*

Elinor staggered as *Glorious* shifted, turned hard to starboard and began a perpendicular pass, something Ramsay called "crossing the bow" and had explained could be a particularly devastating attack. As their guns began pounding the pirate ship, Elinor ignored the fires burning on *Glorious* and *leaned* on the pirate's sails, feeling an ache pass through her as if she were pushing hard on a door someone else stood behind, pushing back. Then she was through, and all four of the main-sails went up in that beautiful green-blue flame. *How many square feet is that? And I know I could do more.*

The green fire flickered, tried to disappear, then returned, not quite as full-strength as before, but still burning brightly. Elinor extinguished the remaining fires on *Glorious*'s deck. No new ones arose. "Attack the deck!" she shouted at Thatcher, who was the only Scorcher she could see. Fortescue was gone, crawled or carried away, and Ross might be behind a tangle of fallen beams where the top of the foremast had fallen, dragging several sailors with it. She had no time to discover his location.

To her dismay, the enemy Scorcher continued to dismiss Thatcher's fires before they could do any damage. The green fires were flickering faster now, and Elinor pressed harder, feeling now as if she were fighting the Scorcher directly, the two of them matching wills, first one gaining headway, then the other. Sweat was running into her eyes and her spine was a streak of agony worse than the spear of wood that had gone most of the way through her arm, and—

—her fire went out.

She collapsed on hands and knees, breathing heavily, feeling as if her spine had been shattered into sharp-edged pieces that ground against each other, stones tearing her flesh. No new fires blossomed on *Glorious*'s deck; perhaps the enemy Scorcher was as exhausted as she was.

The thump of cannons warned her just in time to throw her arms over her head, then another blast of splinters struck her, none as large as the first, but stinging like nettles. She heard more screaming, and pleas for help, and she looked around to see that most of the starboard rail and all of its netting were gone, tangled and hanging over the side of the ship. Thatcher lay nearby, eyes blank and staring, his left arm ripped away and his left leg crushed under the weight of more fallen timbers. Elinor stuffed her fist in her mouth to keep from crying out, or vomiting, or whatever reaction her stricken body might produce.

She looked around and still could not see Ross, though the clouds of smoke rolling across the deck might simply obscure him from sight. *Or he's run.* She forced herself upright against the pain and waved her hands in front of her face, vainly trying to clear the fog away. Flashes of light in the distance signaled more incoming cannonballs, but they whistled overhead, one puncturing the mainsail above her head. *Glorious* was closing the distance between herself and the pirate ship, and surely that was madness, giving their enemy a better opportunity to pound them again. Or did Crawford think they stood a better chance boarding and fighting hand to hand?

A fire, small and weak, erupted near the bow, and Elinor wearily dismissed it. If only she could find that Scorcher... She tried to produce a fire of her own and cried out at the sharp crack of agony that shot down her back. No. She would not be defeated so easily.

She concentrated, telling herself this was nothing, the pain was all in her mind, and this time she summoned a fireball and felt a dull ache rather than a spike. She sent her fire spinning across the gap and saw men fling themselves aside as it lit the grey clouds surrounding them.

No, not all the men. One figure stood, illuminated briefly by her fire, and merely ducked as the ball of fire brushed past him. Quickly, before she could lose sight of him, she set him on fire and then was engulfed herself in crackling, smoking flames. They hurt only briefly, and then her mind remembered she could not be burned and extinguished them before her clothing could do more than smolder. The enemy Scorcher had done the same, and now had disappeared into the fog, or perhaps it was she who had disappeared; the wind had died down, and the ships were sluggishly maneuvering about one another, occasionally exchanging volleys that rarely struck their targets.

Elinor moved across the deck, her eyes stinging from the bitter residue of gunpowder that filled her nose and her eyes and her mouth when she was so incautious as to open it to breathe more deeply. It tasted the way it smelled, bitter and acrid and smoky all at once, and she spat to clear her mouth, then spat again when the first time didn't work. That Scorcher was still over there somewhere, and while he might be immune to fire as she was, she could still keep him distracted. She had no idea how the battle was going, no idea how much damage the two ships had sustained, but since the enemy was still afloat, it was still her duty to destroy it.

A fireball came flying out of the dimness, aimed somewhere over her head. *Fool.* She threw a somewhat more accurate missile of her own and then found herself once again engulfed in flame, which she put out immediately, then stumbled along the deck toward the stern as another fireball struck where she had been standing. Apparently the Scorcher was not the only fool.

Elinor gave up hunting for him and struck out at the sails again; the fire burned a green beacon that, a minute later, *Glorious'* gun crews took advantage of. Elinor watched the fire, too tired to do anything more, and soon after the Scorcher extinguished it. This was not a battle of power but of endurance. Which of them would collapse first? She felt as if her back were burning, an impossibility, but there was no other word to describe the pain that tried to make her bend double to get away from it.

There was so much noise she could hardly concentrate: the pounding of the cannons, the creaking of the sails, the cracking of wood pushed past the breaking point to explode with deadly force, the screams of dying men, and the shouts, faint now, of someone calling out in the tones of one giving orders. If she could see the pirate ship, she might be able to burn the rigging; sailors rarely treated the rigging because the fire retardant compound made the ropes sticky and dangerous at temperatures higher than seventy degrees.

She picked her way past the obstacles littering the deck, stumbled when someone grabbed at her ankle pleading for water, and went to look out across the sea toward the pirate ship, that beautiful fourth-rate Navy ship that had been pressed into service to confuse its previous owners—and, thanks to Crawford's incompetence, had succeeded. She did not know which side of the ship she was on, she was so muddled with pain and noise and confusion, but a flash of light and the scream of another cannonball told her the enemy was out there, somewhere close.

Glorious shot off another volley which seemed to do nothing. The pirates returned fire, and then *Glorious* lurched and shuddered, knocking Elinor forward and over the rail. She screamed and clawed her way back aboard, tearing her nails and the palms of her hands, and lay pressed flat to the deck, her heart racing. The ship lurched again, and then the deck was a slope and Elinor had to press herself into the planks harder because her body was trying to slide headfirst toward— she was still confused, was it the bow or the stern that was sinking?

Sinking. *Glorious* was sinking.

Elinor dragged herself around to face uphill, got to her hands and knees and crawled. The slope was not yet so great as to throw her backward, but it was a struggle to move forward in her exhausted, pain-wracked state. Crawling was the only thing left to her. She had no doubt the survivors would cluster at the bow (or the stern) and the ship's Bounder would carry them to safety. She could crawl that far.

She forced her arms and legs to keep moving, climbed over dead and dying bodies that reeked of blood and gunpowder, realized she was crying tears of pain and shook her head to dash them away. The *Glorious* continued to settle into the water, creaking more loudly now as if crying out for someone to help her, but there was no one to save the ship any more than there were people to save the dying crewmen who would instead spend their final moments fighting to keep the seawater out of their lungs.

The starboard steps to the quarterdeck loomed out of the dimness at her, and she took a moment to orient herself: stern, starboard side, the wheel somewhere to her right. Her vision went black, briefly, and she clung to the steps and tried to breathe without choking until the dizzy sensation passed. Then she dragged herself up the steps, bent double trying to get away from the sharp pain radiating up her spine. The screaming fell away behind her, replaced by the sound of someone talking at almost a normal volume. Momentary confusion gave way to recognition; it was Crawford, several feet ahead of her, giving someone directions.

She tried to stand, fell on her face, and went back to her hands and knees. "Captain, help me!" she cried out, but she could not speak loudly enough that even she could hear herself. She tried again, drawing in a deep breath and almost screaming the words as she dragged herself forward.

The misty gunpowder clouds had begun to clear now that both ships had stopped firing, and Elinor could clearly see Crawford's face, his blond hair in disarray and blood matting his scalp and forehead. There were only two other men standing near him, and as she watched the first took the second by the waist and disappeared. Elinor breathed in a sigh of relief, then choked and hacked to get the grit out of her lungs. The sound finally drew Crawford's attention. His eyes widened, but otherwise he showed no reaction to her appearance nearly at his feet.

"Captain, please help me stand," she said, balancing on one hand to reach the other toward him.

"Of course," he said, but made no move toward her.

The first man came staggering up the companionway, trying not to fall over with exhaustion. He did not notice Elinor. Crawford slung his arm around the Bounder, still looking at Elinor with that unreadable expression, and then they were gone.

Elinor waited. The Bounder did not return. She dragged herself higher on the stern, clung to the taffrail, thought, *He's not coming back*, and looked down to where the waves were barely visible. *He's not coming back.*

Her mind went blank, shut down briefly by a combination of pain and weariness and fear and fury at Crawford, the...the *bastard*, whose hatred of her was so great he would let her die on his abandoned ship. Weren't captains supposed to go down with their ships? No, that seemed unreasonable, but then neither was it reasonable that he might leave behind someone not even mortally wounded. Yet he had.

And she had to get off this ship.

She had a vague memory that simply waiting for a ship to sink beneath the waves and then swimming away was unsafe, though she could not remember why. Possibly the debris would batter her. That brought up another problem: she could not swim. But she would have to learn how quickly, because being captured by the pirates...she knew what they would do to her, doubly damned because she was in the Navy and a woman, and drowning would be a preferable death. So she had to find something that would allow her to float and try to swim away from both ships under cover of this fog before the pirates realized she was there and came after her.

She half slid, half crawled back down the slope of the deck, frantically casting about for something that would float. Well, the ship was made of wood, and wood floated, so she simply needed to find a piece of wood large enough to bear her weight that had been blown free during the fight.

She kicked at planks and found nothing loose, nothing bigger than the sliver of wood she'd dug out of her arm. Remembering that set the wound to aching, and she reached up to touch the spot on her left arm; it was bleeding, but not heavily, and she pressed down on it until she had to let go to use both arms to climb over a pile of rope.

She reached the place where the starboard rail had been blown away and looked over the edge. The sea was far too close now, perhaps ten feet from where she stood. *Glorious* had turned so the enemy ship was on the larboard side, so all she saw was debris floating on the waves, dim in the rapidly dissipating gunpowder clouds. There was the dangling netting, half of it now floating on the waves, hundreds of splinters, a few bobbing planks too small to support her, and, several feet from the ship, a slightly curved section of hull planking about five feet square, though a lopsided square.

Elinor gripped what was left of the rail and leaned forward. Surely it was too distant for her to jump to? But the ship was sinking visibly now, and she had no time to find a better alternative. She backed as far as she could from the splintered gap, thanked Crawford briefly for making her wear trousers, cursed him for putting her in this position, and ran and leaped as far from the ship as she could.

The water struck her like a slap to her whole body, cold and hard, leaving her momentarily stunned. Salt water went up her nose and burned her sinuses, more water went down her throat, and she gagged once before sliding under the waves. The shock of being immersed in the Caribbean waters, of how much colder they were than she had imagined, brought her back to herself, and she thrashed with her arms and legs until her head was above the surface.

Blinking away the burning water, she cast frantically about for her salvation. She saw it only a few feet away just as she went under again. Desperate now, she kicked harder, swung her arms as if she were climbing a ladder, and found herself nearer to the planks, but they were drifting away on the waves, floating out of her reach. Panicked, she kicked out, found something hard under her foot, pushed off it and grabbed the edge of the planks with the tips of her fingers.

She pulled herself up, sobbing, and lay there, her arms outstretched to both sides gripping her makeshift raft's edges, coughing up salty brine and taking in great lungsful of air tinged only slightly with the stink of gunpowder.

She rolled over to see what her foot had found and saw a barrel, upended, bobbing away from her on the waves as if bidding her farewell. What an empty barrel was doing close enough to *Glorious'* deck to be flung free was a mystery she didn't feel like pursuing, in case God was looking out for her and might think she was ungrateful for His gift. She lay back on her raft and discovered the slight curve of its planks eased her back considerably. But she didn't have time to relax; she still had to escape the pirates.

She rolled back onto her stomach and scooted down until only her chest still rested on the raft and her hands clung to its sides. Then she began kicking. She had no direction in mind other than "away," and knew the chances of her finding land, or, miraculously, a friendly ship, were almost nonexistent, but she was determined not to die at the pirates' hands. She kicked, and kicked, and one of her shoes fell off and she discovered her kicking was more efficient if she were barefoot, so she shook her foot until the other shoe slipped loose and sank away from her.

She quickly fell into a rhythm where she kicked until her legs burned as much as her back, then rested, her mind blank, until she felt she could go on again. The waves slopped over her where she lay against the makeshift raft, and now they felt warmer, which probably meant she had grown accustomed to the temperature, and that was a small comfort. Her fingers were white and numb where she clutched the raft, so during her rest times she let go, one hand at a time, and flexed her fingers to restore circulation.

Time ceased to have meaning; there was nothing but intervals of kicking and lying limp across the soggy wood, wondering at what point she would simply slip beneath the waves, exhausted and unconscious. Did it hurt, drowning when you were asleep? After too many of these intervals to count, she left the fog behind and came out under an overcast sky; it looked as if it might rain soon. She heard no cries from the pirate ship, nothing but the slop of waves striking her raft and the stiff wind blowing across her weary body like the whistling of an invisible giant.

After some time, the wind died away and the rain began, comforting warm drops that soon became a torrent, drenching her hair and body and rinsing away the salty crust covering every inch of her. Fresh water gathered in the curve of the raft, and she lapped at it like a dog, undeterred by the slightly tarry, wooden taste imparted by the planks. Even that small draught revived her, and she kicked with greater vigor, shaking her head to clear the rain from her eyes and the hair from her face. She might yet die today, but she would not go quietly.

Through the rain, she saw a cloud that seemed to be sitting directly on the waves, greenish, thick and billowing. Curious, she angled her body to turn the raft in that direction and saw it grow larger and greener, until her fuddled brain finally recognized it as an island. It was too small to be Cuba or Jamaica, both of which were near where *Glorious* had been sailing, but it was still quite large, large enough that it might have fresh water and possibly some kind of food.

Thinking of food made Elinor realize how famished her exertions had left her. Her legs ached so much they were almost numb, her back was still a long streak of agony, her fingers were sore from clinging to the raft. But she was alive. And might continue to be so long enough for someone to rescue her.

She began kicking again, mechanically, while she thought about rescue. Crawford certainly would tell everyone she was dead. She *should* have been dead, the way he'd left her. So the Royal Navy would not be looking for her. Ramsay would—she stopped kicking and pressed her forehead into the soggy wood. This would never have happened to *Athena*. He wouldn't have allowed it. If she were—but that was a line of thinking that would take her nowhere.

She had only two hopes. One was that she might signal a passing ship. That was not unlikely; *Glorious* had been on a well-used shipping route between Saint-Domingue and Port Royal. The other was that there might be a settlement on the island, with seafaring people who might help her reach a town where she could contact the Navy. That also was not unlikely, given the size of the island. Despite her aching, battered body, she felt the beginnings of hope. She might actually survive this. And if she did, she would see Crawford hanged for what she was certain was a court-martial offense.

Her bare toes dashed against something that shifted when she touched it, and she squealed and pulled her feet up before realizing it was sand. She dug her feet in and pushed the raft the rest of the way up the soft, beautifully solid beach until she was past the high-tide mark, littered with seaweed, then she fell down on her stomach atop the raft and prayed the most fervent prayer of thanks she had ever uttered. Then, between one word and the next, she slipped into unconsciousness.

CHAPTER 16

IN WHICH ELINOR MAKES MANY
DISCOVERIES

Elinor woke at dusk to hear the clamor of birds in the nearby trees, calling out sounds she had never heard before. The wind had risen again and the susurrus of leaves blowing against one another nearly drowned out the birds' cries. She pushed herself to her knees, all her muscles shaking from her exertions. There was sand in her nose and crusting her eyelids; she brushed it away, gingerly, and blinked hard to let her tears carry away the rest. When her nose was clear she inhaled with relief at being alive.

The air was full of the scents of a hundred growing things, sweet and green and wet, and the humid post-storm air lay over her skin like a damp, warm blanket. Without the sun's rays, the humidity was easier to endure, less enervating, and she felt her strength returning and was able to stand. Unfortunately, her clothes were still damp, particularly under her armpits and the crotch of her trousers, and when she moved they chafed at her unpleasantly. Still, she was alive, and her back no longer hurt, and her legs were wobbly but strong enough to support her. She really had nothing to complain of.

She looked up the beach to where the sandy shore gave way to black rocks and eventually terminated in the beginnings of a cliff. In the other direction the sand curved away out of sight past a promontory beyond the trees, which grew in a dizzying variety—palm trees with their strange ringed bark, trees she had no name for with straight trunks and broad green leaves, and a dozen others, all growing together in a wild profusion of every shade of green.

She walked toward the tree line and shied away when her approach scared a flock of small brown and red birds out of the canopy. Their flight made a sighing sound like a gust of wind, shaking the trees as they flew away. More cautiously, she went to examine the palm trees. Some of them were coconut palms, their fruit not completely ripe, but by now her stomach was so empty she didn't care.

She walked around one of the trees, thinking. She could not climb the palm's rough trunk, shinnying up like she had seen boys do in Bermuda, and shaking the tree was like trying to shake *Athena*'s mainmast. It was getting too dark to see. She set her hand burning and held it up like a torch, peering up at the distant, shadowed squashed-round shapes, then had an idea. Carefully, she sparked a fire where the stem of one coconut was attached to the tree, then had to dart backward when, with a snapping sound, the fruit burned away from the stem and fell heavily to the ground near her feet.

Elinor snatched up her prize. Its smooth husk was only barely green and she couldn't smell the distinctive coconut aroma. She rapped on it with her knuckles and heard it echo. Now, how to open it? She walked down the beach until she reached the stony shore, then picked her way across more carefully; the stones all looked smooth, but cutting her foot on a sharp rock could be deadly, with no way of cleaning the cut. It made her wonder if the wound in her arm might not fester as well, and she pushed the thought away.

At the far end, where the rocky ridge began, was a shelf about knee-high that was below the high-tide mark, smoothed by centuries of rolling waves. She raised the coconut over her head and threw it onto the rock as hard as she could.

The coconut bounced and rolled toward the incoming tide. Elinor shrieked and dove to retrieve it, clutching it, dripping wet, to her chest. Upon examining it, she discovered a thin crack that flexed a little when she tugged at it with her fingernails. It was now dark enough that if she tried flinging it again she would almost certainly lose the coconut. Sighing, she tucked the hard round fruit under her arm and trudged back toward the palm tree, where she burned off a large frond, which she dragged back down the beach before lighting it on fire.

The crackling warmth soothed her frustration and fear, and for a moment she forgot her hunger long enough to think about lying down naked in the middle of it and letting all her worries burn away. Then she shook her head to dispel the notion. The much larger rock beside the shelf was about waist-high to her when she stood on the rounded stone, and since it was above the tide mark its top was jagged and in some places had a sharp, narrow edge like an axe head. Elinor brought the coconut high above her head and then smashed it down onto one of these edges.

This time, the crack that formed was wide enough for her to insert her fingers and pull it apart. She tore the husk away triumphantly only to discover a second, harder shell inside.

She stared at it, then, screaming, smashed it against the rock, over and over, until with a loud crack it came apart and poured a thin watery liquid all down the face of the rock. She snatched it up and sucked and licked the insides, swallowing what was left of the sweet water with relief. Then she tore at the soft, almost gelatinous innards and devoured as much of them as she could. It didn't fill her, but it eased the deepest aches in her stomach and made her think she could sleep.

No. I can't sleep. I have to send a signal.

She went back to the tree line and, in the light of the burning frond, surveyed the foliage. There were so many of them. She chose a tall one with spreading limbs and fat green leaves the size of her hand, stepped back, and set it on fire. The flames spread slowly through the living wood until the tree blazed high and bright, filling the air with clouds of smoke. It took her some effort to keep the flames from spreading to its neighbors, but eventually she found a shape for the fire that kept it isolated to that single tree. She let it burn while she poked around looking for shelter and found nothing truly suitable. Well, she would simply have to sleep in the open for one night, and in the morning she could explore further.

She swatted the fire away from a nearby palm and sat on the beach near the burning tree, marveling at its beauty. The air was filled with the smell of wood smoke and a sweet odor that had to come from the tree's unique wood. She hoped it was not something valuable—no, it would not be allowed to grow wild if someone could make a profit from it.

She caught herself nodding off and started walking to keep herself awake, rubbing her arms and hissing with pain when she rediscovered the wound in her arm. It had stopped bleeding, in part because her sleeve had stuck to it, and she tore at her sleeve until she worked it free of the shirt, wincing as it pulled away from her injury, then awkwardly bound her arm, using her teeth to help secure the knot.

She rotated her arm, testing the makeshift bandage. It reminded her of Ramsay coming into her bedchamber after the battle, his sleeve bloody, talking about killing and talent and what it all meant, and she wished he were there with her, that she were not so terribly alone. The weight of her abandonment and the terror and pain of making her way to this isolated place struck her like the rising tide, trying to crush her, and she curled in on herself and sobbed out her misery until she was empty, numb with exhaustion and ready to sleep.

She extinguished both fires, found a tree with a broad trunk and welcoming roots to curl up under, and tried to make herself comfortable. Her clothes were dry now from standing near the burning palm frond, but the night air was cool and the wind was strong enough that its constant motion over her skin irritated her. Finally, she gave up, went back down the beach and dragged her raft to her sleeping tree, crawled under it, and was finally able to sleep.

She woke to dim daylight, filtered through the overcast, and the sound of a hundred birds' wings stirring the already unpleasantly humid air. The faint odor of the previous night's fires still hung nearby, waking her hunger. She would have to find something more filling soon.

She relieved herself, feeling vaguely guilty about doing so out in the open, then set out into the forest on a hunt for food and water. She had a notion that water would be more likely found near rock than loam, so she followed the rocky ridge up and around, deeper into the forest. Almost immediately she realized she would never be able to find her way back to the beach unless she began marking her trail, and had a moment's anxiety before laughing at herself and burning a few thin lines in the shape of an arrow into the trunk of a nearby tree. Why she might want to return to the beach, she wasn't sure, but it faced north, and since she had not circled the island to come to its north shore, it was almost certainly facing into the passage between Jamaica and Cuba, where the trade ships went. So it was still her best chance of hailing a ship to rescue her.

She went further inland, marking her trail and marveling at the island's beauty. So many brash, boldly colored flowers, pink and red trumpets calling the insects home. So many birds like tiny, flying jewels that fled at her approach. So many trees smelling of greenness and water that she became thirstier with every breath.

She had to step carefully to protect her bare feet against rocks and fallen branches, but sometimes she was so caught up in the wonder of it all she forgot to be worried about her present situation. There was never silence; when the birds stopped calling out to one another, which happened only rarely, there was the rush of wind through the trees that presaged another rainstorm. She wished she'd thought to turn her raft right side up so it could catch the rain, in case she didn't find another source of water.

As she thought this, she realized what she had believed to be the soughing of the wind was actually much closer to hand, and much more liquid. Water was running somewhere ahead and to her left. She pressed on eagerly and soon found a narrow stream flowing over the rocks that had, over centuries, carved a channel out of the stone that descended down the far side of the cliff in a series of waterfalls. She dropped to her knees and began scooping the cool, delicious water into her mouth, gulping until she was so full her stomach hurt.

She wiped her chin and sat back on her haunches, her head clearer now. Water first, then food. The sailors on *Athena* always claimed no one had to starve in the Caribbean because there was food on every tree. Elinor couldn't see any at the moment, but perhaps she was simply in the wrong place. She decided to move west, away from the ridge, and circle back around to the beach.

She was beginning to see patterns to the tree growth. Palms grew near the shore. The trees with the hand-sized round leaves grew further up, and now she was seeing tall trees with low-growing limbs that in some places brushed the top of her head. Their leaves were glossy and enormous, with deep lobes, and on a whim Elinor reached up and broke one off. It was wide enough that she could use it as a makeshift hat, though from what she could see of the sky it seemed this would be another cloudy, possibly rainy day. She would need more than a single leaf to protect herself from the storm.

She peered up, trying to read the clouds, but instead saw a few pebbly green fruits hanging high above her. Breadfruit. This was a breadfruit tree! She repeated her trick with the coconut palm and soon had two green fruits the size of her head lying at her feet. One had cracked, and she picked that one up and turned it over in her hands. "Don't eat it raw," Stratford had said, "it'll only make you sick." Well, that was certainly not going to be a problem. She held it at arm's length and let fire spread across her hands to surround the rough green surface, which started blackening almost immediately.

A tremor went through her fingers as the crack spread. Now, how long was enough? She turned it over and, her hands still burning, pried open the crack to look at the meat inside. It looked charred and not at all appetizing, but she extinguished the fire and picked at the smoking meat, pulled out a piece and ate it. It tasted like burned potato, but not inedibly so, and she went at it with fingers and nails until she had cleaned out the husk. She was more careful with the second, which came out of the fire nearly perfect, and when she was finished she felt full and revitalized and able to take on any challenges this island would offer. Breadfruit leaf in hand, she continued on her way.

Once she knew what to look for, she found dozens more breadfruit trees, then a straggly clump of papayas, and she took off her waistcoat and used it to carry her stores. She now saw signs of animal life, squeaking when she realized a vine draped over a branch was an enormous snake, but it ignored her, and she gave it a wide berth. She soon became used to the scuttling of small creatures in the undergrowth when it turned out they were no more interested in her than the snake had been. Even so, she stayed alert. The next animal she encountered might be more hostile.

Rain began falling in the late afternoon, and she huddled under one of the evergreens whose branches grew close to the ground and shed a thick, soft carpet of needles that did not prick her feet as long as she was careful. She ate a papaya and planned her next step. She would have to light a bigger fire and hope someone noticed. Then she would start moving around the coast of the island and discover whether it was inhabited. That was still her most likely possibility for rescue. She dozed off under the trees to the comforting sound of rain hissing through the leaves and falling in huge drops off the branches above her.

When she returned to what she had begun to think of as her camp that evening, she was exhausted, but she found a place to put her stores and marked off an area to burn. She felt slightly guilty at destroying so many of the island's beautiful trees, but there was nothing for it if she wanted to survive. She was certain she would not be able to support herself on a diet of tropical fruit for more than a few weeks. She tried not to dwell on the word "weeks."

With her signal burning high and sending great clouds of smoke into the air, she sat on the dry, grainy sand that stuck to absolutely every part of her and marveled at the fire's beauty. There was a part of her that longed to walk into it and let it flow over her and through her. It filled her with joy, and it made her feel invincible, for what human agency could extinguish a fire that strong and hot and fierce? Well, other than herself and that enemy Extraordinary Scorcher. Fighting him had been terrifying, but she had also rejoiced in matching her talent against someone so like her in that one respect.

She resented the fact that he was a pirate. They *should* have been comrades, friends even, and she remembered what Ramsay had said about the difference between an Extraordinary and an ordinary talent. He had become her closest friend somehow, and she had no way of telling him she was alive. How wonderful it would be when she was rescued and returned to *Athena*; even Durrant could not justify giving Crawford another ship when he was responsible for destroying

Glorious, and there was no reason she should not serve with Ramsay again.

A burning palm frond dropped to the sand, followed by a sharp crack and several thuds as a handful of coconuts followed it. It would be interesting to see what coconut tasted like when it was roasted. She extinguished the frond and lay back on the sand. The sun had set after the trees had been burning for only half an hour. Which was a better signal, smoke or flame? Well, now she'd done both.

The fire made it difficult to see the stars, but she knew them well now from the times she had spent on *Athena's* deck, with Ramsay or Stratford or Hays pointing out constellations she had never thought to look for back home. When she left the Navy, she would not settle in London, where the newly installed gas lamps drew the eye away from the skies the way her bonfire did at the moment. She reached out and traced their outlines: Ursa Minor, Draco, Cassiopeia. Someone must have had quite the imagination to see such shapes in such simple outlines.

She blinked, and the stars shifted dramatically. She leaped up, terrified she would find the forest on fire, but it had barely begun to spread past her chosen area. It was time for sleep. Someone would see her beacon and come for her. Perhaps now that she had enough food, she might try a larger beacon of smoke tomorrow.

She extinguished the fire and found herself a more comfortable place to sleep, up the hill near the rocks, where an evergreen's fallen branch made a tent, and a depression on the uphill side made a perfect place for her to stow her food. She drew in her legs, pulled the raft over herself, and fell into sleep.

She woke late the following morning and lay for a few minutes, not moving, because she was comfortable for once and she knew that upon moving all of her abused muscles would complain. Her bladder eventually forced her to rise and tend to its needs, and by the time she was finished there was no point in lying down again.

She still had no way to carry water, so she set off up the hill toward the stream, where she had made a small dam with loose rocks, carried uphill in her waistcoat. Now she was able to scoop water from the pool made by the dam and drink it down without spilling more than a few drops on herself. Not that a few drops would make her look more disreputable than she did. Her clothes looked as if they'd been soaked in the waters of the Caribbean, been dragged across sand and over hills and through thickets of trees, and there was a hole in the knee of her trousers where she'd caught it on a stump of a branch. Her waistcoat was barely recognizable as such. *I am so grateful not to be wearing a gown.*

She took one last drink, wiped her mouth and stood. Toasted coconut this morning, and then a walk along the shore around the promontory to see what lay in that direction.

Rather than fight her way through the thickly-growing trees, she followed the spine of the cliff toward the beach. When she found a flat, broad place where the stone widened, she scrambled atop it to look out across the water for a sign that someone had seen her beacon. The horizon was empty of sails, and she tried to tell herself this was normal. It was to be expected that it would take some time for her signal to be noticed, and crying a few tears of disappointment was irrational, because she would be rescued soon.

She surveyed the rest of the vista, her gaze sweeping across the beach, and was staggered to see a dilapidated rowboat, green with paint or scum, pulled up on the shore some distance away. She was about to race down the hill, heedless of the possibility of falling and breaking her skull, when a tiny voice of doubt captured her attention: if there were no ship at anchor nearby, where had the boat come from?

It was enough to make her pause, then slowly, quietly sidle along until she reached her shelter. She had no reason to assume whoever had come in the boat was hostile, but she was alone and, as far as anyone could tell, defenseless, and it made sense to sit quietly and observe the newcomers before showing herself.

She heard them coming before she could see them—did not want to see them, because that would mean they could see her. Two men, she guessed by the sound of their footsteps crunching along the beach, two voices, one tenor, one baritone, carrying on a conversation she was still too distant to understand. She held tight to the evergreen's trunk to keep herself from sliding or shifting or doing anything that might draw attention.

"—take her to bed w' me tonight." That was the tenor.

"That's nothin' special. She'll spread 'er legs for anyone's got the right price." Baritone.

"I ain't payin' 'er, 'cause she's m' special lady."

"'Ope y' don't get more outa her than y' want. Wouldn't want your fav'rit part to fall off."

"You don't know what the 'ell—wait, there's tracks 'ere."

Silence, except for the scrape-crunch of footsteps on soft sand. "That's just the way the wind blew it," said Baritone. "No footprints."

"Well, there wouldn't be, would there, if the Scorcher 'uz down below the tide. Be all washed away," said Tenor. He sounded defensive.

"Never prove it if 'e did. Maybe it were sum'thin nat'ral what set the fire."

"Gave off that much smoke, and din't burn more than a handful o' trees? Evans'd never believe it."

"Well, I don't see no Scorcher and I'm thinkin' there ain't one to be seen," Baritone said, anger putting an edge on his voice. "They're all madder'n a barrel o' ferrets, maybe he sailed in, set a fire, sailed away."

"You're a bleedin' idiot, you are," said Tenor, sounding smug. " 'S an Extraordinary Scorcher what did that. The forest'd be a pile o' ash else."

Elinor found she was holding her breath and let it out, slowly. They were less than fifteen feet from her. It was a miracle they couldn't hear her heart pounding.

There was silence for about half a minute. "You think it was Dewdney?" said Baritone.

"You know any other Extraordinary Scorchers runnin' around?"

"Nobody's seen 'im since *Olympia* came in, lookin' like it was pounded on by God Himself, and Dewdney near crippled from fightin' another Extraordinary."

"Could be th' other one what done it. The Navy bastard."

"That ship went down wi' all 'ands," Baritone said. " 'Ad to be Dewdney."

Another pause. "Evans ain't gonna like that," said Tenor.

"Just so 'e don't blame it on us, I don't give a damn what he likes."

"You talk big when 'e's not around, don't you?"

"Let's get back. I ain't goin' after Dewdney on me lonesome."

"Me neither. Evans can send out the Movers or some such. Ain't rowin' no more today."

"If ol' Evans 'ad any Bounders, wouldn't 'ave to send us out like this."

"Not Crichton's fault 'e got 'imself shot dead, is it?"

Their footsteps receded. Elinor clung, stiff, to her tree, counting off the seconds until she reached one thousand. Then she slid out from beneath the branch and went back to the ridge in time to see the rowboat pass around the promontory. Her hands were shaking. She sat down where she was until the fear drained away and she could think clearly.

Someone had seen her signal, but not the Navy; the pirates had. Pirates whose ship was anchored out of sight to the west, or—but why send a rowboat when you could simply navigate around to the north side of the island? So, pirates who were camped on the island. Pirates with a leader named Evans, which sounded so familiar. Someone had told her—no, Ramsay had said it once, she could remember him holding his wine glass in those long, clever fingers, leaning back in his chair during supper... Evans, *Rhys* Evans.

Elinor's hand flew up to her mouth, and then she had to wipe bittersweet tree sap from her lips, spitting in disgust. Rhys Evans, leader of the Brethren of the Coast. Rhys Evans who had sent these men to investigate the fire, who controlled the Extraordinary Scorcher she'd fought only days before. Rhys Evans who was near enough that those men were going to report to him.

She had stumbled upon the secret pirate stronghold.

CHAPTER 17

IN WHICH THERE ARE PIRATES

S he had to take a few minutes to calm down again. It was ridiculous. This island had to be mere miles from Jamaica; the Royal Navy patrolled these waters constantly. It was impossible that the pirates could have stayed concealed here all this time. She was up and moving down the hill before she came to her senses. She absolutely could not follow those men. She had no experience in hiding, in moving quietly; it was sheer luck she'd concealed herself from the pirates at all.

She stood at the tree line, under the shade of a coconut palm, and wiped her hands on her trousers to remove the last of the sap. If Ramsay were here, he wouldn't think twice about following those men back to where they were hiding. It would be his duty as an officer of the Royal Navy. Well, she was...not exactly an officer, but she was under orders and that made her as duty-bound as anyone else might be. She had to know if it was merely Evans' ship nearby, or if this was where the Brethren of the Coast hid and issued their orders to every pirate in the Caribbean.

She roasted breadfruit and ate, quickly, then began walking down the beach toward the promontory, planning furiously. She would have to stay concealed within the trees for as long as she could, low to the ground. It might be better to wait until nightfall—no, the sky still threatened rain, and it was possible the overcast would remain after sunset, which would make it nearly impossible for her to find her way since she couldn't light any fires as she went. She could carry no food, nothing that would keep her from running away if that became necessary. She hoped the enemy Scorcher, Dewdney, *wouldn't* make an appearance; if she needed to burn some men in her flight, his intervention might get her killed, or worse.

She stopped short of the promontory, closed her eyes and her fists and chastised herself. This was utter madness. If they caught her, they would torture her, rape her, and eventually kill her, and no one would know to come to her rescue. She was just Elinor Pembroke, gently raised daughter of Josiah Pembroke, completely unsuited to traveling through a tropical forest to spy on a possible pirate stronghold. Elinor Pembroke...who had burned ships and killed men with a talent unmatched by anyone, possibly not even that other Extraordinary Scorcher. Since she had left on this journey she had done so much she would have thought impossible in her former life. This was just one more impossible thing. She took a deep breath, opened her eyes, and continued westward.

She took her time coming around the promontory, not sure she wouldn't still find those two pirates rowing away, but there was merely more beach and sand and trees extending farther west. She went to walk under the palm trees, which slowed her considerably but gave her better concealment. The fallen palm fronds, dry and rustling, were sharp against her already bruised and cut feet, forcing her deeper into the forest to avoid them, but she soon learned to recognize where it was safe to step and began to make better time.

Eventually she left the palms behind for a thick forest of those sturdy trees with the hand-sized leaves that smelled like cool, woody sap and freshly cut grass. They were easier to maneuver through than the palms, and Elinor was able to move even more quickly. The pirates were still nowhere in sight. She heard nothing but the sound of her feet on the bare ground and the wind and the birds she was now so accustomed to that she was startled every time they fell silent. She stopped to relieve herself, then kept walking, observing that the shore had a barely noticeable curve to it, and that in the far distance was another promontory, shaped like a leaping dolphin, after which the island seemed to curve sharply to the left.

It was early afternoon when she reached the leaping dolphin, and she stopped to catch her breath before carefully creeping past it into a cove empty of human life. Here, the trees receded rapidly from the shore, and there was a wide swath of scrub bushes and tiny flowers between the tree line and the white sands of the beach. The beach itself was a perfect C scooped out of the shore and filled with that blue, translucent water that lapped the shores of every harbor in the Caribbean.

She had a moment's longing to run down to the shore and throw herself into the warm water. Then she stepped back into the shelter of the trees and continued on her way, toward a line of rocks extending far out into the blue water, forming the top curve of the C. The line of rocks rose into a sharp ridge blocking her view beyond the point, rising abruptly into a steep cliff crowned with more of those evergreens.

As she walked, she considered the situation before her. Trying to round the point at the water line would be foolish, because she would be completely exposed to the view of anyone on the other side, and that sharp curve prevented her seeing what was there until she had passed the promontory. On the other hand, the ground where she was now had begun to slope up rather steeply toward the ridge, and it might become too steep for her to climb. The need for concealment won the day, and Elinor struggled up the incline, eventually using tree trunks to pull herself up the rise.

Near the top, she rested briefly, waiting until her pulse and breathing were back to normal before crawling over the ridge, pulling herself up and over the steep rise. The trees grew too thickly for her to see anything but glimpses of the blue sea far below, so she edged her way downhill until she reached the tree line. Concealing herself behind a trunk, she was able to take in the scene spread out beneath her.

This was another cove, also perfectly round, but much bigger than the first. Out beyond its mouth, five warships lay at anchor, two of them recognizably Royal Navy ships. One of those ships was missing its topmast and its sails were torn and perforated, its deck and sides a mass of splintered wood. The sight of Navy ships in the pirates' service infuriated Elinor. How many Navy men had died, horribly, so those pirates could sail the seas using those proud ships to terrify and intimidate others into bowing to their demands? None of the ships appeared ready to depart, though Elinor's knowledge of ships was still limited and she might be wrong in that assumption, but their furled sails had a slack look to them that spoke to her of an unreadiness to set sail.

There were two rickety piers jutting out into the harbor, at which a number of boats painted in a wild array of colors were tied, including the scummy green one that had landed on her beach. One of the boats was pulled up on shore and turned upside down, and a couple of men appeared to be doing something to its bottom, possibly caulking it; at this distance Elinor could not tell. Both were bearded and both dressed the same in ragged trousers, loose shirts, and boots, with scarves tied around their heads that made them look faintly ridiculous. They were also both armed with swords at their waists and pistols dangling around their necks that made their appearance far more menacing. What good they thought those weapons would be during boat repair was a mystery. Perhaps they simply felt more comfortable going armed.

The trees ended just past the ridge, baring the rocky slope and giving the cove a naked look. The sand of the beach extended up the shore for some distance, then turned into a rocky incline ending at a sheer cliff that went up several hundred feet, as if it too had been scooped out of the mountain rock like the bay. After observing it for several minutes, Elinor realized it *had* been scooped out of the rock; the cliff face bore marks that, if it had been made of wood, would have indicated someone had carved it, peeling away large chunks without smoothing out the gouges. The rocks comprising the incline looked as if they were the chunks that had been peeled away. Whoever had done this had had a great many Movers at his command, to change the landscape so dramatically.

Nestled into the rocks were five wooden huts that looked cobbled together from whatever driftwood washed ashore. Above these lay what Elinor could only describe as a fortress, its back pressed against the cliff so nothing could get behind it. The tiles of the roof were mismatched but without gaps, probably secure against the worst storms the Caribbean could throw at it. Its tightly fitted, planed boards followed the contours of the rock, and small, slit-like windows looked out over the only path to the only door, where an enormous, heavily muscled man stood, likely a Shaper, bearing two swords, a pistol in his belt, and two pistols hanging fore and back over his shoulder, surveying the entire cove. As Elinor watched, three pirates left one of the huts and walked up to the fortress door, where they were relieved of their weapons by the burly guard before they were allowed to enter.

Elinor slid back over the ridge into the shelter of the trees. She had found the pirate stronghold Durrant had never tried to discover. If she could get this information back to Ramsay, he would know what to do with it. According to those pirates, Evans had no Bounder; perhaps they could trap the ships in the cove, prevent Evans from escaping. Or...

No. It's insanity. But she was there, in place to destroy the fortress and stop Evans entirely. She could burn everything in that cove, perhaps even the ships. Except she had no proof Evans was there now. And their Extraordinary Scorcher Dewdney could be anywhere, even close enough to counter her attack. Better she got the information to Ramsay. If she ever found a way off this island.

She slid back down the incline until it was horizontal enough that she could walk. Back to her beach—oh, no, she couldn't make a big fire again without those pirates returning, and next time they would come in greater numbers. A smaller fire, then, one with less smoke, maybe dry palm fronds on the beach instead of the sap-filled living trees. She was becoming hungry; it was midafternoon now and it would probably be full night by the time she returned. She would—

She realized the noise was too great for her to make alone only a second before coming face to face with the pirate. He held a sack from which peeked a couple of knobby green breadfruits and had both a sword with a broad blade, stained with some kind of juice, and a pistol tucked into his rope belt. The shocked expression on his filthy, bearded face surely mirrored hers. She knew the moment he realized she was female by the way his shock gave way to a lascivious anticipation. He dropped the bag of breadfruits, and Elinor set him on fire.

He fell, screaming, and she ran, tearing down the hill and away, away as fast as she could go, which wasn't fast at all as she still had to watch her footing. The undergrowth tore at the soles of her feet and slapped her legs and face, but she heard shots being fired and knew they were following her. She had nowhere to go, no advantage but her so-narrow lead, and those men were shod and armed and larger than she. She needed somewhere to hide because as spread out as they were, she could not burn them all.

She could hear little above the sound of her feet crashing through the forest and the whistling, panting sound her breath made as she ran, but occasionally there was a gunshot, and shouts behind her and to her left, downhill toward the ocean. They had already cut her off in that direction. She turned and ran uphill. If they hadn't seen her, if all they knew was that she was a Scorcher, she might be able to use that to her advantage and slip away somewhere they would believe she was too heavy and too wide to fit.

She left the hand-leaved trees behind for a thicker forest of evergreens, their branches all low to the ground and too thick for anyone to see through—but the shouts were closer now, and she didn't think she could climb even one of those sturdy, many-limbed trees before they caught her. What she needed was to disappear, like a Bounder, but there was no use thinking like that. *And they certainly do not have a Bounder, or I would be captured already.*

She was moving more sluggishly now, her legs burning with exertion, her feet cut and bleeding. Soon she would have to turn and fight, hoping her fire was enough to kill them all, knowing with dread certainty it was not.

She reached a ridge that looked familiar, though she had never seen it from this height; it was the one where her stream ran, the one that terminated in her beach. If only someone had seen her beacon!

She stumbled and rolled a little way, terror of being caught flooding through her, and she realized she had tripped over a crevice in the rocks, a narrow slit that was all but invisible in the late afternoon light. An idea struck her, and she scrambled back to examine the crevice. It opened up past the entrance into a tiny cave that seemed big enough for her to fit inside, a perfect hiding place. She hesitated. If she climbed into it now they would see she had suddenly disappeared, look more closely at the ground, and find her, trapped neatly for them to capture. She would have to find a way to make them believe she was still running.

She stood still for a moment, clearly silhouetted against the blue clouds filling the eastern sky, then swept her hand across the horizon. As if in reply, a row of trees between herself and the pirates blazed high and bright. Quickly, she set another line of trees burning, in the direction she would be if she had continued to run, and as quickly she struggled into the crevice, scraping her face and arms on its edges. Then she huddled in tight, and prayed they wouldn't trip as she had.

Soon she heard cursing and shouting as men approached from two directions. They didn't seem to be running anymore; they might be as tired as she was. Someone called out, "Go around both ends at once, but go quickly. The Scorcher might try that trick again."

"You saw Morton! Don't want to get caught like that, burned like a roast!"

"You'll do as I say or by damn I'll roast you myself! Now get moving!"

More grumbling, some of it close to Elinor's hiding place, and she squeezed her legs more tightly to her body and tried not to breathe too loudly.

"... damn Scorchers and their damn talent..." said the man who'd complained about being burned like a roast, and then he was past, and then they were all past, and Elinor continued to hug herself tightly because she could not quite believe they weren't simply toying with her.

Once they passed the second fire line, and didn't see her, they might think to search this area more closely. Or they might believe she had hidden in a tree and would spend some time thrashing about trying to flush her out. In either case, she couldn't afford to move because she had nowhere else to go that provided her so much concealment. She would spend the night there and pray fervently that the pirates would eventually give up and go home.

The crevice was damp and cold and smelled like wet stone, and it occurred to her it might have been inhabited, which sent her heart pounding again. She had been lucky all around, so lucky she hoped God would not see it as enough luck and decide not to send a ship her way. They had to come. She could not bear it much longer.

Hours passed. The sun set, and darkness filled Elinor's crevice like damp, black wool that pressed against her throat and her eyelids. She could still hear shouting, though it was far away, and once or twice a gun fired, but then the night was silent. She dozed off, woke herself in terror that she'd snored and they had found her, dozed again, and then fell to shivering too hard to stay asleep.

When the blackness turned to grey and then to pink, it took her several minutes to realize the color meant day had come. She almost couldn't unfold to climb out of her crevice, but once out, she ducked into the shelter of the trees and watched for a long time before she was convinced the pirates were actually gone.

She half-crawled, half-slid down the ridge until she reached the stream and put her whole face in the water to gulp it down. She was exhausted and light-headed, and her body felt as if those pirates had crushed it under their heavy-soled boots all night. The water helped clear her mind, enough that she was able to find her food store and eat several papayas, spitting out the bitter seeds, feeling too weak to break open anything with a more robust exterior.

Finally, she leaned back against the trunk of the evergreen, closed her eyes, and let despair overwhelm her. She was trapped on this island, and at some point those pirates *would* find her and that would be the end. Even if she could safely light another beacon, no one would ever see it. There was nothing else she could do. Ramsay and the rest of *Athena's* men would go on mourning her, possibly, and then forget her, and no one would know about the pirate stronghold because Durrant was too stubborn to look for something hidden just within reach.

She struggled to her feet and stumbled back down to the beach. She was doomed; she might as well enjoy a nice wade in the warm surf. She rolled up her trouser legs, though she wasn't sure why she bothered, since they had already been subjected to far worse than a wetting.

She remembered talking to Ramsay that day they had walked on the beach on Tenerife, the day that had seen the beginning of their friendship, and she stopped ankle-deep in the surf, her cut and bruised feet stinging from the salt water, her toes buried in the squishy wet sand, and let herself cry. It was completely self-indulgent, but she was a dead woman, and if that did not entitle her to cry, then nothing would.

Eventually her tears slowed to a trickle and she wiped her eyes, then grimaced at the sand she rubbed into them. She stooped to rinse her hands in the clear water and dabbed at her eyes, which could endure a little salt, then sighed and looked out across the water toward the empty horizon.

In the distance, like a bird settled on the water stretching its wings to fly, lay a ship, its sails billowing in the wind.

Elinor screamed, clapped her hands over her mouth, then took ten splashing steps toward the ship before sanity reasserted itself and reminded her she could not swim all the way to whatever ship that was. It would have been a true miracle if it had been *Athena*, but all she could tell was that it was one of the Navy's frigates. She sloshed back to shore and ran along the beach, looking for the tallest tree she could find on the tree line, then set that one on fire, made it burn hot and bright against the cool green background, then extinguished it. She set it afire again, put it out, over and over again so its blinking light and drifting smoke would catch their eyes.

The ship came closer, and then, wonder of wonders, lowered its longboat. Elinor ran to the water's edge, waving her hands and shouting, and then her memory dragged up the image of the two Navy ships lying at anchor in the pirates' cove. No one had ever told her how many Navy ships the pirates had captured rather than destroyed. Evans was clever; he might have sent this ship to trick her, make her reveal herself so he could capture her. She had just made an enormous mistake.

She ran for the trees, then stopped with her hands on two trunks, heedless of the sap clinging to her palms. It was too late. If they were pirates and not Navy, they knew where she was and they would capture her no matter where she went. She couldn't live in that crevice forever. Better to face whatever might come, and if that was fatalistic, it was all she could manage after what she had endured the last few days. She walked down to the water's edge once more and bent to rinse the sap from her fingers. If they were pirates, she would kill as many of them as she could manage before they took her.

She stood, watching the boat approach, trying not to hope; most sailors wore slops, whatever was handy, so they and the pirates she'd seen were similar in appearance apart from their grooming, which was not something she could tell at this distance. The longboat came nearer, rowed by a dozen men with someone sitting in the...he was wearing a navy blue jacket with white facings, there was a single lieutenant's epaulette on his shoulder, he even had the hat, he *was* an officer, and now Elinor waded out to meet them, unable to wait a moment longer. They reached her as she was standing waist-deep in water, swaying with the waves that rolled in to shore and reaching out to steady herself on the boat. The lieutenant doffed his hat and bowed without rising.

"Miss Pembroke?" he said. "We've been looking for you."

CHAPTER 18

IN WHICH ELINOR RETURNS
HOME

The ship was *Syren*, a Colonial frigate based in Port Royal, and that was all Elinor learned before she was hustled aboard the ship, ushered to a great cabin identical to *Athena*'s, provided water for washing and a clean, slightly too large uniform (obviously they had no gown for her). She had her injured arm properly bound up and was fed a meal that did not feature any form of Caribbean flora whatsoever.

Near the end of her meal, Captain Horace joined her at the table. He was a round, red-cheeked man of about fifty, with carefully combed black hair and cheerful eyes like black currants. "I cannot believe the Navy saw my beacons," Elinor said, then had to cover her mouth with her napkin because she had spoken with her mouth full of food. Had three days of being shipwrecked been enough to make her entirely forget her manners?

"Beacon? We saw no beacon. The Extraordinary Seer at Admiralty House found you," Horace said, his Colonial accent doing strange things to his long vowels. "It's unfortunate it took so long, but Sight isn't always easy to interpret at first."

"I don't understand. Why would anyone have thought to look for me? Did you not all believe I was dead?"

Horace chuckled, making his cheeks wobble. "All but one. I heard Miles Ramsay made a pest of himself until he got the Seer to pay attention, and then—well, Admiralty House was in an uproar, I can tell you that."

Elinor's heart warmed. Of course Ramsay would not have believed it. He had faith in her—faith past death, apparently. "I suppose losing me would have looked very bad."

"You're valuable as well as being an attractive young lady. Definitely wouldn't want to lose you." Horace smiled and patted her cheek, which to Elinor's surprise did not make her feel patronized. She rather liked the man, though how much of that was due to gratitude for rescuing her, she was not certain. She chose not to dwell on it.

"Where are we going, Captain?" *Please say* Athena.

"Port Royal, first, and I think someone's meeting us there to take you to Admiralty House. *Syren* doesn't have a Bounder, shame about that, but it won't take long. We're about a day out, maybe closer to thirty-six hours, but we'll try to make you as comfortable as we can. I hope you don't mind the uniform. Everyone understands, exigencies of war and that sort of thing, but I think we can find you something better in Kingston before you have to see Admiral Durrant."

"Thank you, Captain, I do appreciate it." The someone meeting her might well be Stratford, if they cared about her comfort at all, and she was going to march into Durrant's office, denounce Crawford, and insist she be returned to *Athena* or...her plan stuttered into failure at that point.

"So, young lady, I'd love to hear what's happened to you, but I imagine that's something Admiral Durrant ought to hear first," Horace said.

"No, Captain, you must send word to Admiral Durrant immediately. The Brethren of the Coast have their stronghold on that island, and if he acts quickly, they might be defeated!"

"The Brethren—?" Captain Horace furrowed his brow at her. "You must be mistaken. This island is right on a major shipping route. They could not possibly go unnoticed."

"I assure you it is true, Captain. Please, have your Speaker communicate this to Admiralty House. The pirates must be given no time to escape."

"Calm yourself, Miss Pembroke. After the ordeal you've suffered, you should not exert yourself. Of course I'll send word."

Now she felt patronized. He did not believe her. He might send word, but it would not be soon enough, and the pirates would not be captured. If only *Athena* had come for her! "We'll arrange for you to meet with Admiral Durrant as soon as possible," Horace added, patting her hand in an infuriating way, "and you can make your report to him."

She almost told him what Crawford had done, but realized in time it might be something the Navy would have to handle internally, and said instead, "Will it be that formal?"

"Oh, they'll sit you down and have you tell your story. Not at all like a court-martial, which you won't have to worry about. Not like poor old Crawford."

"Is Captain Crawford subject to a court-martial?" *Did the Seer discover his treachery as well?*

Horace nodded, leaned back and scratched behind his ear. "Any time a captain loses a ship, there's a court-martial to determine whether he's at fault for it. A formality, plenty of witnesses to say Crawford did everything he could, and now that you've been rescued—he'll be glad to learn he was wrong when he thought you were dead."

Oh, I am certain that is not true. "I know he will be surprised," she said.

"We all were, except maybe Ramsay. Well, my dear, let's find you a place to rest. You look like you could use it. I regret I can't offer you Healing, but probably there's someone in Admiralty House who can do something about your injuries."

Elinor thought of the stab wound on her arm that still hurt when she raised it too high, the cuts and bruises on her feet, the rough scrapes along her arms and left cheek, and nodded. "I will be fine with a hammock, sir," she said.

"I can't make a lady sleep in a hammock! You'll take my bed and nothing more to be said about it."

"No, I am accustomed—"

"Young lady, I've daughters older than you, and you'll do as you're told. Frankly, I don't know what the Navy was thinking, bringing you into this, Extraordinary talent or not."

Something that had been nudging at the back of Elinor's mind finally drew her attention. "Do...have many people learned who I am?"

"Maybe a few. With all the stink Ramsay was raising, couldn't help but reveal the secret to people like me, since I was going to retrieve you and all that. But don't worry. No one thinks any the less of you just because you're serving your country, female or not."

More people who knew...and if one of them made the right (or wrong) connection...it would not take much for word of this to reach her father's ear. She squared her jaw. The secret couldn't last forever; she would simply have to endure when it came out. "Thank you again, Captain."

"Think nothing of it, my dear. Now, if you'd like to come on deck, or nap, or I have some books—anything you like. It sounds as if you had a rough time of it. But then in books like that *Robinson Crusoe* it's always starting a fire that's the hardest, and I guess you wouldn't have any trouble with that!"

He roared at his joke, and Elinor, despite her irritation, laughed at his enjoyment. She felt freer than she had in a month.

The *Syren* made good time, arriving in Port Royal two hours after sunrise the following day. Elinor was standing at the bow, urging *Syren* to move faster with her thoughts, when they passed the famous gibbets, from which two pirates hung in chains, blackened and still stinking. Elinor watched in fascination as a large black bird landed on one of the cages and pecked at some body part inside. She felt only a little disgusted at herself for not being horrified at the sight. *But*, she told herself, *I have killed many men and I am not disgusted with myself over that, so I suppose death itself is no longer terrifying or gruesome to me.*

They sailed past the tip of the island that was formerly the city of Port Royal and came into the Royal Navy dock. Across the bay, Elinor could see the brown and red roofs of Kingston. Its harbor had so many little wooden docks jutting into it that it looked snaggle-toothed, with a fringe of brown-roofed cottages butting up against the shore. Dozens of one- and two-masted boats rowed or sailed across the bay, some of them tacking out of the entrance past *Syren* and out of sight around Jamaica's coast.

The Naval outpost, by contrast, had a random look to it; Elinor recalled that all attempts to resettle the place after the earthquake had ultimately failed. It spoke to British tenacity that they were able to hold on here, in this place where the foundations could shift and drop them into the sea at any moment.

She stood at the bow, one hand on the rail, as *Syren* came about and dropped anchor, looked out across the harbor, and her heart gave a hard, painful thump as she saw, some distance away, a ship whose figurehead and masts and longboat suspended over the waist of the deck were as familiar to her as her own fingers.

She leaned far out over the rail and saw a small figure Skipping toward them, growing larger and larger until it turned into Stratford, who made one last Bound and came running toward Elinor to pick her up around the waist and spin her around, chanting her name until she threw her arms around him and hugged him tight.

"You are no doubt destroying my reputation," she said in his ear. "Or possibly your reputation for sanity." Tears were spilling down her cheeks, and she was fairly certain Stratford's eyes were moist as well.

"Don't care," he said, squeezing her once before releasing her. "A month with no word, and then the word is you're dead—Elinor, I can't tell you how good it is to see you."

"I was hoping you were the one waiting to meet me here, Stratford," she said, wiping her eyes. "May I come back to *Athena*, do you know?" She leaned around him for another look at her beloved ship, so very close now. The paint was different, black with white trim, as if such a thing could fool her.

"I think I should demand an explanation, or possibly an introduction," Horace called out, approaching them with his hand outstretched. He pretended to frown at Stratford, and added, "And just what are your intentions, young man?"

"This is my good friend Midshipman Stratford Hervey, and he is carried away sometimes by his enthusiasm," Elinor said. "Mr. Hervey, Captain Horace."

Stratford shook the captain's hand. "Very much obliged to you, sir, and Captain Ramsay's compliments. I'm to take Miss Pembroke direct to Admiralty House."

"You are to do nothing of the sort, Midshipman," Horace said just as Elinor said, "Mr. Hervey, I cannot possibly appear at Admiralty House in this attire!"

Stratford looked at her in astonishment. "I can't believe you can care about what you're wearing after all this time, El—Miss Pembroke!"

"Nevertheless, I have been forced to wear men's clothing for far too long, and I insist on being properly dressed before I greet the admiral."

"*I* think you look fine," Stratford muttered, then sighed. "All right. We can go into Kingston, but you buy the first dress we find and then we're Bounding away. Lots of people are anxious to see you."

Her own anxiety threatened to choke her. "We will hurry," she said. *I have someone I need to thank for my survival.*

It took some time to find an acceptable gown; Kingston was not nearly as accommodating to English sensibilities as Hamilton was, and Elinor had to depend on Stratford's wheedling charm to convince a shopkeeper to help them, but eventually Elinor was dressed, if somewhat haphazardly, in a respectable brown cotton dress and proper undergarments, though the chemise she purchased gave her no support and made her regret the loss of her old wardrobe.

She felt an unexpected pang removing her borrowed uniform, remembering how her old one had been such a protection while she was shipwrecked, but was determined never to wear one again, since most of the memories associated with it were tied up with Crawford and *Glorious*. She was going to confront him and make him pay for abandoning her to her death. The thought filled her with a fierce pleasure.

She emerged from the great cabin to find Captain Horace waiting with his thumbs tucked into his waistband and Stratford jiggling back and forth with impatience. "I don't know why it takes women so long to dress," he said.

"It is a mystery of the ages, I have no doubt. Good-bye, Captain Horace, and thank you again for coming to my rescue."

Horace clasped her extended hand and bowed over it. "Think nothing of it, my dear. Best of luck with the admiral."

Elinor had barely withdrawn her hand before Stratford clasped her around the waist, and in a blink of insubstantiality they were in *Athena's* Bounding chamber. "But," she said in some surprise, "you said, directly to Admiralty House."

"Well, those were my orders from the Admiralty, but my orders from the *captain* were to bring you here first," Stratford said with a cheeky smile. "Didn't think you'd complain much."

"No, indeed," Elinor said, her heart pounding for no reason she could understand. She was eager to see Ramsay again and thank him for not losing faith in her, but how on earth could she possibly convey her gratitude?

That was it. *Gratitude.* She did not mind owing him her life, but the word made her skin crawl. It was what her father had always demanded of her. Feeling that way toward her dear friend—it was a barrier between them, and it made her feel awkward about seeing him again. She would simply have to pretend it did not exist. She would not let it ruin their friendship. Her heart would not stop pounding.

She strode through the mess deck behind Stratford as quickly as her narrow skirt would allow. Perhaps there were things she would miss about her uniform, after all—no, showing her legs to anyone who cared to look was not worth the freedom of movement. The lower deck, the door to the gunroom, the stairs to the upper deck—they had seen more fighting, the formerly pristine planks of the deck were scarred from the gun carriages recoiling against the blast, but it was all so familiar she wanted to cry again.

"Milady! Miss Pembroke!"

She couldn't tell who had shouted first, but in an instant the deck was trembling with the shouts and cheers of dozens of men, and then she really did cry. Feet pounded above and men crowded in at the companionway, waving and laughing, and she waved back and wiped away tears of happiness, then laughed at herself for being so moved by the cheer and approbation of a ship's worth of sailors.

"Come along, Elinor," Stratford said, pulling on her arm, and she waved one last time and let him draw her through the lobby and into the great cabin, where Beaumont stood looking out the windows and Ramsay sat at the table, going over some papers with a pen in his hand. He looked up as they entered, and a burden she didn't know she was carrying fell away as he greeted her with one of those wry little smiles. "Miss Pembroke," he said, "welcome back."

"It is... it is good to see you, Captain," Elinor said, feeling unaccountably weepy again. She stretched out her hand to him. "I understand I have you to thank for my rescue."

He clasped her hand, put his other hand over both of theirs and squeezed briefly, then released her. His firm, warm hand gave her more comfort at that moment even than seeing *Syren* on the horizon, and she wanted to cling to it. "I knew you weren't dead. Everything else was merely detail. Sit down, please. Mr. Hervey, thank you for your services. You're dismissed."

"Sir," Stratford said, then turned on his heel and left, but not before tipping his hat at Elinor.

Ramsay watched him go with a look of amused exasperation. "That young man has entirely too much exuberance," he said.

"That's probably for the best, if you can harness it," Beaumont said.

"No doubt." Ramsay met Beaumont's eyes, and the two traded looks Elinor could not read. Beaumont looked back out the window again, then said, "Let me know how it—those lists work out," and left the room.

"What lists are those?" Elinor asked.

Ramsay shrugged. "Stores, supplies. Checking the purser's log, double checking the watch list. Occasionally they all have to be done at once. It's not important." He pushed the paper aside and leaned back in his chair. His eyes looked tired, as if he'd spent the last three days without much sleep.

"How did the Seer find me, Captain? You said he needed something to focus on."

He chuckled. "I had your parasol. Then I harassed the admiral's Extraordinary Seer until he had a useful Vision of your location. Though I suppose the most useful Vision was the first one, the one that proved you weren't dead and I wasn't wasting everyone's time. It felt as if it took half a lifetime."

"I felt the same. It was a long three nights, and—oh, Captain, I found the pirate stronghold!" She had come close to forgetting in her anxiety about getting home, and now it was the only thing she could think of.

Ramsay looked at her with narrowed eyes. "What pirate stronghold?"

"The place where Rhys Evans and the Brethren of the Coast make their plans and send out their orders. I found it, Captain. It is right there under Admiral Durrant's eye, and it would take hardly any effort to destroy them! Did not Captain Horace tell the admiral?"

"The pirate stronghold." Ramsay ran his hands through his hair. "Miss Pembroke, are you sure your ordeal hasn't..."

"You believed I was not dead and you cannot now credit what I have learned? Shabby behavior, Captain."

"I...no, you're correct." He stood and paced to where Beaumont had been standing. "Crawford was awfully insistent that you were dead, you know," he said as if this were the conversation they'd been having. "It was extremely satisfying to prove him wrong, but I did wonder at his certainty, and then his look of fear when he learned the truth."

"That is because Captain Crawford is a...a rat bastard who left me to die on his sinking ship," Elinor said. The memory made her furious all over again.

Ramsay spun to face her, eyes blazing, and said, "He did *what?*"

"He spoke to me, looked me in the eye as his Bounder took him away, and did not send the man back even though he knew I was alive and not mortally injured. I am certain that is against some Article of War or other, is it not? Because I would quite cheerfully see him hanged, for that and for...other things."

Ramsay came back and took Elinor by the shoulders, rather roughly. "Did he offer you insult?"

"No, Captain, it was merely that we disliked each other, and that grew into hatred, and he said things I could not abide. And then he left me to die."

Ramsay released her and said, "I apologize, I should not have handled you like that, but I—You know I have no love for Crawford, but I had assumed he would not take advantage of you."

"No, he did not. I think it is unfortunate he did not die when *Glorious* sank, and now I feel rather guilty for having such bloodthirsty thoughts."

"Then we're both guilty of that." Ramsay turned back to the window, then brought his hands down hard on the sill. "Miss Pembroke," he said, "there is no way we can bring this accusation against him."

Elinor leaped to her feet, knocking her chair over. "*What?* But...is he not to bear responsibility for what he did? I am perfectly willing to testify to the truth."

Ramsay turned to face her, reclining against the windowsill with his arms crossed over his chest. "It's your word against his, and he still has his uncle's favor."

Elinor kicked her chair hard with the sole of her shoe, making it slide an inch or two toward the door. "And yet he is to face court-martial for losing his ship. I would think I am at least as valuable a weapon as *Glorious* was."

"*You are not a weapon,*" Ramsay said. "Though Admiral Durrant might actually respond to that argument, much as it pains me to admit it."

"Then that is the argument we will make."

"Miss Pembroke, I don't think I'm explaining this very well. If you accuse Crawford of attempted murder—which is what this is—he'll deny it, of course, and the admiral will take his side, even if he knows the truth of what happened. Covering something like that up—both Admiral Durrant and Crawford would face a civilian trial for complicity in the attempted murder of an Extraordinary. What all that means is if you or I try to press the issue, we might encounter some fatal accidents to prevent us giving away the secret. So there's no way to see Crawford receives justice for what he did to you."

"I cannot believe he will not—will the court-martial at least prove he was negligent in the battle?"

Ramsay shook his head. "Possibly. He should have known *Olympia* had been captured by pirates; every one of our ships that goes missing is reported to the fleet. Other than that, I couldn't say. I haven't heard any whispers about negligence."

"But he...he ignored their lack of signals! He allowed them to come right—"

"Nothing, Miss Pembroke. Not one word. I take comfort in the fact that Admiral Durrant doesn't have a ship to give him."

"But I will testify at his court-martial, will I not? I saw the whole thing, Captain!"

Ramsay rubbed his eyes as if they ached. "Your status in the Navy is ambiguous. The Admiralty may rule you're ineligible to testify, either because you're not an officer or because you're not a man. The First Lord might even think he's doing you a favor by keeping your existence a secret, not that that matters now."

She felt a chill pass through her. "What do you mean?"

"I'm afraid it's my fault. Rescuing you meant more people had to know your identity and why it was so important we retrieve you. Captain Horace, the Extraordinary and the other two Seers at Admiralty House... it's not many, but you know how hard it is to keep a secret once more people know it."

Now she felt sick as well as cold. So she was a weapon, after all. "I suppose I am valuable enough that compromising my identity was worth the cost," she said.

"That's how Admiral Durrant thought. I assure you, your rescue was personal for... for every man on this ship."

She remembered the welcome the sailors had given her, the smile with which he'd greeted her, and felt better immediately. "I missed you all so very much," she said, and bent to right her chair and sit down, twining her fingers in her lap. "Captain Ramsay," she said, looking down at her hands, "why did you not have me returned here?"

Ramsay was quiet for so long she wondered if perhaps she had not spoken loudly enough. She glanced up to see he had turned to face the window again, his head bowed. "I tried, Miss Pembroke," he said quietly, "God knows I tried. I argued the point with everyone I knew inside the Admiralty. I argued the point with the First Lord himself. Lord Melville was extremely sympathetic, but refused to countermand Admiral Durrant on the grounds of...I don't remember, some nonsense or other about jurisdiction which I am certain the First Lord has disregarded any number of times when it suited him."

"Then—"

"What it came down to was that the First Lord assigned you to *Athena* because I was convenient, not because she was a superior ship best fitted to your abilities or anything else he said that day. You were an interchangeable piece as much as any of us are, and I should never have encouraged you to believe otherwise."

Elinor clenched her hands together so tightly they felt numb. "I understand I am under orders to serve where the Admiralty dictates," she said, "but I am not a thing, and I do not believe I am interchangeable. This ship *is* where my abilities will always be most effectively used. Had it been *Athena* and not *Glorious* that encountered that pirate ship, even had we had no other Scorchers but myself, that battle would have ended with that pirate at the bottom of the sea, because I know and trust you and everyone aboard this ship, and I would not have been scrambling to cover the deficiencies of my comrades. And *you* would not have been deceived by such a simple ruse. Crawford is a fool, and he deserves to have no ship, though I cannot wish it to be at that cost." She went to where Ramsay stood and put her hand on his shoulder. "I will not allow the admiral to remove me from *Athena* again," she said.

He turned his head slightly, enough that his eyes could meet hers. "And what makes you believe you have that power?"

"Because I think he is afraid of me, and I think I can use that. Because I will make him see reason. I survived three days on that island, Captain. I was chased by pirates and slept in a crack in the rock while they hunted me. Admiral Durrant is *nothing* beside that."

Ramsay had turned away when she said the word "pirates," and now he let out a long sigh that sounded as if it came from the deepest recesses of his soul. "I would like to hear that story," he said, "one day in the far future when we can both laugh about how close you came to death, but right now I think you should see Hays, and then we should talk about this pirate stronghold you've discovered, and *then* we can decide how you should speak to the admiral."

CHAPTER 19

IN WHICH ELINOR BEARDS THE
ADMIRAL IN HIS DEN

Elinor felt the deficiencies of her wardrobe the moment she stepped out of Admiralty House's Bounding chamber. Many of the servants and slaves passing through the hallway, stepping around her with heads lowered, wore dresses or skirts made of the same brown cotton as her hastily purchased clothing. Her hair was arranged loosely on her head with only those few pins she had been able to scavenge from her bedchamber on *Athena*. Embarrassing, to be so grateful for her carelessness, but without them she would have been forced to braid her hair as if dressing for bed, or leave it hanging around her shoulders like a child, and she wanted—needed—Admiral Durrant to take her seriously.

"But—you *must* accompany me!" she had exclaimed to Ramsay.

"I haven't been summoned. And I am not your commanding officer, not as far as the Admiralty is concerned."

"I—" In all her imaginings, when she faced Durrant, Ramsay stood with her. Now all her proud words about standing up to the admiral flew out the window with the salt breeze.

Ramsay had taken her by the shoulders, firmly, his blue eyes intent on her face, his hands like an anchor. "Miss Pembroke, you are more than his equal, and what's more, you have right on your side, and that always seems to give you confidence. This cannot be worse than walking into the Board Room at the Admiralty in London and telling Lord Melville you want to serve in the Navy, can it?"

She laughed. "No, I suppose not. But if Crawford is there, it will be hard not to spit in his face."

He released her and smiled that tiny, wry smile. "If you do, I'll deeply regret having missed it."

Now she led the way, Stratford trailing behind her, toward the entrance hall, her footsteps slow and quiet. Brave words aside, she was not looking forward to this encounter. If she could not convince Durrant of the need to attack the pirates, of the vital importance of returning her to *Athena*...she would simply have to convince him, that was all.

"I'm taking you back to *Athena* whatever the admiral says," Stratford murmured.

"You will not, if he assigns me elsewhere, because I will not see you hang for mutiny," Elinor whispered back.

"That's not mutiny. And it's hardly wrong, if you're going where you're supposed to be."

"Stratford, I will not see you or any of *Athena* harmed on my account. The captain will find a solution, if it comes to that. But I hope I will be returning with you with Admiral Durrant's blessing."

They reached the entrance hall, as thronged with uniformed men as ever. A captain standing near the door noticed her, jerked in surprise, nudged his companion, and pointed surreptitiously. Conversations ceased, except for a few whispered comments as those who did not know her were enlightened by those who did. Ramsay was right; her anonymity was gone.

Elinor's heart, which had been thumping like a rabbit fleeing the fox, sped up to flutter hummingbird-fast. Nearly twenty men in the room, and every one of them knew the truth: the Extraordinary Scorcher was a woman, and how many steps was that information to the knowledge that she was Elinor Pembroke, Josiah Pembroke's daughter? She curtsied to them all, the merest bob, and turned on her heel, hands clutching her gown in a desperate attempt to keep them from shaking.

Her walk through the halls to the admiral's chamber felt like a gallows march. Every man stopped what he was doing to watch her pass. She had no idea what they saw in her, because she was afraid to meet their eyes. She hoped they took her rigid silence for indifference to their attention, for aloofness, and silently prayed for the kind of calm strength of presence Ramsay always had, no matter to whom he was speaking. When she put her hand to the iron doorknob, her fingers trembled hardly at all. She took a last deep breath, turned the knob and pushed the door open.

Crawford stood by the fireplace, leaning against the mantel and looking down at the clean, empty grate. His head came up at her entrance. Durrant was nowhere to be seen.

Elinor felt the blood drain from her face in sheer surprise, and a moment of irrational terror flashed through her before common sense reasserted itself. *Crawford* ought to be afraid of *her.* Abandoning a member of his crew, even intentionally, might be passed over as the exigencies of the moment, but she now knew that the attempted murder of an Extraordinary could mean prison or even death. Crawford must be—what was Beaumont's phrase?—*pissing his trousers* wondering what she might do.

"If you try to press the issue, you might face a fatal accident," Ramsay had said, but the temptation to attack Crawford was so great Elinor had to press her lips together to keep from screaming accusations at him before filling the grate with his ashes.

"I am glad you are not dead," Crawford said, too formally, his jaw clenched.

"So am I," said Elinor, feeling her body sing with the desire to fill itself with fire.

"It was...an unfortunate mistake...that you were left behind."

"A mistake I am certain you regret."

Crawford nodded, a touch too vehemently. "I hope you do not bear me any ill will."

Elinor's eyebrows rose. She wanted to laugh at his brazen, bald-faced effrontery. *No ill will?* "I see no reason why I should, if it was an... unfortunate mistake."

Crawford stiffened. Elinor continued, "And I am alive despite my ordeal, so I do not believe any good will come of either of us dwelling on the incident."

Crawford now looked as if he were not certain what she was saying. Elinor smiled and came toward him, stretching out her hand and saying, "Come, Captain, we should be friends."

Blinking in surprise, Crawford reached to take her hand, then jerked away with a curse as flames sparkled along Elinor's fingers. She gasped in pretended shock and shook her hand, causing droplets of liquid fire to spatter Crawford's uniform jacket. "I beg your pardon, Captain," she said in tones of sincere apology. "Occasionally deep feeling causes me to manifest my talent unexpectedly. I *do* hope you were not injured." She made the gemlike fire vanish and ostentatiously wiped her hand on her skirts.

Crawford brushed at the front of his jacket, now speckled with spots of char. "I...no, Pem—I mean, *Miss* Pembroke," he said, and he sounded afraid rather than angry, which satisfied Elinor down to her core.

The door behind Crawford opened, and Durrant entered. "You're early," he said to Elinor, and to Crawford, "I hope you've made your apologies. It was all very unfortunate."

"Yes, sir, and I believe Miss Pembroke...bears me no ill will," Crawford said, his face absolutely still.

"Good. No sense holding a grudge, when no malice was intended," Durrant said. Elinor was certain he knew nothing of what had actually transpired on *Glorious'* ravaged quarterdeck. So Crawford had been afraid to tell Durrant the truth, which meant he was doubly afraid Elinor might give away his secret. So long as he was more afraid of what Elinor might do to him personally, it was unlikely he would try to silence her.

"I completely agree, sir," she said, and smiled sweetly at Crawford, who went as white as her sister Amelia once had.

"Now, Miss Pembroke, I would like to hear your account," Durrant went on, seating himself but offering her no chair. Elinor was glad for it; standing made her feel confident, as if she had some sort of dominance over the admiral.

"Well, Admiral Durrant, I was able to swim to an—"

"No, Miss Pembroke, I was referring to the battle. I wish to know what your actions were so we can determine if you were negligent."

Her mouth dropped open. "I, negligent?"

"You are effectively an officer and bound by the Articles of War. If you displayed cowardice, you could face court-martial."

She wanted to burn him. She wanted to burn the room and everything in it. Cowardice? She had spent nearly all her endurance until her back wanted to split open, had saved Fortescue from the enemy Scorcher's fire...though did that count as bravery, when he had almost certainly drowned? "I assume I am not to feel insulted by the accusation of cowardice," she said, her voice trembling with rage.

"This is a formality," Durrant said, his eyes giving his tongue the lie.

Elinor saw the trap. They would find her guilty, would ship her back to England—they could not afford to execute her no matter what she had or had not done—and Crawford would not be convicted in court-martial, because they would not allow her to testify against him, and she seemed to be the only one who knew the truth of how he had failed.

"I think," she said, "and I say this with all due respect, Admiral Durrant, but I think you are not qualified to judge whether I, an Extraordinary Scorcher, performed to the best of my abilities. I can tell you I was able to ignite three thousand square-feet of fire-resistant sail and you will not realize how...extraordinary...that is. I can tell you I fought another Scorcher who shared my abilities to a standstill, and you will not know that such an action would be impossible for any of my fellow Scorchers on *Glorious*. I can recount any number of smaller events, including saving Mr. Fortescue from immolation, and you will not know whether I could have done more. So I believe, Admiral, that such questions should be deferred to someone who is my peer."

Durrant was as white as Crawford had been. "You dare—"

"Admiral, *you* are the one who accused me of possible negligence. I should be asking you how *you* dare."

Durrant's eyes darted to her waist, and Elinor realized her hand was once more on fire. *How odd, that my lie to Crawford should turn out to be true.* She extinguished it and met Durrant's eyes once more, trying to project Ramsay's cool indifference when the fire was raging inside her begging to be freed.

With a visible effort, Durrant brought himself under control. "I take it you mean no insult," he grated.

"No more than you did, sir. I believe we have simply misunderstood one another."

"Indeed." He laid his hands flat on the mirror-bright surface of the table and spread his fingers wide. "I am convinced you acted to the fullest of your capacity, Miss Pembroke. I see no need for further questions."

"Thank you, Admiral Durrant. Now, sir, I wish to discuss with you the pirate stronghold on the island where I was shipwrecked."

Durrant smiled at her unpleasantly. "Captain Horace relayed your claim. Do you expect me to believe a lone woman found what the entire Fleet of the Americas could not?"

It is not as if you were looking very hard for it. Elinor wished she dared put her disdain for him into words. So he hadn't heeded her warning, after all. "Please listen to my story," she said instead, and recounted the details of her adventure, beginning with the arrival of the two pirates on her beach. Durrant's expression went from disdain to surprise to a calculated cunning that worried Elinor. When she was finished, he said, "Did you see Evans?"

"I would not recognize him if I did. But I saw the captured Navy ship that attacked *Glorious*, so even were it not for the words of those two pirates, I would still conclude that this secret location is important to the Brethren."

"It couldn't be large enough to contain every pirate in Evans' fleet," Crawford said.

"It wouldn't have to be," Durrant said. "The pirates loyal to Evans have home ports all over the Caribbean. But the Brethren themselves, the leaders, they have to have somewhere to meet, to work out their strategies. More than one place, for them to have eluded our search for so long."

"You're not saying you believe this wild tale?"

"I doubt Miss Pembroke, with her inexperience in naval matters, could make up such details as she's recounted." Durrant glanced at

Elinor with an appraising air. "It's unfortunate her information is irrelevant."

"I beg your pardon, Admiral, but how is that?" Elinor said, outraged.

"Don't get testy with me, young lady. The pirates failed to capture you. You are an enemy Scorcher, therefore Evans will know his location has been compromised, and will already have moved to a new stronghold. We have no way to know where that is."

"But...but I cannot believe..." Elinor was struck by inspiration. "Surely our Seers could use whatever he has left behind to locate him!"

Durrant waved his hand dismissively. "He'd have destroyed anything useful. There's no point."

"Admiral, it is certainly worth looking! There are many ships in Port Royal—one of them could visit the place and investigate. It would take very little effort."

"It's a waste of time, Miss Pembroke."

"Was it a waste of time to search for me, when there was no reason to believe I lived?" The fire began to bloom along Elinor's fingers, and she struggled to control her anger and frustration. "Admiral, think how much of an advantage this will give you if Evans has been careless. Your strategies will be even more effective, and you will know better how to direct the fleet. If nothing comes of it, you are none the worse for it, correct?"

Durrant eyed her narrowly, then sighed. "Very well, but I don't expect we'll find anything. Captain Horace can stop by on his way to Saint-Domingue. And I will set the Speaker reticulum to watching for unusual ship movement. Will that satisfy you?"

"I do not care about my satisfaction, only about finding the Brethren."

"Evans is crafty," Crawford said. "We've searched for him for seven years and found nothing. What makes you think this will be any more successful?"

"I have faith in the Royal Navy's abilities," Elinor said, "and it is possible, is it not, that Evans may make mistakes now that he has been discovered once?"

Durrant shrugged. "As you say, it's worth investigating." He seemed to have forgotten his earlier objection to her plan. "Now, we must decide where you will be assigned next. We have only two other fourth-rates, true—*Glorious* was a hard loss."

"I will return to *Athena*," Elinor said.

Durrant leaned back in his chair and clasped his hands in front of him. "You have no authority to dictate your postings, Miss Pembroke."

"I will return to *Athena* because it is the only sensible choice, Admiral." Her voice was calm, her hands steady, and she could feel Ramsay's presence, hear his voice saying *You have nothing to fear*.

"Is it, now."

"Yes, sir." She took a step forward and clasped her hands behind her back. Her hair was beginning to fall down, but she ignored it. "You said we have few fourth-rate ships, but I do not believe a ship of that size is suited to my abilities. Most of the pirate ships are far too maneuverable for a fourth-rate to successfully engage, which means I will be almost useless because I would not be able to efficiently affect the enemy." She clenched her hidden fists together, hoping his lack of knowledge about her talent would prevent him seeing the inconsistencies in this statement.

"Anything smaller than a frigate would not have the firepower to stand up to the larger pirate ships alone, which would mean I would effectively be the sole weapon, and that would be a waste of my talent. That leaves the Fleet's fifth-rate frigates, and were I assigned to any of them but *Athena*, I would have to endure days or even weeks of teaching the crew not to fear me. I am known to the officers and crew of *Athena*, and we have proven how well we suit. So, Admiral, I suggest that my returning to *Athena* is the only sensible course of action."

Crawford's eyes narrowed. "And your attachment to its captain is irrelevant."

Elinor's face flushed. "It is true Captain Ramsay is my friend," she said, "but I hope you are not implying I would compromise the Navy's trust in me by suggesting I serve anywhere but where I will be most effective."

Durrant pursed his lips, his tongue moving inside his mouth as if he were trying to remove a bit of food from between his teeth. "Very well," he said. "Your logic is sound. I will send Ramsay his orders soon. And I had better not regret this."

Elinor had to stop herself from smiling like a fool. "You will not, Admiral Durrant, I assure you that you will not."

Durrant nodded. "Dismissed, Miss Pembroke."

She curtsied to Durrant, curtsied to Crawford after a moment's hesitation, then left quickly, before the admiral could change his mind. *Going home, going home, going home* sang a silly chorus inside her head. She had won. She had stood up to Durrant and bent him to her will. It was hard not to skip down the passage like a child racing home for a promised treat.

She came into the entrance chamber and called out, "Mr. Hervey," and a man standing near the front door, the only man in the room not dressed in a uniform, turned abruptly.

"*Elinor*," he said, striding toward her, and Elinor stopped, her whole body gone numb in an instant.

It was her father.

CHAPTER 20

IN WHICH ELINOR HAS AN
UNWELCOME SURPRISE

"Y ou disobedient *child*," her father said, his voice low and
harsh. "Do you have any idea what you have done to our
family? To your *mother*?" He grabbed her upper arm and
squeezed.

Elinor cried out and reflexively tried to pull away, but without
success. She barely felt the hard pressure of his hand; she was numb
with shock and the beginnings of fear. He could not have found her so
soon. He could not be there. Uniformed men stared at their tableau
and whispered, but no one stepped forward to intervene.

"Papa," she began.

"Do not address me. I do not wish to hear a single word from you.
You will return with me immediately, and we will attempt to mitigate
the unparalleled disaster you have brought upon yourself. Everyone
knows what you have been about, Elinor. They know you have spent
untold hours *alone* with the worst kind of reprobates the Navy can
dredge up. Lord Copley himself took great pleasure in telling me
where you were; can you imagine my humiliation? Your reputation is in
ruins. You have stained the Pembroke name with your behavior—think
of what you have done to your sister—do you believe *any* man will

want a wife who may be as ungoverned and wanton as her degenerate sister?"

She yanked on his hand, harder, and he crushed her arm with his grip. "Papa, I have done nothing to sully my reputation, I have been—"

"I told you to be silent." He began dragging her toward one of the hallways leading off the entrance. "We will find a Bounder to take you back to London; I cannot bring myself to call it your home, since your actions prove you think little of those who reared and cared for you."

"No." Where was Stratford? He must have been called away. He could not have known she would need him.

She began struggling, drawing more attention to herself, but still no one said a word. Frantically, she slapped at her father's hand, realizing only when it was too late that her own hand was on fire. Mr. Pembroke thrust her away from him, clutching his burned hand to his chest. "*How dare you!*" he shouted. "You *dare* use your vile talent on your own father!"

"It... it was an accident, papa, forgive me. Forgive me!"

He examined his hand closely. Elinor did not think it looked badly burned, but the fury in his eyes told her it was the same to him as if she'd burned it off entirely. "Ungoverned, ungrateful *wretch*. I thank God for all our sakes Lord Huxley is still willing to offer you the protection of his name. You will have to demonstrate your gratitude to him. Redeem yourself, and someday I may forgive you for your arrogant selfishness."

"No," Elinor whispered, her eyes filling with tears. "I will not return with you."

"You have no choice in the matter. I am your father and you will do as I say."

"I beg your pardon," said a familiar, perfectly composed voice, "but Miss Pembroke is not going anywhere."

"Who the devil are you, interfering in a private matter?" Mr. Pembroke said.

"Captain Miles Ramsay," Ramsay said, coming to stand close behind Elinor. His warm, strong presence at her back was like an anchor, steadying her against the fear her father always instilled in her.

239

"I'm Miss Pembroke's commanding officer. I take it you are Mr. Pembroke."

"The idea that my daughter is a member of His Majesty's Navy is simply ridiculous," Mr. Pembroke said. "She has no commanding officer. She owes her obedience to *me*."

"Miss Pembroke is of age and an Extraordinary and therefore allowed to enter into contracts in her own name. She has served valiantly in several battles. The Navy believes her to be one of its own."

"I came here to speak to Admiral Durrant. He'll listen to reason, or I'll bring suit against him for abduction."

"I chose this path, papa—"

"If you will not be silent, I will silence you myself!"

"Do not make threats against Miss Pembroke," Ramsay said, his calm tone turning to anger.

Elinor did not have to see Ramsay to know he would fight this battle for her as surely as she knew she could not allow him to. She looked at her father's face, contorted with fury, and remembered that long night curled up in the crevice of the rock, and could not understand why she had ever feared him.

"I will not be silent!" she shouted. "You have belittled me, and mocked me, and told me I should be grateful for your attention, paltry as it was, and I owe you *nothing*. I will not return with you, papa, I will not marry according to your dictates, I will not behave as you demand so you will be covered in my reflected glory. And I feel no remorse for taking the action I did!"

"You dare speak to your father—"

Elinor laughed. "My father? Had you ever behaved toward me as a father should toward his daughter, we would not now be having this conversation. I might have remained at home, meek and biddable, living an empty life. So I must thank you for being the impetus that brought me to a place I love, surrounded by people who respect me and my talent."

She snatched at his wrist and brought his burned hand up to hang, unresisting, between them. "My talent, papa. You thought only of my talent in the abstract, didn't you? As a chapter in your ongoing thesis? You never realized what the world would think of me. Did you know if

I am so much as threatened, my *attacker* will be brought up on charges before a court of law regardless of what I do to him in my defense? That's how valuable I am, papa, and if you dare lay a hand on me again, I will destroy it and no one, *no one*, will step in to defend you."

She flung his hand away from her. "Speak to the admiral if you must. He doesn't like me much, and I am certain you will both have much to talk about with regard to my character. But he will never grant your request, because I am needed here."

Mr. Pembroke's face was the color of old brick and his mouth hung open, his jaw slack. He rubbed his wrist as if she'd already carried out her threat. "You are nothing to me," he whispered. "I disown you. Never return, do you hear? I never want to see your face again. From this moment I have only two daughters."

"I think, in a sense, that is all you have ever had," Elinor said.

Mr. Pembroke's jaw twitched. He pushed past Ramsay like a blind man, striding back toward the entrance hall.

"Mr. Hervey, take Miss Pembroke back to the ship," Ramsay said in a low voice. "I think I will make sure he doesn't cause more trouble." He squeezed Elinor's shoulder briefly, then went off after her father.

"Clap on," Stratford said, and there was a moment of insubstantiality and she was on *Athena* again. She didn't need to see the unique symbol of the Bounding chamber; she could tell by the smell of Dolph's cooking and the way the ship rocked on the harbor waves that she was home.

"I didn't know where you were," she said.

"I went for the captain as soon as I saw there was trouble," Stratford said. "Was that truly your father?"

Elinor laughed bitterly. "Did you not hear? He disowned me. I have no father." She pushed open the door of the Bounding chamber and crossed the empty mess deck, propelled by a confusing mixture of emotions. Her family had cast her off—she had finally, *finally* stood up to her father—Ramsay had come when she needed him—she was back on *Athena*, this time for always—*where am I to go when this war is over? Does Selina despise me?*

The thought was enough to turn all those emotions into tears, and she sped up her pace, ignoring Stratford's questions. "I cannot," she said, "do not ask me," knowing that did not make sense, and fled to the privacy of what was once again her bedchamber.

It did not appear Ramsay had used it while she was gone. He must have been certain she would come back someday, to give up his comfort for over a month when there was no need for it. She sat on her bed and covered her face with her hands, but no more tears came. Of course not; why would they? She had won two battles today, three if you included intimidating Crawford, which still stirred her heart with fierce joy.

She pictured her father's face, as shocked by her sudden and violent outburst as the fox must be when the hen turns and savages him. She regretted nothing she had said. She had been entirely right about everything, except possibly for her assertion that she could burn him with impunity. Well, if Ramsay had got away with murder...except her talent was far more terrifying than his, and it was possible the government might actually put her to death if they thought she was capable of indiscriminate killing. She let her hand burn and turned it about, marveling at the colors. She would simply have to avoid killing anyone who was not a pirate. It was such an absurd thought that she laughed.

"If you're capable of laughing, I will assume you aren't consumed with remorse," Ramsay said, his voice muffled by the door.

"I will never feel remorse for what I said," Elinor said, opening the door to find Ramsay smiling at her. Something about him looked different—his hair, perhaps? "I should have said it all years ago."

"Mr. Hervey was in such distress when he arrived I thought I might need to rescue you from a dragon," Ramsay said. "But it seems you didn't need rescuing."

"I could never have stood up to him had you not been there. You gave me courage."

"Then I'm happy to have been of use after all." He smiled again, and bowed.

That was it. All his teeth were perfectly straight. Why he had had the crooked one fixed after all this time—but then, Elinor knew something of what it was like to finally be driven to fix a problem you had been living with for years.

"Your father went back to London, as far as I could tell," Ramsay went on. "He didn't speak with the admiral. I assume he was serious about his threat to disown you."

"He is always serious about his threats. It is how he makes them convincing."

Ramsay leaned against the door frame. "And he threatened to make you marry?"

"Yes. But I refuse to marry merely to be some breeding animal." Elinor's hands flew up to cover her mouth. "I cannot believe I said anything so indelicate to you!"

Ramsay laughed. "Well, you *have* been spending a great deal of your time among sailors. You'll be drinking grog next."

"That will never happen, I assure you, Captain."

"I feel some anxiety about asking you this question, but did I have Mr. Hervey abduct you?"

Elinor shook her head, feeling that warm joy fill her chest again. "I am assigned to *Athena*, Captain," she said.

Ramsay closed his eyes and gave an exaggerated sigh of relief. "I'm glad to hear it, because I told Dolph to set you a place at the table, and you know how I hate to look foolish."

⚶

AFTER HER MIDDAY MEAL, WHERE SHE RELATED HER CONVERSATIONS with Crawford and with Durrant and caused Ramsay nearly to choke on his mutton with laughter, Stratford took her into Hamilton for another shopping trip. She had chosen a gown and a nightdress before realizing she did not have sufficient funds to pay for them. Humiliated, she was about to hand them back to the shopkeeper when Stratford dipped into a little purse and put down a few coins. "Stratford!" she exclaimed. "I cannot accept! You ought not to spend your money on me."

Stratford shook his head. "It's your pay."

"It is not. You are making things up so I will accept your charity."

"It's not charity either. Captain said, she should have drawn her pay weeks ago, probably doesn't know she's due it, don't let her drink it all away."

"Stratford!"

"Thought that would draw you out. I made that last bit up, but the rest is true. I just forgot to give you it before." He slapped the purse into her palm.

"I—but this seems too much."

"I wouldn't know, except I hear they pay Extraordinaries very well."

"But I...made other arrangements for my remuneration."

Stratford shrugged. "I wouldn't know about that."

Elinor felt the purse again. She was certain the Admiralty considered her eventual fifteen-thousand-pound payment in lieu of her salary as well as her prize money. This "pay" had come directly from Ramsay's pocket.

Face burning, she watched the shopkeeper wrap her purchases in brown paper. She should not accept. More gratitude, making a barrier between them. What must he think of her, that she was so helpless? And yet there would be no point to confronting him; he would insist, with that infuriating calmness, that it was her pay, that she owed him nothing but a thank-you for having procured what was due her. She reached out to accept the parcel and had it taken from her by Stratford, who mock-scowled at her for not allowing him to be chivalrous and then returned them to *Athena* before she could object.

She folded the gown into her new trunk, looked at it for a little while, then closed the lid and stood there with her hand on it. She could not understand why this disturbed her so much. If the situation were reversed...she pictured herself paying for Ramsay's uniform and smiled despite herself. It simply felt so...intimate, as if he had stood in the shop and paid for the gown himself. She simply could not accept; it was improper for her to accept such a gift even from her friend.

The alternative is that you continue to wear this shabby brown dress that no doubt makes you look like a streak of dirt, with those sun-browned hands and face, she told herself. *How mean-spirited, to reject his friendship over something so insignificant.* She opened the trunk, removed the new gown and changed her clothes. If he could lie about the money, she could pretend she believed the lie. She refused to consider her disquiet more deeply.

She spent the rest of the afternoon reacquainting herself with *Athena*, cheerfully greeting the seamen who hailed her, spending half an hour watching Bolton and his mate repair damage from their last battle ("Would'ha gone quicker w' you here, missie"), pretending pleasure at Selkirk's effusive welcome. She avoided Livingston, though his expression disturbed her, made her reach for a memory she could not quite identify. Hays was quietly pleased to see her again and had stories of his travels in the hills of Jamaica, searching for *Nesopsar nigerrimus* and *Euphonia jamaica*.

She sat down to supper with Ramsay, Beaumont, Livingston, and Sampson Brown, the sailing master, and enjoyed even Livingston's company, though he smirked unpleasantly when he caught her eye. She still had the feeling she was forgetting something when she looked at him. She was still thinking about it when Ramsay pushed back from the table and said, "Dolph, clear this away, and Mr. Beaumont, if you'd be so good as to bring out the big map."

Elinor stood to move out of Dolph's way and bumped into Livingston. "I beg your pardon," she said, just as he said, "I beg your pardon" and stepped to one side, an unpleasant smile on his lips. Elinor pretended not to notice. He had the look of a man with a nasty secret who was waiting for someone to pay him not to reveal it. Well, whatever secrets he had were nothing to her.

Lord Copley himself took great pleasure in telling me where you were, her father said in her memory. *Lord Copley wants great things for his son,* Ramsey had said.

The memories echoed so loudly that she was startled when the Ramsay of the present said, "Miss Pembroke, won't you join us?" She nodded, too stunned to speak, and took her seat and leaned forward to examine the map of the Caribbean now spread on the table.

"This is the island where you discovered the pirates, Miss Pembroke," Ramsay said, tapping the map near the eastern coast of Jamaica. "Admiral Durrant is correct that Evans will not have left anything that could be used to See his location, doubly so because he is himself an Extraordinary Seer. Arthur?"

Beaumont was sitting with his head tilted slightly back and his eyes wide open but sightless, indicating he was Speaking to someone. They all waited, Elinor somewhat impatiently, until Beaumont lowered his head and said, "That was Harris at Montego Bay. No unknown ships have passed in the last twenty-four hours. If Evans is going that way, they'd have seen him before now."

"He might not have sailed within sight of land," Livingston said.

"Also possible, Mr. Livingston," Ramsay said, "which is why I'm not discounting the possibility that the pirates headed for Cartagena or Maracaibo. What's important is that Evans had to leave in a hurry, and that should make him careless.

"So there are two ways we can track him. It is possible all the Brethren left in convoy, which means we'd be looking for four or five ships traveling together instead of a single ship, and that will make them much more visible. Unfortunately for us, Evans is clever, and it's more likely he told his men to make their own way to wherever the new hiding place is."

"Which makes him virtually impossible to find," Livingston said with a sneer.

"But thanks to Miss Pembroke," Ramsay said, "we know something about the Brethren's ships, namely, that one of Evans' fellow Brethren has a captured Navy ship, one of our fifth-rates like *Athena*. The Fleet of the Americas isn't large, and our ship movements are known to the Speaker reticulum to facilitate their information gathering. Which means our second method of tracking Evans, and the more likely method, is to look for Navy ships in places where no Navy ship should be."

"I thought Admiral Durrant was going to do this," Elinor said.

"He is. He's also not going about it quickly." Ramsay pushed his hair back from his face. "Admiral Durrant is an excellent tactician, and despite our disagreements I have always respected his successes in this war. However, he can be overly cautious, and he doesn't like innovation. He'll send word to the Speaker reticulum to keep their eyes open for unknown ships, and if they turn up anything, he'll act on it, but he won't put any more effort into it than that. If we can locate Evans' new stronghold, however we manage it, he'll put up a token resistance and then act on it as if it was his own idea."

"You hope. Sir," Livingston said.

"I am certain of it, Lieutenant," Ramsay said, his voice going cool.

Elinor, watching Livingston closely, saw his lip curl briefly before he nodded his acknowledgement of Ramsay's authority.

Beaumont threw his head back again, and Ramsay and Livingston went silent, waiting. Elinor kept her eyes on Livingston, her hands clenched in her lap under the table. He dared—

"Durham at Santiago de Cuba," Beaumont said, and he was smiling. "An unscheduled Navy frigate passed the observation point, traveling east, yesterday evening exactly at sunset."

Ramsay jabbed his finger at the map. "Right there, going east. Gentlemen, any predictions?"

They all leaned over the map. Elinor peered beneath their arms, slightly annoyed.

"Could be anywhere along the coast of Cuba," Beaumont said. "Any Spanish port would give the pirates shelter."

"That would make them impossible to find," said Livingston.

"Let's assume for now that this is not impossible," Ramsay said. He traced a line along the map. "Most of Saint-Domingue is still in turmoil; Evans could take advantage of that. There are any number of coves along that coast."

"Could they have reached Port-au-Prince?" said Livingston. "Based on how fast they were traveling...yes," he said, answering his own question.

"No one's seen them there, but as the captain said, they're—excuse me," Beaumont said, and tilted his head back again.

"I still say we should be looking at the Cuban coast," Livingston said. "Isn't there someone at Ymia?"

"I don't believe Mr. Beaumont knows that Speaker, unfortunately," said Ramsay. "If his other contacts know nothing, I will have to visit Admiralty House in the morning and see what I can discover. Still, Mr. Livingston, we have eliminated the west as their possible destination, and I call that success."

"Mole Saint Nicolas, Captain," said Beaumont, "and they saw an unknown frigate pass going eastward at seven a.m. today."

Ramsay and Livingston exchanged glances, their mutual animosity forgotten for the moment. "Saint-Domingue?" Livingston said.

"They're traveling fast," Ramsay said. "They might be going as far as Puerto Rico."

"We're never going to find them. The Speaker reticulum doesn't extend all the way eastward along the northern coast of Saint-Domingue."

"Don't lose hope yet, Mr. Livingston. Arthur, what about Port de Paix?"

"Westin's not responding, Miles. I think he has the late watch and he won't be awake for another hour."

"I see. I suppose this means we will wait. Mr. Livingston, would you mind taking over for Mr. Fitzgerald on the quarterdeck? We'll call you when there's news."

Livingston's lip curled, just enough to be a sneer without being insubordinate, but he nodded and left the room. When he had left the room, Ramsay closed his eyes and said, "If I were a swearing man, which I am not, I think I could blister the paint off the wall right now."

Elinor giggled. He looked down at her, raised his eyebrows and said, "Should I bring you a tankard of grog, Miss Pembroke?"

"It is not as if you actually swore in front of me, Captain. I hardly think my amusement makes me indelicate."

"Miles, you will have to do something about him," Beaumont said. "The men have started to notice and it's hurting morale. They're going to think you're weak."

"If you have a suggestion, I'd like to hear it."

Beaumont shook his head. "Send him before the mast. Strip him of rank for a few weeks. Or months. Confine him to quarters. Have him flogged."

"There are political problems with all of those suggestions."

Elinor pushed back from the table. "Please excuse me, gentlemen, I think I will take a short walk if we are to wait an hour for further information."

She went up on deck and stood for a moment, breathing the night air mixed with *Athena*'s distinctive scent of canvas and tar and something indefinable she had never smelled anywhere else. It seemed the day had one more confrontation in it.

She moved past the wheel and the mizzenmast to join Livingston where he stood near the rail. "Mr. Livingston, good evening," she said.

Livingston continued to gaze out over the rail. "I suppose you're ecstatic to be back on this hulk."

"I would take issue with two of those words, but I feel so much gratitude toward you, I cannot find it in me to argue semantics."

He looked down at her, confused. "Gratitude?"

"Yes. Have you not heard? My father came to Admiralty House this morning. Someone had told him where I was, and he came to take me back to London."

Livingston smiled at her, nastily. "Did he now? I'm sure that was distressing."

"Oh, for a moment only. You see, I have never been able to stand up to my father. Not until today. It's liberating, not being afraid anymore."

The nasty smile disappeared. "I don't see why you owe me gratitude," he said.

Elinor put a confiding hand on his arm. "It was something my father said," she told him. "About how Lord Copley was so very obliging as to tell him where I was. And I thought, why would the Viscount care about me at all? Then I remembered—he is your father, is he not? So, of course, *you* must have told him."

Livingston pulled his arm from her grasp. "I think you are confused," he said.

"And *I* think you are not a fool," Elinor said. "You dislike me. You thought to ruin me by telling the world where I was. You succeeded, Mr. Livingston. My reputation is shattered beyond repair. When I return to England, as I eventually must, it will be to near-universal disapprobation. So you may congratulate yourself on having succeeded at your goal."

"I—I admit nothing."

"You *understand* nothing, Mr. Livingston." Elinor raised herself on tiptoe to whisper in his ear. "We both know what you have done. What you fail to grasp is that I now have nothing left to lose. There is nothing more society can do to me. I am free, Mr. Livingston, free from fear, and I have you to thank for it."

"You're mad."

"What, because I can thank you for ruining me? Perhaps. But I think I am sane. Shall we ask Captain Ramsay to decide for us?"

Now Livingston looked a little afraid. "This has nothing to do with him."

"It does, though. You see, my father intended to take me back to London, which would have deprived the captain of a powerful weapon he has taken some pains to reclaim. I think if he knew you were responsible for that state of affairs, he would be angry. And I think he would be interested in turning that anger on you."

"He can do nothing to me."

"Oh, come now, Lieutenant, we both know that is not true. I think you have given him cause to finally rid himself of you. I wonder how happy your father will be to find you have destroyed your career?"

Livingston grabbed her by the arm, exactly as her father had done that morning. "You will say *nothing* of this—"

Elinor brought her other hand around, blazing, and grabbed his wrist, making him cry out with pain and release her. "You forget yourself," she said coldly. "Touch me again and you will receive worse."

Again unconsciously mimicking her father, Livingston clutched his injured arm to his chest. "Don't tell him," he said, breathing heavily. "My father—I'll do anything—"

"Stop belittling Captain Ramsay," Elinor said. "Humble yourself and make it clear he has your respect and obedience. No more sneering or speaking ill of him behind his back. *Athena* is my home, Lieutenant, and you are trying to tear her apart. Start behaving like a man instead of a spoiled child, and I will say nothing to anyone. Continue as you have done, and the captain learns of your…indiscretion. Do we have an understanding?"

Livingston nodded rapidly. "I beg your pardon," he began.

"Please do not apologize to me," Elinor said, "for what you have done. I truly am grateful not to have this beam hanging above my head. Thank you."

She went back down the companionway, feeling strangely afloat. So few hours had passed since she entered Admiralty House that morning, and yet how much had happened, how many burdens had fallen from her back. Livingston was nothing compared to Durrant, who was nothing compared to her father, and she had faced all three and won, though she thought Livingston's change of heart would not last forever. Even so, it was a victory. Elinor plucked at her skirt. He would never know it, but she had repaid Ramsay's gift in her own way.

Fitzgerald opened the door to the great cabin just as she had her hand on the knob. "Excuse me, Miss Pembroke," he said, and held the door for her before hurrying off. Ramsay, Beaumont, and Brown were all leaning over the table, intent on the map.

"Have you learned something, gentlemen?" she asked.

"Probably," said Ramsay. "Beaumont Spoke to Westin at Port de Paix minutes ago. No unknown ships have passed there in the last twenty-four hours." He was smiling.

"You seem excited about what does not sound like good news. Do you not want the Speakers to observe Evans' ships?"

"It's as important what they *don't* see. Gentlemen, if you'd join us?" He said this last to Fitzgerald and Livingston, who jostled each other trying to enter the room at the same time. Elinor found herself wedged between Ramsay and Brown, looking down at the colorful map.

"Port de Paix is here, on the coast of Saint-Domingue," Ramsay said, pointing. "This is Mole Saint Nicolas here, to the west. Evans' ship was seen off that point, going east, which put him along the northern coast, and that would mean he'd have passed Port de Paix before midmorning today. Except Westin says they haven't seen it."

The other men all exchanged glances. "I feel there is something I am missing," Elinor said.

"If the pirate ship didn't pass Port de Paix, there's only one place it could be going," Ramsay said. He pointed at a spot on the map Elinor had thought was a smudge. "They're on Tortuga."

CHAPTER 21
IN WHICH THERE IS A GREAT
DEAL OF PLANNING

"I beg your pardon, but they could still have gone around the northern side of the island to stay out of sight of Port de Paix, sir," Livingston said, deliberately not looking at Elinor.

Ramsay opened his mouth to reply, gave Livingston a suspicious look, and said, "There are two more observation points, at Fort St. Louis and Le Cap, but Mr. Beaumont doesn't know anyone there. We'll have to wait until morning to see what Admiralty House can tell us. I hate waiting on this."

"The pirates probably aren't going anywhere," Fitzgerald pointed out.

"With an Extraordinary Seer as their leader?" Ramsay said. "Every minute that passes is a minute in which he might See what we're planning."

"I beg your pardon, gentlemen, but what does this mean?" Elinor said. "Surely we must have more concrete proof than this, which is—I beg your pardon—based on reasoning and not on direct evidence. Not that I mean to belittle your work, and I am certainly convinced of your conclusions, but I daresay Admiral Durrant will not launch an offensive without more facts than this."

"He'll want visual confirmation," agreed Beaumont, "and honestly, it's going to take some doing to prove they're on Tortuga."

All the men nodded or murmured in agreement. Elinor said, "I am afraid I don't understand. I thought Tortuga was a notorious pirate stronghold."

"Emphasis on 'was,' " said Fitzgerald. "Tortuga's buccaneers were cleaned out by the end of the seventeenth century. It's all plantation owners and farmers now. France made sure that was all it would ever be, since they were afraid it might be a rallying point for the upsurge in piratical activity after Evans appeared. But now that it's owned by the freemen of Saint-Domingue...could be the Tortugan land owners saw a benefit to providing a sanctum to Evans' men."

"I don't know," Livingston said, "The rebel unrest might have spilled over into greater lawlessness, true, but I think Port de Paix would have noticed that kind of traffic. Tortuga's harbor is almost directly opposite it."

"Could the pirates be using a different harbor?" Elinor asked.

"Nothing else there," said Brown, who had been frowning over the map as if plotting a course for *Athena*. "North shore's rocky right down to the waterline. No place for even a sloop to dock, let alone a handful of warships."

"But he could make a harbor, could he not?"

All the men except Ramsay, who had gone to stand by the window, stared at her as if they were trying not to give in to hoots of derision. "Miss Pembroke, it's not as simple as digging a hole in the sand," Beaumont said, kindly enough that Elinor was irritated until she remembered they had not been privy to her conversation with Ramsay about the pirate cove.

"I forget you gentlemen did not see what I did," she said, and briefly explained what she had observed on her island. Their looks of carefully concealed disbelief melted into surprise.

"That sounds impossible—not to contradict you, Miss Pembroke, it's simply hard to imagine how many Movers one would have to have to do such a thing," Fitzgerald said. "Cracking the stone alone would be...it's simply mind-boggling."

"I agree," Elinor said. "But I heard the pirates refer to Evans sending his Movers to apprehend Dewdney, and I infer he must have many if he expects them to shepherd an Extraordinary Scorcher back to the fold, let alone capture one. And we have no idea how many years ago he might have begun excavation. It might be a stronghold of long standing."

"They have an Extraordinary Scorcher?" Livingston exclaimed, then snapped his mouth shut tight as if he had remembered he was afraid to speak to Elinor.

"I think there is much the captain and I have failed to share with you," Elinor said, glancing at Ramsay for permission, but he continued to stare out the windows toward the dock, so she related the rest of the details of her time on the island, leaving out her terrifying flight and the night spent huddled in the crevice.

Fitzgerald sat down heavily in his chair before she was halfway finished. Beaumont and Livingston stared at her, the first in amazement, the second in a kind of frightened awe. Brown continued his study of the map, apparently not heeding her, but when she finished, he said, "Always knew you were a Navy man at heart," which made Elinor smile and blush.

"An Extraordinary Scorcher. An army of Movers, some of whom might be Extraordinaries themselves. And who knows what the hell—I beg your pardon, Captain—who knows what else he might have," said Livingston. "And that's all after we dig him out of his man-made, probably fortified harbor. *And* we'll likely have to fight off his ships before we can even get to that point. I apologize for being so pessimistic, but this doesn't look easy. The one advantage we have is that he doesn't have any Bounders, and that seems almost too lucky."

"Talent's not evenly distributed," Brown said. "We've almost no Scorchers but a grundle of Speakers. Not impossible that Evans don't have many Bounders."

"Let's hope that's still true when it comes to an attack," said Livingston.

"If we can get Admiral Durrant to agree to an attack—he's a good strategist," Fitzgerald said.

"Good with sea battles. I doubt he's ever planned an assault on a fortified position."

"Mr. Livingston," Elinor said, causing Livingston to jerk with surprise, "why are you certain Evans will have fortified his stronghold? I saw no fortifications in the one I observed."

"Oh. Ah, Miss Pembroke, you—and I mean no disrespect to your observational powers—you probably wouldn't have," Livingston said. He seemed to be growing used to the idea that she was not going to start hurling accusations at him. "They would have been higher than the shoreline and likely concealed. You said there was a cliff, correct? The best location for an emplacement would be somewhere defensible like that. If he had enough Movers to carve that cliff side, he'd have enough to build stone emplacements and set some large cannons into them.

"And a shore-based battery is deadly to ships—they can find their range easily without having to compensate for the movement of the deck, not to mention supporting larger cannons that have a greater range than ours do."

"You terrify me, Mr. Livingston." Elinor felt faint at the idea of *Athena* coming under fire like that. "How does anyone defend against such things?"

"Brute force," said Fitzgerald. "Or a raiding party to take out the cannons from the shore side."

"That is what I have been thinking," Elinor said. "I do not see why I should not find my way there and set—"

"You will not be mounting any one-woman raids, Miss Pembroke," Ramsay said, still looking out the window.

"But I assure you—"

He turned to face her, and there was no humor in those blue eyes. "*It will not happen*, do you understand me? Even you can't burn stone, and if you encounter that Dewdney, you will be far too busy fighting him to do us any good. So stop considering it. There's no point in planning an assault strategy when we don't know what we're facing.

"In the morning I will go to Admiralty House with...Mr. Livingston"—again, he gave Livingston a narrow-eyed look—"to verify that Evans' fleet didn't continue along the coast of Saint-Domingue. After that...I have a few ideas, depending on the admiral's available talents, but we can discuss that in the morning. So I suggest you all take yourselves off to bed or watch, and we'll discuss further after breakfast tomorrow morning. Miss Pembroke, if you wouldn't mind waiting?"

Elinor took her seat at the table while the lieutenants left and Brown rolled up the map and stowed it away, saying, "Navy man," and nodding at Elinor as he left.

Ramsay remained silent until the room was empty but for the two of them, then continued silent, looking out the window again, until Elinor became impatient and said, "Did you ask me to stay behind because you wished an audience for your reverie?"

He chuckled and shook his head, then came to take his seat next to her. "I have been trying to decide how to ask you what you did to Livingston. No, decide whether I *should* ask you, since I might need to deny knowing whatever it was."

"I? I think you are mistaken, Captain. I did nothing to Mr. Livingston." *Exactly true.*

He raised his eyebrows at her. "Livingston leaves the room, you follow him, he returns and is suddenly, inexplicably polite and respectful to me. I'm not sure what other conclusion I can draw."

"I walked on the quarterdeck and came back. It was a pleasant night and it made me feel at peace. Perhaps Mr. Livingston had a similar experience."

"You're not going to tell me, are you."

"Because there is nothing to tell."

Ramsay rolled his eyes and stood to walk back toward the window. "Well, you have my thanks, if it turns out he's had as complete a change of heart as it seems."

"I certainly hope he has, Captain."

"I could order you, as your commanding officer, to tell me."

"You could, Captain, but I would disobey, you would have to order me flogged, the crew would all mutiny, and you would end your days marooned on some tiny Caribbean island eating nothing but raw breadfruit and unripe coconuts."

"Raw breadfruit is indigestible."

"Then coconuts it will have to be."

Ramsay laughed. "Miss Pembroke, it is good to have you back aboard."

"I am happy to be here, Captain Ramsay. I have missed our conversations."

"So have I." His eyes met hers and his smile faded, replaced by a more serious expression. "I—" he began, then blinked a few times and gave her a wry smile. "I hope I have success at Admiralty House tomorrow. Admiral Durrant isn't happy with me right now, and it will take a great deal of incontrovertible evidence to get him to agree to my plan. No, to *Livingston's* plan, as I intend him to be my mouthpiece. The Admiral respects Lord Copley...unfortunately it's Admiral Durrant's unthinking deference to titles that put us in this position. Mr. Livingston's father is a viscount; Admiral Durrant wants Crawford to be ennobled; I am only an upstart with more talent than I deserve—"

"I do not understand how Lord Ormerod can be your cousin if you are not noble."

"Third cousin. Our...let me see...we have the same great-great-grandfather, some craftsman or other, not wealthy but able to support his family well enough. He had two sons, one of whom manifested Moving talent; that son was given a title and property, you know how it goes, or maybe you don't—"

"Of course I do. My father has spent his life tracking the intersections of talent with nobility. The ancestors of two-thirds of the talented nobles in England received their titles in service to Charles II. I am surprised *you* have not been offered a title, since the King and now the Prince Regent are so profligate with them."

Ramsay shuddered. "The Regency Bill was supposed to deny the Regent power to award peerages. How I wish that provision had remained—but talent must be rewarded, and who knows how long the King may be incapacitated by his Extraordinary Discerner talent? I cannot imagine what it must be like, feeling what everyone around him feels, unable to distinguish between his own emotions and theirs... I should not pity my king, but it's hard to feel anything but compassion for his condition.

"At any rate, I've managed to keep far away from England for the last seven years, away from anyone who might think my naval rank and prize money aren't reward enough for an Extraordinary. I wouldn't mind becoming an admiral someday, but an earl or a marquess...no. I have trouble imagining myself as some sort of lord. Harry loves it, let him have it. At any rate, I'm descended from the brother who didn't manifest. There was no talent in that side of the family until I came along, and I—" All the chairs except Elinor's lifted into the air at once and came down neatly aligned along the table. "More talent than I deserve, from the admiral's point of view."

"I suppose if you were a lord, Admiral Durrant would heed your words better."

"True. Though I'm not sure the end would be worth the means."

"So what is your plan? Or should I not ask?"

Ramsay shrugged and came to sit down next to her, the chair scraping itself away from the table without being touched. "I'm going to prove the pirates are on Tortuga. I'm going to ask for one of the admiral's Bounder spies to sneak in and retrieve some object for the Extraordinary Seer to focus on. Then I'm going to have the Seers produce drawings of Evans' stronghold and its fortifications. And then I'm going to give it all to Admiral Durrant, or have Mr. Livingston do it, and ask for his advice." He smiled at her. "A little humility goes a long way, with the admiral."

"Then I imagine you must have great difficulties in dealing with him."

Ramsay's eyebrows climbed practically to his hairline. "Miss Pembroke! You shouldn't take such liberties with your commanding officer's character."

Elinor smiled with her eyes cast down, demurely. "I have those difficulties myself, Captain, so I do not think it much of a character flaw."

Ramsay laughed and struck the table with the palm of his hand, one resounding smack. "I suggest you get some sleep, Miss Pembroke. Once we convince the admiral that action is both needed and possible, I want you present for the planning council. I'm certain Admiral Durrant will want you to play a role in the assault."

ELINOR SAW LITTLE OF RAMSAY OVER THE NEXT THREE DAYS. WITH no new orders forthcoming, the officers spent most of their time trying to maintain discipline over nearly three hundred men. Though the sailors had their pay and were allowed to go into Kingston in small groups to spend it, they were still aboard most of the time, the gunnery crews practicing to improve their speed, the others busy with their duties, painting the ship or cleaning the copper bottom. When not thus engaged, they drank, and ate, and played music and told stories, and Elinor was certain they were also gambling, though Ramsay disapproved of it.

Elinor, however, had little outlet for practicing her talent, as burning the harbor and the other Navy ships was frowned on, and she was frequently bored. Stratford was kept busy taking people to and from Admiralty House and other locations, so he was unable to procure her new books. Walking along the harbor at Port Royal, as she was not permitted to go alone into Kingston, lost its appeal approximately five minutes after she touched solid ground. Most of the livestock had been slaughtered, removing even the slight entertainment of watching them eat and relieve themselves.

She finally took to standing at the taffrail and flinging fireballs out and away, trying to increase her range and accuracy. This proved to be a popular activity, and the sailors began hunting down things that could float for her to aim at. When the noise became too loud, whoever the officer of the day was would shoo everyone away, and Elinor would go back to the great cabin and fidget, or lean out one of the windows and drop handfuls of liquid fire into the ocean and watch it boil.

She was engaged in entertaining the crew on the afternoon of the third day when a calm voice said, "I had no idea you wanted to be a performer. Perhaps you could go on the stage when your naval service is finished."

She extinguished the fire she was holding and said, "Captain, I do not believe I have ever been so excruciatingly bored in my entire life."

Ramsay chuckled. "Back to work," he shouted, and the crowd dispersed, muttering. "They'll have something more engaging to do soon," he said, "as will you. We're going to Admiralty House to discuss strategy."

"You have persuaded the admiral?"

"*Mr. Livingston* has persuaded the admiral. Mr. Livingston has continued to be respectful, obedient, helpful, and filled with all manner of other virtues that terrify me, since I'm waiting for him to revert to type."

He paused and raised his eyebrows at her, offering her the opportunity to speak; when she looked innocently back at him, he shook his head in mock-despair. "I've commended his performance to the admiral, and honestly, he deserves most of it. I didn't realize he could actually think. With him making some valuable contributions and me being at my most persuasive with the Seers, we managed to get quite a few drawings of Evans' stronghold."

Elinor let out a long breath of relief. "Then it is there."

"It is," Ramsay said, but he didn't sound happy.

"Something is wrong."

"I'd rather not give you the details until you can see the drawings yourself, but...it won't be easy."

"I still think I—"

"If you're about to say you want to go in alone and burn the place to the ground, I don't intend to listen. It would be suicide, Miss Pembroke, and as we have other options, we're not going to entertain that one."

"And am I to play a part in these 'other options'?"

"I think so. Come, let's join the others and see what Admiral Durrant has in mind."

Five other captains waited in Admiral Durrant's Board Room when they arrived, among them Horace, who smiled and nodded at Elinor. She knew none of the other captains; Crawford was not present. The men stood around the table in varying degrees of awkward silence, all of them except Horace unwilling to meet her eyes.

Elinor gripped her skirt in her hands and twisted it until it wrinkled, then tried to smooth the wrinkles out. Ramsay stood next to her, as calm as if he were at a picnic, hands behind his back and head tilted slightly. It was a bad idea, her being here, they did not need her—

"Gentlemen, Miss Pembroke, pray have a seat," Durrant said, entering the room and flinging himself into his chair at the head of the table without waiting for anyone to follow his instructions. He looked tired and angry, with his clothes in disarray and his teakwood face more lined than usual. A knot of apprehension formed in her stomach. He did not look like a man who anticipated victory.

Ramsay held Elinor's chair for her then sat down beside her. Elinor leaned over and whispered, "Is the admiral—"

"Be silent, Miss Pembroke, or I'll have you removed," the admiral said, slamming his fist down on the table. She shied away from him in surprise. "You're all here because your ships are either anchored at Port Royal or are stationed near Saint-Domingue, and that's going to matter in this action. Thanks to the diligent work of Lieutenant George Livingston, we've located Rhys Evans' secret stronghold." His voice was hoarser than usual, and Elinor almost thought he had been crying, if she had not been certain he was incapable of tears.

Durrant snapped his fingers at Sullyard, who had followed him into the room, and the man moved around the table, laying sheets of paper in front of each captain and Elinor. His hand brushed the nape of her neck as he leaned past her, and she bent away from him, furious and humiliated. He dared touch her!...but of course he dared, because she could not burn him without the admiral seeing it and throwing her out of the meeting, or worse. His hand on her neck trailed further down, caressing her back, and she scooted forward in her seat, praying he would move on soon.

Then Sullyard hissed in pain and bent, his hand dropping from her back to clutch his foot. Beside her, Ramsay was studying his papers and paying no attention to Sullyard's strange behavior.

Elinor looked at Sullyard's elegant shoe, at the thin leather and the unnecessarily high heel, looked at Ramsay's stout Hessian boot, just sliding back beneath his chair, and could not resist saying, "Oh, Mr. Sullyard, I imagine those shoes do pinch terribly, do they not? Perhaps you should have *chosen more wisely*." Sullyard straightened, glared wordlessly at her, and continued moving around the table.

Impulsively, Elinor reached out and found Ramsay's hand, resting on his knee under the table, and clasped it briefly in thanks. His attention never strayed from the papers in front of him, but his fingers curled around hers, gripping them for a fraction of a second when she would have let go.

The room suddenly seemed unaccountably warm, all those bodies in one place, the windows closed against the sunny Bermudan afternoon, and when he released her hand she raised it to her cheek, wondering if she looked as flushed as she felt. She could still feel his hand on hers. She busied herself with the papers Sullyard had given her, wishing for a breeze to cool her face.

She spread the four pages out so she could see them all at once. One was a map depicting a coastline, on which was centered a circular bay with its entrance on the east side. The second was a drawing of a tiny settlement, with rough huts and a larger building of unfinished logs that resembled the fortress she had seen on her island, and four ships drawn up in the vast harbor.

The third showed the same view as the second, but from farther away, as if the observer were in a boat and had rowed himself well out into the bay. High up on the cliff walls to either side of the settlement were rough stone boxes from which protruded cannons, at least six cannons on each side. The artistry of all three drawings was exquisite, making Elinor wonder if drawing was a skill all Seers were expected to master. The fourth drawing was much rougher and seemed to be a line drawing of a frigate with what Elinor could only describe as flaps along both sides and a strangely elongated stern.

"The stronghold's almost all the way to the west on the northern shore," Durrant continued, "and—damn it, Sullyard, where's the bloody map?"

Elinor refrained from flinching, or covering her mouth, or doing anything else that would make her look missish in front of these men, but Durrant's anger was beginning to frighten her. She had never seen him so close to losing control. She kept her eyes carefully averted, thinking he might decide to be infuriated by her presence, and focused on the map Sullyard was now unrolling from where it hung above the fireplace.

"Tortuga," Durrant said, stumping over to the map and smacking it hard with his slim wooden baton. "Here's where the cove is. It's sheltered and it has emplacements on the outer side as well as the inner. Look at the pictures and you'll see the wall of the cove protects it on the north so the harbor's nigh impossible to see when you're sailing past."

He indicated spots on the map with his baton. "There's a battery of guns in that north wall facing the sea, don't know how the hell he managed that, and another to the east of the cove's mouth, and then a shore battery inside the cove facing east, the guns pointed at the entrance. It's wide enough that he can get those four ships and more inside, and he dug the whole damn thing out himself, or rather, with his Movers, or so Miss Pembroke says." He glared at her, and she forced herself to return his gaze with a calm, indifferent demeanor.

"Right now, Evans is holed up inside with some or, if we're lucky, all of his captains. Nice, secure location, but it's a rat trap for those damned rats. We're going to blockade them in there and hammer away at the ships, so they won't have any way to escape, then send a detachment of Marines in to finish the job."

Durrant traced a curved line over the northern coast of Tortuga. "Current flows east to west here, so we'll sail around the south side of Tortuga and up to where that current will bring us straight into the mouth of Evans' bay. Nothing easier."

"Beg pardon, Admiral Durrant," said one of the captains, "but what about the emplacements?"

"What about them?"

The captain looked at his nearest neighbor. "Um...they'll keep pounding on us the whole time we're attacking the pirate fleet."

"We won't ever be in reach of the western battery. Eastern battery, we'll send *Breton's* Marines to take that out from the cliff side. And the inner emplacement, the one inside the cove, their own ships may get in the way, but if not, Miss Pembroke will keep it burning so they won't be able to fire at us."

Elinor shifted uncomfortably as every eye in the room was fixed on her. She glanced down at the drawings. "I beg your pardon, Admiral Durrant," she said, "but I cannot burn stone, and I do not believe—"

"You'll follow orders, or by God I will ship you back to England myself!" Durrant roared.

Elinor shut her mouth tight. The urge to terrify him with fire was so great she had to grip her hands together under the table. Ramsay, close beside her, tensed. Something was very wrong.

"Yes, sir," she said when she had regained a measure of control.

"Does anyone else wish to speak out?" Durrant said.

"Sir, is there enough room for all of us to maneuver in front of the cove's entrance?" asked another of the captains. Elinor waited for the explosion, but it never came, which made her angry. Apparently it was permissible for him to shout at *her* for questioning his plan, but let one of his precious captains, his *men*, raise a concern...

"Plenty of room," Durrant said. "We'll have Speakers communicating when and where you'll make your passes. You have something to add, Carruthers?" This last was directed at a portly red-haired captain who seemed unperturbed by Durrant's aggressive tone.

"Evans is an Extraordinary Seer," he said in a deep bass rumble. "He's been able to track our ships all along. How do we know he won't see us coming?"

"One of Lisbon's Extraordinary Seers has learned to do the same thing Evans does," Durrant said. "Evans is using the captured Navy ships as a...a generalized focus, or whatever the hell she calls it, and compelling Visions of all the ships that match that shape, then working out which Vision is important. We know he has *Olympia*—or he had before *Glorious* beat seven kinds of hell out of her. Captain Horace found her abandoned on that island of Miss Pembroke's. They also have *Tarsus* and *Melpomene*, which gives Evans a fourth-rate and two frigates to focus on.

"I don't mind telling you the man is some kind of damned savant to be sorting out the Visions of our fleet from all the other ships of their classes all over the world, but sort them he does. So we'll be altering the lines of your ships before we go, which should make them impossible for Evans to track, and we're also counting on the sheer mass of information he has to go through to hide the fact that we've disappeared.

"Now, get back to your ships and ready yourselves. Have your carpenters make the alterations indicated. Doesn't have to be pretty, just obvious. We have to do this quickly, before Evans Sees what we're up to. I'll be joining Walters on *Breton*. We're leaving Port Royal at noon tomorrow to meet with the rest of the fleet at Port de Paix on the first of July."

He rose from his chair and left the room before anyone else could stand. The captains began trading glances, some of them even looking at Elinor with what appeared to be apologies. So Durrant's behavior *was* erratic, and it was not her imagination.

Ramsay offered her his arm and she almost had to run to keep up with his pace. "I think we'll make a stop before returning to *Athena*," he said. He dragged her, clutching her drawings, through a doorway into a long, high-ceilinged room. It looked as if it might once have been a ballroom, with hooks in the ceiling from which chandeliers might have hung, brass sconces lining three of the four walls, and a fine parquet floor like interlaced trellises. The fourth wall was entirely made of tall, white-framed windows that looked out over the same lawn and garden Elinor had glimpsed from the admiral's board room.

Whatever the room's original purpose, it was now entirely given over to rows of wooden chairs, most of them occupied by men in uniforms of pale blue coats with rows of brass buttons, white shirts with high collars and cravats gone limp in the Caribbean heat, and nankeen trousers tucked into shiny brown leather boots. Each chair was pulled up to a small desk that looked almost like a child's toy, stacked high with sheets of poor-quality greyish paper and supplied with a brass inkwell and a jar filled with pens.

Many of the men had their heads tilted slightly back in the attitude of someone Speaking to another. Some were scribbling rapidly on sheets of paper, waving them in the air to dry them, then folding them in half and writing something on the outside. Young boys dressed in a cut-down version of the Speaker uniform waited to take those folded papers, then either put them in one of the cubbies that lined the other long wall, or ran out through the north or south door as if being chased.

The room was eerily silent except for the scratching of pen nibs and the occasional patter of feet across the trellis parquet. With the bright Bermudan summer sun pouring through the closed windows, it was also hot and smelled of unwashed bodies and ink. Sweat started to prickle under Elinor's arms.

Next to the north door stood a lieutenant in Speaker uniform, with the addition of a three-cornered hat with a cockade in Speaker blues. Ramsay crossed the room to speak to him, pulling Elinor in his wake as if he'd forgotten she were there. "Did the admiral receive a communication from Whitehall in the last hour?" he said.

"I can't tell you about private communications, Ramsay, and there's no way you can charm it out of me," the man said.

"I don't want to know the details. I only want a yes or no answer, Mitchell. One word."

Mitchell started to look twitchy. He glanced at Elinor, looked back at Ramsay and then his gaze snapped back to Elinor's face. "She the Scorcher?" he said in a low voice.

"Yes, she—"

"Captain, I am standing right here. I beg your pardon, Lieutenant Mitchell."

Mitchell looked confused. "Is she or isn't she?"

Elinor made an exasperated noise. "She is," Ramsay said, amused.

Mitchell looked furtively around the room. "Show me?" he said, finally addressing Elinor.

"I beg your pardon again, Lieutenant, but...show you what?"

Mitchell fluttered his hands. "Do something fiery."

Ramsay made a strangled sound that was probably a suppressed laugh. Elinor repeated, "Something...fiery?"

Mitchell nodded. Elinor sighed. She held up one hand and let the fire flow over it, its gemlike colors instantly soothing her annoyance. She could feel more eyes on her from the room at large as men who were not engaged in Speaking to someone caught sight of the spectacle. "Is that what you had in mind?" she said.

Mitchell seemed transfixed by the display. Elinor extinguished the flame and lowered her hand, and he caught his breath. "That's beautiful," he said, and the simple admiration in his voice made Elinor ashamed of her frustration with him.

"Thank you," she said.

Mitchell came out of his reverie and stepped closer to Ramsay.

"Admiral had two messages from Whitehall about forty and forty-five minutes ago," he said in a low voice. "Can't tell you who they was from, but...I can tell you Harkins took the messages."

"I owe you again, Mitchell," Ramsay said.

"Just bring the girl around again sometime," Mitchell said, and smiled at Elinor with a friendly and admiring interest that made her feel flustered. It was rare that men looked at her with that expression; she knew she was not hideous, but she was certainly no beauty like Amelia, and in any case most of the men she met these days looked at her with more fear than romantic interest. And the lieutenant was attractive, if a bit too dim to be interesting to her. Still...

Ramsay nodded to Mitchell and left the room as quickly as he'd come, pulling Elinor after him. "'Bring the girl around sometime,'" he muttered.

Elinor, surprised, said, "Is something wrong, Captain?"

"No. Well, yes, but—wait a moment." They entered the front hall, and Stratford leaped to his feet. "Mr. Hervey, please take us back to the ship. We'll discuss it there," Ramsay said to Elinor.

Back in the great cabin, Ramsay threw his hat at one of the couches and paced in front of the windows. "Pray, tell me what's troubling you, Captain?" Elinor said, sitting at the table and removing her bonnet.

"Harkins knows only a few people at the Admiralty," Ramsay said, finally coming to a stop, "and those few are...I think Admiral Durrant received news about Crawford's court-martial, and it wasn't good news."

"Do you mean Captain Crawford was convicted?"

"That is the only thing I can think of that would make the admiral lose his temper like that. Either someone else saw what you did on *Glorious,* or he was held accountable for not recognizing *Olympia* as a captured ship, or...it could be any number of things. I'm surprised, actually, since it sounded like Crawford fought as long as anyone could be expected to...but I'm not the one he had to answer to."

"So...he might hang."

"Possibly."

Elinor found that her earlier bloodthirstiness with regard to Crawford's fate had dissipated. "What will this mean for us? For the attack on the pirates?"

"Nothing, I hope. But it might compromise the admiral's judgment. Distract him." Ramsay ran his fingers through his hair, pushing it away from his face. "Most of his plan is sound, except for him expecting you to burn the emplacement. I don't know what he was thinking."

"Captain, I am certain I can at least do *something*. I will know more when I see them with my own eyes. Though these drawings are remarkably fine."

"They had better be. We're staking our lives on them," Ramsay said.

CHAPTER 22

IN WHICH THERE ARE MORE PIRATES

E linor had never seen a blacker night. High clouds covered the sky, promising no rain, which was just as well since she was not certain she could maintain a large fire during a downpour. All *Athena*'s lights were extinguished, and with the warm dampness of the Caribbean night, Elinor felt as if she were wrapped in damp, black wool, her fingers on the larboard rail the only things reminding her that she stood on a ship's deck, straining her eyes for the signal.

Athena's normal sounds of creaking rope and chuffing sail seemed muffled, as if she knew she were sneaking up on an enemy that could turn her into so many splinters and scraps of canvas. Elinor shuddered at the thought of proud *Athena* destroyed, her crew scattered across the grey waves—she put the image far from her. It was inviting bad luck to think such thoughts, and she clenched the rail and pictured instead stone boxes filled with fire and screaming pirates.

She still had not seen the emplacements; it had been full night when they came around the eastern end of Tortuga and doused all their lights for their run at the pirate stronghold. How the ships managed to keep track of one another in the darkness was a mystery to her, but Ramsay and Horace seemed not at all concerned about a collision, so she laid her worries aside.

She was beginning to think she would see the emplacements only after their cannons had begun firing, those little flashes of light marking their location, and then she would...she still had not decided on a strategy. Fireballs seemed haphazard, if the emplacement looked as Ramsay had described in a hasty sketch not nearly as good as the ones the Seers had produced—a slit no taller than that of a gun port, with cannons ranged inside, probably iron cannons she was incapable of melting. She would be blind, effectively, unable to see the pirates manning the cannons inside, but it was what Admiral Durrant wanted, and she was under orders. Privately, she had made up her mind to burn the ships if she possibly could.

A breeze had risen, unusually chilly in the darkness, and she shivered and wished she had a shawl or a spencer or something a civilized woman no doubt would never be without. She could not light a fire without giving their position away to the enemy. Unless Evans already knew their position—this was the true obstacle, not knowing what Evans knew.

The hasty alterations did distort the ships' beautiful lines; whether those changes would be enough to defeat the pirate's Sight, no one could guess. The Admiralty Seers had confirmed that there were now five pirate ships in the harbor and that there had been no unusual activity all day, but suppose this was part of Evans' plan?

Elinor smelled wood smoke and snatched her hands away from the rail before it could ignite, hoped her briefly burning hands had not made them a target. She had made such progress with controlling her fire, with not setting herself alight unconsciously, but it seemed her control was not yet perfect, and that frustrated her. Suppose she were actually in contact with someone when she caught fire? When this was all over, she would have to practice more diligently.

When this was all over. Suppose they did manage to kill Evans and some or all of his captains—what then? Would the Navy still have need of her? Napoleon had yet to be defeated, and surely the Navy would have a hand in that. Elinor rubbed her goose-pimply arms and breathed in the calming, muggy salt air. She didn't want to think about it. She would *have* to think about it, soon, because she needed to have a plan for when the war was over. She couldn't go back to her family because even Selina wouldn't want her, and there was nothing for an Extraordinary Scorcher to do in peacetime, except...no, there was nothing—

"It's going to be another ten minutes before we can hope to see the signal," Ramsay said. "You should go below, where it's warmer."

"I prefer not to stumble about the cabin in the dark, Captain," she said, but she already felt warmer just having him nearby. "And this is so peaceful, this quiet time. It is hard to believe in war, and death, on a night like this."

"I know what you mean. When I was much younger I used to climb the rigging to the royal truck—all the way to the top—and weave my feet and hands through the ropes and sway with the ship. Then there was the Flying—it's dangerous, Flying at night like this, which is probably why I enjoyed it so much."

"I do not commonly think of you as reckless."

"I was, as a youth. Then it wasn't fun anymore, somehow."

Elinor shifted position and looked up at Ramsay, a dark silhouette next to her. "May I ask how old you are, Captain?"

"Thirty. I feel older, sometimes, since I've held this rank since I was one-and-twenty. I was probably too young for it, and I can't imagine there weren't others more deserving of making post, but try telling that to an Admiralty that likes rewarding its Extraordinaries beyond what they deserve."

"I cannot imagine you were not deserving of the rank."

He chuckled. "Let's say I grew into it."

"I would say I wish I had known you at twenty-one, but I'm afraid you would have found we had little in common, as I was still in the schoolroom."

"Now I'm having the devil of a time not asking *your* age."

Elinor laughed, quietly. "I turned twenty-two seven days ago. The day of my rescue, in fact."

"I see. Yes, we would have had little in common. How fortunate for both of us that we met now and not nine years ago."

His voice sounded strange in the murky darkness. Elinor was momentarily confused by the lack of light, uncertain where she stood or where Ramsay was in relation to her. She put her hand out to grasp the rail and found his warm, solid hand instead. "I beg your pardon," she said, and slid her hand away, feeling an unaccountable reluctance to let him go.

"Admiral Durrant has asked us to hold back," Ramsay said, his voice still echoing strangely, "to allow you a better line of sight on the emplacement. Though between the two of us, I'd wager he doesn't want *Athena* to come up covered in glory again."

"Has there been any word of Captain Crawford?"

"Nothing that I've heard, and I honestly don't want to know. Did you see a light?"

Elinor strained her eyes into the blackness. The Admiral had sent a longboat ahead of the ships to anchor near the mouth of the harbor and light a shielded lantern to mark where they should make their turn. "I see nothing, Captain."

"I've been staring out into nothing for so long I'm seeing sparks. Unless those are real."

"No."

He sighed, and Elinor felt him lean on the rail beside her. "I don't like waiting," he said. "Never have. When there's something you want to do, and you can't because it has to happen at the right time or everything will be ruined...and yet you're ready, inside, to do or say whatever it is...am I making sense? Because I think I may be spouting madness."

"I understand you perfectly, Captain. Though I cannot say I have ever had difficulty in waiting for things."

"Then you're far more patient than I."

"I have had very little control over my life until recently. It is hardly patience when you simply cannot have the things you want."

"And what do you want?" The strange echo was back, some effect of the night air, and in her memory she heard her sister asking a similar question some three months earlier. She was confused, again, and were it not for the movement of *Athena*'s deck she might have thought herself standing alone with Ramsay on some hilltop, surrounded by a starless sky. She shivered, but not from cold.

"I thought I wanted freedom," she said, "but now I have it and I am still...I am not dissatisfied, Captain, you must never think I do not want to be here, but I feel as if there is something I would want if only I knew what it was."

"I understand you, though I can't say I've ever had that problem."

"You are always certain of what you want?"

"Always," Ramsay said. He shifted his grip on the rail and the edge of his hand pressed against hers. "Though knowing what I want doesn't always mean getting what I want, unfortunately."

The words *And what is it you want, Captain?* were about to pass Elinor's lips when a tiny gleam caught her eye. She reached out and gripped Ramsay's arm. "I see a light."

"Where?"

"There—oh, how foolish of me, I'm pointing—" She reached up to his shadowy face and took hold of his chin, then turned it until she was sure it was aligned with hers. He reached up and took her fingers away, squeezed her hand gently, and released her.

"I see it. Thank you." Then he was gone, and she could still feel the pressure of his hand on hers, the warmth he left behind in contrast to her chilled arms and face. She looked out at the light, then up the cliff side, trying to imagine where the Marines were creeping along toward the unsuspecting emplacement. The Marines' Speaker was in communication with the one on Durrant's flagship, *Breton*, to let them know when the emplacement was secure, and then Durrant's Speaker would send the message to all the ships, and then the fighting, and the dying, would begin.

She heard the cry of a seabird, far to larboard, a long dying *caaaaaw* followed by faint hooting sounds—an owl? Impossible. Though the land was on the larboard side, and who knew what birds might live on Tortuga...

...on the solid rocks where even trees did not grow...

...and the night blossomed with fire arching high above, and before Elinor extinguished the eight burning orbs that fell toward their fleet she saw three vessels sailing around the western side of the enormous harbor, coming about to aim their cannons at the incoming Navy ships, and another two, no more than dim shapes, coming up fast from the harbor's mouth.

Suddenly the air was filled with the thunder of cannon fire that seemed to come from everywhere at once. Elinor saw flashes of fire in the cliff side, high above, then heard the whistling scream of cannonballs hurtling at them. Most flew past harmlessly, but a few struck their targets, and to the deafening booms of the cannons and the shriek of the flying cannonballs were added the screams of dying men.

She was too stunned to respond. Another arc of fireballs flew toward them, this one aimed at the ships nearest the harbor, and she extinguished them reflexively, unable to remember what she was supposed to do. *The emplacement. What an idiotic strategy.* The emplacement that was to be her target was silent, unable to fire because Evans' own ships were in the way. She looked up the eastern cliff toward the flashes that marked the position of the enemy cannons. The Marines had failed, for whatever reason, and now those cannons were turning the Navy ships into scrap wood.

Fires erupted on the decks of the most distant ships, *Breton* and *Chariot*. Elinor absently extinguished them as she cast about for something, anything, she could do. The pirates were outside her range, though she strained desperately to reach them, furious at Durrant's plan that kept *Athena* so far from the front of the battle. At least it seemed Dewdney was not present; she would have had far more difficulty countering his fires.

She gripped the rail as *Athena* began the turn to come about, moving away from the deadly seas, and made her fumbling way toward the quarterdeck, her eyes on what little she could see of the emplacement. If *Athena* would only stop rocking about for two minutes! Finally, she reached the stern, locked one arm about the taffrail, and flung a fiery missile easily ten feet across at the distant sparks high on the cliff.

It lit their corner of the battle in gory clarity for several seconds before splashing against the emplacement, forcing a brief pause in the firing pattern. *Exordia*, which had been sailing nearest *Athena*, had taken two hits, one of which had been a lucky shot that clove her top mainmast in half. Her sailors were busy cutting themselves free of the debris and the helmsman seemed not to know what to do, for *Exordia* continued to sail into the bay instead of turning aside to allow the front rank of ships to maneuver to engage the pirates.

All was darkness again for half a minute until the enemy Scorchers sent up another volley of fireballs. They had clearly been instructed to provide light for their ships to target the Navy vessels, because their fires always coincided with another broadside from the three pirate ships—one of them, infuriatingly, a former Navy frigate—slamming the ships in front, raking their decks with a full battery of shots while the Navy vessels could only fire off their front guns.

The battle was happening at such a distance Elinor could only tell it was *Chariot* that was listing to one side and drifting into the path of *Breton,* which was desperately trying to maneuver itself into a position to fire its dozens of 18-pounder guns at the enemy. It was only her imagination that made it seem as if the ships were staggering in confusion.

Then the emplacement fired again, and Elinor threw another fireball at it, and another, but nothing she did could make the battering stop completely. Her fires were splashing off the stony surface without doing more than forcing the defenders temporarily back. She dismissed another cluster of enemy fireballs and wanted to scream with frustration. She should be burning those ships, giving *Breton* and *Chariot* time to regroup, and yet all she could do—

"The Marines are all dead, or as good as," she heard Beaumont shout over the furor of cannons and screams. "Evans knew we were coming! There are at least seven ships!"

"*Breton* and *Hornet* are both trapped between our ships and the harbor, and *Chariot's* not going to survive another broadside!" Ramsay roared at him.

"Captain, I can—" Elinor called out.

"Stay where you are and that is an order, Miss Pembroke! Find a way to shut down that emplacement!"

"But—" Furious, Elinor shut her mouth. She had *not* been about to suggest she go in alone and it was unfair of him not to listen to her. Durrant's plan had been too careless, too dependent on things not going wrong. It was *stupid* and now men would die for it.

She summoned another fireball, but instead of flinging it, she focused on telling it to move, to fly up the cliff and hover near the emplacement to give her light. The fortification was too far away for her to make out details, but she could see the dark smudge where the cannon bores emerged from the stone, and it was enough. She thought, *Well, if I am wrong about this, it is not as if anyone knows enough about Scorchers to criticize.*

What she needed was a long, thin tongue of fire, and if there were anything to burn in the area, she could set it alight and shape it into the right form. But perhaps the highly diffuse ball of fire might be enough. She closed her eyes. There it was, her other self, far away and very quiet, but when she spoke to it, the fire sprang to greater life.

She spread it flat, rolled it like dough, spun it into a spear and ran it into the slot as hard as she could. A narrow space, then it opened up, and she released the fire and let it expand as fierce and hot as it wanted, it was so *beautiful* and desperate to grow, and she heard the seabirds' cawing cries again and realized they were the voices of dying men. She opened her eyes and saw that faint glow on the far-off cliff. Her heart was pounding with exhilaration. *I need something else to burn.*

"Captain!" she shouted. "What else am I to do?"

Ramsay was deep in conversation with Beaumont and did not hear her until she came nearer and shouted at him again. "The emplacement!" he called out over the noise of screams and thunder.

She shook her head. "It is done!"

Ramsay glanced at the cliff. "Use your initiative, Miss Pembroke!" He ran forward to speak to the helmsman.

The enemy Scorchers were still sending up fireballs. *Chariot* was foundering, directly in *Hornet*'s path now, but *Breton* had extricated herself and was making way for *Syren*. But the pirate ships were advancing, and they seemed to know exactly where to be to avoid taking any hits from the Navy ships. Another two pirate ships had begun to emerge from the harbor—what strategy had Evans formed, what had he Seen? He had known enough to summon more ships to fight them. How could he possibly have known they were coming?

The emplacement was silent, fire still glowing along the thin open line. Elinor half-ran, half-stumbled toward the bow. The battle raged far ahead—still too far? She reached out to set the nearest pirate ship alight and felt relief and fierce pleasure when the deck lit with flame. The sails, next—they had been treated, so it was more of an effort, but she—

The deck fire went out. *Dewdney.*

Elinor lit the deck a second time and *leaned* into it, and felt a pressure leaning back, as if she and Dewdney were on opposite sides of the same door, fighting to see who could push it open first. She could feel the fire being twisted, contorted out of shape in its conflict to decide which master to serve, but it would be her, she would not allow this man to defeat her, *would not*—

The pressure vanished so abruptly she had to fling her arms about the rail to keep from going over. She screamed her triumph, not that anyone could hear her over the rest of the battle cries.

Then, in the distance, she saw fire break out on *Exordia's* deck, and on crippled *Chariot's* masts and sails. She loosed control of her fire to extinguish the new ones and felt hers go out with a snap. Furious, she lit it again and saw the same fires spring up again on the Navy ships, then all three went out as she and Dewdney repeated their gruesome dance. They might be at this all night—but no, the pirate ship was out of her reach again, because *Athena* was moving farther out to sea.

She abandoned her attack and raced back down the deck to look for Ramsay, who had disappeared. "Why are we moving away?" she demanded of the helmsman.

"Comin' ab't," he said in a hoarse voice, barely audible over the cannon fire. "Tekkin' *Chariot's* place."

"But *Chariot* cannot move! We are going too far away, Mr. Wynn! I cannot burn them from here!"

"You'll have to wait," Ramsay said from behind her, taking her by the shoulders and firmly moving her out of his way. "Stay below until I send for you."

"I will *not* stay below!"

"You *will* obey orders, Miss Pembroke, or you will get decent men killed with your recalcitrance! Don't think you are the only weapon in this fight!" Ramsay's eyes blazed at her, the only bright thing in this dim world, and she felt as if he'd slapped her.

He said I wasn't a weapon. I suppose he was wrong.

Without another word, she ran down the companionway and into the great cabin, where she leaned on the window frame and tried to see something that would burn.

She cursed herself, her lack of understanding of naval warfare, her inability to look at the way the ships were moving and understand what it meant, because she was useless at this distance and did not understand the strategy in any case. All she knew was that *Chariot* was certainly sinking, and would not be able to move out of anyone's way. *Athena* would be forced to stay far away from the battle, and Elinor would be unable to fight, and for all she knew Ramsay would face a court-martial and be hanged for not taking the fight to the pirates. And she could do nothing about any of that.

No. She still had one choice left to her.

Before she could talk herself back into reason, she left the great cabin and went down to the mess deck and into the officers' gunroom, shoving past sailors carrying their wounded shipmates down the companionway or running up the steps, newly Healed, to rejoin the fight. Hays was in the process of Healing someone's broken leg.

The sound of battle was as loud here as it was above, but was not tuned to a higher pitch by the screams of injured men; Elinor saw white faces, heard a few moans, but the more severely injured had been rendered unconscious by Hays' touch. The ship lurched again, forcing Elinor to grab hold of the door frame. "Dr. Hays, I am looking for Mr. Hervey," she said.

"I'm right here, Elinor," Stratford said from behind her. "What are you doing down here?"

"I need to talk with you about something important," Elinor said, pushing him out of the gunroom and into the quiet darkness of the empty deck, where the sounds of fighting and dying were muffled by planking and the sea. "Stratford, I need you to take me to shore."

"Are you mad? I'm not taking you anywhere near there. Captain would have a fit *and* we'd both get killed."

"No. We won't. Their ships are all moving out of the harbor and there cannot be anyone left there. And even if there were, it would not matter, because our fleet will be destroyed if I cannot burn those ships, and I cannot reach them from here. By the time *Athena* has maneuvered into position, it will be far too late for far too many men. Please, Stratford. It will take only a few minutes. Half an hour at the most, and no one will be shooting at us."

"No. Elinor, no. The captain wouldn't allow it."

"The captain told me to use my initiative."

"He didn't mean going into the middle of a battle."

"I am a weapon, Stratford. The middle of a battle is where I belong." She felt like a weapon, fire bound up inside her waiting to be unleashed on the enemy.

Stratford clutched at his hair with both hands and turned away from her. "Why can't you wait until we're within range again? It can't be that long."

Elinor swore, causing Stratford to stare at her in astonishment. "Come with me," she said, and pulled him up the ladders to the deck, then hauled him along toward the bow until they were well out of sight of the quarterdeck. "Look," she said, waving her hand at the distant battle. "They are *dying* and all we can do is watch. I cannot stand by and allow that to happen. *Please*, Stratford."

Stratford put both hands on the rail and looked down at the water below. Now that *Athena* was out of range of both the cliff-mounted and ship-mounted guns, and her wounded had mostly been treated, the noise level had dropped considerably, though the shouts and commands that flew through the air had an extra urgency about them. The smell of gunpowder, the residue that burned her eyes, made her feel as if she were standing with those distant fighters, staggering under the brunt of another attack. "What about that Scorcher?" Stratford said.

"I will be better able to fight him if I am not also at the edge of my reach," Elinor said, hoping it was true.

Stratford shook his head. "We go in, we go out. No heroics, all right? And if I hear about this from the captain, I'm blaming it all on you."

"Your unchivalrous behavior pleases me. Thank you, Stratford."

He shrugged, shaking his head again, and put his arm around her waist. "Never Skipped with a passenger before," he said. "You might want to close your eyes if you get dizzy."

Before Elinor could draw breath to answer, she felt momentarily insubstantial, and then she was *falling*. How had she forgotten about the falling? She clapped a hand over her mouth to hold back a scream.

Then she was again nonexistent, then the harbor and the ships were closer and she was falling *again*. It looked as if the harbor was hopping toward them between blinks, like a giant toad, the shoreline its mouth and the cliffs rising around it the warts on its back. Elinor did feel dizzy, but she was afraid to close her eyes, afraid Stratford might overshoot or drop her or something else that would make this whole venture meaningless.

Then they came out of a Skip close to the ground, and when they dropped, it was only a foot's distance, and Elinor stumbled but caught herself before she fell on her face. They stood at the water's edge, facing the log fortress Elinor recognized from the Seers' drawings.

While the noise of battle was greater here than on *Athena*, it was still distant enough that the fortress and the huts drawn up near it could have been a quiet island community, if a small one. There was no sand on this beach; the rock sloped down into the water at a rather sharper angle than a natural beach would have, and gravel took the place of sand, hard and pebbly beneath Elinor's thin-soled shoe. Somewhere above was the harbor emplacement, still silent, and across the harbor one ship, the largest, lagged behind the others, firing its bow chasers into the darkness.

"So start your fires, and let's be off," Stratford said, looking around nervously. "This place is unnatural."

"I know." Elinor reached out, testing her limits. She had been correct; all the ships were close enough. It was unfortunate she could not burn all the ships at once, but the thought made her spine ache with preemptive pain, so she concentrated on the nearest one, thinking to roust Dewdney from wherever he was hiding.

The deck obediently began burning down its whole length, and soon the distant triumphant shouts turned into screams. She let it burn for a minute. No Dewdney. She turned her attention to a different ship and was filled with unease. This was far too easy. The Extraordinary Scorcher had to be somewhere. None of the Navy ships were on fire, so what could he be doing?

Stratford stepped in and grabbed her elbow. "Elinor, we need—"

She heard several distant popping sounds, and Stratford grunted and sagged, pulling Elinor down with him. "What—" she began, pulling out of his grasp, then said, "Stratford, get up. Get up!"

He looked at her, his eyes huge and glassy in the dim light from the distant, burning ship, and worked his lips soundlessly a few times. "Back," he said.

More popping, this time louder and closer and sharper, and it wasn't popping at all, it was musket fire. Elinor looked away from Stratford and saw a cluster of dark figures running toward them and shouting unintelligibly. Pirates, but—*oh, no. From the emplacement.* It had been so dark and still that she had forgotten it would still have been manned, against the chance the Navy made it into the harbor, and now those pirates were headed directly for them.

She pulled on Stratford's arm, trying to help him rise, and he scrabbled at the rock with his left hand, pushing at it. "We need to Bound back to *Athena*," she said, "please, Stratford, I know you can do it, *please* don't give up!"

He looked at her again, said "Try...tomorrow," and then the weight of his arm, the boneless, unresisting weight, told her he was gone. Elinor clutched at his hand. If she held on tightly enough, he would come back. He always came back.

Hard boots on bare rock came nearer. She was beginning to understand what they were saying, enough of it, anyway, to know they realized she was female and alone and defenseless, that they had shot her friend and now they were going to have fun with her.

She released Stratford's hand, stood and turned to face the men, who had slowed down now and were jostling each other as if working out who would have fun with her first. They were man-shaped shadows to her uncomprehending brain. Shadows in the darkness, and Stratford's body was still warm at her feet. Her pain and guilt at being responsible for Stratford even being here in this godforsaken place to be shot became fury, though whether at herself or at the pirates, she did not know.

The men did not even have time to scream before she turned them into white fire, pure white with no trace of yellow or orange, and the heat of it battered at Elinor as no heat had done for many weeks now. It felt good, comforting, and she knelt at Stratford's side and patted his hand. "Forgive me," she whispered. "I wish my apology mattered at all."

Then she stood, and contemplated the white fire. It was not beautiful. It was like bone and white ash and it felt like despair, and it seemed to be fueled by something other than the bodies of the men it consumed. She watched it, unable to think, unable to grieve, until it went out as abruptly as if it had never been.

Facing Elinor, beyond the piles of ash and twisted weaponry that had been six pirates, stood a young man, a barefoot adolescent, dressed in too-long trousers held up with rope and a torn, striped shirt missing one sleeve. He wore a scarf wrapped around his head and long dark hair brushed his shoulders. He stood with his thumbs thrust into his waistband, though the gesture looked less like defiant insouciance and more as if he didn't know what to do with his hands. His eyes were large and very dark, as if he had no irises, and they were fixed on her with a disturbing stillness.

"I like your fire," Dewdney said.

CHAPTER 23

IN WHICH ELINOR RELEASES
THE FIRE

"Why aren't you on a ship?" Elinor said. It was the only thing that came to mind; standing over Stratford's body, other questions like *Who are you?* and *Why are you so young?* seemed irrelevant.

"Mr. Evans don't like me scaring the crew," Dewdney said. He ran his thumbs along his waistband, around to the front, back to his sides. "Lost track o' where I was, once, set one o' his ships afire. You know how it is. They only take me now if he shoots some'un to make 'em obey."

Elinor nodded, thinking, *If I agree with him, he will keep talking, and I can determine how to kill him before he kills me.* Too much time was passing. The pirate ships were moving farther away. "How did Mr. Evans know the Navy was coming?" she said.

Dewdney's black eyes darted to something beyond Elinor's shoulder, then back to her face. "He had sentries watchin' the coast o' Saint-Domingue when them ships disappeared from his Sight. Don't always need Sight to know what's happening. You ever burn a man from the inside?" He smiled, pleasantly, as if they were talking about the beauties of nature that did not surround them.

"I have not," Elinor said. *Ordinary sentries. Such a foolish oversight,* she

283

thought, wishing she could take Durrant by the collar and drag him to where he could watch the destruction his stupid plan had wrought.

Dewdney's smile wavered. "Why not?" he demanded.

She realized he was mad, and her heart started to beat faster, preparing her to run, not that there was anywhere to run to. "I did not know it was possible," she said, being completely honest and hoping he believed her.

"I can show you," he said, his smile broadening. "We could try it on one o' them Navy captains. Evans lets me have 'em, when he's done with 'em."

"I would prefer a different target." At any moment he would turn his fire on her, and she was certain he could find a way to burn her despite her immunity. She prepared to counterattack, letting the fire inside her rise and burn hotter.

"Then a pirate," Dewdney said with a shrug. "They're none of 'em like us. Don't much matter who."

Elinor imagined she could feel the ships slipping away, though she could not afford to look and see whether that was true. "Are we so different from them?"

Dewdney's smile froze. "You don't see it," he said, and Elinor lashed out with her fire at the very instant he struck at her.

It was cool, for the moment, flickering blues and blacks she knew to be fire only because her heart recognized it, for it resembled an earthly fire as much as her white pyres had. She could feel it battering at her, looking for a way to break through her defenses. She could feel her own fire doing the same to Dewdney, ruby and lapis and gold and opal trying to consume him. It hurt already, trying to attack and defend both at once, and she tried to take a step toward him and the black fire stabbed at her, enough to make her cry out in pain and waver.

Dewdney's fire was a pressure that threatened to sink her into the ground like a nail into soft wood, and her spine screamed at her to stop, stop now before it snapped. She stepped backward, involuntarily, to keep her balance, and her foot pressed against something soft. Stratford. Her dear friend, who had given in to her arguments and was dead for it, and her momentary grief turned into anger. If she gave in, if she let Dewdney consume her, he would have died for nothing. She let that anger boil up into fury and let it pour out of her, and now it was Dewdney who staggered under the pressure of her attack.

Then her fire filled him, and she knew his madness and the fear that drove him, knew how he had killed his family when he manifested, not by accident, but by his love for its power and his pleasure in hearing people scream as their flesh bubbled off their bones. She heard him laugh, an uncomplicated, joyous, insane sound, and his fire washed over and around her like an ocean wave that boiled and scalded her. She clenched her teeth on a cry. She could not allow his fire to take her.

She pressed harder, fueling her fire with her pain and sorrow, willing it to burn hotter than had ever been possible for her before, and it scoured away all her emotions until the fire was everything, it was all she was, and for a moment she forgot why it was so important that she destroy this tiny figure before her, because the fire was all that mattered.

Abruptly, the pressure of his attack disappeared, the black fire vanished, and to her shock he opened himself to her fire and let it burn through him. He laughed again, and she felt his profound relief and joy at being set free from the madness that had burned inside him as surely as the fire had. Then he was gone, and her fire burned only an empty shell until it was ash and splintered bone.

With her target vanished, Elinor came back to herself, swaying with exhaustion. She was unable to maintain her fire, which dwindled and dissipated in the wind that stirred the ash of Dewdney's remains. She looked down and saw that most of Stratford's left arm had been burned away. Well, he no longer needed it. She realized she was naked and was too tired to care.

She looked out across the harbor and saw the pirate ships moving away. The largest ship—it had to be Evans' ship, did it not?—was still closest to her. Tears ran down her cheeks; she was so tired, too tired to do what she had come for, and Stratford's sacrifice was for nothing.

Use your initiative, Miss Pembroke, Ramsay said in her memory. He would be furious if he knew she had given up so quickly. No, worse— he would be *disappointed,* and she could not bear that, even if he did think she was a weapon. She reached inside herself and drew on resources she did not realize she had until Dewdney had revealed them, and let the fire build up again until it burned hot and bright. Then she released it on the ships.

All seven pirate ships erupted in flame, sails, rigging, hulls, decks, from Evans' ship to the one farthest away, the one whose crew she could see boarding one of the Navy ships through her fiery second self. She drew that fire back enough that it would not burn whichever of the Navy's ships that was, putting an imaginary wall between the two that let not even heat pass.

Men tried to extinguish her, and she slapped at them contemptuously, because she was the fire and they could not touch her. She knew her human body was once again burning with all those gemlike colors that flashed before her eyes, blinding her, but she could feel every inch of her extended fiery body and laughed, because sight was irrelevant, hearing was unimportant, all that mattered was the fire.

A ship creaked under the tremendous pressure with which she bore down on it, and felt the planking bend and snap and cry out before she devoured it utterly, casting tiny bodies into the waves that she chose not to pursue. Somewhere in the fire that had been her mind she remembered it was the ships that were important, the ships and the guns they carried.

She focused on another ship and made the iron of the cannons go red and gold and melt into puddles that burned whatever they touched, felt another ship's sails disintegrate, and laughed again because she had never felt such intense pleasure, such joy in her talent, and she wanted more of it. She drew on those reserves again and found a ship's powder store and made it explode like a thousand cannons going off at once. The smoke of its explosion caressed her distant body, and with the heat pouring off her, she created drafts that made that smoke curl and flow in the darkness.

The ships were vanishing, one by one, and she looked around for more targets and saw other ships dancing on the waves, and reached out to touch one—but no, that was wrong, she could not remember why but she knew it was wrong, and she cried out in disappointment because there was only one left, the nearest one, and it was burning rapidly and would soon sink beneath the water where even she could not burn it.

Her body was diminishing to a single, small form on a rocky shore, and cried out again because the fire was fading and she could not bear to lose it. She had so little to feed it, just that body, and she let the fire rise up inside her because it was beauty and power and it was hers and she knew it loved her and would kill her if she did not subdue it. And she did not want to subdue it.

Someone spoke to her. The fire roared in her ears so she could barely hear it, but there it was, a voice she knew but could not recognize:

elinor. come back.

come back. you are not a weapon. you are not the fire. come back.

your work is finished. come back. come back to me.

please

Then there was a hand, clasping hers, and she remembered she had a body, and terror filled her because her body was falling apart, carried away by the fire. She desperately clung to the hand as it gripped hers, bringing the fire back to her heart, feeling bone and muscle reform in a way she hoped would leave her recognizably human. She clutched at that hand like a lifeline, pulling her through the waves to solid ground, and then the fire was gone, and she fell hard on the rocks, blind, unable to catch herself.

Her back hurt so badly she was sure it must be broken. She curled in on herself, keening with her need to crawl away from the pain, to leave her body behind until it was not one spike of burning agony—but she had already tried to leave her body once, and she would endure any amount of pain to keep herself solidly anchored in it now.

Someone was making her move, lifting her arms and bending them to force them through sleeves of a rough, heavy fabric. She could feel the night air now, the wind picking up and blowing hair into her face and flowing across her bare legs. She shivered once, then could not stop shivering, and the same someone put an arm around her waist and held her tight. "Hold on," the man said, and made her put her arms around his neck, and he jumped and did not come down again.

She screamed, and clutched the man's neck, and the wind was

stronger against her legs and arms because they were Flying, and she realized that Ramsay had come for her. He had one arm around her waist and was holding her tight against his body, muttering words she could not make out, but he didn't seem to be speaking to her, so she held on tighter and blinked to clear her vision, which was going from dark grey to a paler grey that might be Ramsay's shirt.

Then he dropped her.

The only thing that saved her was her death grip around his neck. He plummeted, his arm around her waist going loose and his muscles all relaxing at once. She screamed again, louder and longer this time, and he jerked and his flight leveled out. His arm went around her waist and crushed her against his body so she could feel his heart pounding as hard as hers was.

"I beg," he said in her ear, his voice raspy and far away, "beg pardon, I can't...just a little farther, Miles...don't let go, don't let go..."

That last did seem directed at her, so she buried her face in his shoulder and prayed they would both survive this flight. Tears of pain streaked her face, and she tried not to cry out loud for fear of distracting him.

Ramsay muttered again, unintelligibly, and he made a wide, curving turn to the left which dragged at her body and tried to pull her away from him. She kicked with her legs, trying to regain her balance, and Ramsay wobbled as if he might drop her again, but then he hit something hard, and Elinor fell away from him and landed on the bright security of *Athena*'s deck.

She rolled onto her side, her hands pressing flat against the planks, forcing her body to straighten against the pain, then made it onto her hands and knees. Other hands helped her stand, held her up when her legs would not support her. She closed her eyes, fighting the pain radiating from her spine throughout her body. Ramsay's jacket hung to the middle of her thighs, it was open a little over her breasts, but she could not find it in herself to care about her modesty.

"Take her below," Ramsay said, again in that unfamiliar, rasping voice. "Set a course to rendezv—"

There was a moment's silence, then the hard thump of something hitting the deck, and she heard dozens of men surging forward, exclaiming. She opened her eyes and saw that Ramsay had collapsed, and she pushed through the crowd of men surrounding him, and screamed.

The entire right side of his body was blackened and blistered, huge reddish bubbles of flesh and blood. The burns streaked his neck and across his chin and the side of his face; most of his hair on that side was gone, and his ear was burned past recognition. His waistcoat and shirt had melted into the burns and his trousers had a gaping, char-edged hole extending from his waist almost to his knee, revealing more burned flesh below. His arm, and his hand...she could not bear to look, could not stop looking. His eyes were partly open, unseeing. He was not breathing.

She screamed again, and again, and could not stop herself scream-ing. Someone tried to pull her away, and she fought him, mindlessly, clawing and panting in her desperate attempt to reach Ramsay's body, thinking in her madness that if she could reach him, she could undo the damage she had done. *We left Stratford behind* flashed through her mind, and then she was nothing but a mad thing, a weapon that had killed everyone she had ever loved. Someone put a cool hand on her wrist, and everything went black.

CHAPTER 24
IN WHICH ELINOR DECIDES
TO LIVE

She woke in darkness, feeling soft fabric against her legs and buttocks and warm, rough cloth around her arms and chest. A deep breath told her she was in her bedchamber on *Athena*, the lamp unlit, its warm, stuffy confines like a recently used tomb. The jacket she wore, and it was all she wore, smelled of ash and cook fires and roasted meat—she fell out of her bed and vomited onto the floor, uncontrollably expelling bitterness and thick saliva until she was wrung out and empty.

She crawled back onto her bed, then sat up and tore Ramsay's jacket off her body and threw it hard against the far wall, heard it strike with a soft thud and then hit the floor with a softer one. She curled naked on her bed and stared into the blackness, the image of Stratford's lifeless body, eyes open and blank, alternating with Ramsay's blackened form like the most detailed paintings Dewdney might have produced if his mad, evil genius had run to art rather than fire. She felt as if the tears had all been burned out of her; she wondered if, having poured so much fire into her attack, she could ever spark another fire again.

She wondered if she would even dare to.

Finally, feeling as if she were performing an act of penance, she reached out to light the lamp. A throbbing pain traveled down her back, but the tiny fire kindled and the lamp filled the room with its orangeish glow. She watched it for a while, until its black inverse blinded her when she closed her eyes, then extinguished it and went back to lying curled up on her bed. His bed, that he'd given up to her because he was a gentleman. His bed, his cabin, his ship. He'd given her so much and she had given him death.

Lying there in the oppressive darkness, she remembered their last conversation and felt like a fool. *I feel as if there is something I would want if only I knew what it was,* she had said, and the whole time he was standing right next to her and all she had needed to do was reach out and say, *You. I want you.* Those few words might have changed everything.

She began shuddering uncontrollably and pulled the blanket over herself, though she did not feel cold. Or it might have changed nothing. It would not have stopped the pirates taking them by surprise and it would not have obviated the need for her to move in closer to burn the enemy ships. Likely everything would have happened just as it did, except that Ramsay would have known she loved him, and he might have...what? Embraced her, rejected her, turned away in embarrassment? Perhaps it was better this way, after all.

The smell of vomit crept into her nostrils and fought with the smell of muggy wood and the fainter smell of smoke. Elinor lit the lamp again, stood on wobbly legs, and went to the cupboard. Her evening gown hung there, its pink silk and white gauze out of place on this rough ship so distant from the drawing rooms of London. She could not bear the thought of wearing it, but she had foolishly got rid of the ugly brown cotton, and now it was the only clothing she had. She destroyed everything she touched, didn't she?

She had burned the last of her undergarments, so she wormed her way into her gown and hoped it was sufficiently opaque. The waistband was tight around her ribs, but not uncomfortably so. She straightened her gown, ran her fingers through her hair in lieu of a comb, also missing, and with a deep breath went barefoot into the great cabin.

It was empty, silent, and dark. Moonlight streamed through the windows; the threatening storm had passed, leaving the sky clear and bright as if it had only been waiting for the battle to be over to appear. Tortuga lay off the starboard side, just a sliver of it, and there were no ships except a black hump in the distance too regular to be stone. She touched the glass as if she could reach out and push the pirate ship beneath the waves. Or it might be one of the Navy's, might be poor, doomed *Chariot*.

She knew nothing of how the battle had passed after she—hadn't one of the pirate ships boarded one of theirs? If only Admiral Durrant had taken her into his planning, if she had been allowed to burn the ships without resorting to— She made herself stop. It was wrong, it was evil, for her to try to make this disaster the fault of anyone but herself.

She left the great cabin and went up on deck, too weary to care if the sailors hated or feared her now. She could hear them moving about the deck, quietly, as if they still hoped to hear their dead captain's voice calling out commands over their murmured conversations. She passed Wynn, the helmsman; he didn't even look at her, not that she blamed him.

She trailed her fingers along the mizzenmast and went to the strangely empty stern, stood at the taffrail and looked out. Navy ships stood at rest on both sides of *Athena*, their lights burning brightly. Even with the light from the waxing gibbous moon, it was too dark to see the damage that had been done to them. *Syren's* stern lamps glowed over her name, easily read because she was within shouting distance of *Athena*, and to starboard she saw *Exordia* and *Breton*. What would the admiral say to her? Would he realize how she had lost control, send her back to England for execution? She almost certainly deserved it. She was dangerous to everyone around her.

She looked down, far down to where *Athena's* hull disappeared into the dark water. Perhaps she should save them the trouble, and herself the pain, of a public execution. The humiliation, she could bear, just one more part of her penance. Not that she would be around to endure it, not for long, anyway. She remembered struggling to reach her raft, the sharp bite of salty brine in her nose and sinuses and the bitter taste of it in her mouth, and shuddered. She might deserve death, but she would not seek it out.

"Going to a party, Miss Pembroke?" Lieutenant Beaumont said, coming to join her at the taffrail.

"I have no other gown, Lieutenant. I apologize for my appearance of frivolity."

"You seem hard on your clothing. Drowning, fire."

"I suppose so." His words were light, even playful, but his voice was tight and angry. *His best friend is dead. He ought to hate me. I deserve it.*

"That was quite the show you put on. No one knew you were that...powerful."

"I did not know either, Lieutenant. I assure you..." What? What could she tell him? That she regretted her rash behavior? That she would never do it again? What difference would it make?

"Admiral Durrant is pleased with you. Said you controlled the fire so *Breton* wasn't singed despite the pirate ship being latched on for a boarding party. Very impressed."

"I am sure I am grateful for his consideration." Of course Beaumont had spoken to the admiral; he was in command of *Athena* now. She was surprised Durrant could still be impressed with her, knowing Beaumont's account of what she had done to her commanding officer. But Durrant had never cared for Ramsay, so perhaps he counted his life as small loss. Elinor's eyes burned from having stared unblinking into the darkness for so long. She wished Beaumont would leave her alone to her grief, not that he would feel she was entitled to mourn for the man she'd killed.

"What you did to him," Beaumont began, then gripped the taffrail with both hands and bowed his head. "He never believed you were dangerous, no matter what I said. He should have listened to me."

Elinor nodded, unwilling to trust her voice—but then, what could she possibly say to that?

"But I suppose it doesn't matter now, does it? And I think—if I'm correct, I think you hate yourself right now more than I ever could. If your feelings are engaged as I suspect."

Elinor prayed he could not see her blush in this dim light. So he'd seen it before she had. Perhaps Ramsay had, too, and had kept silent so as not to embarrass her. Always the gentleman. She turned her head to look at Beaumont. "I assume I will be going back to London soon. If the admiral decides the pirate threat has been mostly eliminated."

Beaumont met her eyes. He looked surprised, though she could not see what about her words was surprising. "I imagine you could stay, if you wanted to."

"There's nothing left for me here, Mr. Beaumont."

In the moonlight, his eyes narrowed. "Nothing to keep you here?"

"What would you have me say, Lieutenant?"

His mouth opened, formed a word he closed his lips over. "I suppose...nothing. If you have no reason to stay. I thought...but I suppose I was wrong. Better you leave than stay here out of gratitude —that's a poor repayment." He pushed away from the taffrail, leaving Elinor gazing at him in confusion. "Miles will be waking up soon. I should be there when he does."

It was as if a cold ocean wave had struck her, driving her down into the frozen depths where she could neither speak nor see. "What?" she managed.

"Hays says he ought to have someone there he knows well to help him orient. That was some Healing he did. Never seen the like before, which I'm glad of."

Elinor was finally able to draw breath. "I thought I killed him," she whispered.

"What was that, Miss Pembroke?"

"He was dead," she said, more loudly, "he wasn't breathing, and I...I thought I killed him."

Beaumont's expression went from angry to startled, and then full of sympathy, in one second. He reached out to take her hand. "Miss Pembroke, I beg your pardon," he said. "They took you away before— he wasn't breathing, true, and his lungs were fair sco—singed, but nothing Hays couldn't manage. Some scarring, but he's not dead. You —oh, no wonder you said there was nothing—" He began pulling her along. "Come with me. You can see for yourself."

"No," Elinor cried, tugging her hand free. The blessed relief of knowing she had not been responsible for two deaths melted away into horror and anguish and a different kind of crushing guilt. "I cannot see him, I cannot bear it, he will—" and she fled past the helmsman, down the companionway, and into the dark, stinking confines of her bedchamber.

She stood, breathing heavily, her eyes squeezed shut. Scarred, Beaumont had said. She had hurt him so badly, permanently damaged him, and she would eventually have to see him and know how he hated her, how her lack of control disgusted him, he who had tamed his impulses so he would not use his talent to hurt others. The thought stabbed at her heart.

She lit her lamp and used Ramsay's ruined jacket, speckled with burn marks and striped with ground-in char, to mop up the vomit—how strange that there was so little of it—and wadded it up and threw it out the window in the great cabin. Then she went back into her bedchamber and hid, leaving the door open a crack to air the room out. She sat on her bed and let random thoughts drift through her mind. Someone would have to go for Stratford's body. She would need another gown; she could not wear this one for every day; it was completely inappropriate.

She would have to speak with the admiral. Could she find a way over to *Breton* before Ramsay was recovered enough to see her? If she could avoid him entirely...maybe that was what he wanted as well, not to be reminded of who had damaged him. Was his arm whole again? Had Hays been able to save his hand? She tried not to think of that blackened ruin, told herself, *It is not so much a handicap for him, he is so skilled at Moving*, and hated herself for once again trying to find ways to make all of this less her fault.

The door of the great cabin opened. Footsteps sounded on the floor boards, and a light bloomed, then another, until bright light cast a glow through her open doorway. Elinor sat on her bed, her pulse drumming inside her ears. Footsteps, again, then silence. Then Ramsay said, "Arthur said you wouldn't come to me, so I thought I'd come to you instead."

He didn't sound angry. He sounded as calm and unruffled as he always did. Elinor closed her eyes tight until she saw sparks, opened them, and stepped through her door.

Ramsay stood at the window, his profile cast into shadow by the arrangement of the lamps. He wore only a shirt and trousers, neither of which were burned, and his boots looked untouched by fire. He turned his head slightly when she entered, then gave her a more direct look that left the right side of his face in shadow. "You look beautiful," he said. "I've seen that gown hanging in that cupboard a dozen times, but I never thought I would see you wear it."

It was so much not the greeting she was braced for that she stammered, "It...I have no other gowns, Captain, and...I hoped you would not think...it is not as if I am happy, you know."

"I know. I can imagine." He went back to looking out the window. "I want you to see," he said after a long moment in which Elinor wondered if there were any point to her fleeing back to her bedchamber, or out the door. It was a ship; where could she run to that he would not eventually find her? "I think it will be better if you don't continue to torture yourself with possibilities."

He turned to face her fully, and stepped into the light shed by the overhead lamp. She clenched her teeth on a cry. Shiny pink scars streaked with red ran along his chin and down his neck, up the edge of his face and into his bare scalp where the burnt hair had been shorn away. His ear, undamaged and too pale, looked out of place among the scars. His right hand was bandaged, loosely, each finger wrapped separately, and the bandaging continued up into his sleeve, the cuff unfastened to allow the bandages to pass through easily.

With his eyes still fixed on her, he reached up with his left hand and tugged the neck of his shirt to the side to reveal more scar tissue on his shoulder that seemed to extend down toward his chest. "There's only so much Healing can do with burns," he said. He sounded so apologetic she wanted to fling herself out the window. "But Peregrine repaired my ear, and my lungs and throat are undamaged."

"I am so glad," she said, and cursed how strange and distant her voice sounded. It was wrong, it was all wrong, he was supposed to hate her, not...not *explain* as if this were all something that had simply happened, like a hurricane or some other natural disaster no one could predict.

Ramsay took a deep breath and turned to face the window again. "I will be going to London in the morning, as soon as there's a Bounder to spare," he said. "Peregrine knows a specialist he thinks might be able to restore my hand and arm, though I likely won't have full functionality, but then it's not as if that's a problem for me."

He laughed, a short, tense laugh—he sounded nervous, why nervous? How could he think he owed her *anything*? "So I...Miss Pembroke, I..." He laughed again, and turned to face her, his good hand pushing his hair back from his face. "I told you I was bad at waiting, didn't I? And this does not seem the right time, but I have to tell you, that is, to ask—I realize I'm not the best prospect, and I'm certainly not as handsome as I was, not that I ever was much to look at, but I wonder if you would consider—if you would accept—"

Realization burst over Elinor, what he was trying to say, and she was so overwhelmed with conflicting emotions of guilt and sorrow and happiness and relief that she burst into tears and said, "How, *how* can you think I would love you less because you have a few scars, when I am the one who gave them to you? Miles, why do you not hate me for hurting you so? I despise myself so much for my lack of control, and I —you should have let me burn, you should have, because I do not deserve your sacrifice!"

Blind with tears, she heard him approach her, footsteps crossing the floor, and then he put his arm around her and drew her close. He smelled of soap and freshly laundered linen and not of blackened flesh, and it made her cry harder. "Elinor, you were disintegrating in front of me," he said, only just audible over the sound of her weeping. "I could barely see your face. I was shouting at you, and you didn't seem to hear me, so I did the stupidest thing I've ever done in my life and reached into that fire to find whatever was left of your hand. And then I held onto it. *My* choice, Elinor. It hurt like the devil, and I would do it again if I had to, because there is nothing in this world I would not do for you."

"No, I am too dangerous—"

"So was I, once. My self-control came at the cost of a man's life. You are far luckier than I."

"I will never use my talent again, never!"

"You won't be able to keep that vow. Darling, listen to me." He put two fingers under her chin and lifted her head so her tearful eyes could meet his. "If all you will ever feel when you look at me is self-loathing, if all you will ever see are these scars, then I will leave this room, and you will never see me again because I refuse to torment you so. But I don't want that. I love you, Elinor. I want to spend the rest of my life with you. Please, love, forgive yourself, if only for my sake. Don't make me walk away from you."

Elinor drew a great, shuddering, calming breath, and blinked away tears because by now her arms were around Ramsay's waist and she did not want to let go. "Stratford is dead," she said.

"I know. We'll both have to bear the burden of guilt for that. I should have specifically instructed him not to take you anywhere."

"It was so stupid. I should have realized there were men in that emplacement."

"I know. As I said, we both have a measure of guilt there."

She laid her cheek against his shoulder and breathed in the bright, clean smell of him. "I think you are handsome and your scars make you more so."

"You can tell all the other wives you have a husband who will walk through fire for you."

"I do. I cannot now remember if I have said that I love you."

"You did, actually, but it was a rather tear-riddled confession and I was too startled to fully appreciate it. So if you want to say it again—"

"I love you." She looked up at him. "I think you should kiss me."

His eyebrows went up. "Isn't that somewhat improper?"

"I have only been kissed once before, and I did not enjoy it. I would like to see if your kiss is better."

He laughed and ran his fingers across her skin, down her hairline and along her jaw, so gently. "I make no promises," he said, kissing her forehead lightly, making her close her eyes with pleasure. "But I think —" he kissed her cheek, just as lightly—"you will not be disappointed," and his lips brushed against hers, the faintest pressure that made her inner fire rage with a need for more, so, impatient, she pulled his head down so she could kiss him instead.

CHAPTER 25

IN WHICH ALMOST EVERYONE
HAS A HAPPY ENDING

So much happened in the next seven days that Elinor
remembered it as a blur, punctuated by bright, still moments
she would never forget:

Miles returning after far too many hours in London with the right
cuff of his jacket limp and empty, then comforting her as she sobbed;

Stratford Hervey in his shroud, lying with *Athena*'s other dead as
Miles read out the service, then Bounded away to be returned to his
grieving parents;

Admiral Durrant's shaking hands as he congratulated her on her
victory, with no word of blame nor reference to his nephew's death
sentence, commuted to transportation;

and Selina's face when she entered her drawing room and found
Elinor there, her surprise and then tearful joy unmarred by anger or
reproach.

A small but prominent notice in the pages of *The Times*,
announcing the upcoming marriage of one Captain Miles Ramsay,
Extraordinary Mover, to Miss Elinor Pembroke, Extraordinary
Scorcher, appeared quietly one day that week. Elinor showed it to
Miles at the breakfast table. "It is the only notice I will give him," she
said to Miles, who looked grim. He had wanted no notice at all, had

been angrier at Mr. Pembroke's treatment of his second daughter than Elinor was, but had bowed to her wishes. "If he or mama chooses to attend, I will not turn them away. But I think they will not."

Selina and her husband would be there, and Miles's father, and Arthur Beaumont and Captain Horace to serve as witnesses, and a few others of Miles's acquaintance, but neither Elinor nor Miles wanted a great fuss. They intended to return to *Athena* directly afterward in lieu of a wedding trip. They had already traveled much farther than anyone Elinor knew could imagine.

The eighth day was unexpectedly cool and rainy for July in London. Elinor rubbed her bare arms and shivered as their carriage left the Admiralty for the quiet London neighborhood where Miles had found a church with a priest enthusiastic about performing their marriage ceremony. "It was quite warm six days ago when I ordered this gown," she complained, picking at the dove-grey silk. "I did not realize I should have purchased one of wool."

Miles smiled and tucked her under his arm. He looked wonderful in his dress uniform, his hat in his lap, his hair newly trimmed and swept back from his face so those blue eyes would draw everyone's attention. "If we were home, and you were warm, I wouldn't have this excuse to put my arm around you."

"I should upbraid you for your impertinence, but I find my time in the Navy has made me rather wanton. I hope you do not mind it."

He brought his left arm around to draw her even closer to him. "You know," he said, "that night at Harry's party, I wanted to ask you to dance with me."

She gasped. "And I was so awful to you."

"I thought you might think I was making fun of you. Then I regretted not asking the whole rest of the night."

"I wish I could tell you I would have said 'yes'. But you are right. I likely would have become even more offended, and then I would have said truly awful things to you, and you would have hated me, and we would never have become friends—"

"Or I would have liked your defiant spirit, and fallen in love with you immediately, and gone to my knees and begged you to marry me right there."

She laughed and laid her head on his shoulder. "I much prefer the way you actually did it."

"What, me stammering and not knowing what to say, and terrified that I was wrong and you didn't actually care for me?"

"You standing there, so handsome, looking at me as if I were your heart's desire."

"Which you are." The carriage came to a rattling, bouncing halt, but Miles, not releasing her, pushed back her bonnet and brushed her forehead with one of those light kisses that made the fire at her center leap up in response. "Are, and always will be."

The beautiful little church, like a miniature cathedral, and its walk were slick with rain, the short grass emerald green under the lenses of a million tiny drops, so Miles took her hand and swept them both from the street to the door so rapidly the rain had no time to fall on them. They were the last to arrive, though their guests did not seem impatient; the slender young priest, on the other hand, was fairly bouncing with excitement. Elinor supposed his normal routine did not include performing the marriage of two Extraordinaries.

She and Miles walked together down the aisle to stand in front of the man, who beamed at them and began speaking almost before the witnesses could arrange themselves, then had to pause when Elinor realized she was standing on the wrong side: "Dearly beloved, we are gathered together here in the sight of God..."

She listened to the service, had a smile for Selina's husband John as he handed her over to Miles, responded at the proper time with the proper words, then Miles slid a thin gold band over her finger, saying "With this ring I thee wed, with my body I thee worship." There was a look in his eyes that said he intended to show her exactly what that meant, and she heard the rest of the service in a daze.

Afterward, Selina embraced her tightly, happy tears in her eyes, the swell of her belly pressing against Elinor, and Elinor clung to her briefly, shedding a few tears of her own. She was kissed on the cheek by her new father-in-law, a tall grey-haired man who had his son's blue eyes, then she turned to greet Miles' friends and saw a portly figure leaving the church, trailed by a woman who looked over her shoulder at her daughter and raised her hand once in farewell. Elinor caught her breath. Perhaps he had changed his mind. *Or, more likely, I married well enough to suit him*. She felt no sorrow at his absence.

"We will have your wedding breakfast at Wrathingham House, and I do not wish to hear your demurrals, Elinor," Selina said, "for I am certain I will not see you again for a long time, if you are going back to the Navy."

"I will not fight you, Selina," Elinor said with a laugh, "but now that I have no fear of discovery, I will probably return more often, if our new Bounder can bring himself to lay hands on me."

"Is he so very young, then?"

"He is full three-and-forty years old and has never been to sea in his life. I believe he is afraid I will break."

"Breakfast, yes, Lady Wrathingham—"

"You must now call me Selina, Miles."

"All right, Selina, but we mustn't linger because it's just gone four o'clock where *Athena* is and I should be there immediately after sunrise."

The door opened, letting in grey, watery light and a slim young man shaking drops of water from his flat cap. "Captain Ramsay?" he said.

Miles turned, and the young man advanced down the nave to hand him a rolled sheet of paper, bow, and leave as quickly as he had appeared.

"Strange," Miles said, flicking the dangling seal with his thumbnail and turning away to read the letter.

"Selina," Elinor said, "I hope I can see Jack and Colin before—"

"*Damnation!*" Miles roared. Selina and Elinor both gasped. The priest said, "Captain!" Beaumont covered his mouth to hide a smile. "Good heavens, Miles, what on earth is the matter?" Elinor exclaimed.

He turned back to face her, waving the letter as if hoping to make the words fly off the page and disappear. "This," he began, "this is—it's completely irregular, far too informal, but they do it this way sometimes if they think you're likely to pretend you didn't get the message —just read it, Elinor."

Elinor took the paper from him and scanned its contents, and blanched. "But I don't want to be a countess!" she said.

Selina gasped. "Oh, my dear, a *countess?*"

"It's not the sort of thing you refuse," said Miles. "And I guarantee you, my being created Earl of Wherever-it-is—"

"Enderleigh."

"Wherever-it-is is meant to reward *you*, Elinor. The Regent may respect and admire you as a fellow Scorcher, but he doesn't like to give titles to women in their own right, so the instant you were safely married—"

"Congratulations," Lord Wrathingham said, extending his hand to Miles and not flinching when he saw the stump. "I'm only surprised they didn't elevate you sooner, Extraordinary war hero and so forth."

"Because I'm good at staying out of the way, that's why," Miles said, grimly.

"Let us go and have breakfast," Selina said, "you and all your friends, and there will be plenty of time to fall into despair later."

The rain had stopped and the clouds had begun to drift, revealing fragments of a sky bluer than the Caribbean Sea. Miles assisted Elinor into their carriage and the two of them rode silently for a quarter of a mile before Elinor said, "But I don't want to be a countess!"

Miles laughed. He flattened the paper, which had become rather crushed in his grip, and put it away inside his uniform jacket. "It could be worse. You could be a duchess."

"That is not much worse. I am so awkward in society, and I do not see how we are expected to maintain an earl's household on my fifteen thousand and whatever you have invested in the funds."

"I do have quite a tidy sum saved, you know. Though you seem to be an expensive woman, always needing new gowns and the like." She poked him in the side and he pulled an injured face. "In seriousness, we will have income from whatever property is attached to the title. Gifts —we'll be expected to host a gala when we finally return, a celebration of our well-deserved nobility, and our guests will be generous with their welcoming gifts. And I think some of these titles come with a lump sum."

"That is terribly wrong, when we are at war and trying to support our troops and our Navy."

Miles shrugged. "I have no control over the profligacy of our king and his Regent. What I *do* know is that a title does not preclude serving in the Navy, so until this war is over, or they have no more need of us, we won't be leaving *Athena*. Imagine if that letter had been a notice that I had become an admiral instead."

"But if you were an admiral, your career would be truly secure. I would much rather you were an admiral than an earl."

"I think you may be the only woman in England who has ever said those words."

"Then I am the only sensible woman in England. At the moment, I am relieved no one is coming to drag us away from our home and send us off to this drafty manor, wherever-it-is."

"Enderleigh."

"Wherever that is." She leaned against his shoulder and sighed. "I suppose I can endure being Countess of Enderleigh if I may also be the wife of Miles Ramsay."

"I would have to insist on it."

Breakfast was a happy, raucous affair, for Lord Wrathingham was a cheerful man who did not stand on ceremony, who loved to tell stories of his time in the Army and trade jests with the Navy men. Selina pretended to blush and chastise her husband when he became too exuberant, but her fond smile told everyone how she truly felt. Elinor watched Miles roar at one of her brother-in-law's jokes and thought, *Stratford would have loved this.* The idea filled her with sorrow, but not with pain.

Then they were back at Admiralty House to return to *Athena*, and Elinor was beginning to feel the exhaustion of having been awake for more than twenty hours. She watched first Beaumont, then Miles vanish along with the new Bounder, whose name she could not remember, then a minute later grasped the man about the waist and felt, not Stratford's smooth transition, but an abrupt jerk that rattled her teeth. "I beg your pardon," he said. In the dim light of the Bounding chamber he looked terribly embarrassed, so she merely smiled at him and exited the room.

Miles had vanished. The deck was sparsely populated with sleeping bodies in slightly swaying hammocks, as it was nearly six a.m. and only the starboard watch was asleep. The distant murmur of working men made her smile with contentment. Still home. She removed her shoes and made her way silently through the rows of hammocks, apologizing to the one man she jostled out of sleep. Then she was up the steps and into the great cabin, which was lit dimly by the pale pink of the rising sun.

Someone put his hand on her waist and spun her around. "Mrs. Ramsay," Miles murmured in her ear, "welcome home."

"My home is wherever you are, Captain Ramsay." She put her arms around his neck and returned his kiss.

He smiled and bent to lay his forehead against hers. "Even if it is a cold, drafty manor with fireplaces that smoke?"

"Even then."

She felt herself rise off the ground until her stocking-clad toes barely brushed the planks. "Even if all I have to offer you is a narrow bed in a narrow, windowless room that smells of damp wood and tar?"

His single hand was busy unfastening her gown, something his Moving could not easily do, and she reached out to stroke his scarred cheek. "Even then. *Especially* then."

He laid the stump of his wrist over her hand where it rested on his face. "Even if I ask you to share that bed with me?"

"I would have to insist on it," Elinor said.

ACKNOWLEDGMENTS

This book would not have been possible without the encouragement and support of many people, especially Jacob Proffitt, Jana Brown, and Hallie O'Donovan, the latter of whom rose to unparalleled heights of diplomacy in discovering at least fifteen new and gentle ways to tell me I was wrong. Sherwood Smith kindly went over the final version of this manuscript and was equally kind in pointing out my many mistakes; any remaining errors are due either to narrative necessity or my own failings.

A full listing of reference materials would be impractical here, but for anyone who would like to be better able to picture *Athena*, I recommend *The 32-Gun Frigate* Essex, by Portia Takakjian. The USS (later HMS) *Essex* was an American-built frigate, and her construction is somewhat different from that of similar English-built ships of the time, so I used her as a basis for the "new" construction Ramsay refers to. For an interactive view of a similar ship, the HMS *Trincomalee*, visit http://hms-trincomalee.co.uk/ and take a virtual tour.

THE TALENTS

THE CORPOREAL TALENTS: Mover, Shaper, Scorcher, Bounder

MOVER (Greek τελεκινεσις): Capable of moving things without physically touching them. While originally this talent was believed to be connected to one's bodily strength, female Movers able to lift far more than their male counterparts have disproven this theory in recent years. Depending on skill, training, and practice, Movers may be able to lift and manipulate multiple objects at once, pick locks, and manipulate anything the human hand can manage. Movers can Move other people so long as they don't resist, and some are capable of Moving an unwilling target if the Mover is strong enough.

An EXTRAORDINARY MOVER, in addition to all these things, is capable of flight. Aside from this, an Extraordinary Mover is not guaranteed to be better skilled or stronger than an ordinary Mover; Helen Garrity, England's highest-rated Mover (at upwards of 12,000 pounds lifting capacity), was an ordinary Mover.

SHAPER (Greek μπιοκινεσις): Capable of manipulating their own bodies. Shapers can alter their own flesh, including healing wounds. Most Shapers use their ability only to make themselves more attractive, though that sort of beauty is always obvious as Shaped. More subtle uses include disguising oneself, and many Shapers have also been spies. It usually takes time for a Shaper to alter herself because Shaping is painful, and the faster one does it, the more painful it is. Under extreme duress, Shapers can alter their bodies rapidly, but this results in great pain and longer-term muscle and joint pain.

Shapers can mend bone, heal cuts or abrasions, repair physical damage to organs as from a knife wound, etc., make hair and nails grow, improve their physical condition (for example, enhance lung efficiency), and change their skin color. They cannot restore lost limbs or organs, cure diseases (though they can repair the physical damage done by disease), change hair or eye color, or regenerate nerves.

An EXTRAORDINARY SHAPER is capable of turning a Shaper's talent on another person with skin-to-skin contact. Extraordinary Shapers are sometimes called Healers as a result. While most Extraordinary Shapers use their talent to help others, there is nothing to stop them from causing injury or even death instead.

SCORCHER (Greek πιροκινεσις): Capable of igniting fire by the power of thought. The fire is natural and will cause ordinary flammable objects to catch on fire. If there aren't any such objects handy, the fire will burn briefly and then go out. A Scorcher must be able to see the place he or she is starting the fire. Scorcher talent has four dimensions: power, range, distance, and stamina. Power refers to how large and hot a fire the Scorcher can create; range is how far the Scorcher can fling a fire before it goes out; distance is how far away a Scorcher can ignite a fire; and stamina refers to how often the Scorcher can use his or her power before becoming exhausted. The hottest ordinary fire any Scorcher has ever created could melt brass (approximately 1700 degrees F). When she gave herself over to the fire, Elinor Pembroke was able to melt iron (over 2200 degrees F).

Scorchers are rare because they manifest by igniting fire unconsciously in their sleep. About 10-20% of Scorchers survive manifestation.

EXTRAORDINARY SCORCHERS are capable of controlling and mentally extinguishing fires. As their talent develops,

Extraordinary Scorchers become immune to fire, and their control over it increases.

BOUNDER (Greek τελεταχύς): Capable of moving from one point to another without passing through the intervening space. Bounders can move themselves anywhere they can see clearly within a certain range that varies according to the Bounder; this is called Skipping. They can also Bound to any location marked with a Bounder symbol, known as a signature. The location must be closed to the outdoors and empty of people and objects. Bounders refer to the "simplicity" of a space, meaning how free of "clutter" (objects, people, etc.) it is. Spaces that are too cluttered are impossible to Bound to, as are outdoor locations, which are full of constant movement. It is possible to keep a Bounder out of somewhere if you alter the place by defacing the Bounding chamber or putting some object or person into it.

An EXTRAORDINARY BOUNDER lacks most of the limitations an ordinary Bounder operates under. An Extraordinary Bounder's range is line of sight, which can allow them to Skip many miles' distance. Extraordinary Bounders do not require Bounding signatures, instead using what they refer to as "essence" to identify a space they Bound to. Essence comprises the essential nature of a space and is impossible to explain to non-Bounders; human beings have an essence which differs from that of a place and allows an Extraordinary Bounder to identify people without seeing them. While Extraordinary Bounders are still incapable of Bounding to an outdoor location, they can Bound to places too cluttered for an ordinary Bounder, as well as ones that contain people.

THE ETHEREAL TALENTS: Seer, Speaker, Discerner, Coercer

SEER (Greek προφητεία): Capable of seeing a short distance into the future through Dreams. Seers experience lucid Dreams in which they see future events as if they were present as an invisible observer. In order to recognize the people or places involved, Seers tend to be very well informed about people and events and are socially active. Their Dreams are not inevitable and there is no problem with altering the timeline; they see things that are the natural consequence of the current situation/circumstances, and altering those things alters the foreseen event. Just their knowledge of the event is not sufficient to alter it.

No one knows how a Seer's brain produces Dream, only that Dreams come in response to what the Seer meditates on. Seers therefore study current events in depth and read up on things they might be asked to Dream about. Seers have high social status and are very popular, with many of them making a living from Dream commissions.

An EXTRAORDINARY SEER, in addition to Dreaming, is capable of touching an object and perceiving events and people associated with it. These Visions allow them not only to see the past of the person most closely connected to the object, but occasionally to have glimpses of the future. They can also find a Vision linked to what the object's owner is seeing at the moment and "see" through their eyes. Most recently, the Extraordinary Seer Sophia Westlake discovered how to use Visions attached to one object to perceive related objects, leading to the defeat of the Caribbean pirates led by Rhys Evans.

SPEAKER (Greek τελεπάθεια): Capable of communicating by thought with any other Speaker. Speakers can mentally communicate with any Speaker within range of sight. They can also communicate with any Speaker they know well. The definition of "know well" has meaning only to a Speaker, but in general it means someone they have spoken verbally or mentally with on several occasions. A Speaker's circle of Speaker friends is called a reticulum, and a reticulum might contain several hundred members depending on the Speaker. Speakers easily distinguish between the different "voices" of their Speaker friends, though Speaking is not auditory. A Speaker can send images as well as words if she is proficient enough. Speakers cannot Speak to non-Speakers, and they are incapable of reading minds.

An EXTRAORDINARY SPEAKER has all the abilities of an ordinary Speaker, but is also capable of sending thoughts and images into the minds of anyone, Speaker or not. Additionally, an Extraordinary Speaker can Speak to multiple people at a time, though all will receive the same message. Extraordinary Speakers can send a "burst" of noise that startles or wakes the recipient. Rumors that Extraordinary Speakers can read minds are universally denied by Speakers, but the rumors persist.

DISCERNER (Greek ενσυναίσθηση): Able to experience other people's feelings as if they were their own. Discerners require touch to be able to do this (though not skin-to-skin contact), and much of learning to control the skill involves learning to distinguish one's own emotions from those of the other person. Discerners can detect lies, sense motives, read other people's emotional states, and identify Coercers. Discerners are immune to the talent of a Coercer, though they can be overwhelmed by anyone capable of projecting strong emotions.

An EXTRAORDINARY DISCERNER can do all these things without the need for touch. Extraordinary Discerners are always aware of the emotions of those near them, though the range at which they are aware varies according to the Extraordinary Discerner. Nearly three-quarters of all Extraordinary Discerners go mad because of their talent.

COERCER (Greek τελενσυναίσθηση): Capable of influencing the emotions of others with a touch. Coercers are viewed with great suspicion since their ability is a kind of mind control. Those altered are not aware that their mood has been artificially changed and are extremely suggestible while the Coercer is in direct contact with them. By altering someone's emotions, a Coercer can influence their behavior or change his or her attitude toward the Coercer.

Coercers do not feel others' emotions the way Discerners do, but can tell what they are and how they're changing. Many Coercers have sociopathic tendencies as a result. Unlike Discerners, Coercers have to work hard at being able to use their talent, which in its untrained state is erratic. However, Coercers always know when they've altered someone's mood. Coercers do not "broadcast" their emotions, appearing as a blank to Discerners. Because Coercion is viewed with suspicion (for good reason), Coercers keep their ability secret even if they don't use it maliciously.

An EXTRAORDINARY COERCER does not need a physical connection to influence someone's emotions. Extraordinary Coercers are capable of turning their talent on several people at a time, and the most powerful Extraordinary Coercers can control mobs. The most powerful Extraordinary Coercer known to date is Napoleon Bonaparte.

ABOUT THE AUTHOR

Melissa McShane is the author of more than twenty fantasy novels, including the novels of Tremontane, the first of which is *Servant of the Crown;* The Extraordinaries series, beginning with *Burning Bright;* and *The Book of Secrets,* first book in The Last Oracle series. She lives in the shelter of the mountains out West with her husband, four children and a niece, and three very needy cats. She wrote reviews and critical essays for many years before turning to fiction, which is much more fun than anyone ought to be allowed to have. You can visit her at her website **www.melissamcshanewrites.com** for more information on other books and upcoming releases.

For news on upcoming releases, bonus material, and other fun stuff, sign up for Melissa's newsletter at http://eepurl.com/brannP

CPSIA information can be obtained
at www.ICGtesting.com
Printed in the USA
LVHW041554130619
621125LV00002B/370